fangirl

1

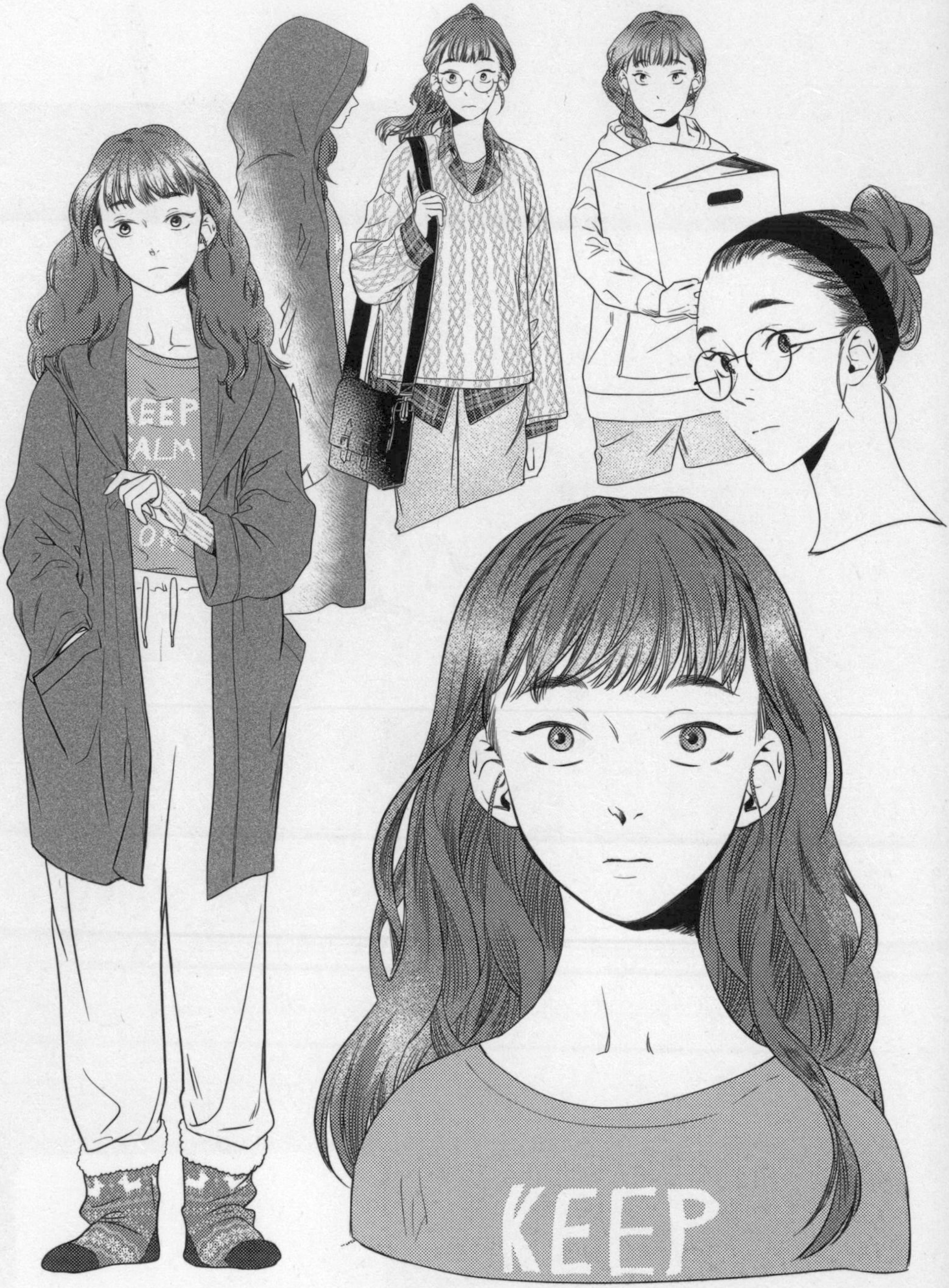
KEEP
KEEP

fangirl

Based on the
bestselling novel by

RAINBOW
ROWELL

Adapted by
SAM MAGGS

Illustrated by
GABI NAM

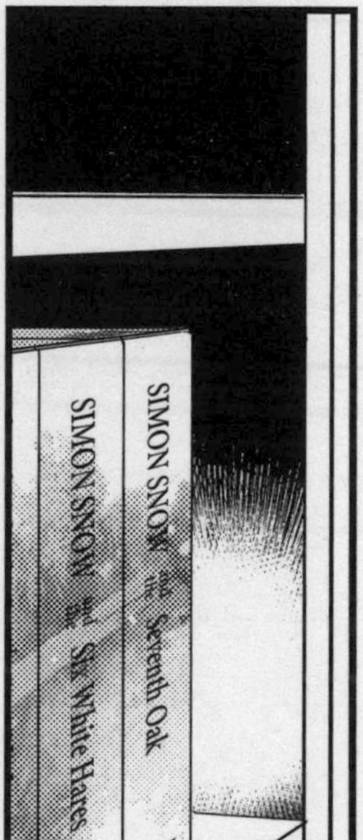
SIMON SNOW and the Seventh Oak 7
SIMON SNOW and the Six White Hares 6

ENCYCLOWIKIA · COM

🔍 EXPLORE ⌄

Article   Talk   Read   View source   View history

The Simon Snow Series

The Simon Snow Series
From Encyclowikia, the people's encyclopedia

This article is about the children's book series.
For other uses, see <u>Simon Snow (disambiguation)</u>

Simon Snow is a series of seven fantasy books written by English philologist Gemma T. Leslie. The books tell the story of Simon Snow, an 11-year-old orphan from Lancashire who is recruited to attend the Watford School of Magicks to become a magician. As he grows older, Simon joins a group of magicians – the Mages – who are fighting the Insidious Humdrum, an evil being trying to rid the world of magic.

The Simon Snow books have sold more than 380 million copies.
The eighth and final entry in the series is set to be released next May.

fangirl

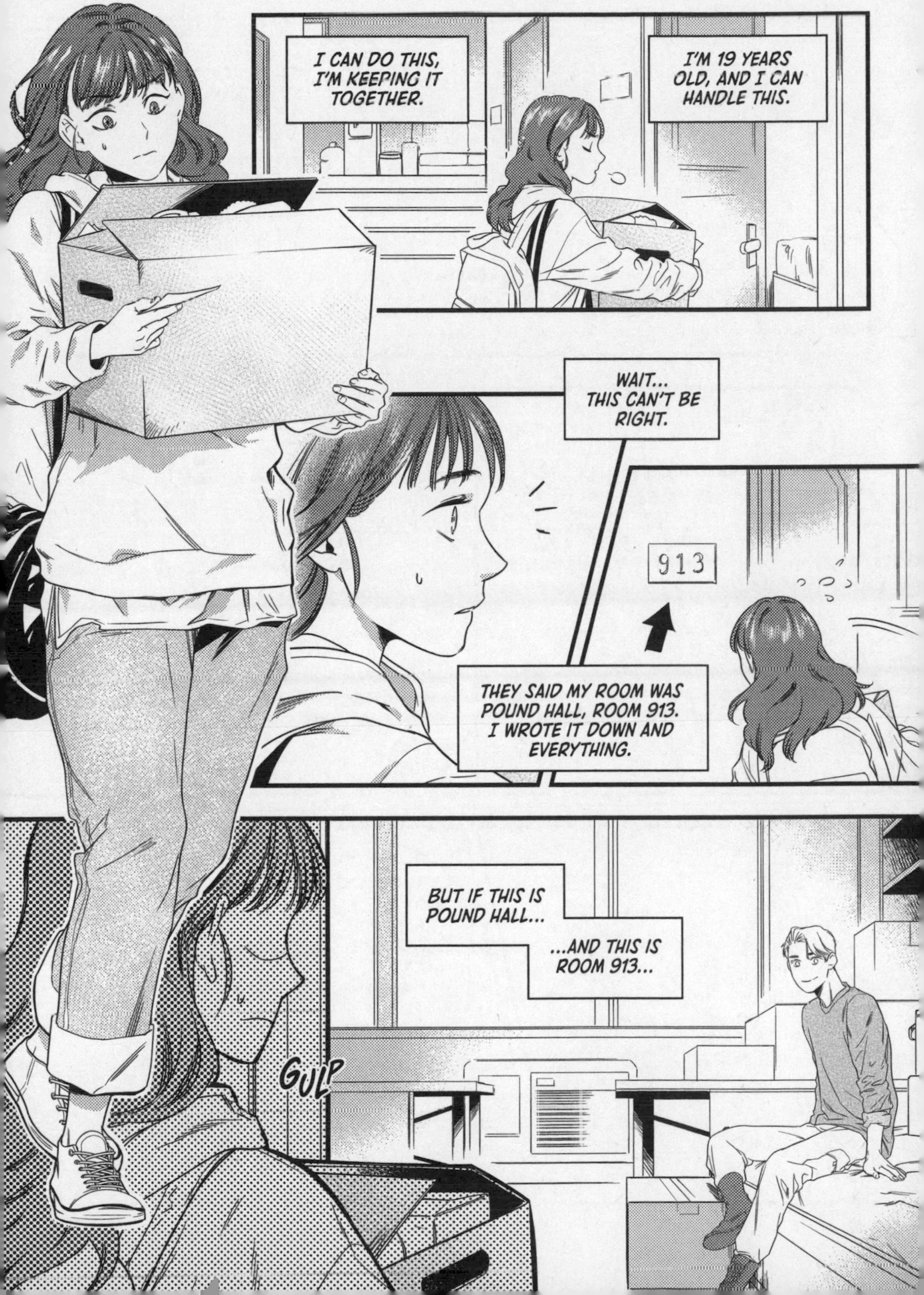
I CAN DO THIS, I'M KEEPING IT TOGETHER.
I'M 19 YEARS OLD, AND I CAN HANDLE THIS.
WAIT... THIS CAN'T BE RIGHT.
913
THEY SAID MY ROOM WAS POUND HALL, ROOM 913. I WROTE IT DOWN AND EVERYTHING.
BUT IF THIS IS POUND HALL...
...AND THIS IS ROOM 913...
GULP

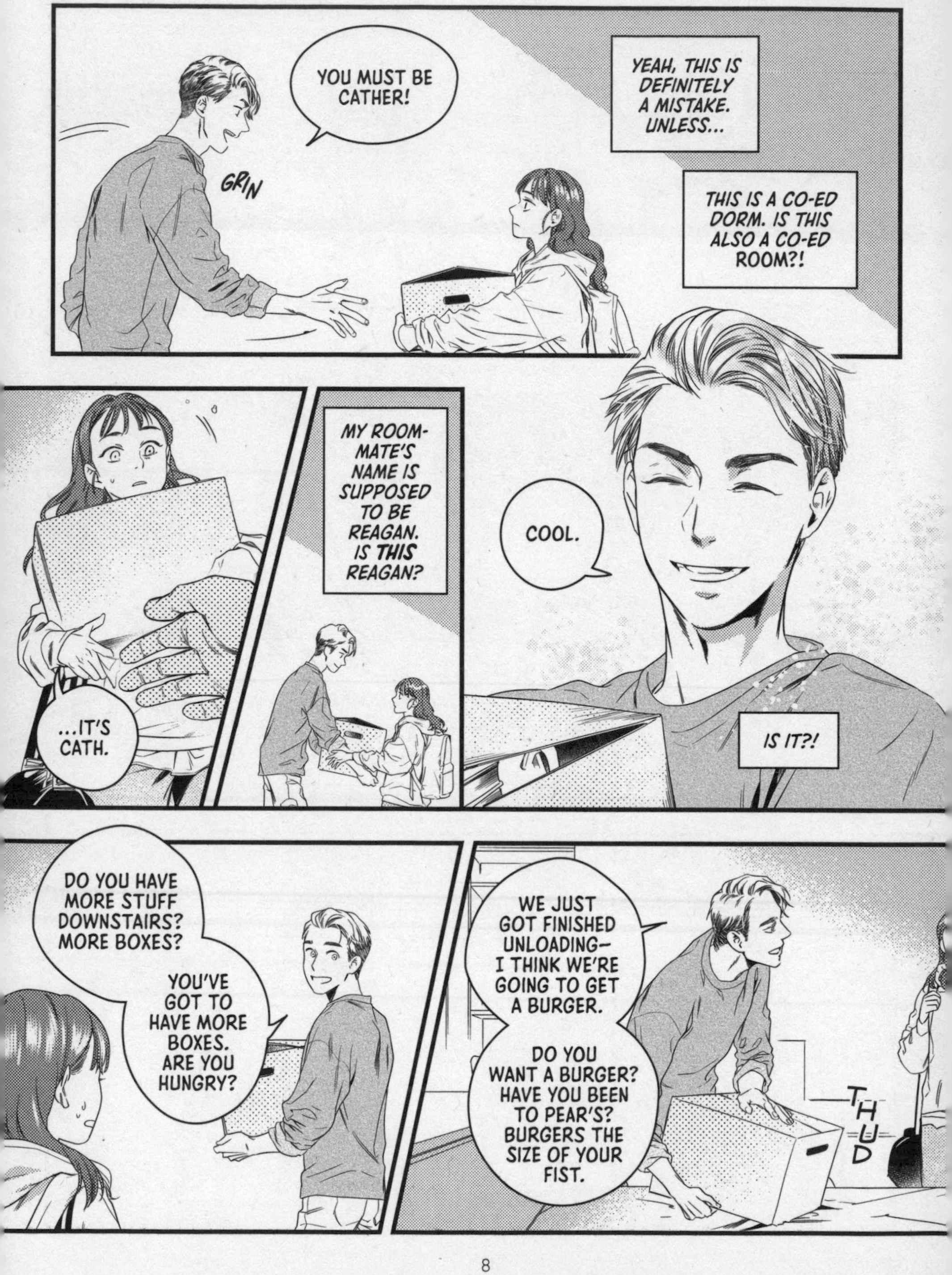
YOU MUST BE CATHER!
GRIN
YEAH, THIS IS DEFINITELY A MISTAKE. UNLESS...
THIS IS A CO-ED DORM. IS THIS ALSO A CO-ED ROOM?!
...IT'S CATH.
MY ROOM-MATE'S NAME IS SUPPOSED TO BE REAGAN. IS **THIS** REAGAN?
COOL.
IS IT?!
DO YOU HAVE MORE STUFF DOWNSTAIRS? MORE BOXES?
YOU'VE GOT TO HAVE MORE BOXES. ARE YOU HUNGRY?
WE JUST GOT FINISHED UNLOADING— I THINK WE'RE GOING TO GET A BURGER.
DO YOU WANT A BURGER? HAVE YOU BEEN TO PEAR'S? BURGERS THE SIZE OF YOUR FIST.
THUD

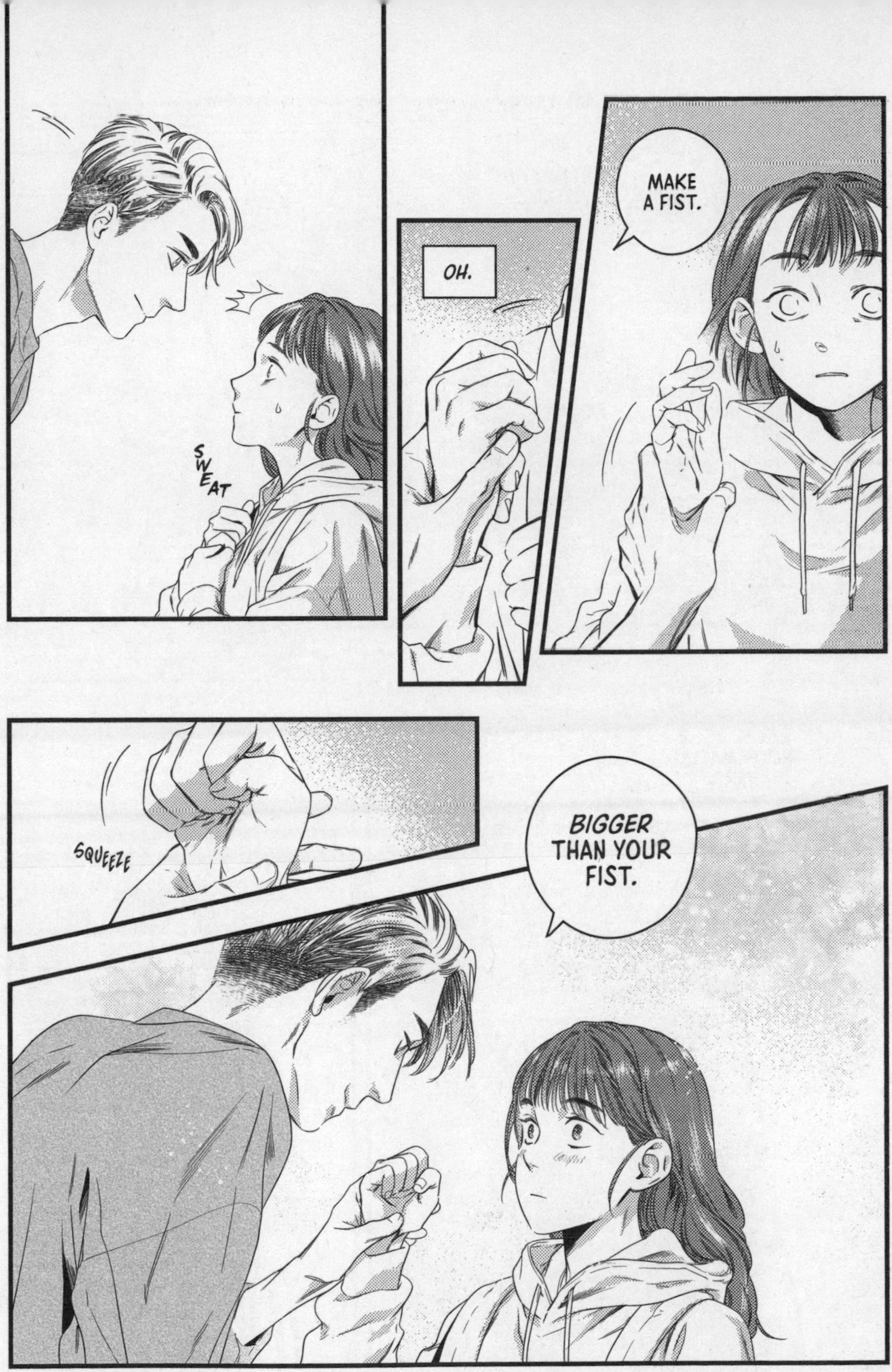
SWEAT
OH.
MAKE A FIST.
SQUEEZE
BIGGER THAN YOUR FIST.

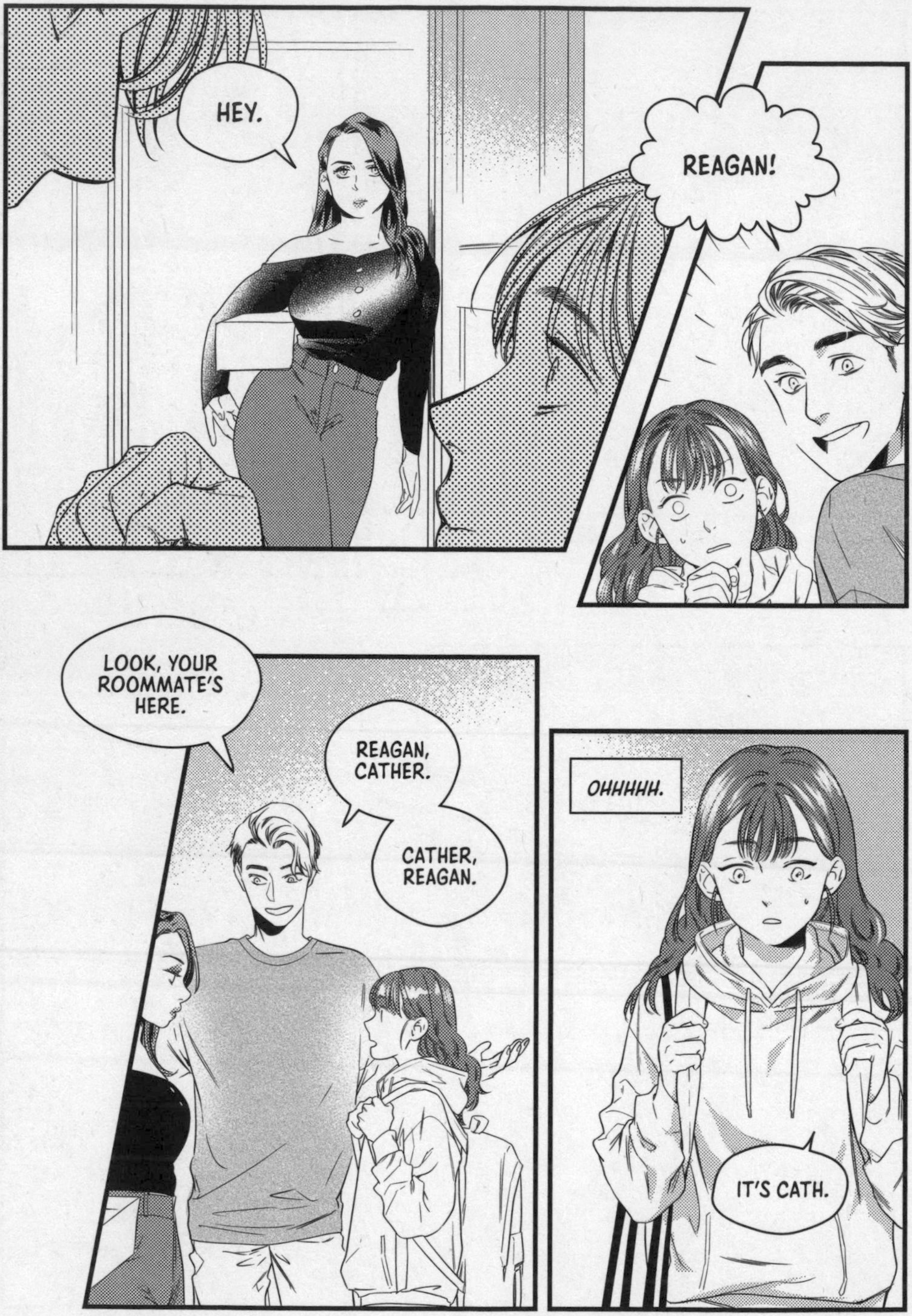
HEY.
REAGAN!
LOOK, YOUR ROOMMATE'S HERE.
REAGAN, CATHER.
CATHER, REAGAN.
OHHHHH.
IT'S CATH.

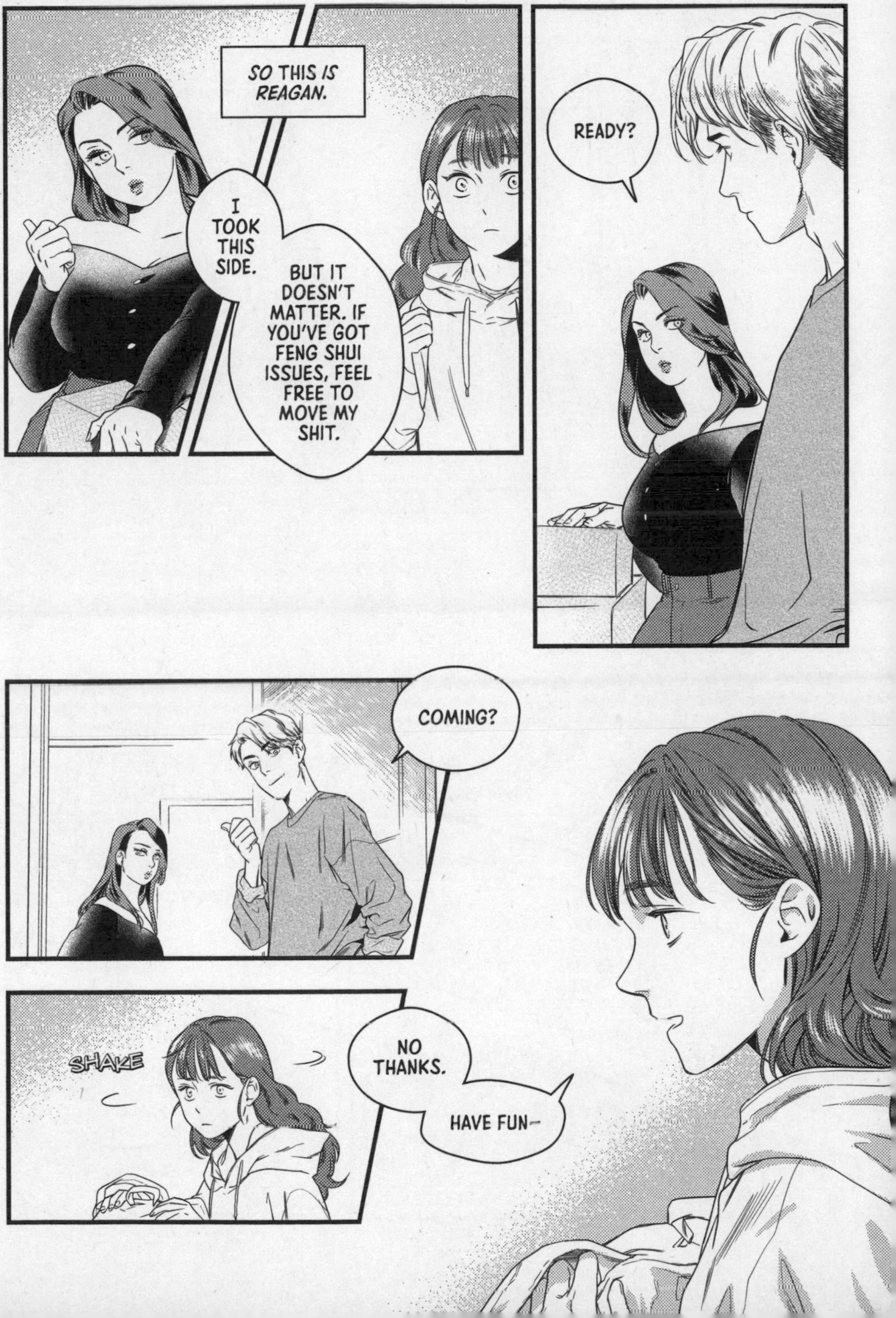
SO THIS IS REAGAN.
I TOOK THIS SIDE.
BUT IT DOESN'T MATTER. IF YOU'VE GOT FENG SHUI ISSUES, FEEL FREE TO MOVE MY SHIT.
READY?
COMING?
SHAKE
NO THANKS.
HAVE FUN—

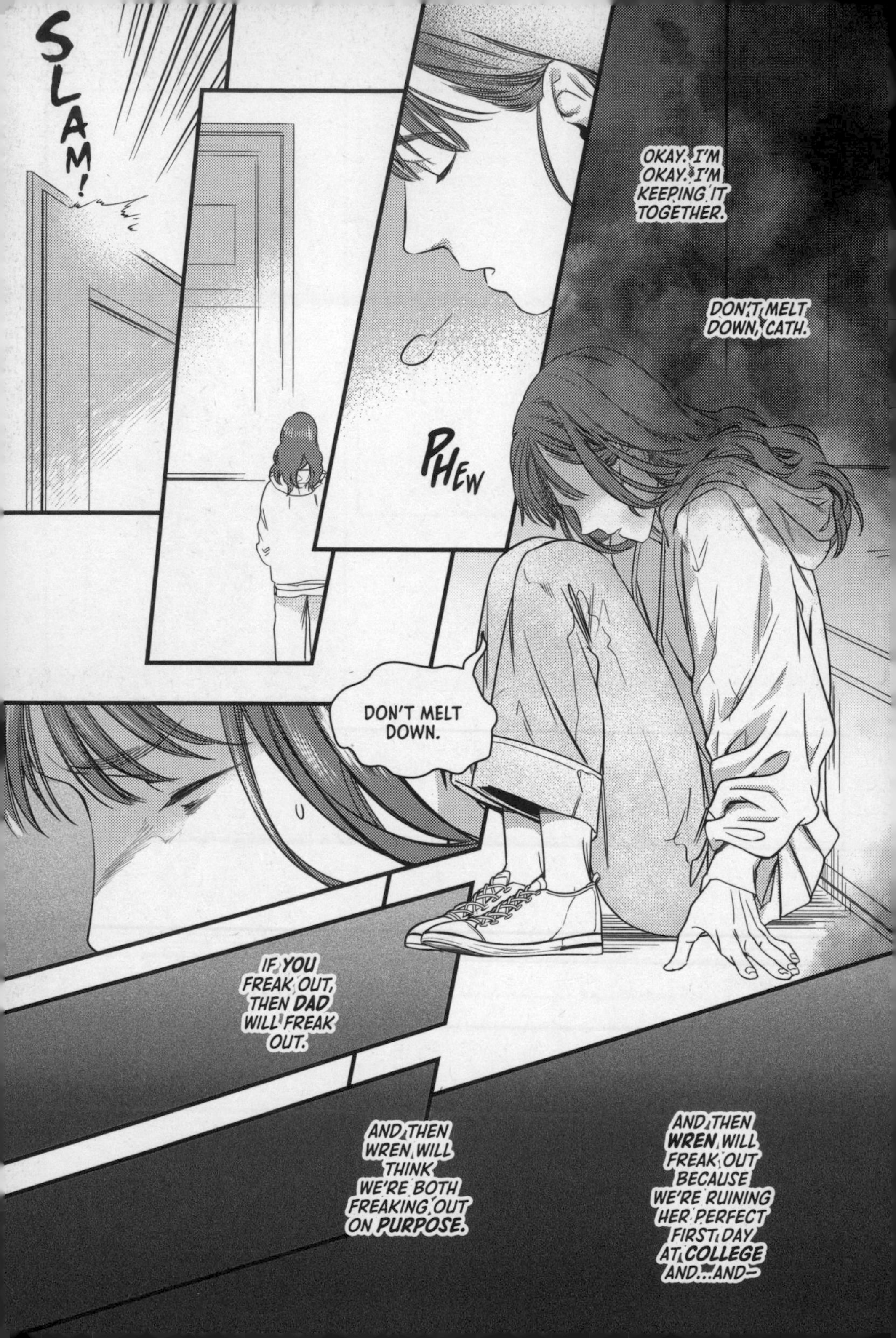
SLAM!
OKAY. I'M OKAY. I'M KEEPING IT TOGETHER.
DON'T MELT DOWN, CATH.
PHEW
DON'T MELT DOWN.
IF YOU FREAK OUT, THEN DAD WILL FREAK OUT.
AND THEN WREN WILL THINK WE'RE BOTH FREAKING OUT ON PURPOSE.
AND THEN WREN WILL FREAK OUT BECAUSE WE'RE RUINING HER PERFECT FIRST DAY AT COLLEGE AND...AND—

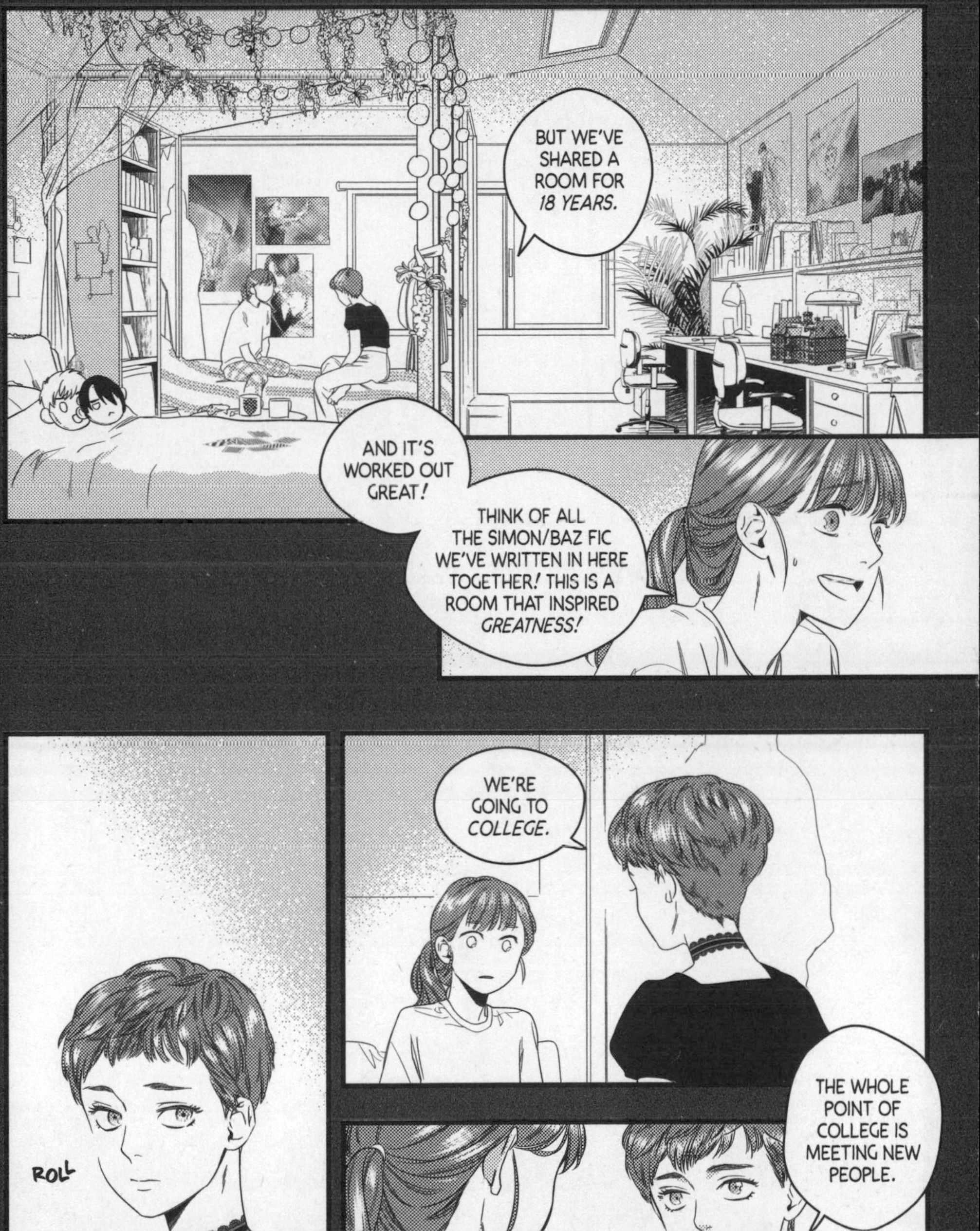
BUT WE'VE SHARED A ROOM FOR 18 YEARS.
AND IT'S WORKED OUT GREAT!
THINK OF ALL THE SIMON/BAZ FIC WE'VE WRITTEN IN HERE TOGETHER! THIS IS A ROOM THAT INSPIRED GREATNESS!
ROLL
WE'RE GOING TO COLLEGE.
THE WHOLE POINT OF COLLEGE IS MEETING NEW PEOPLE.

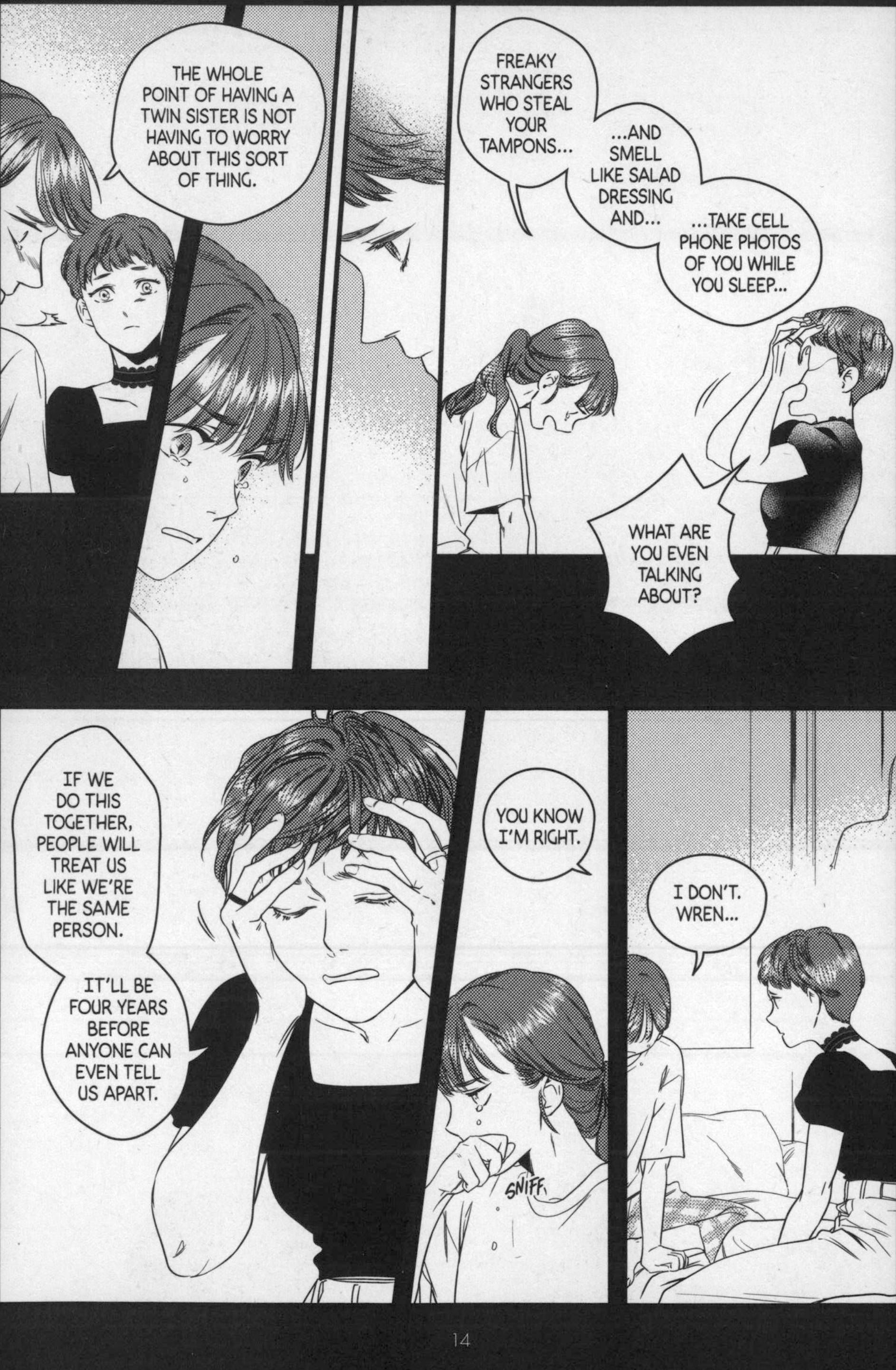

THE WHOLE POINT OF HAVING A TWIN SISTER IS NOT HAVING TO WORRY ABOUT THIS SORT OF THING.
FREAKY STRANGERS WHO STEAL YOUR TAMPONS...
...AND SMELL LIKE SALAD DRESSING AND...
...TAKE CELL PHONE PHOTOS OF YOU WHILE YOU SLEEP...
WHAT ARE YOU EVEN TALKING ABOUT?
IF WE DO THIS TOGETHER, PEOPLE WILL TREAT US LIKE WE'RE THE SAME PERSON.
IT'LL BE FOUR YEARS BEFORE ANYONE CAN EVEN TELL US APART.
YOU KNOW I'M RIGHT.
SNIFF
I DON'T. WREN...

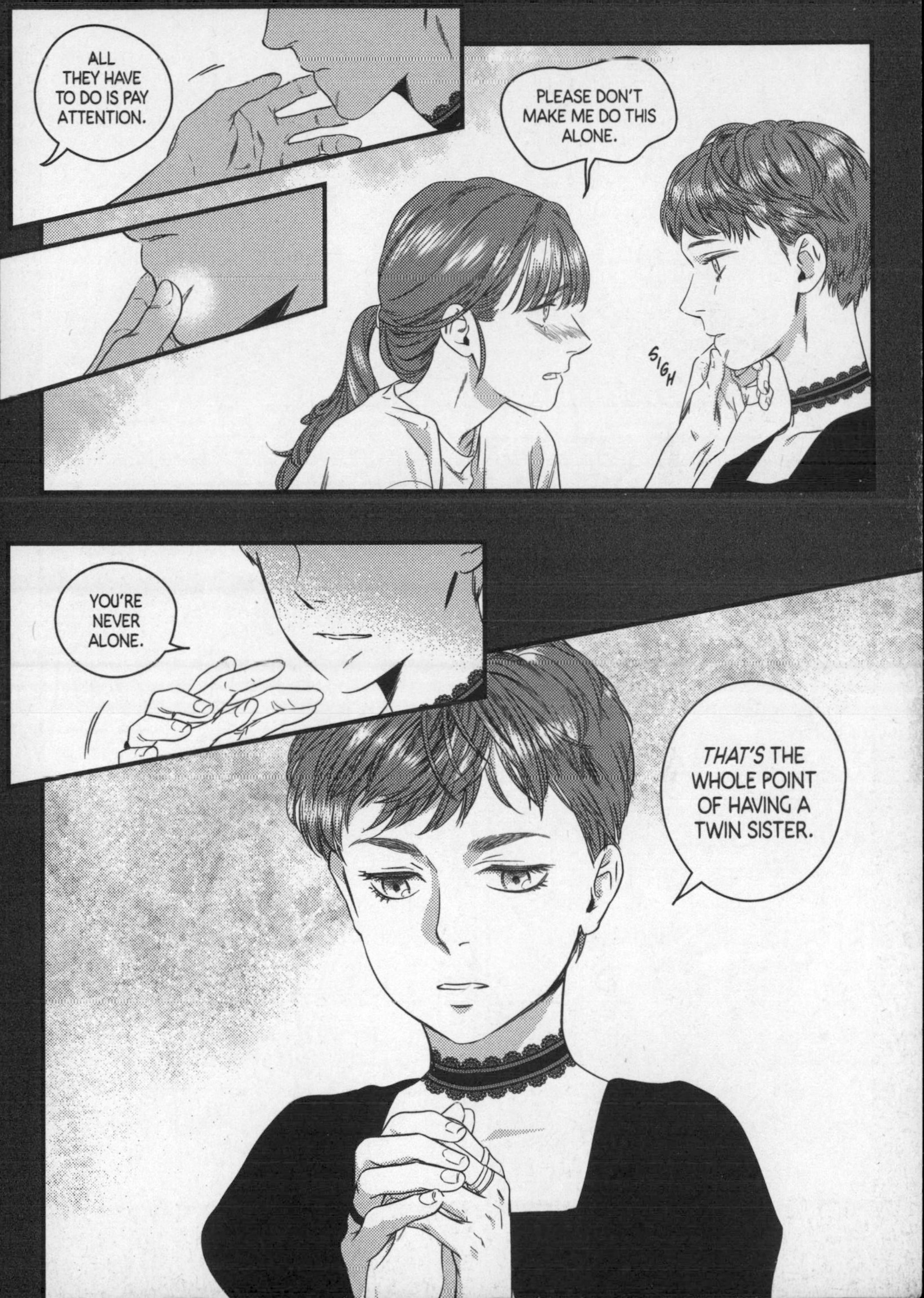
ALL THEY HAVE TO DO IS PAY ATTENTION.
PLEASE DON'T MAKE ME DO THIS ALONE.
SIGH
YOU'RE NEVER ALONE.
THAT'S THE WHOLE POINT OF HAVING A TWIN SISTER.

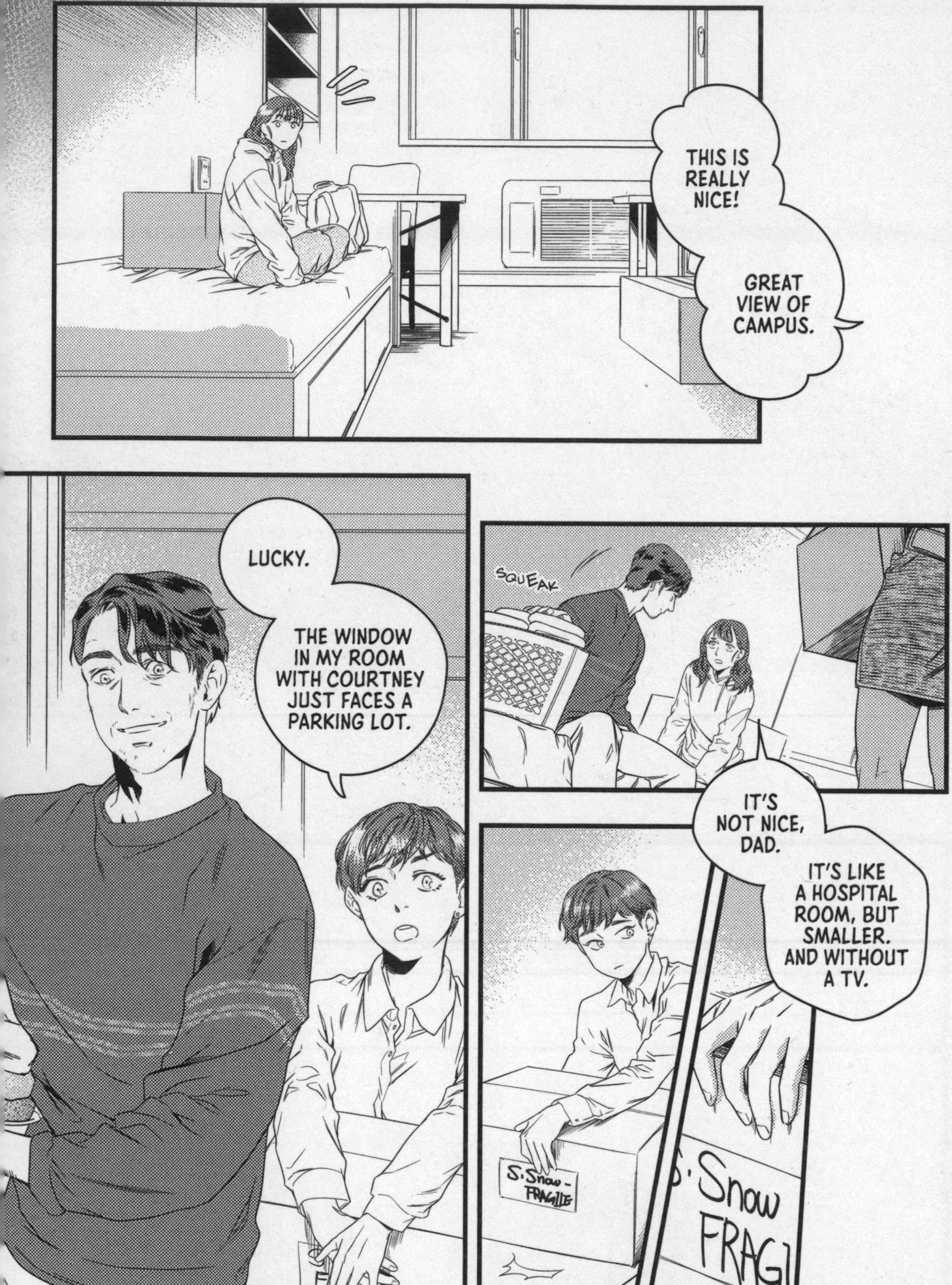
THIS IS REALLY NICE!
GREAT VIEW OF CAMPUS.
LUCKY.
THE WINDOW IN MY ROOM WITH COURTNEY JUST FACES A PARKING LOT.
SQUEAK
IT'S NOT NICE, DAD.
IT'S LIKE A HOSPITAL ROOM, BUT SMALLER. AND WITHOUT A TV.
S. Snow - FRAGILE
S. Snow FRAGI

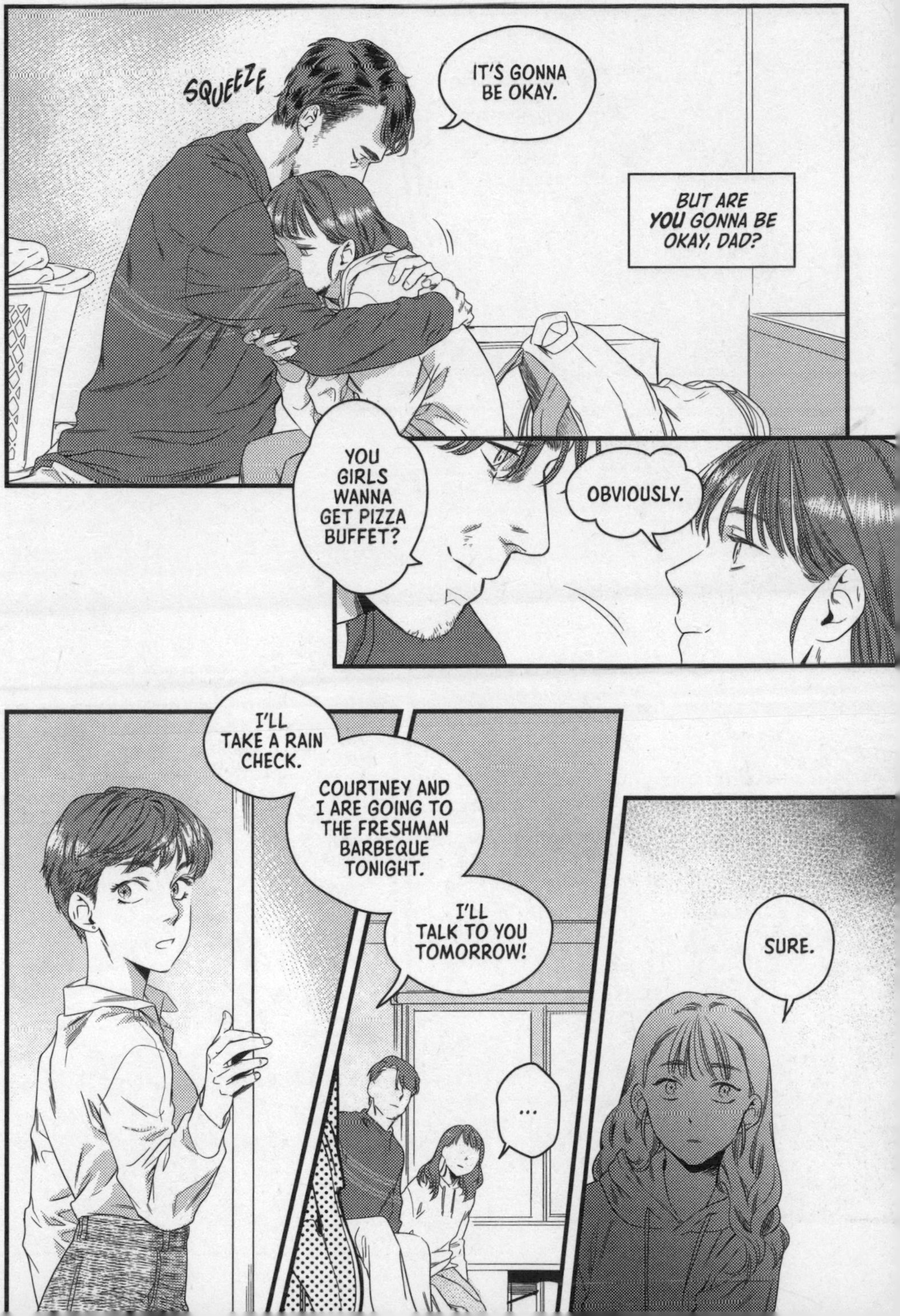
SQUEEZE
IT'S GONNA BE OKAY.
BUT ARE YOU GONNA BE OKAY, DAD?
YOU GIRLS WANNA GET PIZZA BUFFET?
OBVIOUSLY.
I'LL TAKE A RAIN CHECK.
COURTNEY AND I ARE GOING TO THE FRESHMAN BARBEQUE TONIGHT.
I'LL TALK TO YOU TOMORROW!
...
SURE.

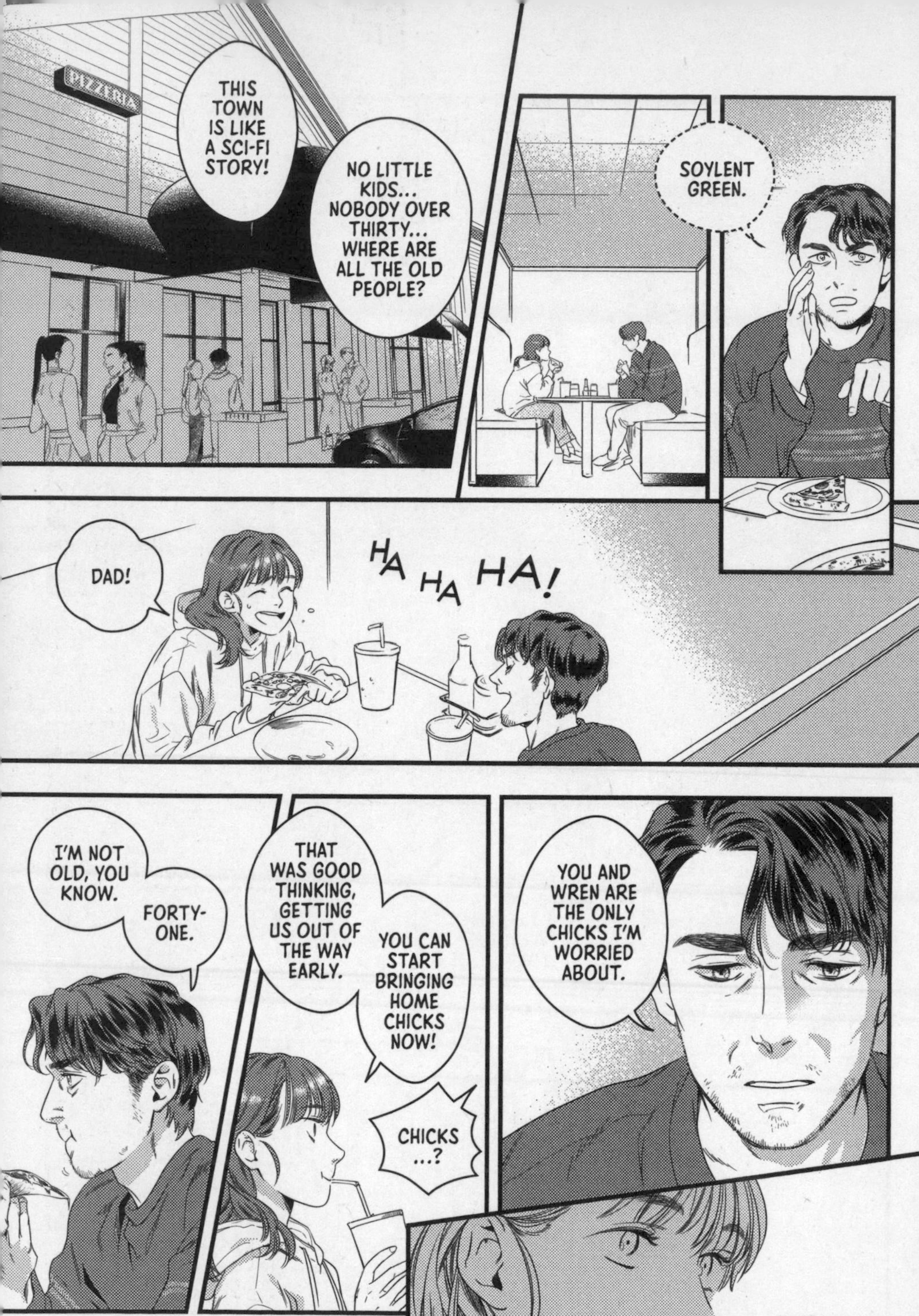
PIZZERIA
THIS TOWN IS LIKE A SCI-FI STORY!
NO LITTLE KIDS... NOBODY OVER THIRTY... WHERE ARE ALL THE OLD PEOPLE?
SOYLENT GREEN.
DAD!
HA HA HA!
I'M NOT OLD, YOU KNOW.
FORTY-ONE.
THAT WAS GOOD THINKING, GETTING US OUT OF THE WAY EARLY.
YOU CAN START BRINGING HOME CHICKS NOW!
CHICKS ...?
YOU AND WREN ARE THE ONLY CHICKS I'M WORRIED ABOUT.

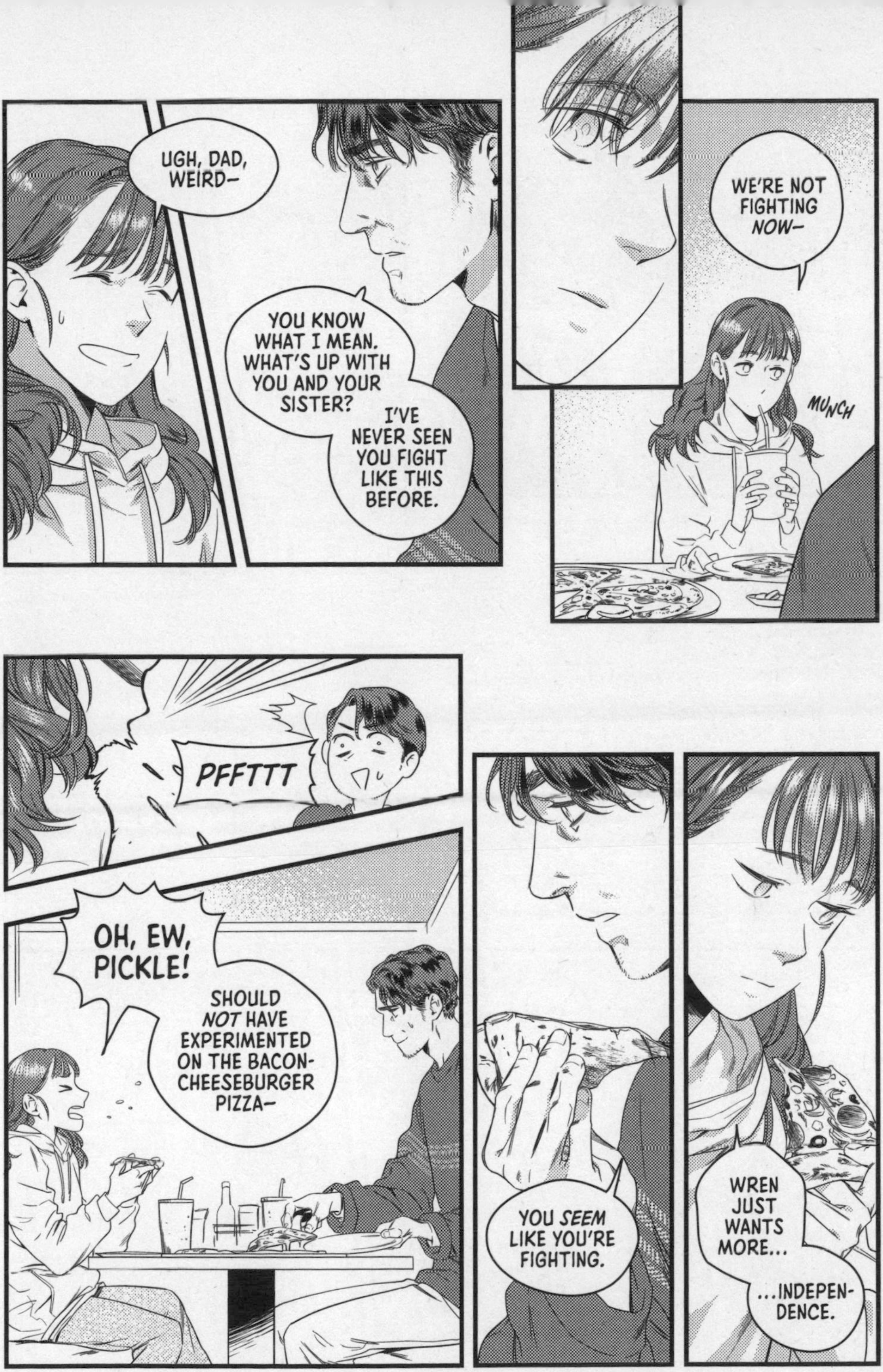
UGH, DAD, WEIRD–
YOU KNOW WHAT I MEAN. WHAT'S UP WITH YOU AND YOUR SISTER?
I'VE NEVER SEEN YOU FIGHT LIKE THIS BEFORE.
WE'RE NOT FIGHTING *NOW*–
MUNCH
PFFTTT
OH, EW, PICKLE!
SHOULD *NOT* HAVE EXPERIMENTED ON THE BACON-CHEESEBURGER PIZZA–
YOU *SEEM* LIKE YOU'RE FIGHTING.
WREN JUST WANTS MORE...
...INDEPEN-DENCE.

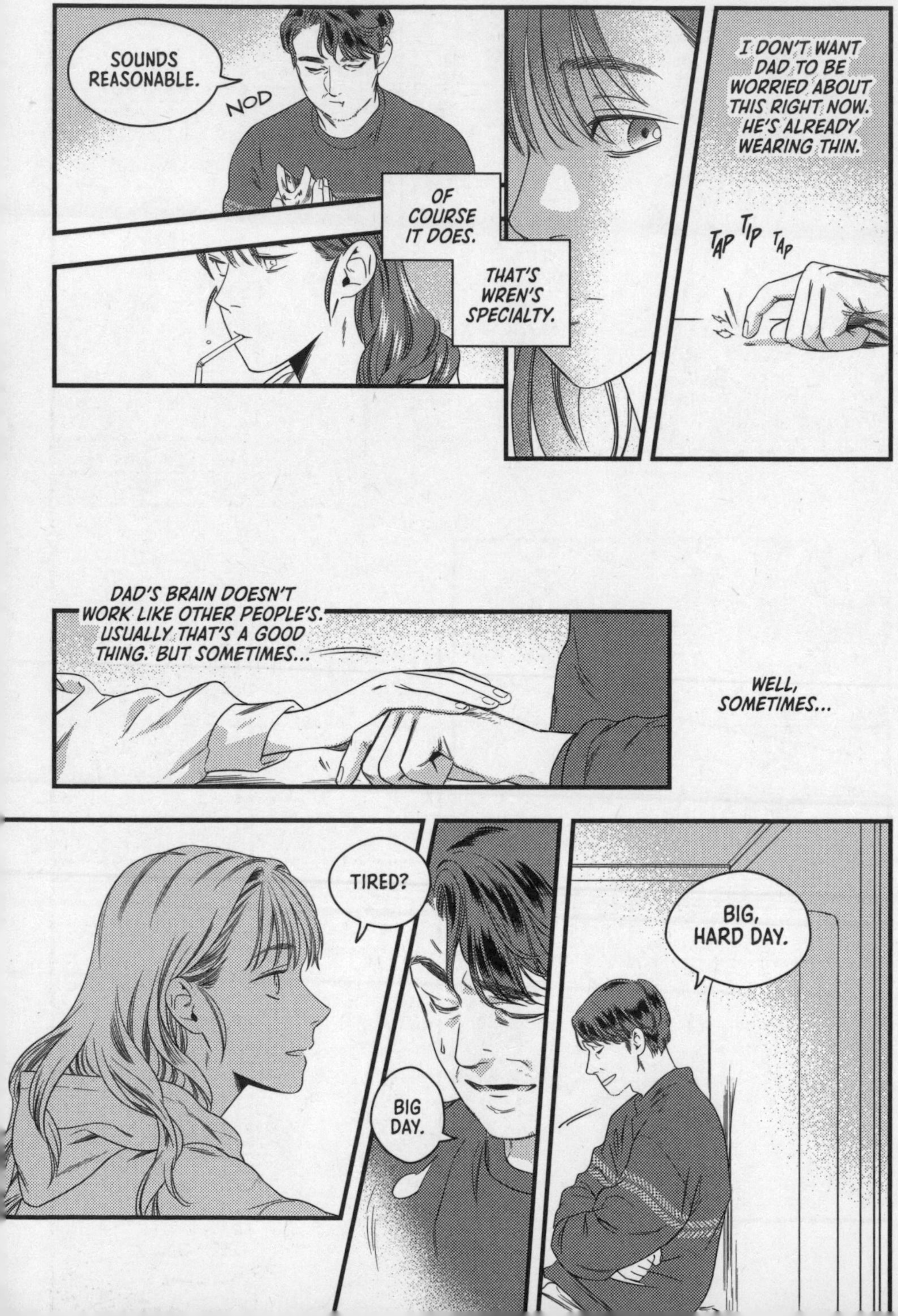
SOUNDS REASONABLE.
NOD
OF COURSE IT DOES.
THAT'S WREN'S SPECIALTY.
I DON'T WANT DAD TO BE WORRIED ABOUT THIS RIGHT NOW. HE'S ALREADY WEARING THIN.
TAP TIP TAP
DAD'S BRAIN DOESN'T WORK LIKE OTHER PEOPLE'S. USUALLY THAT'S A GOOD THING. BUT SOMETIMES...
WELL, SOMETIMES...
TIRED?
BIG DAY.
BIG, HARD DAY.

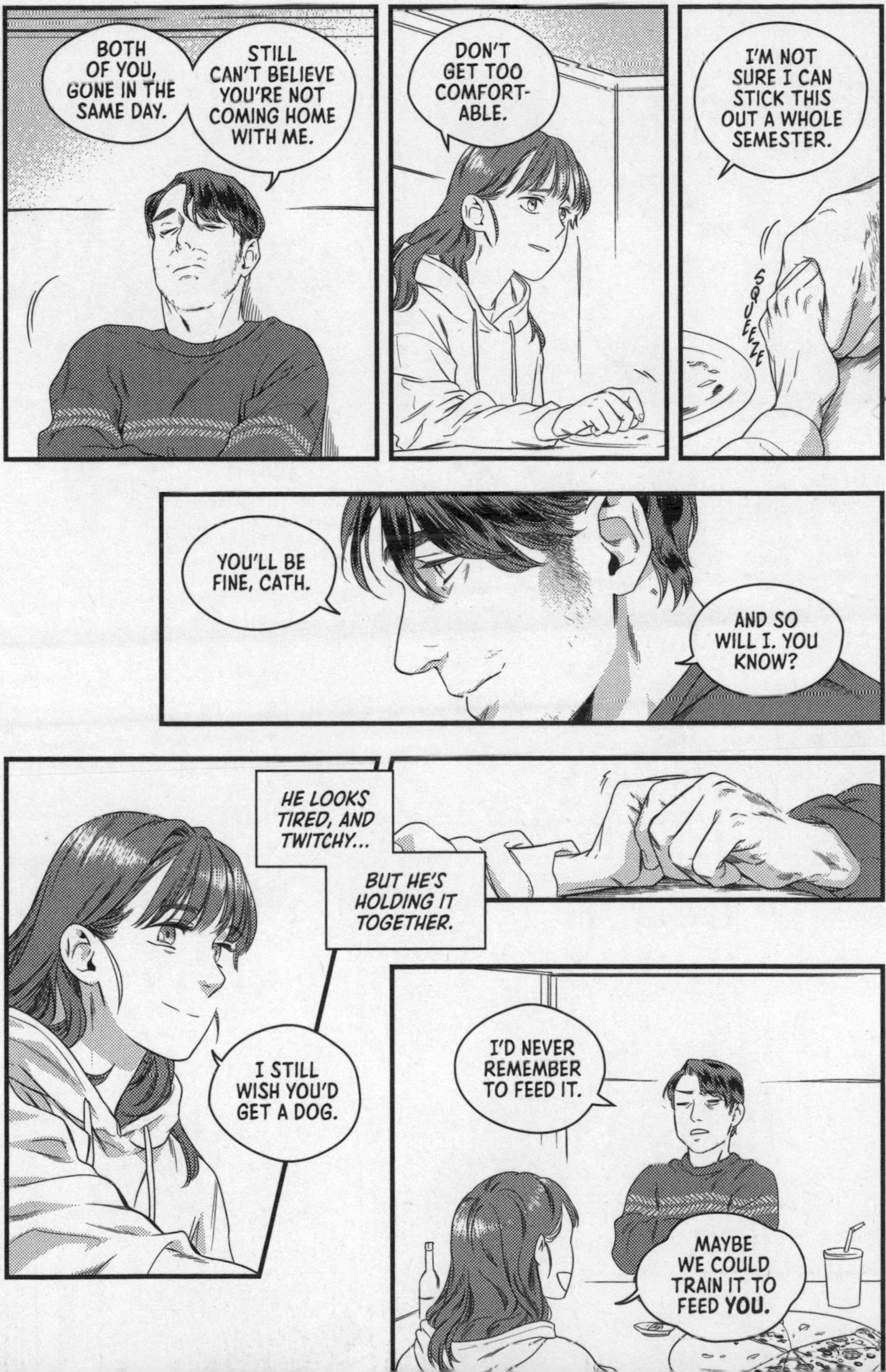
BOTH OF YOU, GONE IN THE SAME DAY.
STILL CAN'T BELIEVE YOU'RE NOT COMING HOME WITH ME.
DON'T GET TOO COMFORT-ABLE.
I'M NOT SURE I CAN STICK THIS OUT A WHOLE SEMESTER.
SQUEEZE
YOU'LL BE FINE, CATH.
AND SO WILL I. YOU KNOW?
HE LOOKS TIRED, AND TWITCHY...
BUT HE'S HOLDING IT TOGETHER.
I STILL WISH YOU'D GET A DOG.
I'D NEVER REMEMBER TO FEED IT.
MAYBE WE COULD TRAIN IT TO FEED YOU.

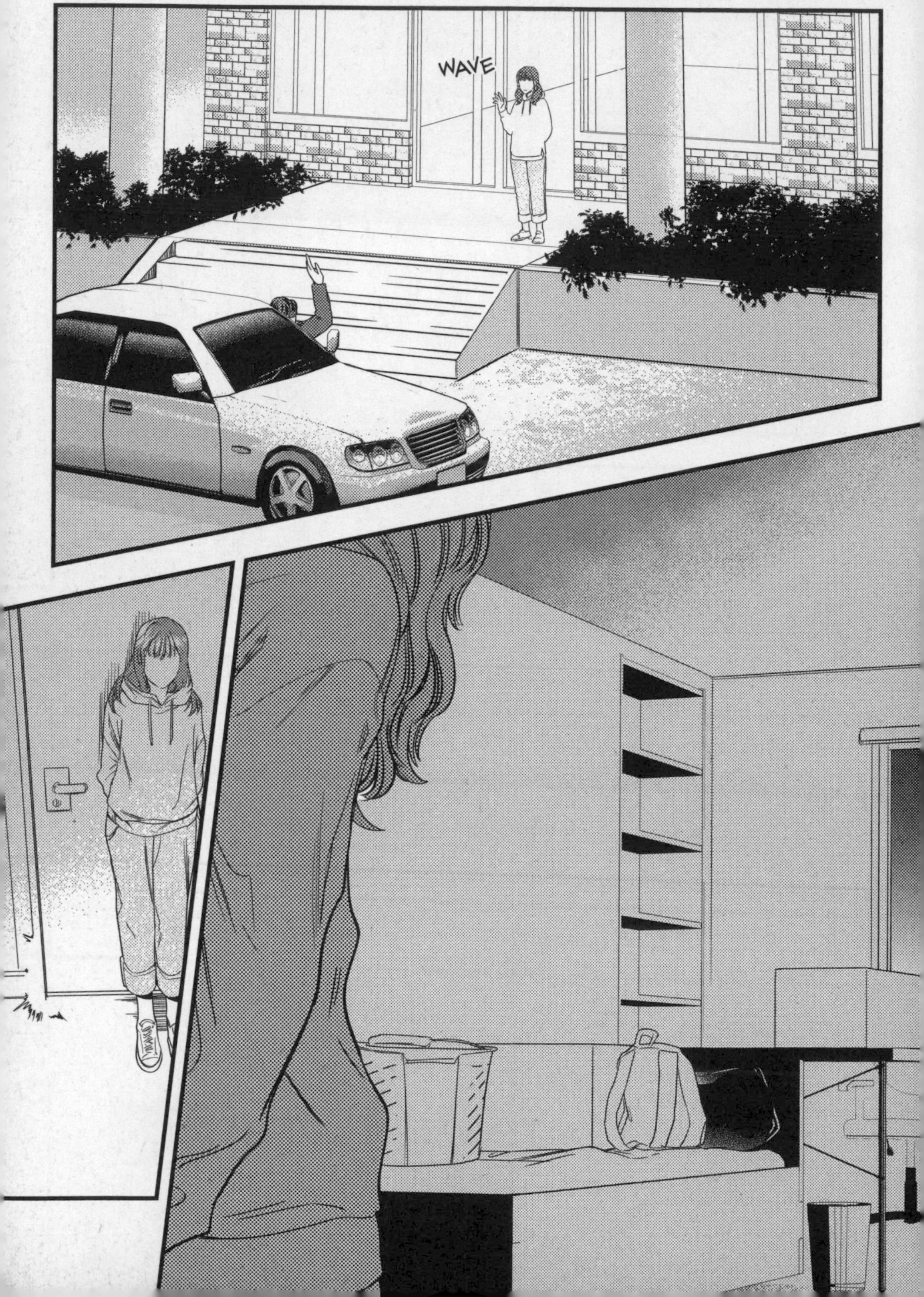
WAVE

MEET
SIMON
AND
BAZ!

As created by **Gemma T. Leslie**
in her best-selling *Mage's Heir* series

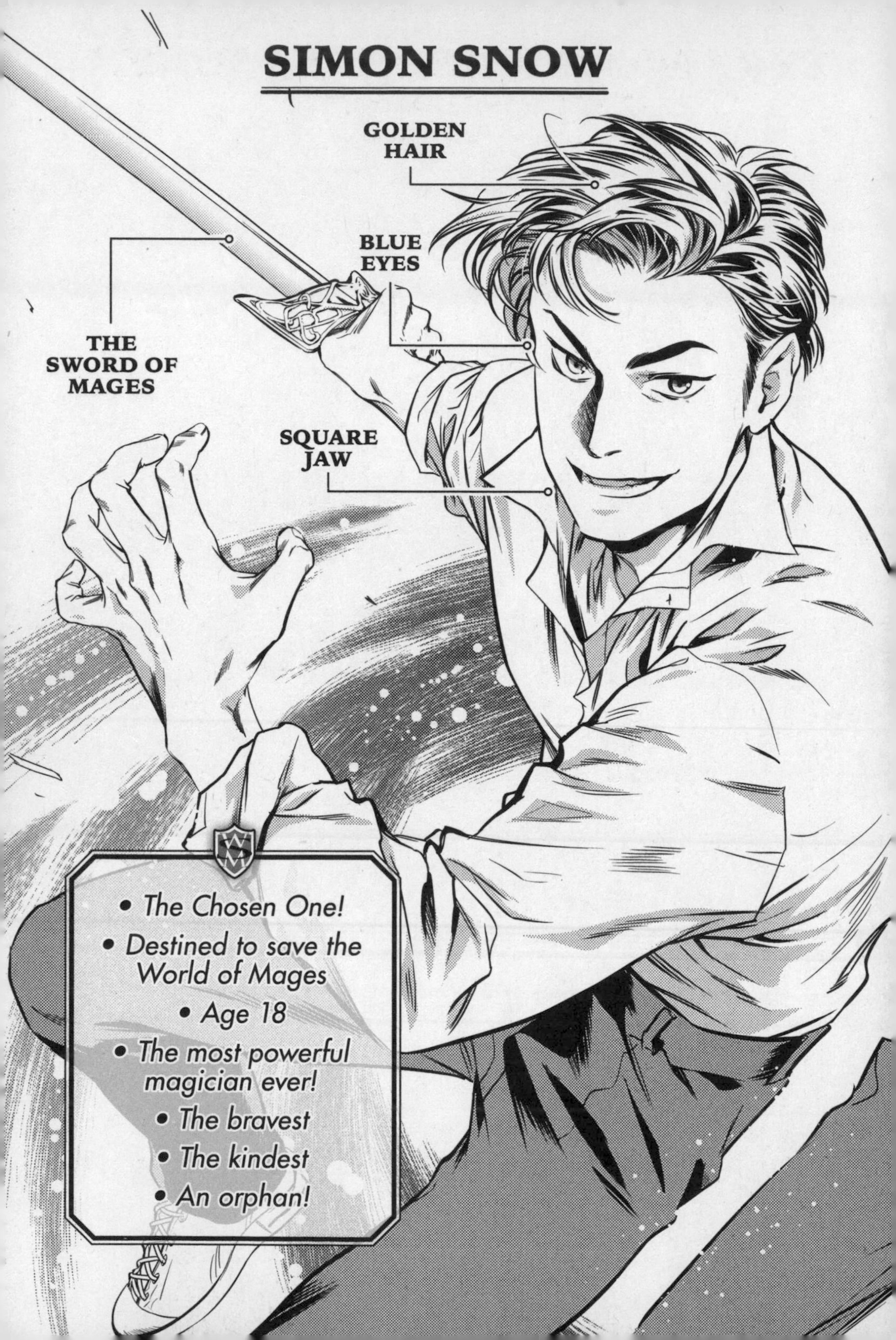
SIMON SNOW
GOLDEN HAIR
BLUE EYES
THE SWORD OF MAGES
SQUARE JAW
• The Chosen One!
• Destined to save the World of Mages
• Age 18
• The most powerful magician ever!
• The bravest
• The kindest
• An orphan!

TYRANNUS BASILTON "BAZ" GRIMM-PITCH

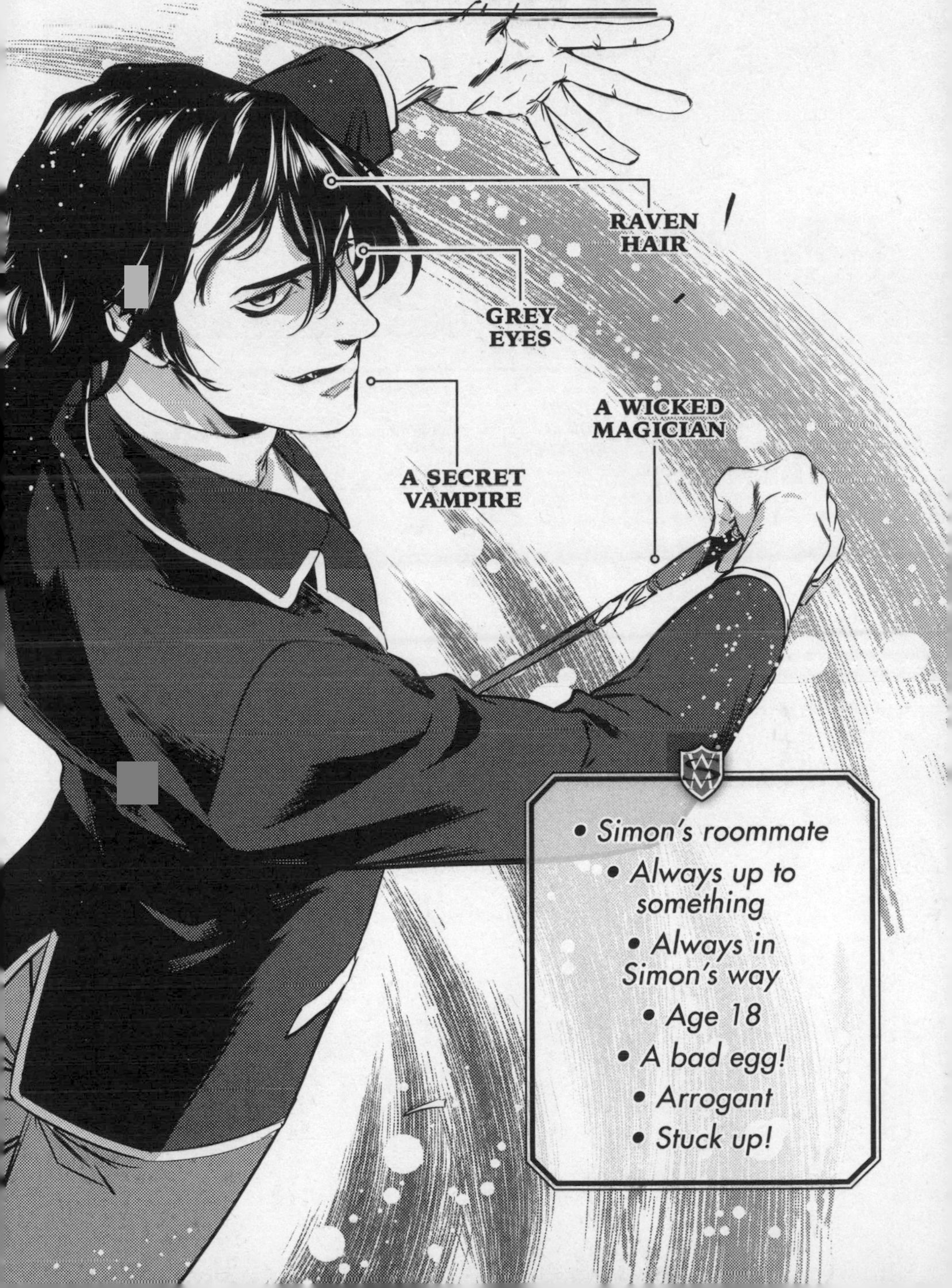
RAVEN HAIR
GREY EYES
A SECRET VAMPIRE
A WICKED MAGICIAN
• Simon's roommate
• Always up to something
• Always in Simon's way
• Age 18
• A bad egg!
• Arrogant
• Stuck up!

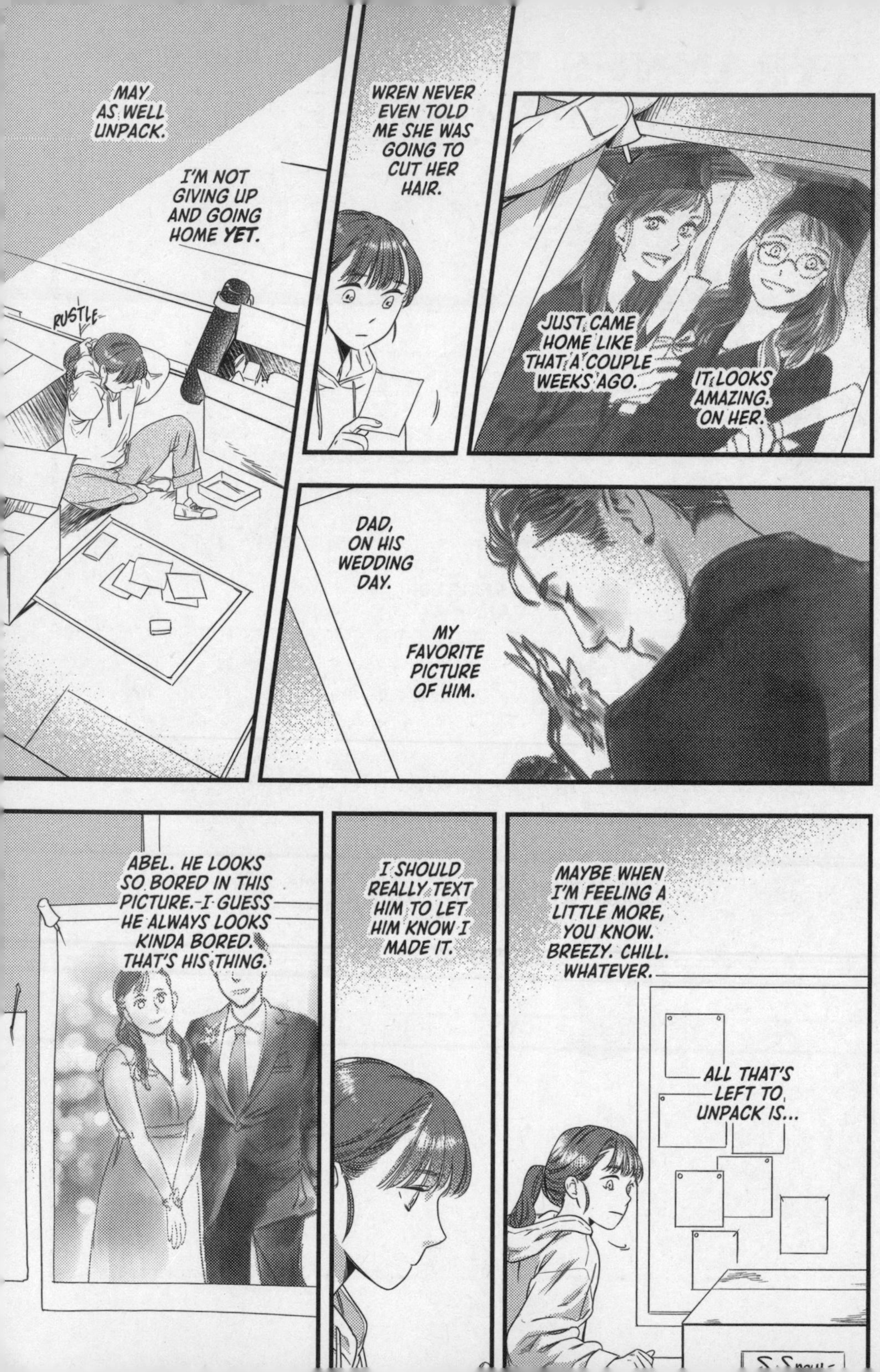
MAY AS WELL UNPACK.
I'M NOT GIVING UP AND GOING HOME YET.
RUSTLE
WREN NEVER EVEN TOLD ME SHE WAS GOING TO CUT HER HAIR.
JUST CAME HOME LIKE THAT A COUPLE WEEKS AGO.
IT LOOKS AMAZING. ON HER.
DAD, ON HIS WEDDING DAY.
MY FAVORITE PICTURE OF HIM.
ABEL. HE LOOKS SO BORED IN THIS PICTURE. I GUESS HE ALWAYS LOOKS KINDA BORED. THAT'S HIS THING.
I SHOULD REALLY TEXT HIM TO LET HIM KNOW I MADE IT.
MAYBE WHEN I'M FEELING A LITTLE MORE, YOU KNOW. BREEZY. CHILL. WHATEVER.
ALL THAT'S LEFT TO UNPACK IS...

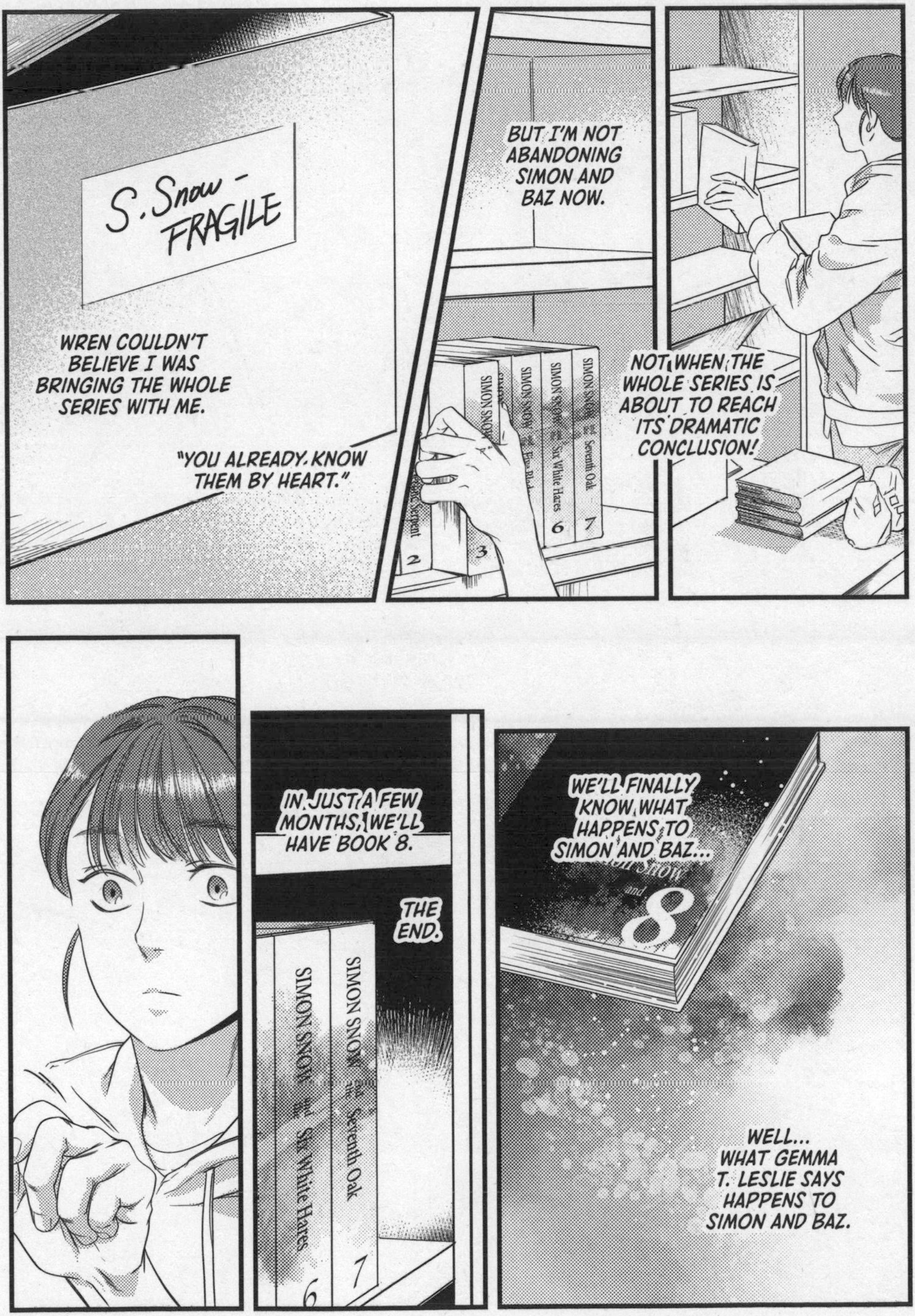
S. Snow - FRAGILE
WREN COULDN'T BELIEVE I WAS BRINGING THE WHOLE SERIES WITH ME.
"YOU ALREADY KNOW THEM BY HEART."
BUT I'M NOT ABANDONING SIMON AND BAZ NOW.
NOT WHEN THE WHOLE SERIES IS ABOUT TO REACH ITS DRAMATIC CONCLUSION!
IN JUST A FEW MONTHS, WE'LL HAVE BOOK 8.
THE END.
SIMON SNOW and Seventh Oak 7
SIMON SNOW and Six White Hares 6
WE'LL FINALLY KNOW WHAT HAPPENS TO SIMON AND BAZ...
8
WELL... WHAT GEMMA T. LESLIE SAYS HAPPENS TO SIMON AND BAZ.

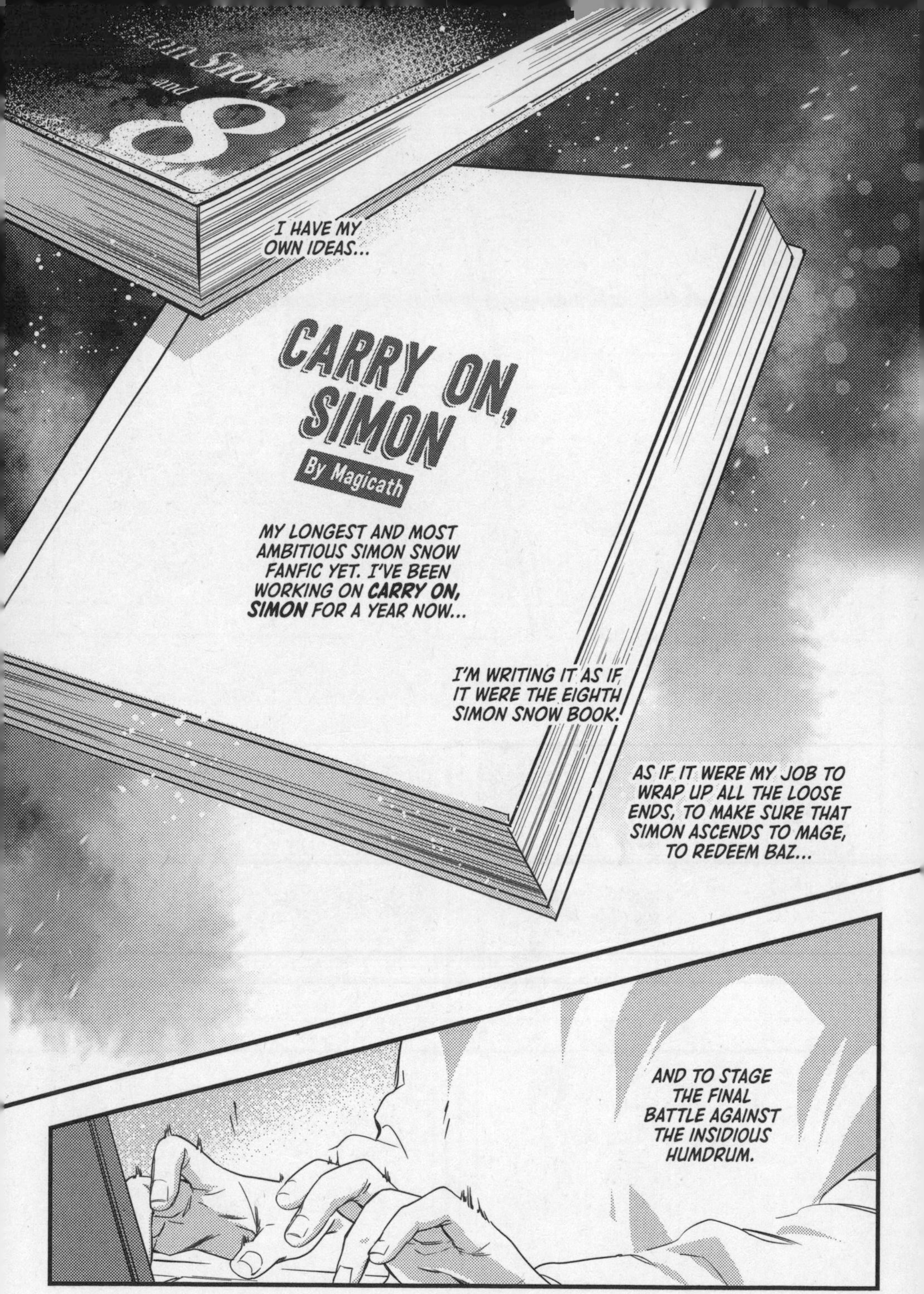
I HAVE MY OWN IDEAS...
CARRY ON, SIMON
By Magicath
MY LONGEST AND MOST AMBITIOUS SIMON SNOW FANFIC YET. I'VE BEEN WORKING ON **CARRY ON, SIMON** FOR A YEAR NOW...
I'M WRITING IT AS IF IT WERE THE EIGHTH SIMON SNOW BOOK.
AS IF IT WERE MY JOB TO WRAP UP ALL THE LOOSE ENDS, TO MAKE SURE THAT SIMON ASCENDS TO MAGE, TO REDEEM BAZ...
AND TO STAGE THE FINAL BATTLE AGAINST THE INSIDIOUS HUMDRUM.

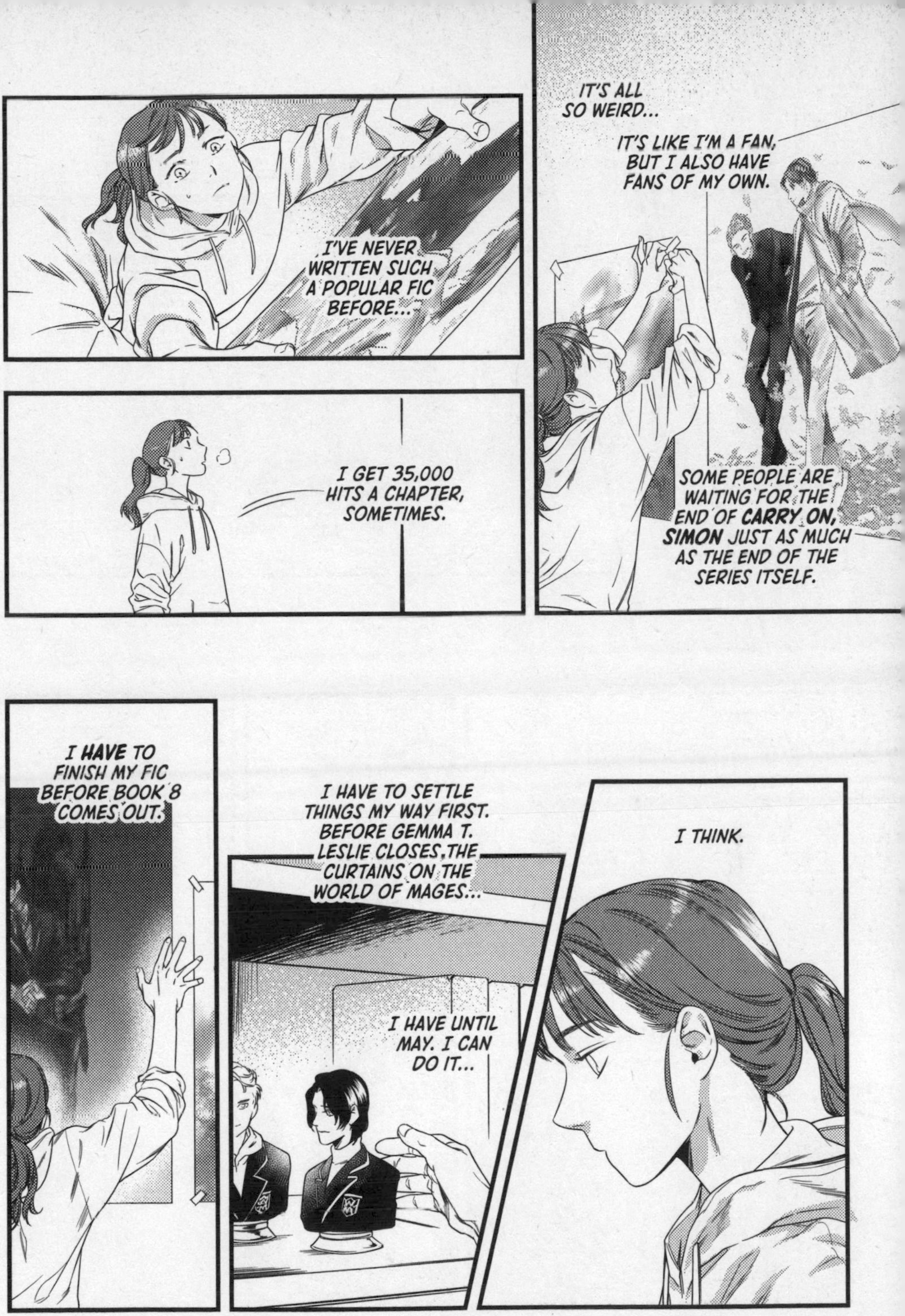
I'VE NEVER WRITTEN SUCH A POPULAR FIC BEFORE...
I GET 35,000 HITS A CHAPTER, SOMETIMES.
IT'S ALL SO WEIRD...
IT'S LIKE I'M A FAN, BUT I ALSO HAVE FANS OF MY OWN.
SOME PEOPLE ARE WAITING FOR THE END OF **CARRY ON, SIMON** JUST AS MUCH AS THE END OF THE SERIES ITSELF.
I **HAVE** TO FINISH MY FIC BEFORE BOOK 8 COMES OUT.
I HAVE TO SETTLE THINGS MY WAY FIRST. BEFORE GEMMA T. LESLIE CLOSES THE CURTAINS ON THE WORLD OF MAGES...
I HAVE UNTIL MAY. I CAN DO IT...
I THINK.

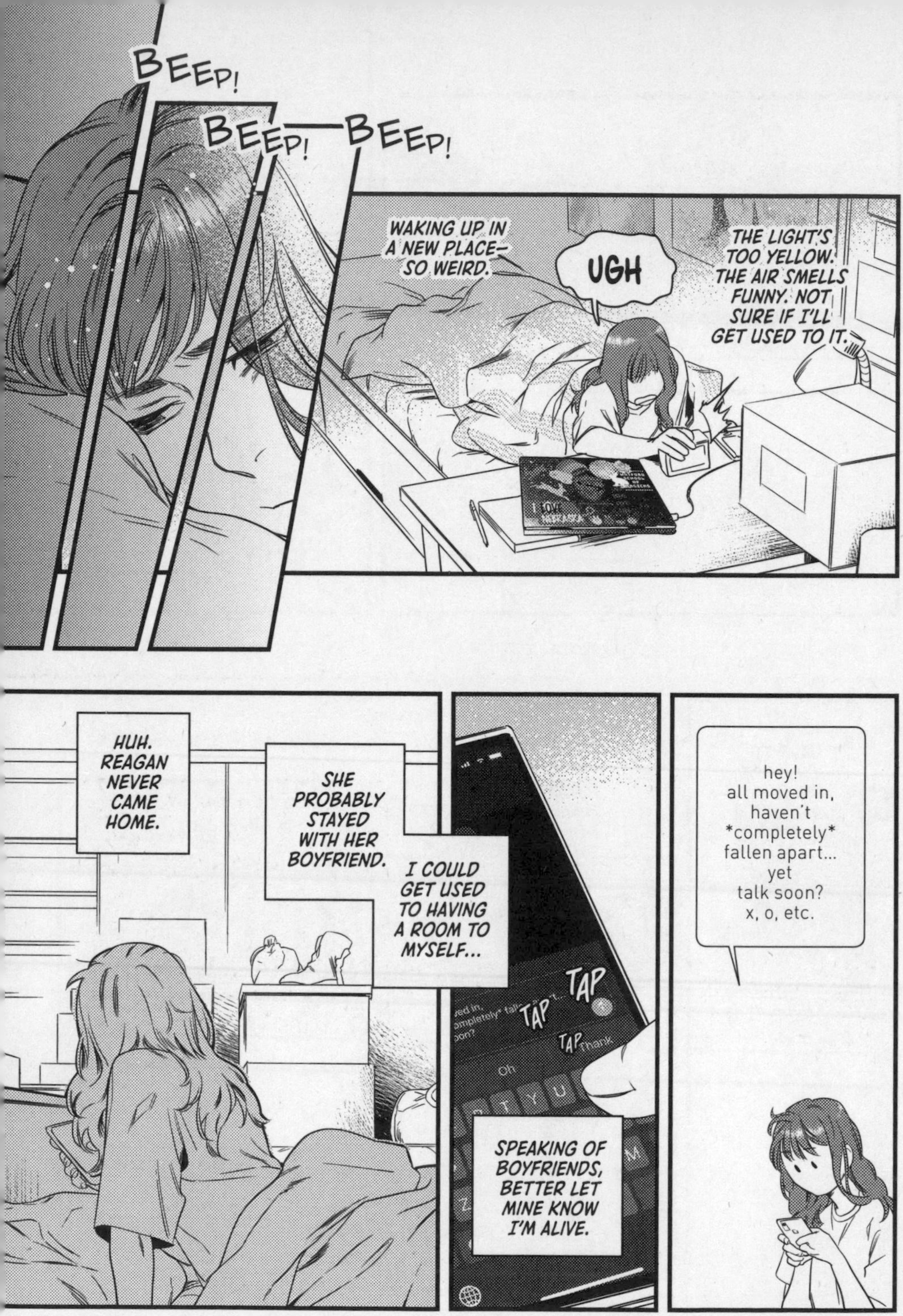

BEEP!
BEEP!
BEEP!
WAKING UP IN A NEW PLACE— SO WEIRD.
UGH
THE LIGHT'S TOO YELLOW. THE AIR SMELLS FUNNY. NOT SURE IF I'LL GET USED TO IT.
I LOVE NEBRASKA
HUH. REAGAN NEVER CAME HOME.
SHE PROBABLY STAYED WITH HER BOYFRIEND.
I COULD GET USED TO HAVING A ROOM TO MYSELF...
TAP
TAP
TAP
SPEAKING OF BOYFRIENDS, BETTER LET MINE KNOW I'M ALIVE.
hey! all moved in, haven't *completely* fallen apart... yet talk soon? x, o, etc.

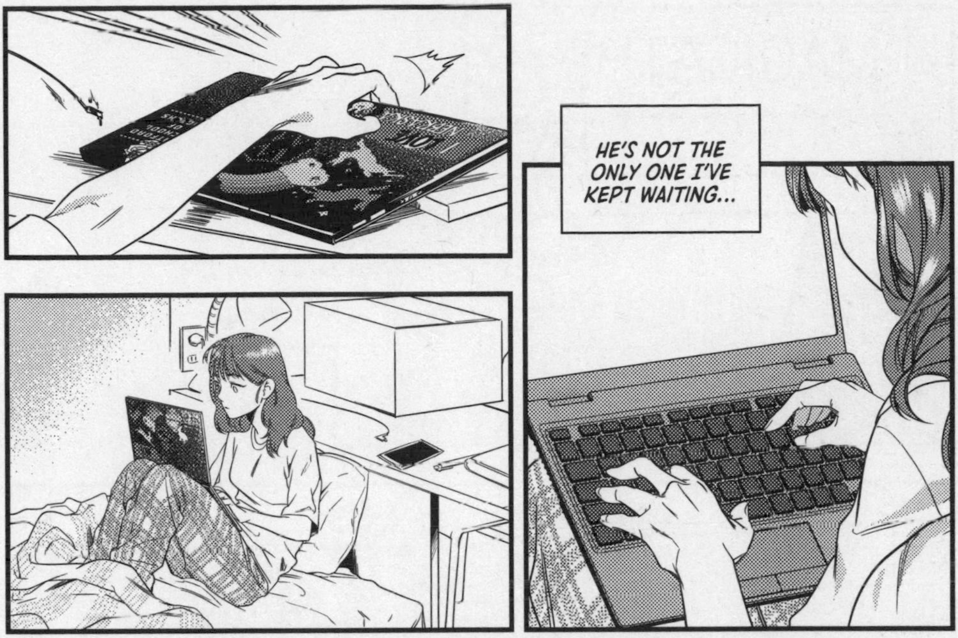
HE'S NOT THE ONLY ONE I'VE KEPT WAITING...

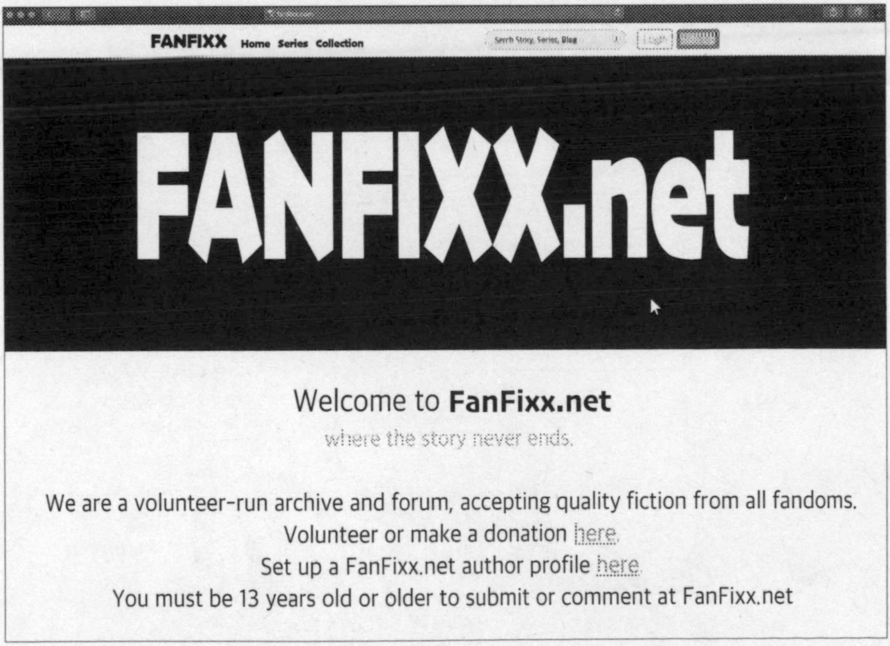
FANFIXX
Home Series Collection
Serch Story, Series, Blog
FANFIXX.net
Welcome to **FanFixx.net**
where the story never ends.
We are a volunteer-run archive and forum, accepting quality fiction from all fandoms.
Volunteer or make a donation here.
Set up a FanFixx.net author profile here.
You must be 13 years old or older to submit or comment at FanFixx.net

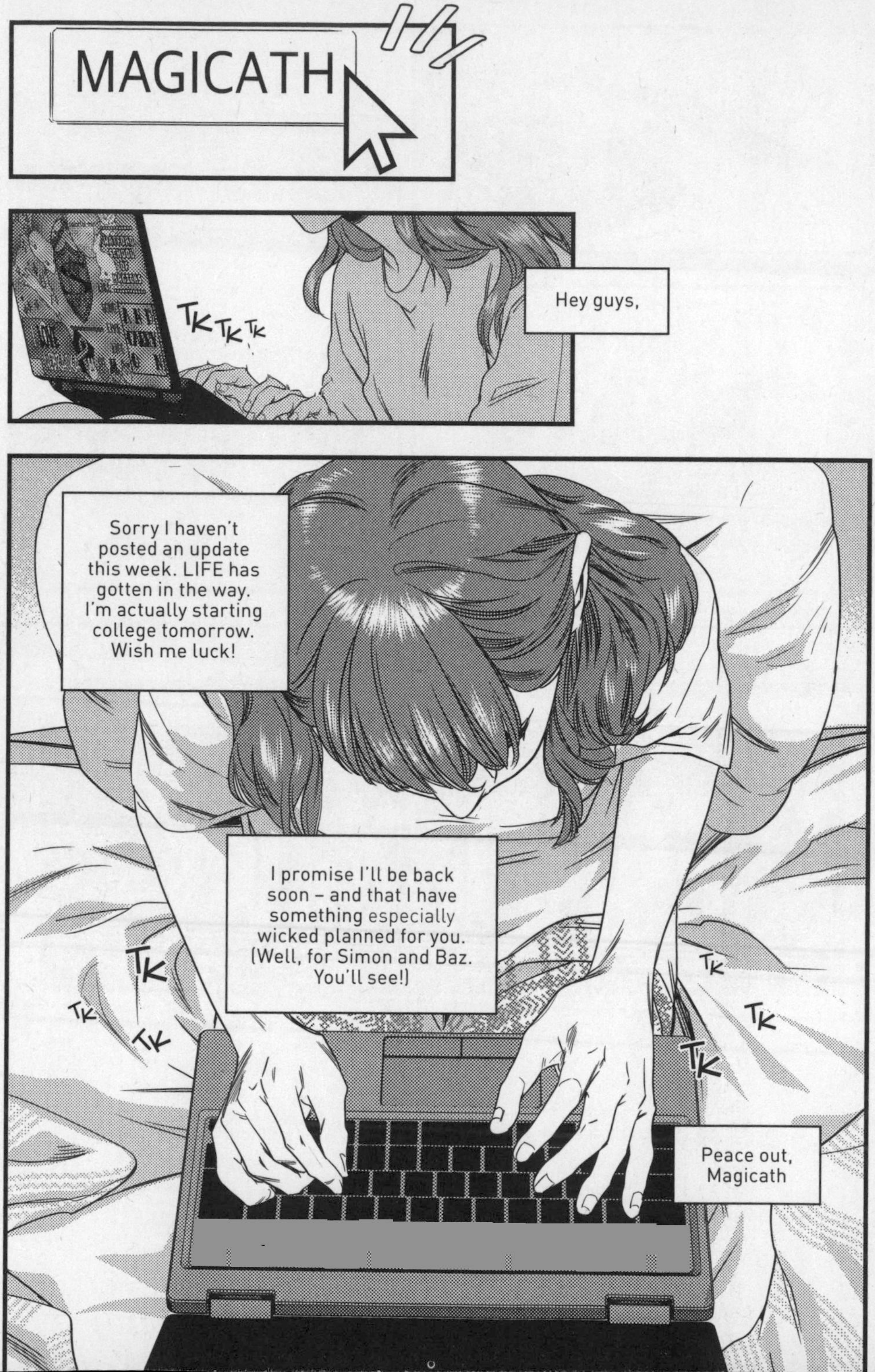
MAGICATH
TK TK TK
Hey guys,
Sorry I haven't posted an update this week. LIFE has gotten in the way. I'm actually starting college tomorrow. Wish me luck!
I promise I'll be back soon – and that I have something especially wicked planned for you. (Well, for Simon and Baz. You'll see!)
TK
TK
TK
TK
TK
TK
Peace out, Magicath

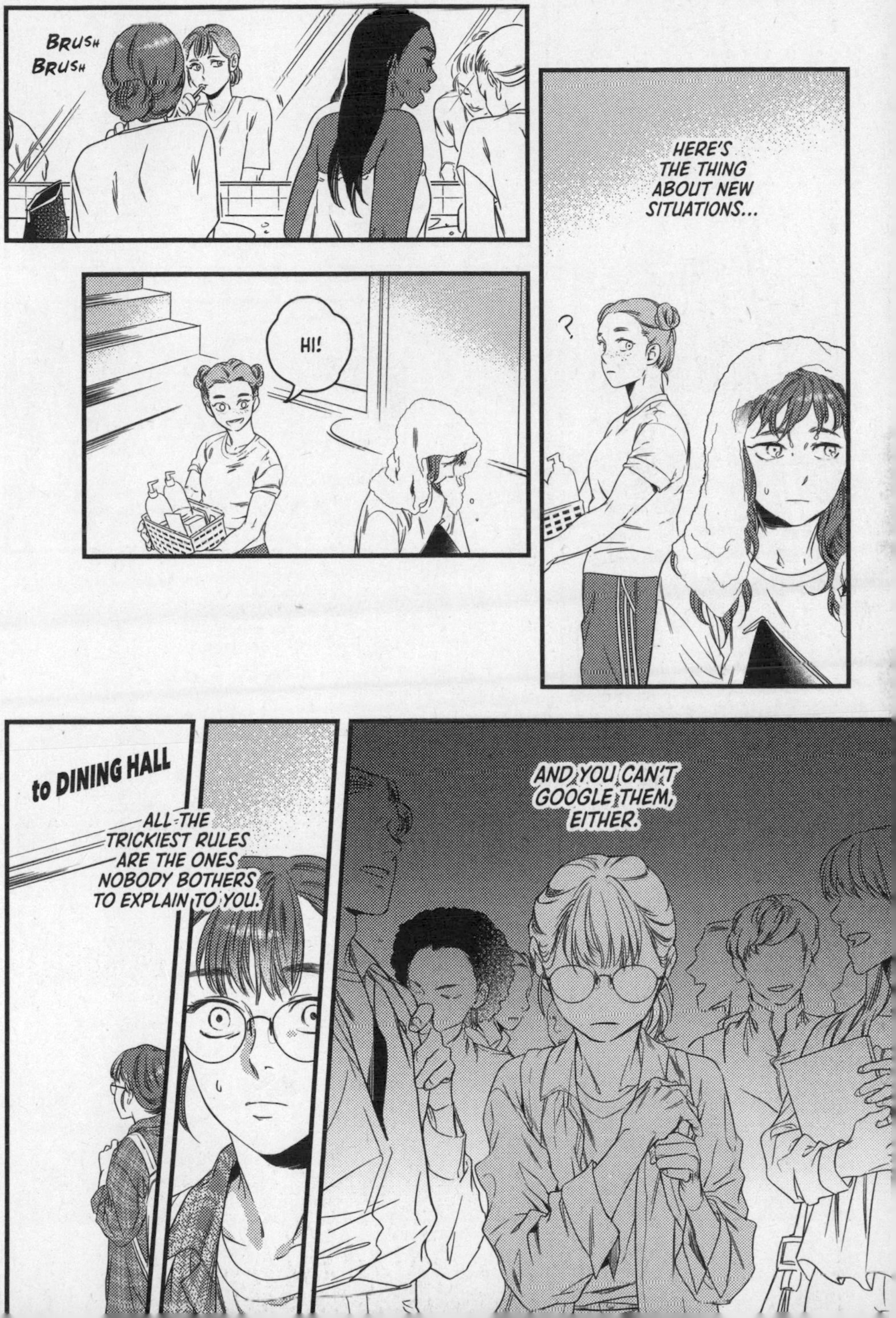
BRUSH
BRUSH
HI!
?
HERE'S THE THING ABOUT NEW SITUATIONS...
to DINING HALL
ALL THE TRICKIEST RULES ARE THE ONES NOBODY BOTHERS TO EXPLAIN TO YOU.
AND YOU CAN'T GOOGLE THEM, EITHER.

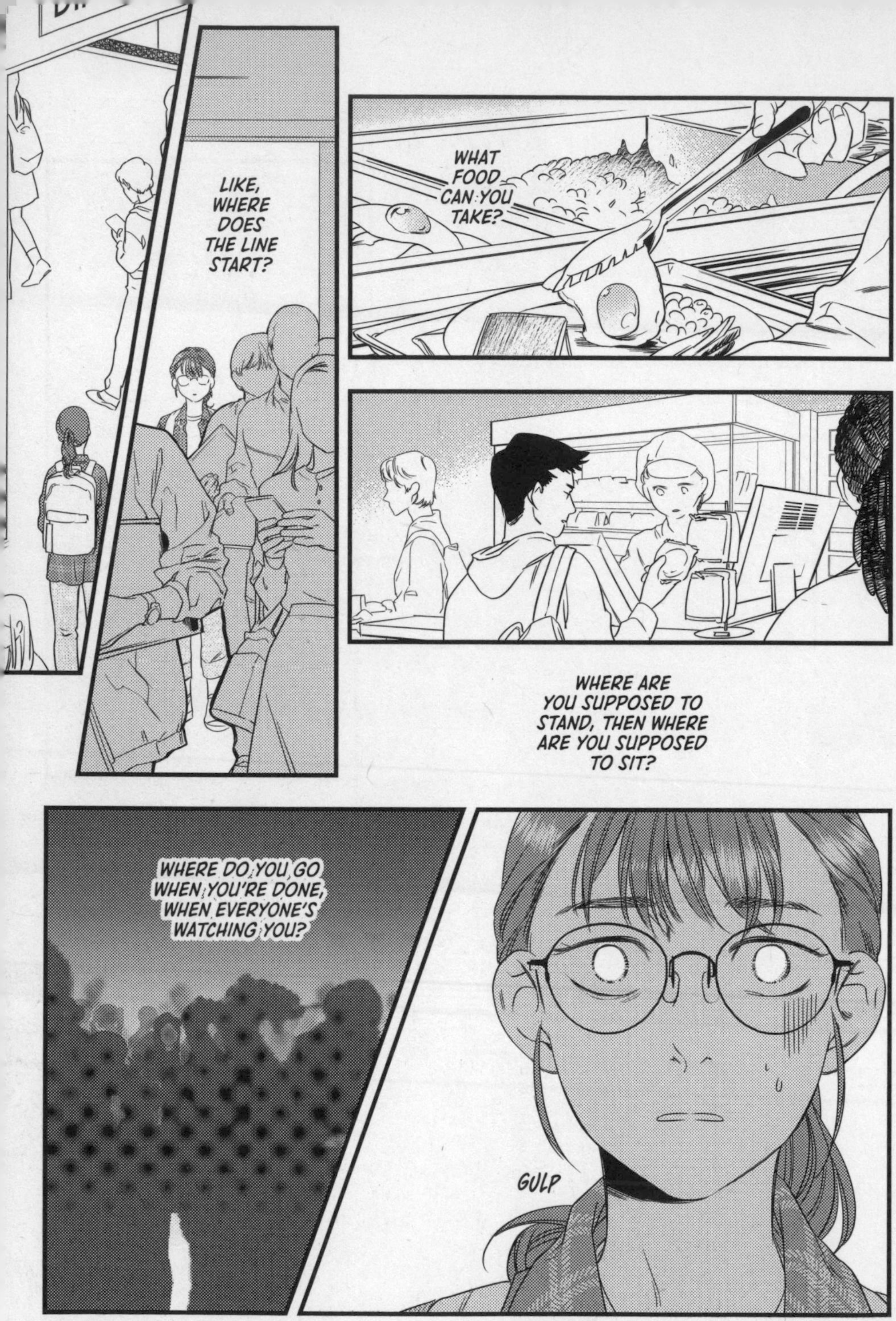
LIKE, WHERE DOES THE LINE START?
WHAT FOOD CAN YOU TAKE?
WHERE ARE YOU SUPPOSED TO STAND, THEN WHERE ARE YOU SUPPOSED TO SIT?
WHERE DO YOU GO WHEN YOU'RE DONE, WHEN EVERYONE'S WATCHING YOU?
GULP

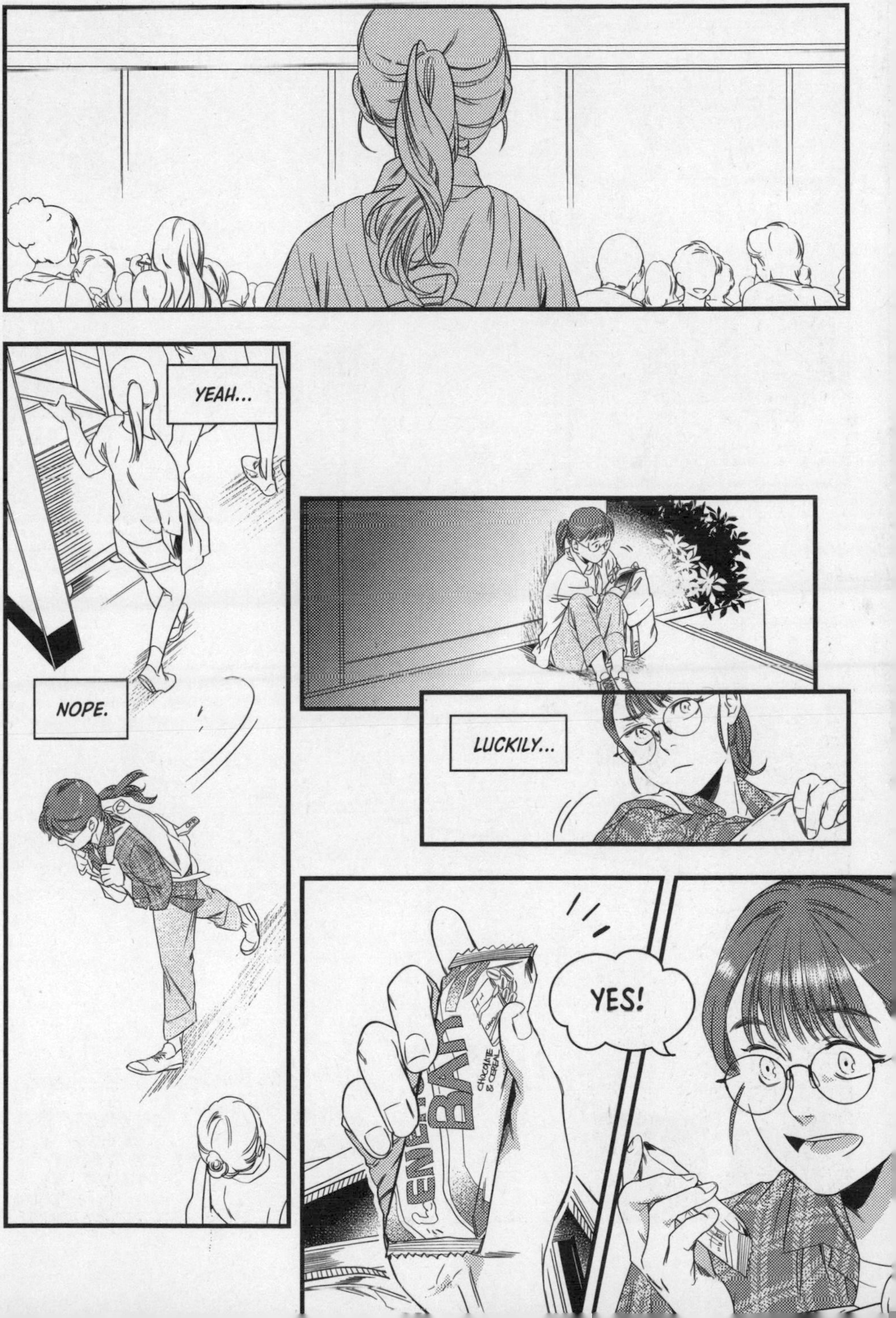
YEAH...
NOPE.
LUCKILY...
BAR
CHOCOLATE & CEREAL
YES!

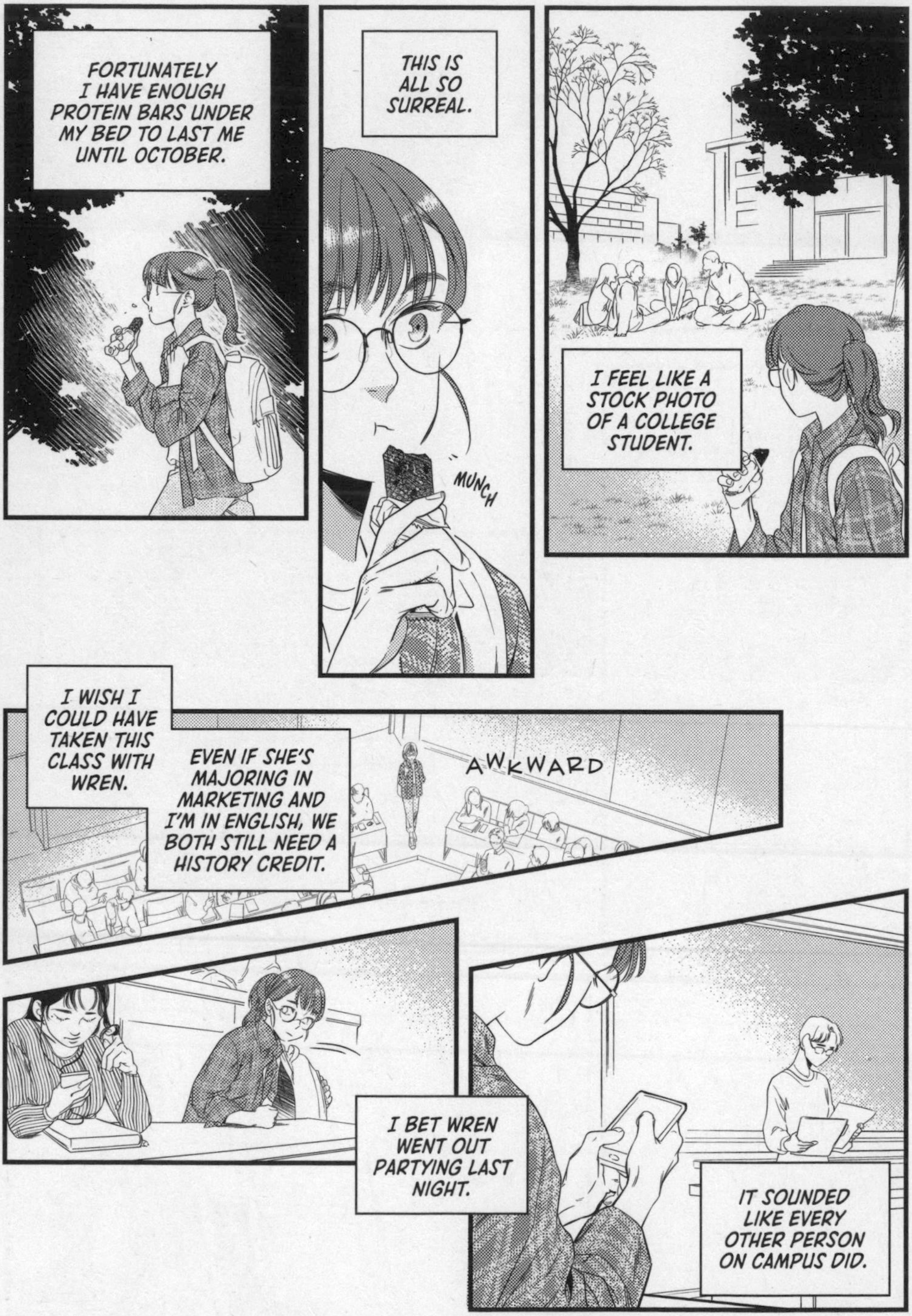
FORTUNATELY I HAVE ENOUGH PROTEIN BARS UNDER MY BED TO LAST ME UNTIL OCTOBER.
THIS IS ALL SO SURREAL.
MUNCH
I FEEL LIKE A STOCK PHOTO OF A COLLEGE STUDENT.
I WISH I COULD HAVE TAKEN THIS CLASS WITH WREN.
EVEN IF SHE'S MAJORING IN MARKETING AND I'M IN ENGLISH, WE BOTH STILL NEED A HISTORY CREDIT.
AWKWARD
I BET WREN WENT OUT PARTYING LAST NIGHT.
IT SOUNDED LIKE EVERY OTHER PERSON ON CAMPUS DID.

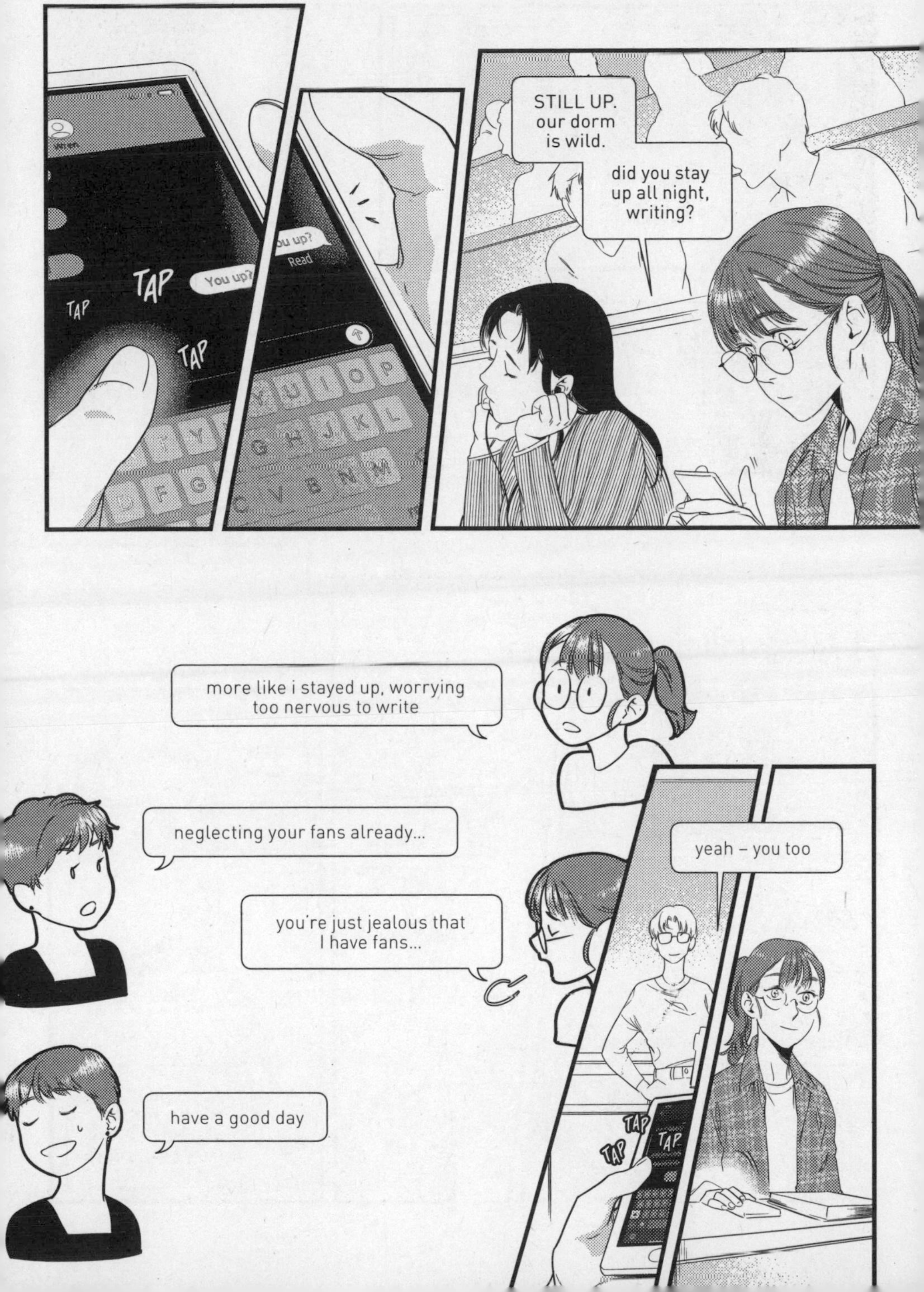
TAP
TAP
You up?
TAP
Read
STILL UP. our dorm is wild.
did you stay up all night, writing?
more like i stayed up, worrying too nervous to write
neglecting your fans already...
you're just jealous that I have fans...
have a good day
yeah – you too
TAP
TAP
TAP

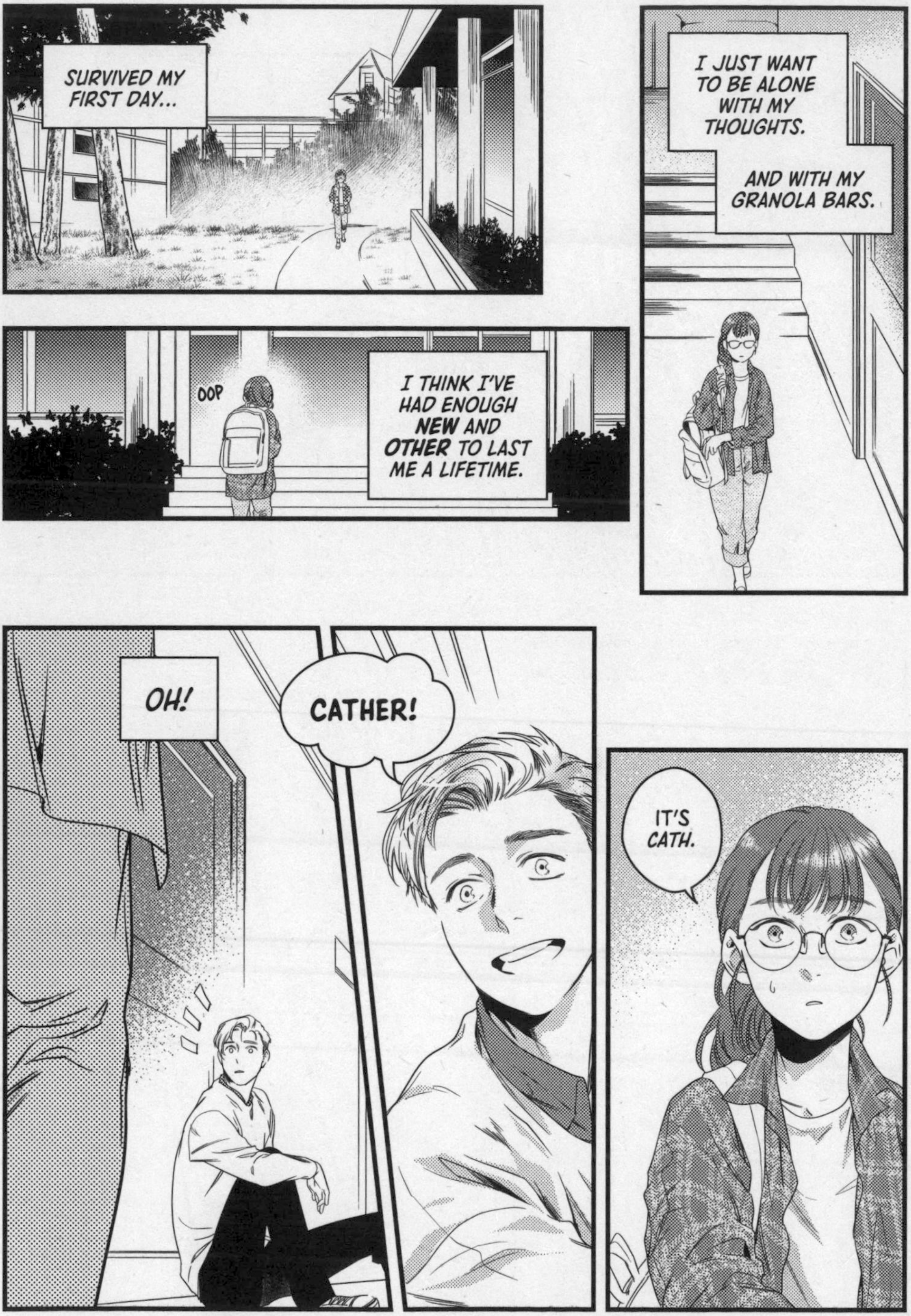
SURVIVED MY FIRST DAY...
DOP
I THINK I'VE HAD ENOUGH **NEW** AND **OTHER** TO LAST ME A LIFETIME.
I JUST WANT TO BE ALONE WITH MY THOUGHTS.
AND WITH MY GRANOLA BARS.
OH!
CATHER!
IT'S CATH.

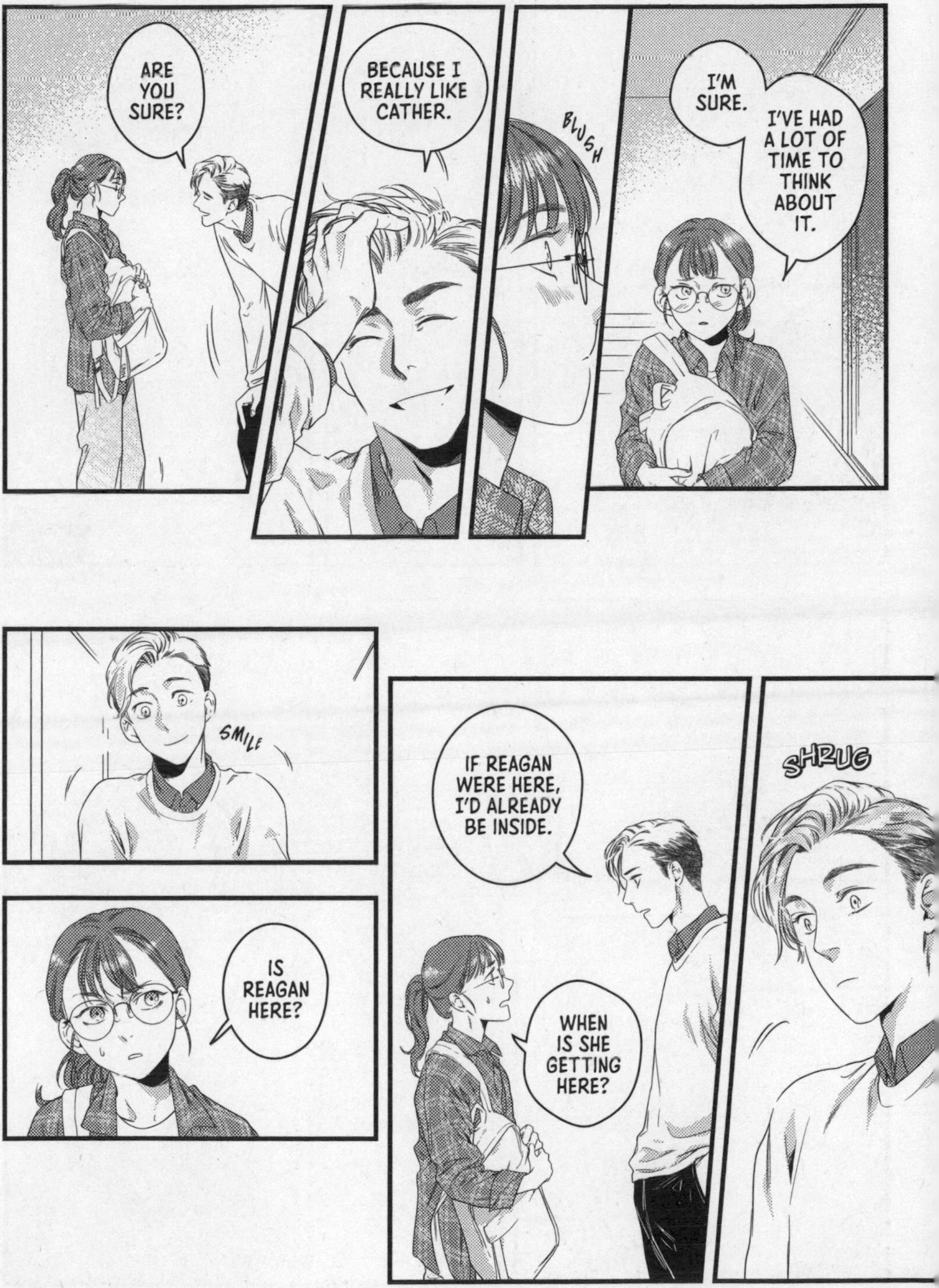
ARE YOU SURE?
BECAUSE I REALLY LIKE CATHER.
BLUSH
I'M SURE.
I'VE HAD A LOT OF TIME TO THINK ABOUT IT.
SMILE
IS REAGAN HERE?
IF REAGAN WERE HERE, I'D ALREADY BE INSIDE.
WHEN IS SHE GETTING HERE?
SHRUG

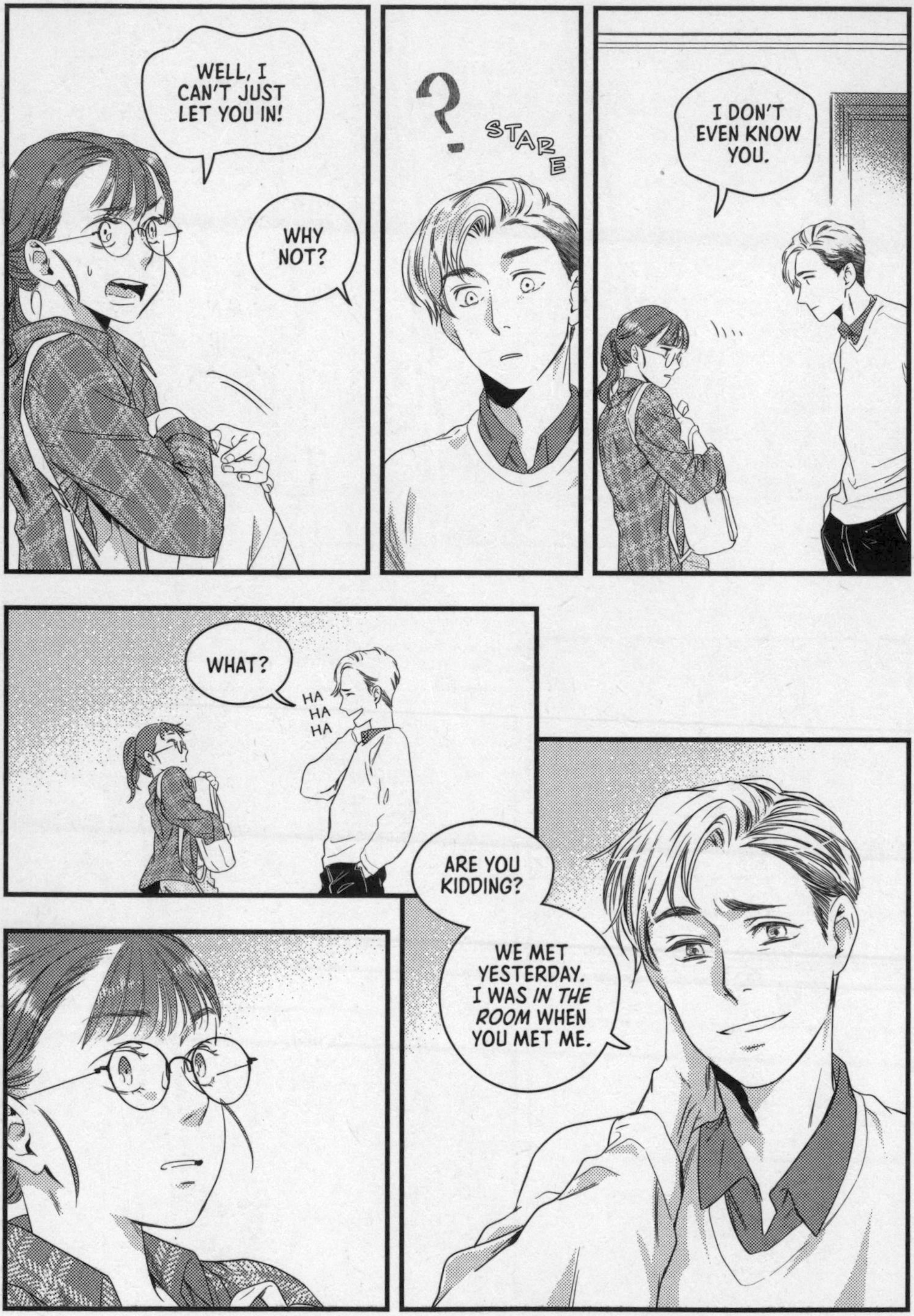
WELL, I CAN'T JUST LET YOU IN!
WHY NOT?
?
STARE
I DON'T EVEN KNOW YOU.
WHAT?
HA HA HA
ARE YOU KIDDING?
WE MET YESTERDAY. I WAS *IN THE ROOM* WHEN YOU MET ME.

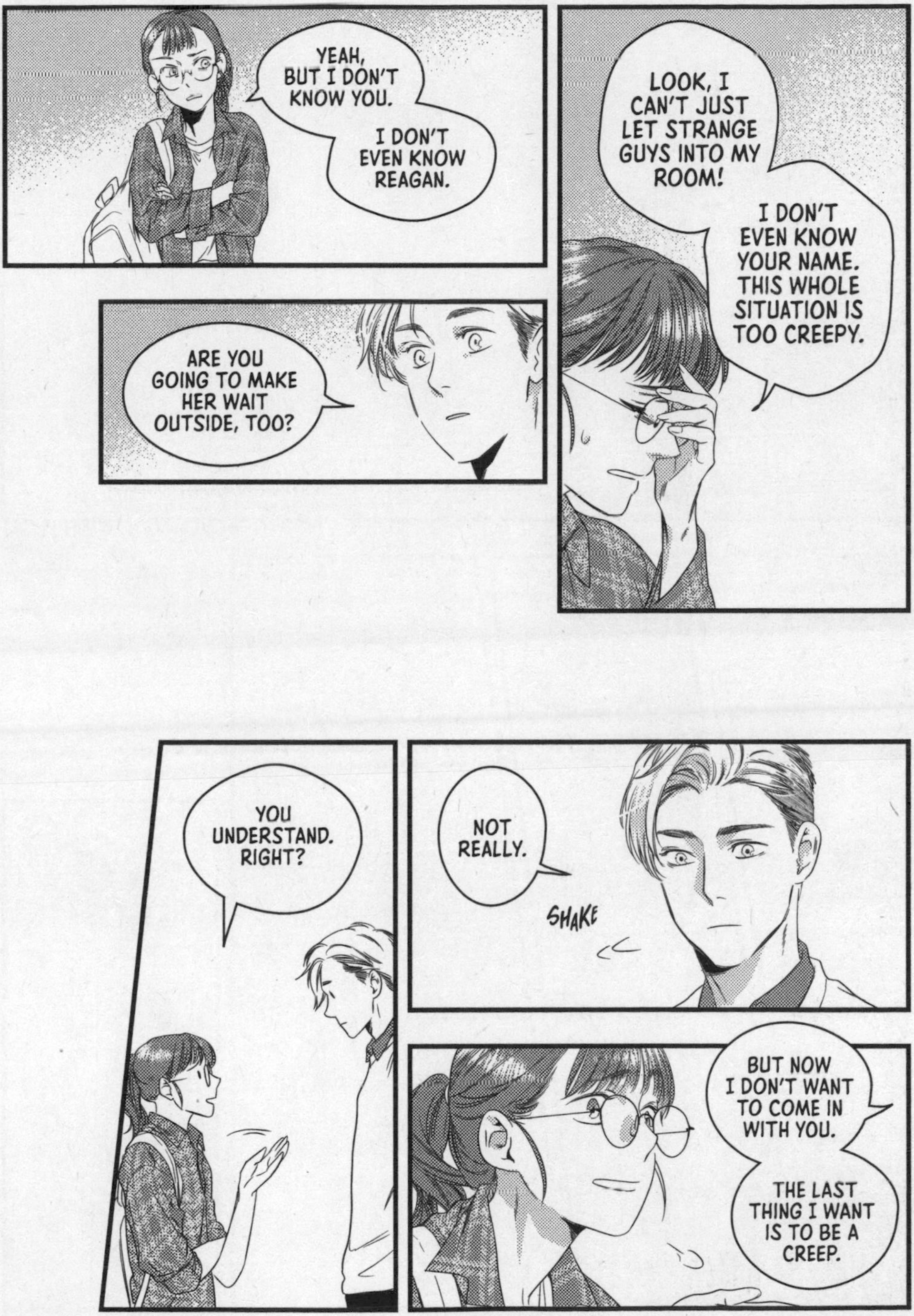
YEAH, BUT I DON'T KNOW YOU.
I DON'T EVEN KNOW REAGAN.
ARE YOU GOING TO MAKE HER WAIT OUTSIDE, TOO?
LOOK, I CAN'T JUST LET STRANGE GUYS INTO MY ROOM!
I DON'T EVEN KNOW YOUR NAME. THIS WHOLE SITUATION IS TOO CREEPY.
YOU UNDERSTAND. RIGHT?
NOT REALLY.
SHAKE
BUT NOW I DON'T WANT TO COME IN WITH YOU.
THE LAST THING I WANT IS TO BE A CREEP.

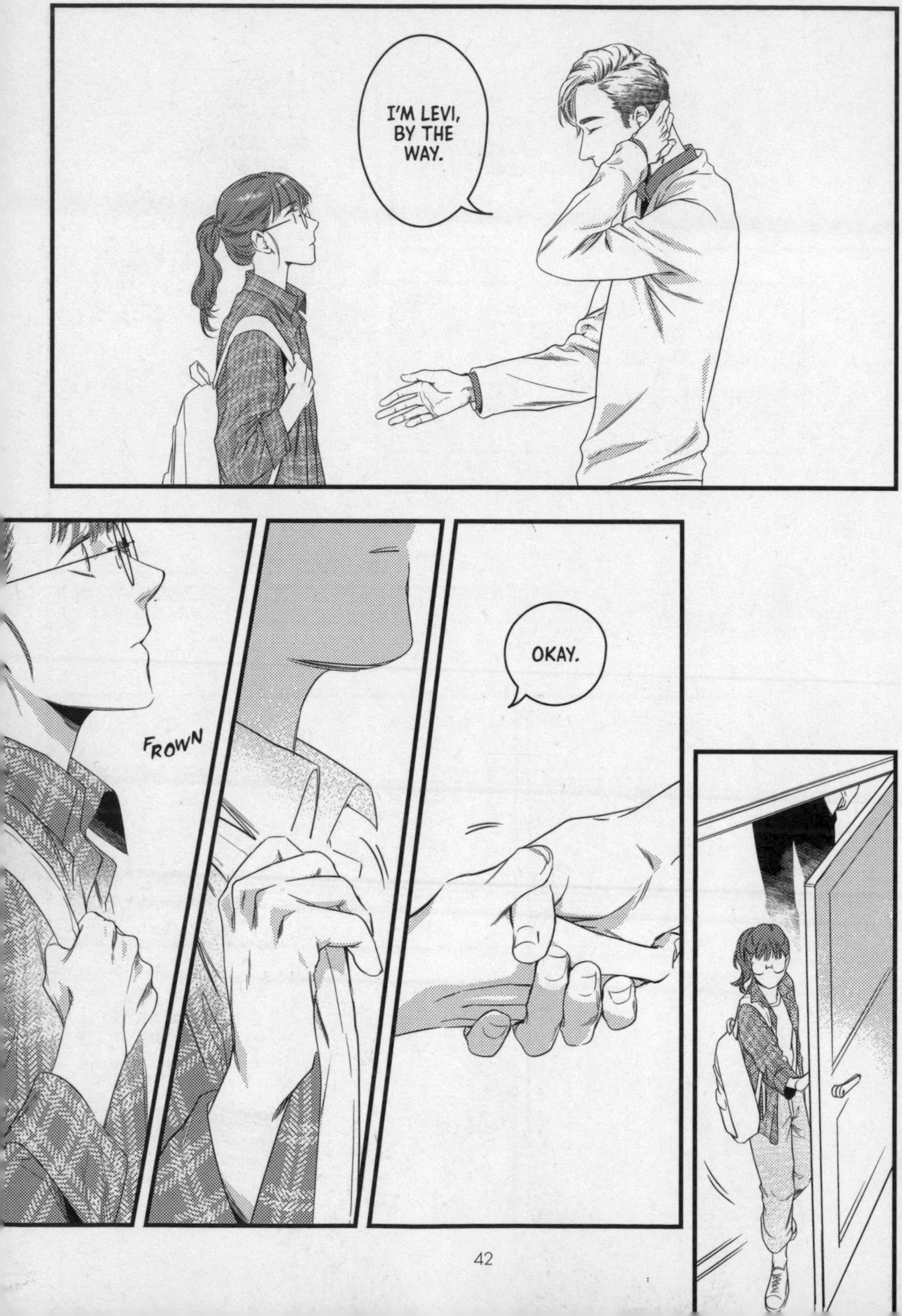
I'M LEVI, BY THE WAY.
FROWN
OKAY.

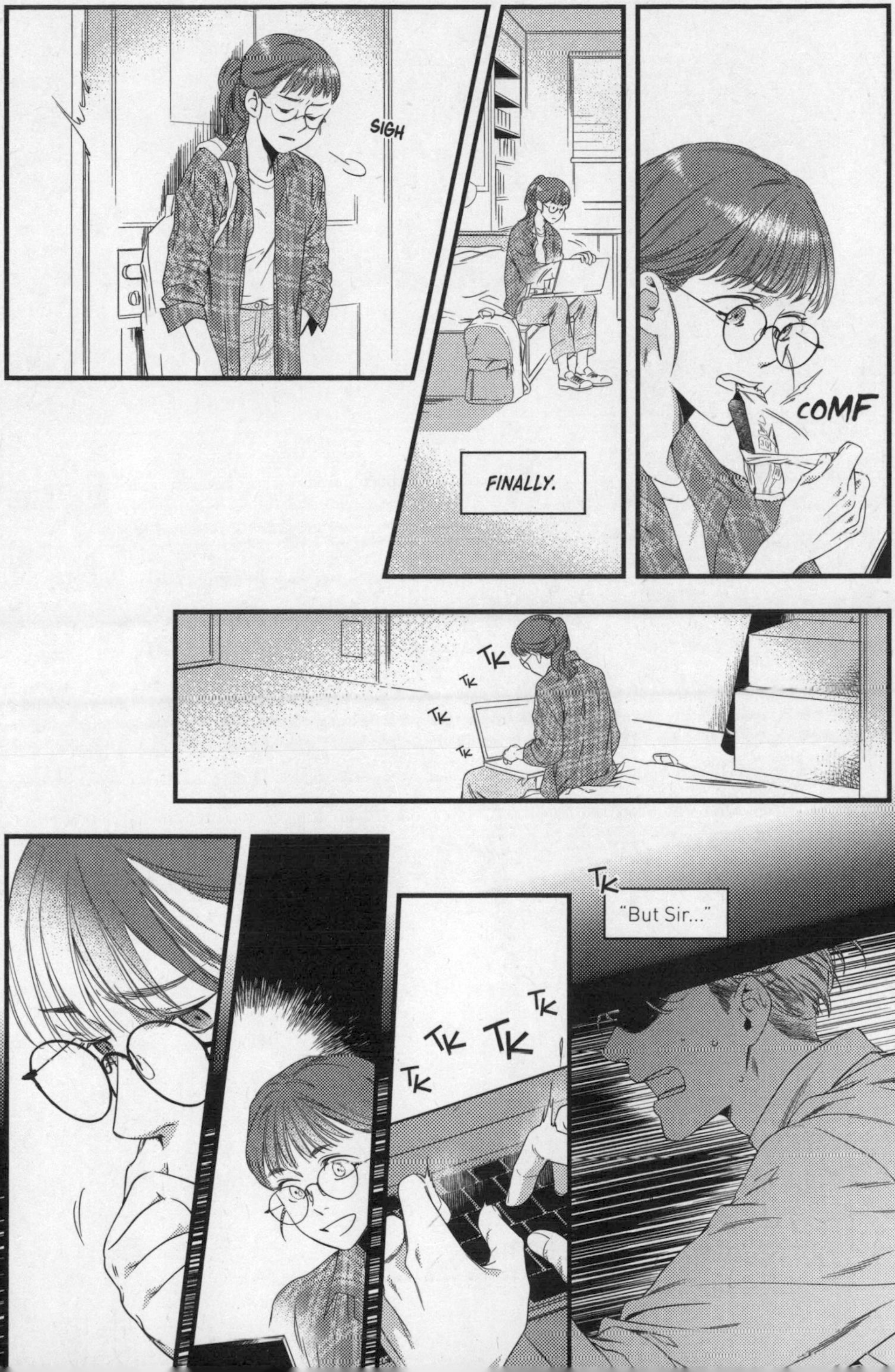
SIGH
FINALLY.
COMF
TK
TK
TK
TK
TK
TK
TK
TK
TK
"But Sir..."

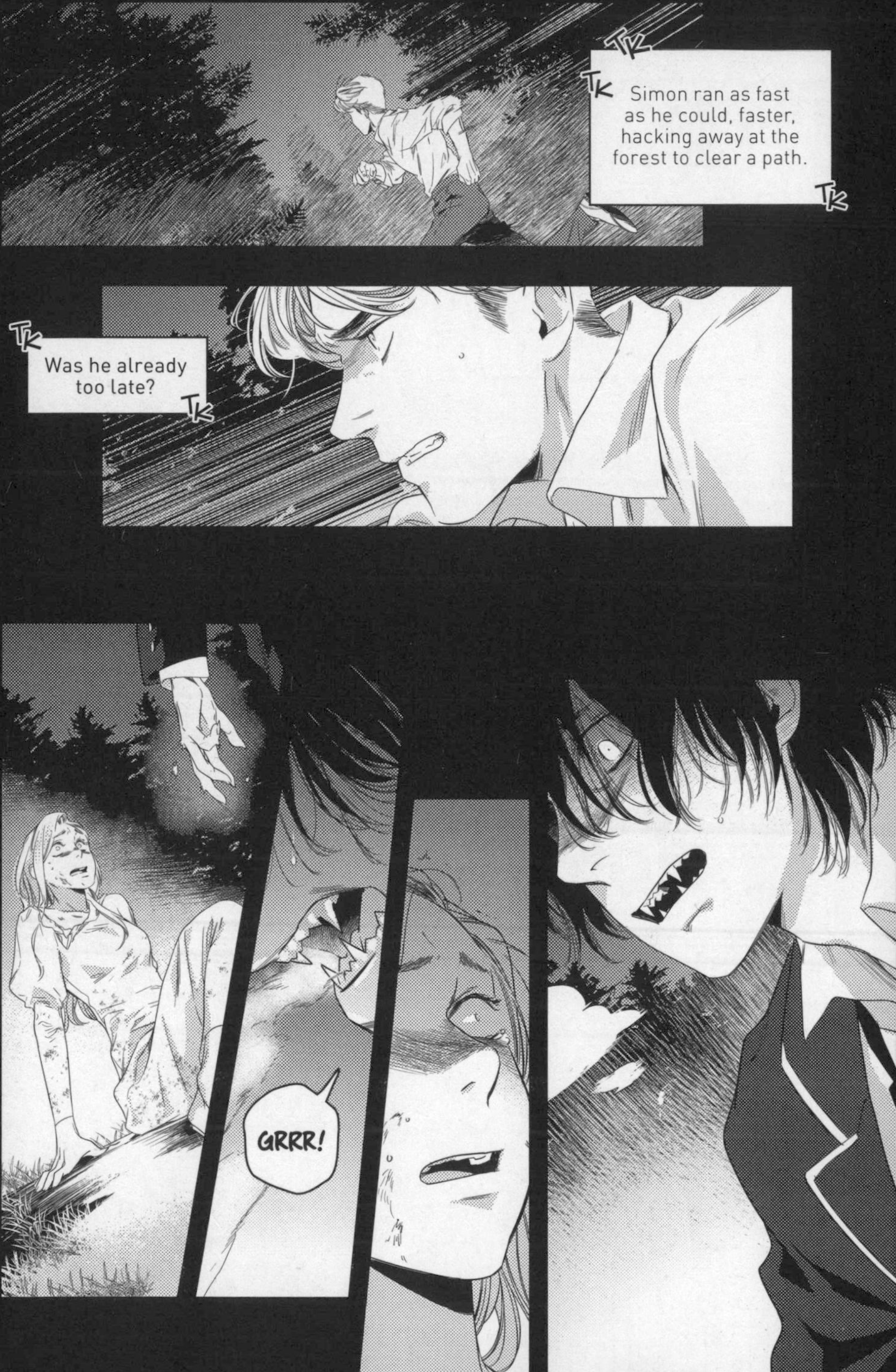
TK
TK
Simon ran as fast as he could, faster, hacking away at the forest to clear a path.
TK
TK
Was he already too late?
TK
GRRR!

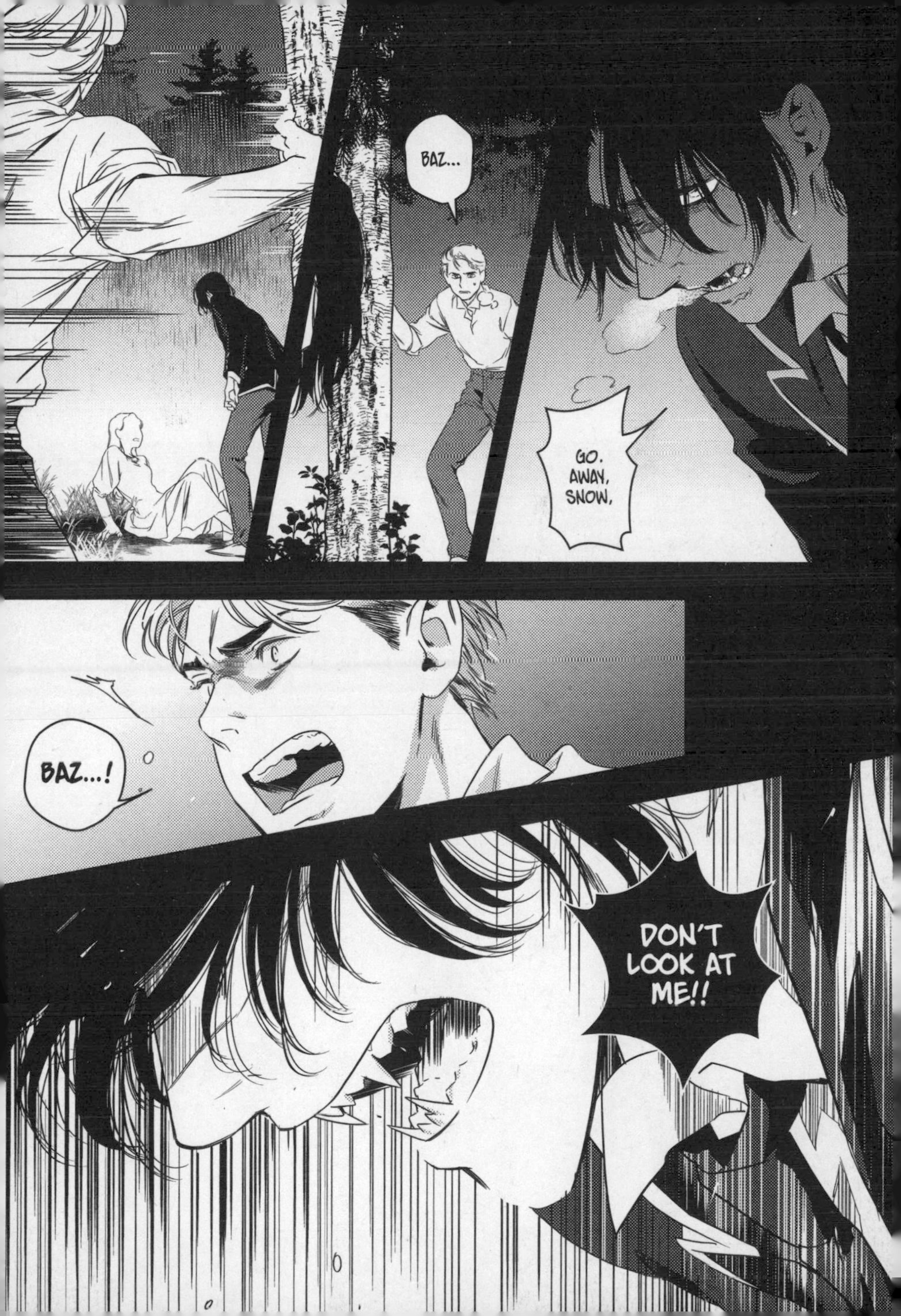
BAZ...
GO. AWAY, SNOW.
BAZ...!
DON'T LOOK AT ME!!

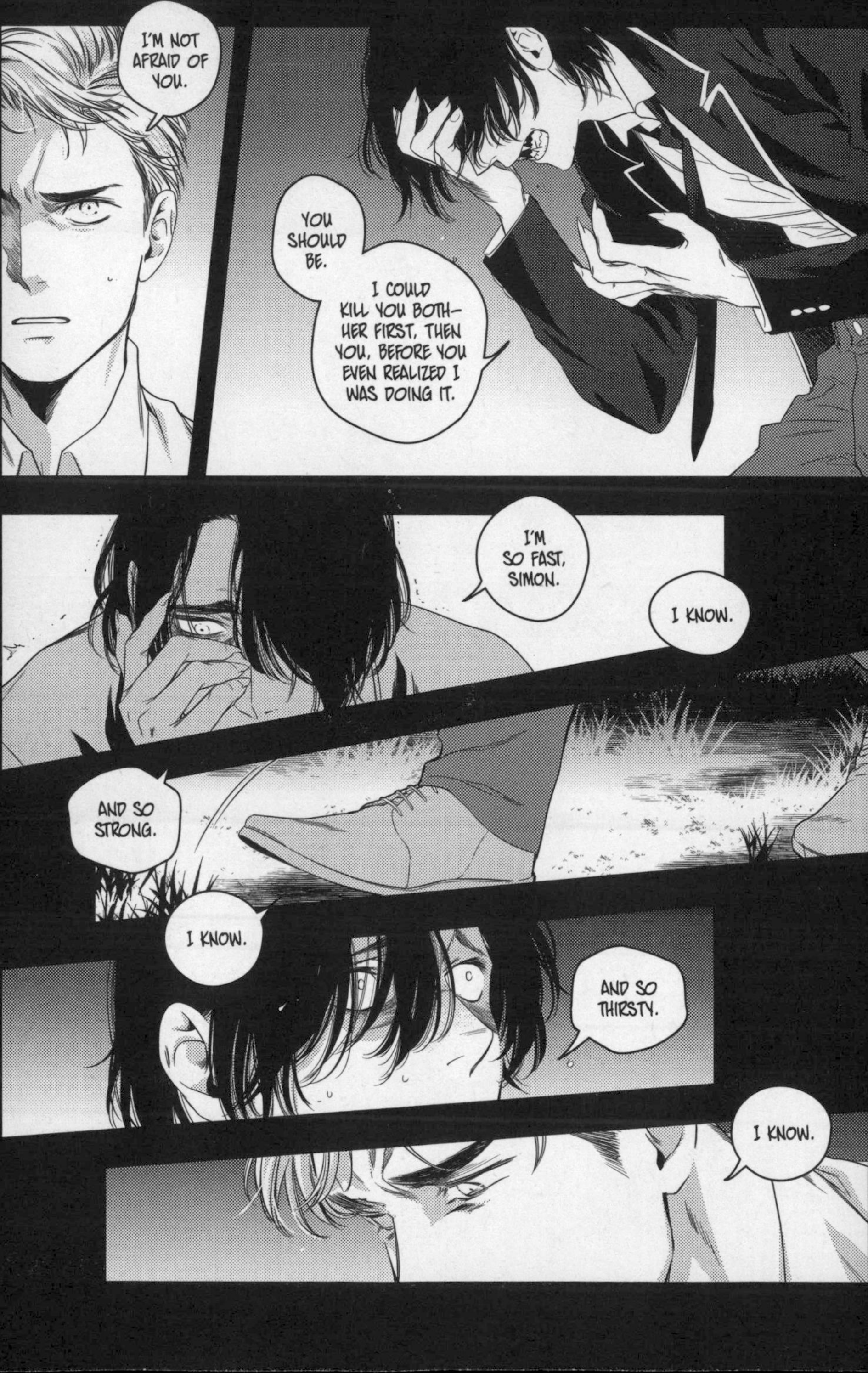
I'M NOT AFRAID OF YOU.
YOU SHOULD BE.
I COULD KILL YOU BOTH—HER FIRST, THEN YOU, BEFORE YOU EVEN REALIZED I WAS DOING IT.
I'M SO FAST, SIMON.
I KNOW.
AND SO STRONG.
I KNOW.
AND SO THIRSTY.
I KNOW.

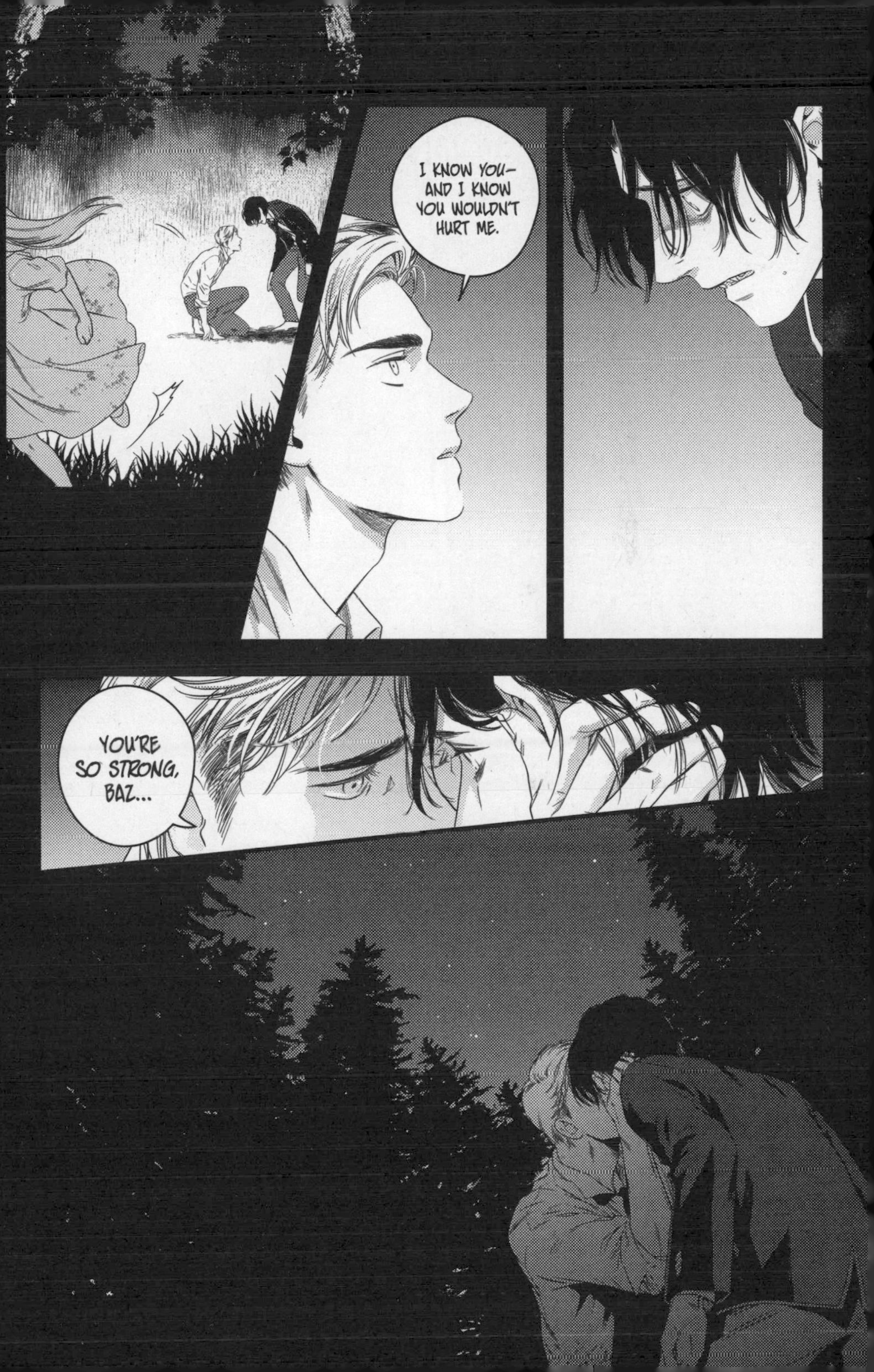
I KNOW YOU—
AND I KNOW
YOU WOULDN'T
HURT ME.
YOU'RE
SO STRONG,
BAZ...

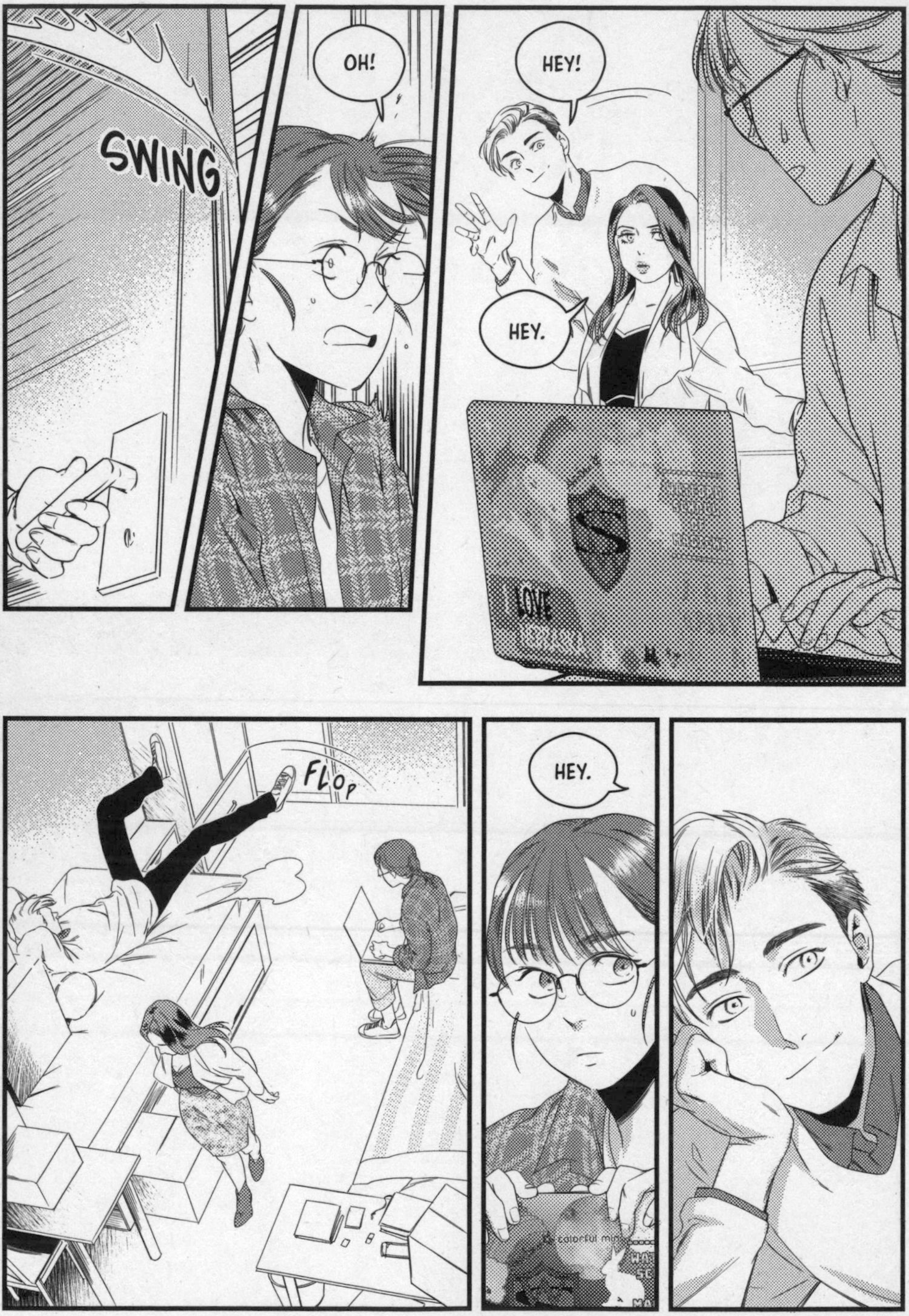
SWING
OH!
HEY!
HEY.
LOVE
FLOP
HEY.

HOW WAS YOUR FIRST DAY?

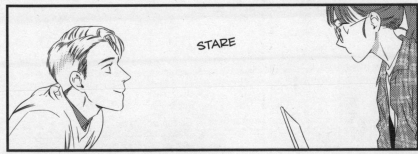

STARE

OH, ME?

FINE.

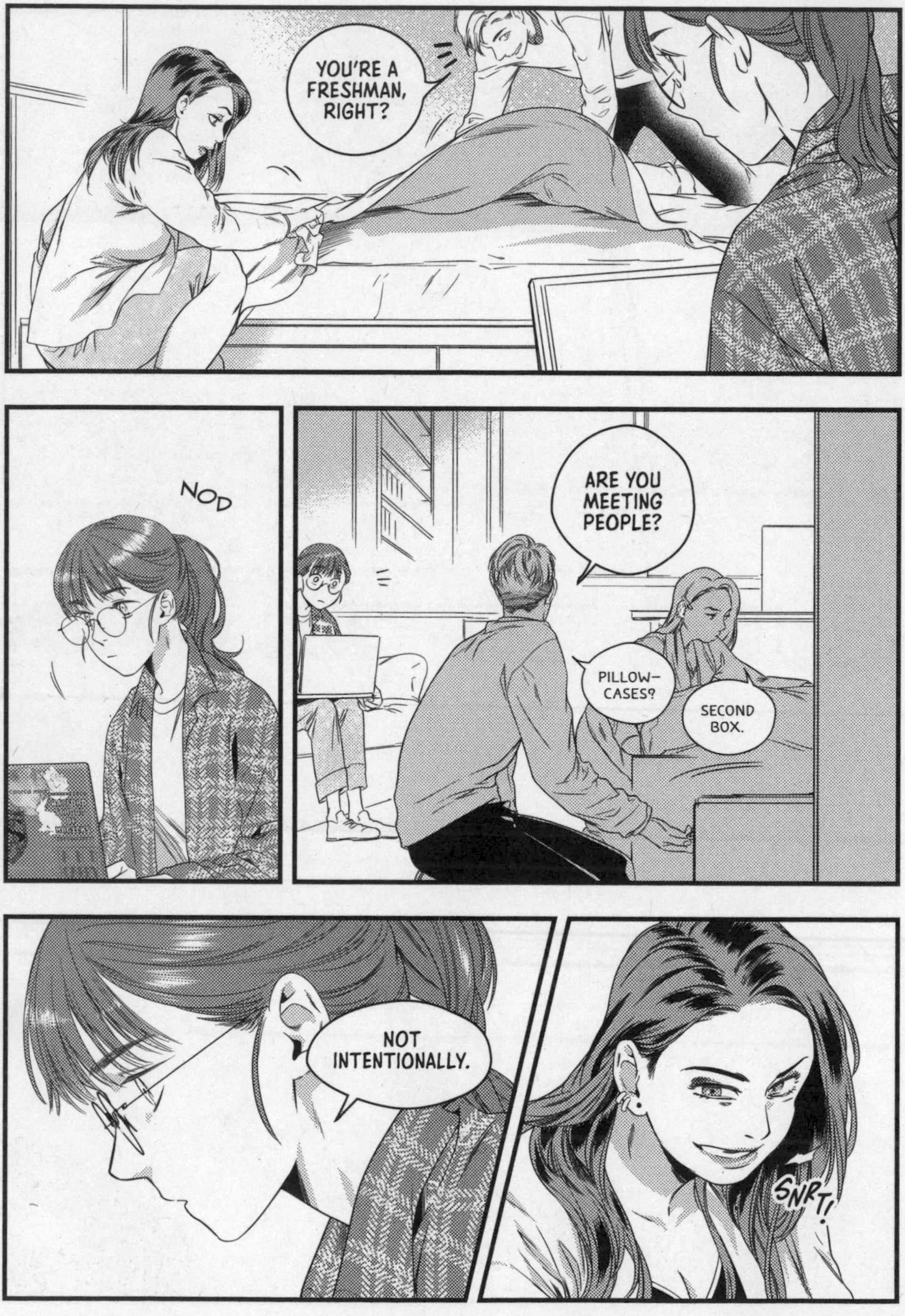
YOU'RE A FRESHMAN, RIGHT?
NOD
ARE YOU MEETING PEOPLE?
PILLOW-CASES?
SECOND BOX.
NOT INTENTIONALLY.
SNRT!

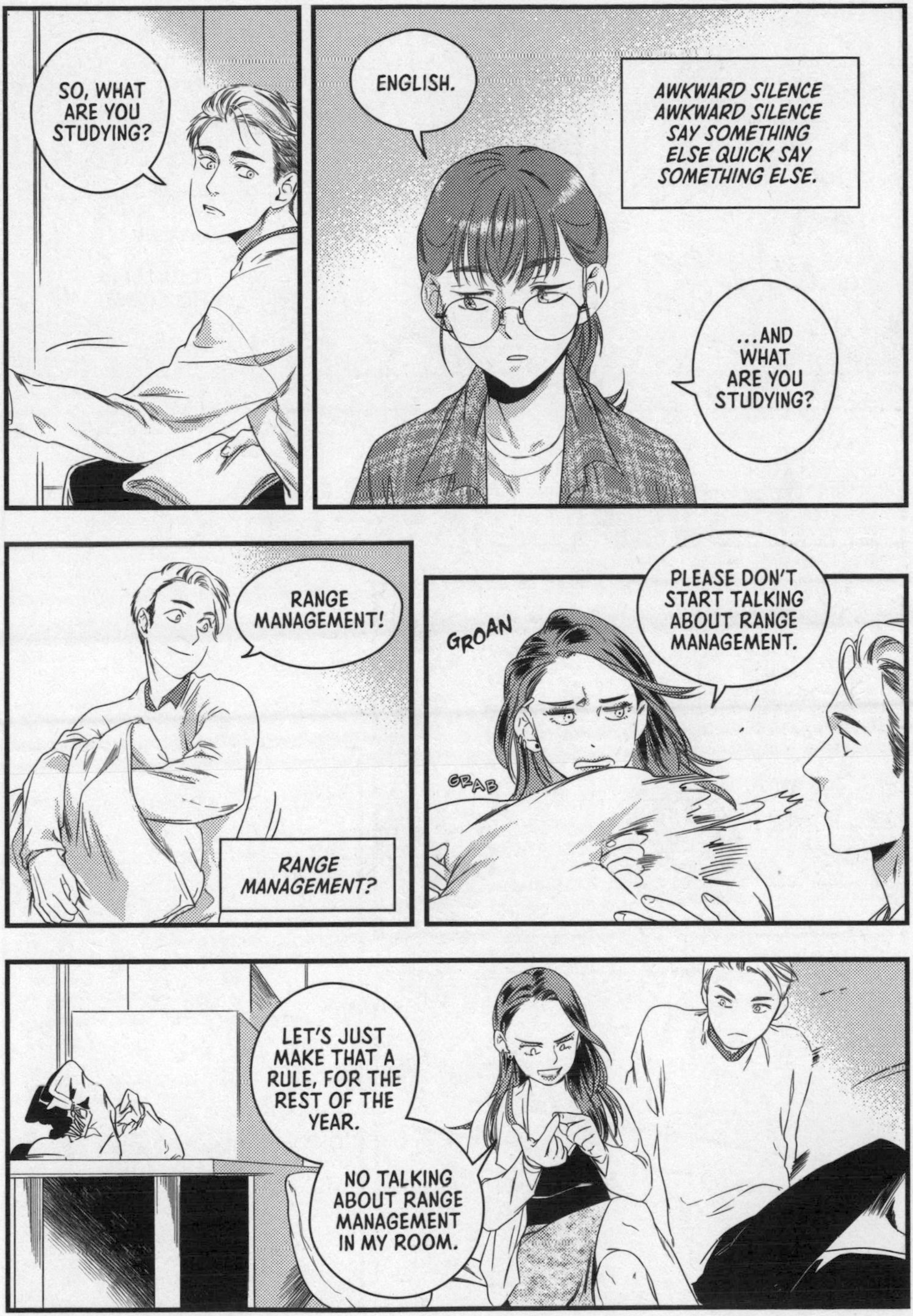
SO, WHAT ARE YOU STUDYING?
ENGLISH.
AWKWARD SILENCE AWKWARD SILENCE SAY SOMETHING ELSE QUICK SAY SOMETHING ELSE.
...AND WHAT ARE YOU STUDYING?
RANGE MANAGEMENT!
RANGE MANAGEMENT?
GROAN
PLEASE DON'T START TALKING ABOUT RANGE MANAGEMENT.
GRAB
LET'S JUST MAKE THAT A RULE, FOR THE REST OF THE YEAR.
NO TALKING ABOUT RANGE MANAGEMENT IN MY ROOM.

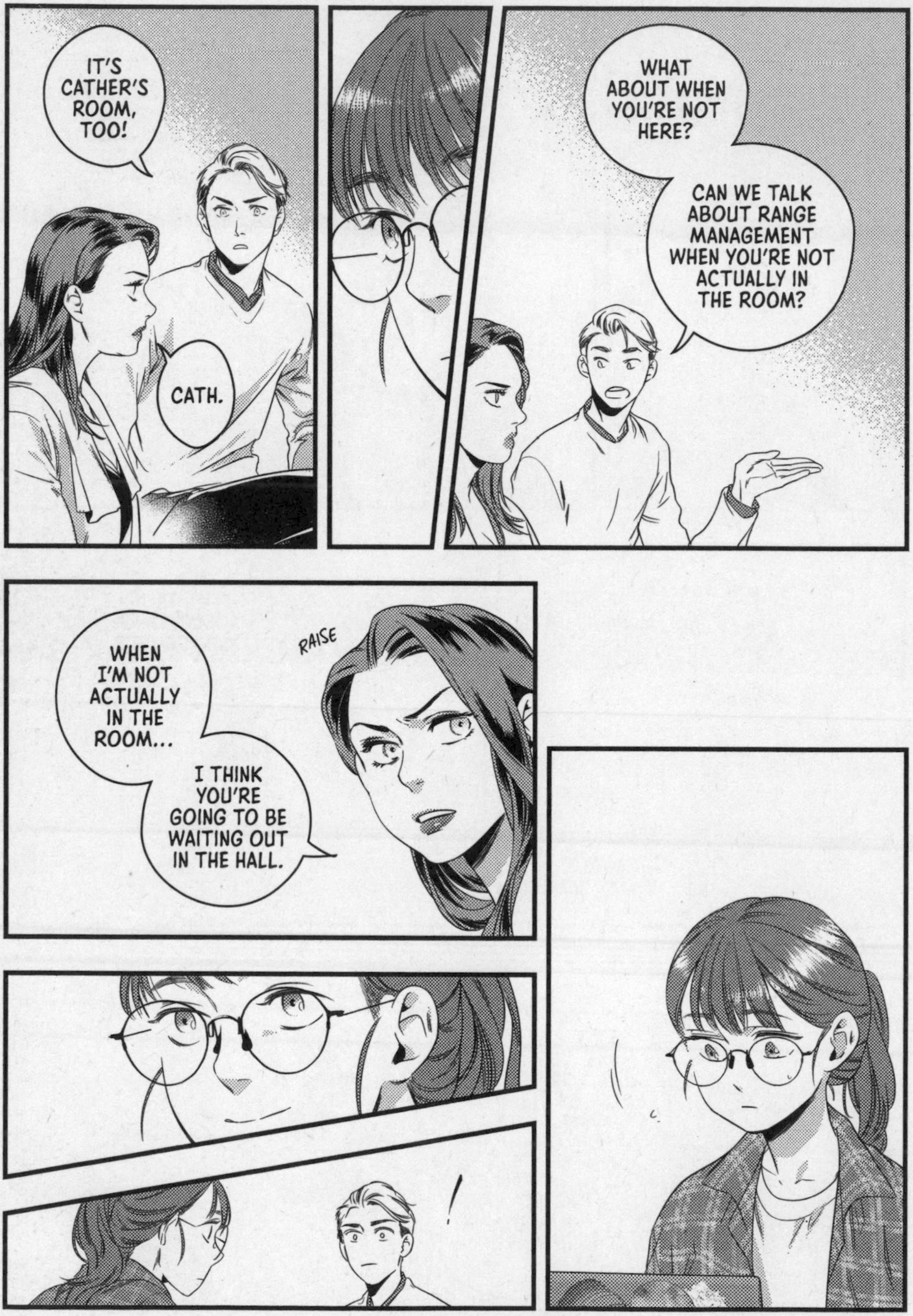
IT'S CATHER'S ROOM, TOO!
CATH.
WHAT ABOUT WHEN YOU'RE NOT HERE?
CAN WE TALK ABOUT RANGE MANAGEMENT WHEN YOU'RE NOT ACTUALLY IN THE ROOM?
RAISE
WHEN I'M NOT ACTUALLY IN THE ROOM...
I THINK YOU'RE GOING TO BE WAITING OUT IN THE HALL.
!

MEET
SIMON
AND
BAZ!

As reimagined by **Magicath**
in *Carry On, Simon.*

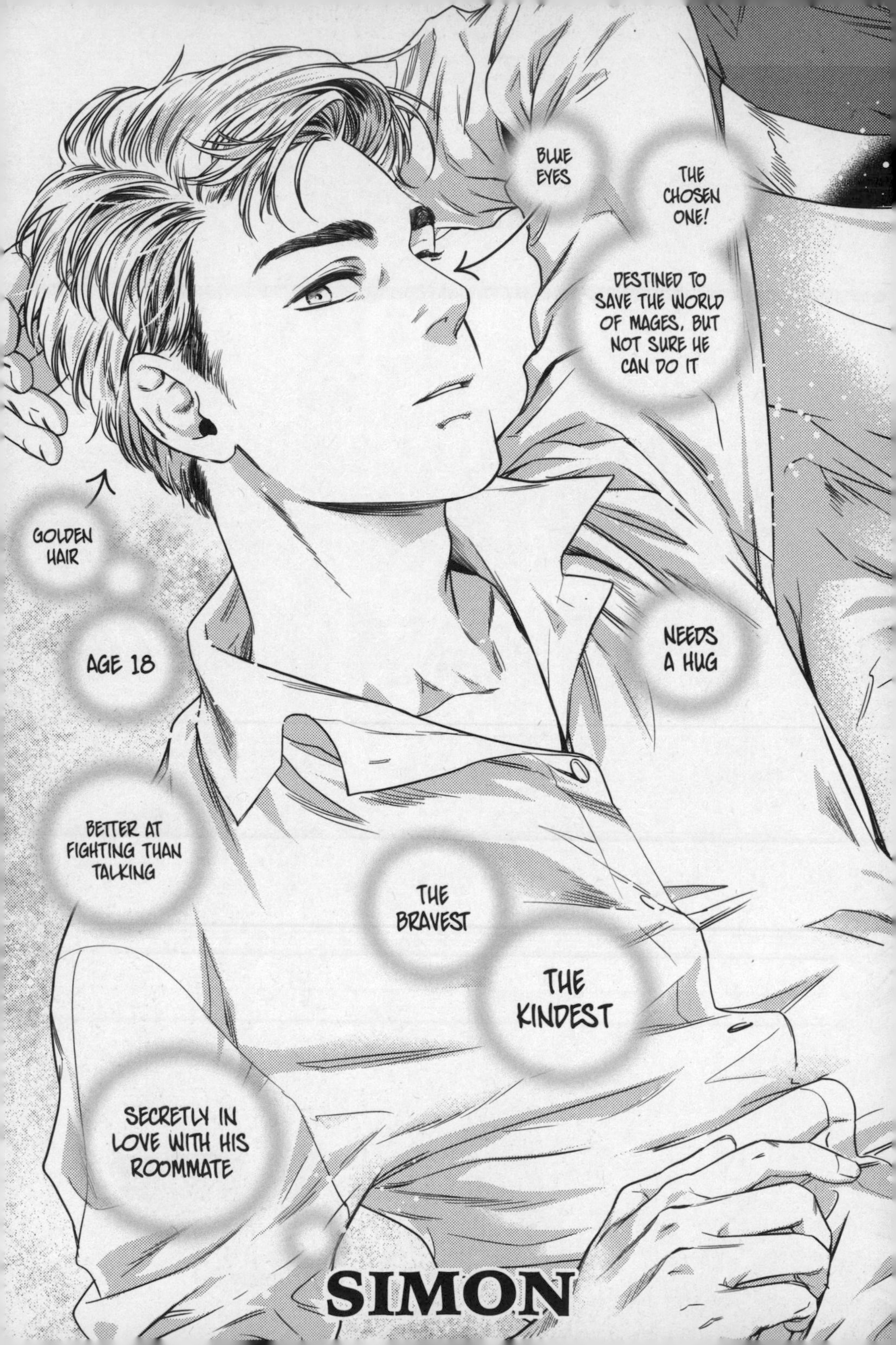
BLUE EYES
THE CHOSEN ONE!
DESTINED TO SAVE THE WORLD OF MAGES, BUT NOT SURE HE CAN DO IT
GOLDEN HAIR
AGE 18
NEEDS A HUG
BETTER AT FIGHTING THAN TALKING
THE BRAVEST
THE KINDEST
SECRETLY IN LOVE WITH HIS ROOMMATE
SIMON

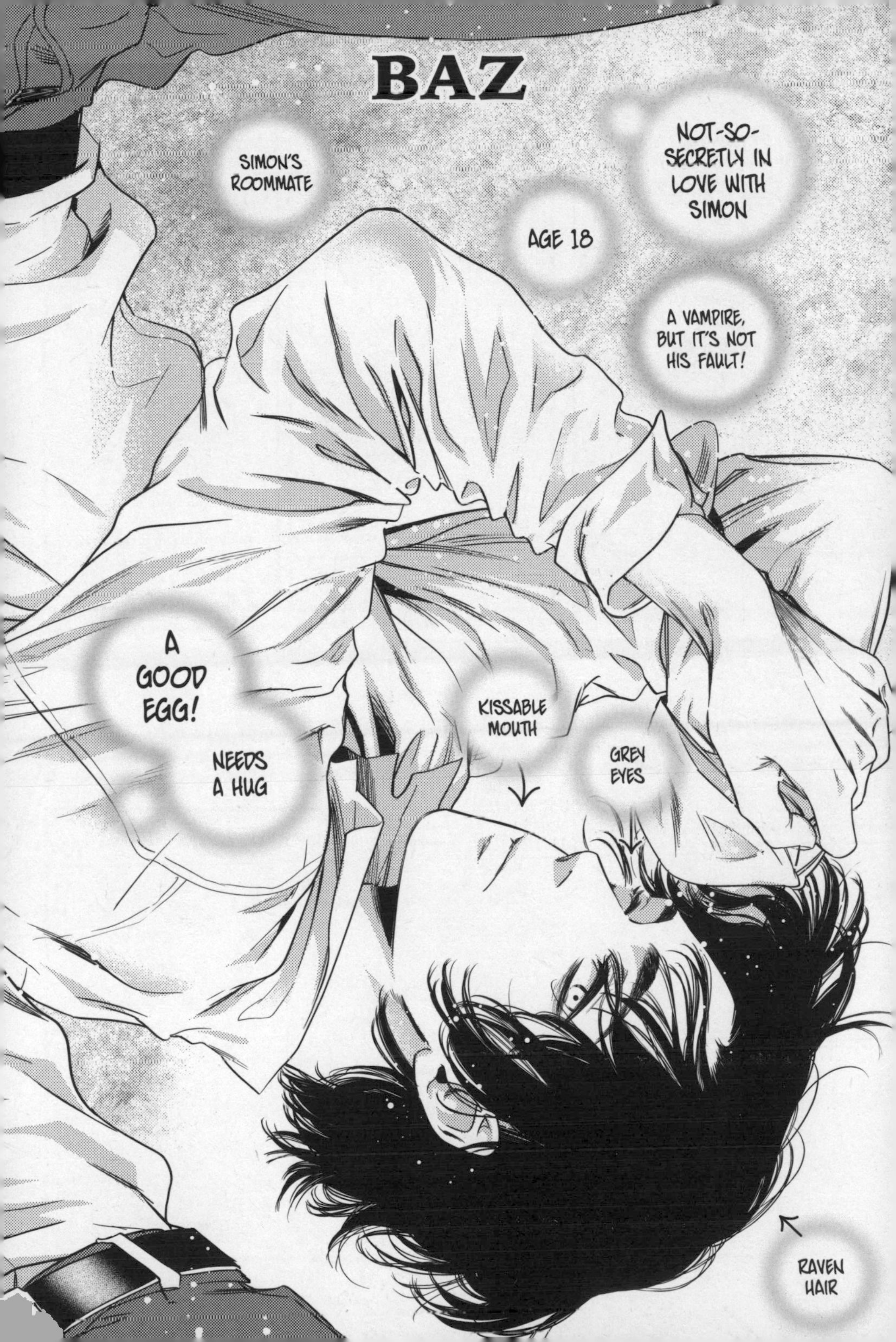
BAZ
SIMON'S ROOMMATE
NOT-SO-SECRETLY IN LOVE WITH SIMON
AGE 18
A VAMPIRE, BUT IT'S NOT HIS FAULT!
A GOOD EGG!
NEEDS A HUG
KISSABLE MOUTH
GREY EYES
RAVEN HAIR

I'M NOT USED TO BEING ALONE...

I WONDER WHAT ABEL'S UP TO.

You up?

Sorry, so late. I'll txt you!

how's missouri? i miss u i'll fly get it!

TAP

TAP

nebraska is fine

everyone here has really expensive water bottles

TAP

MAYBE DAD IS HOME.

HEY, DAD, JUST CALLING TO SEE HOW YOU'RE DOING. CALL ME BACK WHEN YOU GET THIS.

NO.

I COULD TRY...

Wren

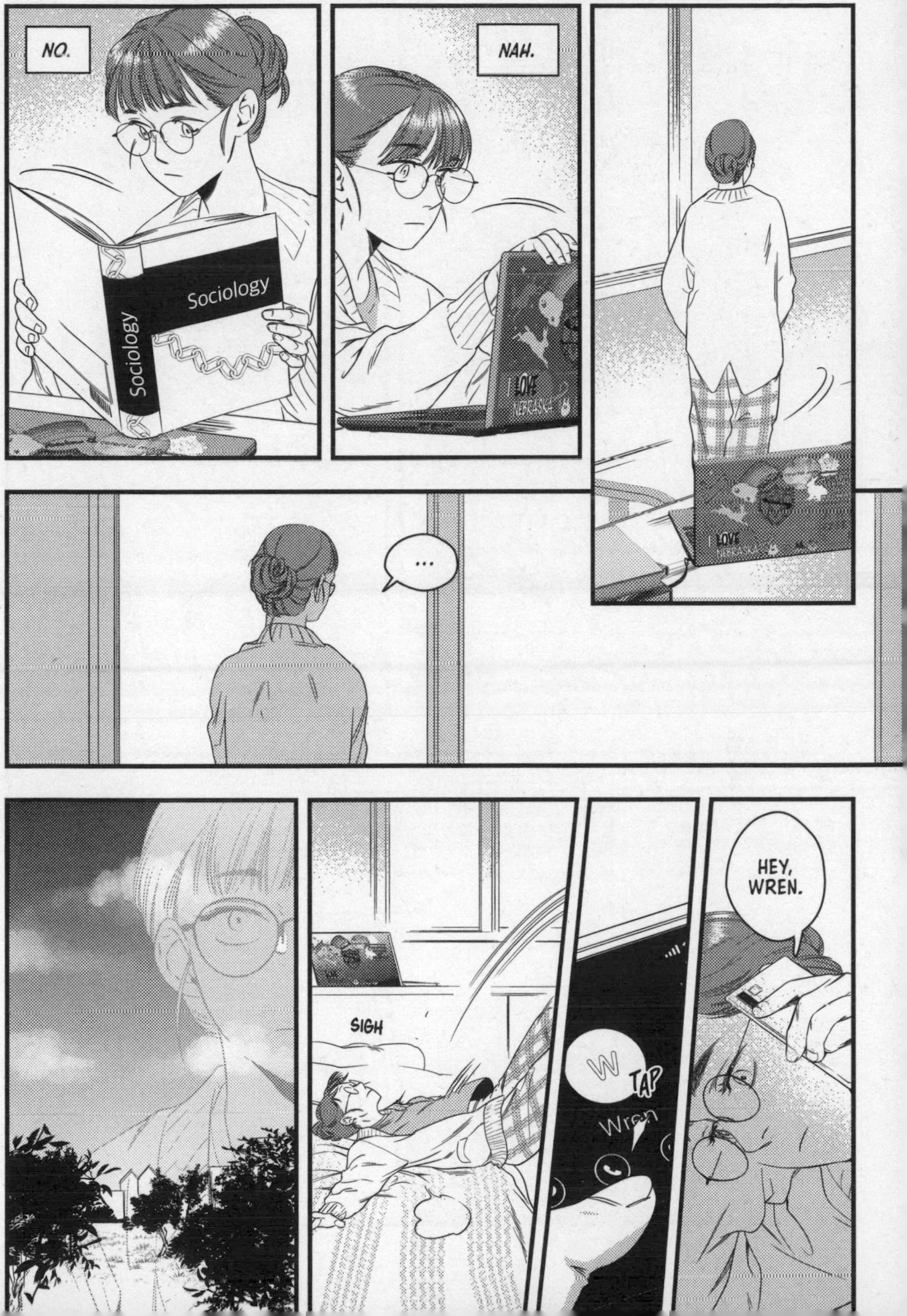
NO.
Sociology
Sociology
NAH.
I LOVE NEBRASKA
I LOVE NEBRASKA
...
SIGH
W
TAP
Wren
HEY, WREN.

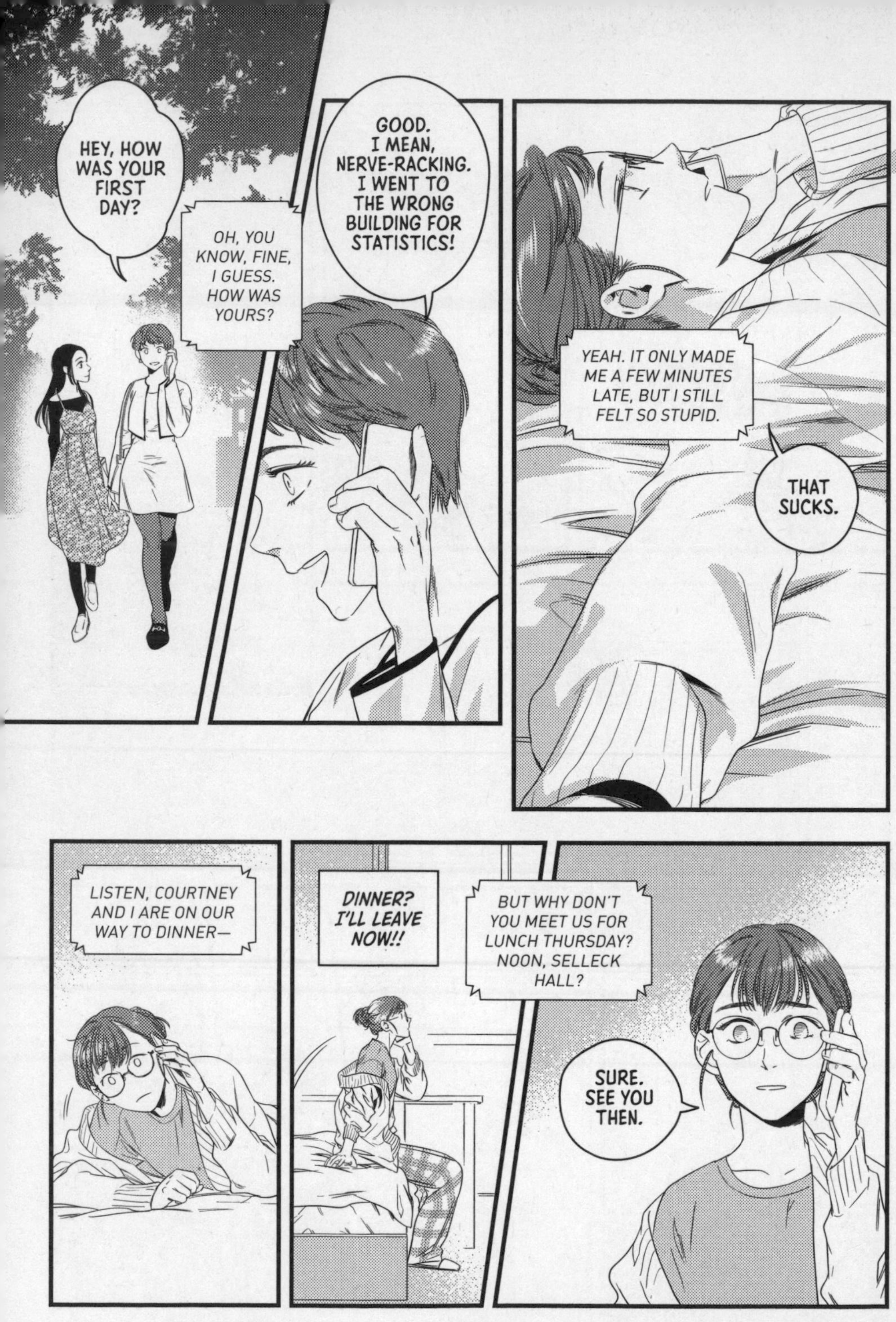
HEY, HOW WAS YOUR FIRST DAY?
OH, YOU KNOW, FINE, I GUESS. HOW WAS YOURS?
GOOD. I MEAN, NERVE-RACKING. I WENT TO THE WRONG BUILDING FOR STATISTICS!
YEAH. IT ONLY MADE ME A FEW MINUTES LATE, BUT I STILL FELT SO STUPID.
THAT SUCKS.
LISTEN, COURTNEY AND I ARE ON OUR WAY TO DINNER—
DINNER? I'LL LEAVE NOW!!
BUT WHY DON'T YOU MEET US FOR LUNCH THURSDAY? NOON, SELLECK HALL?
SURE. SEE YOU THEN.

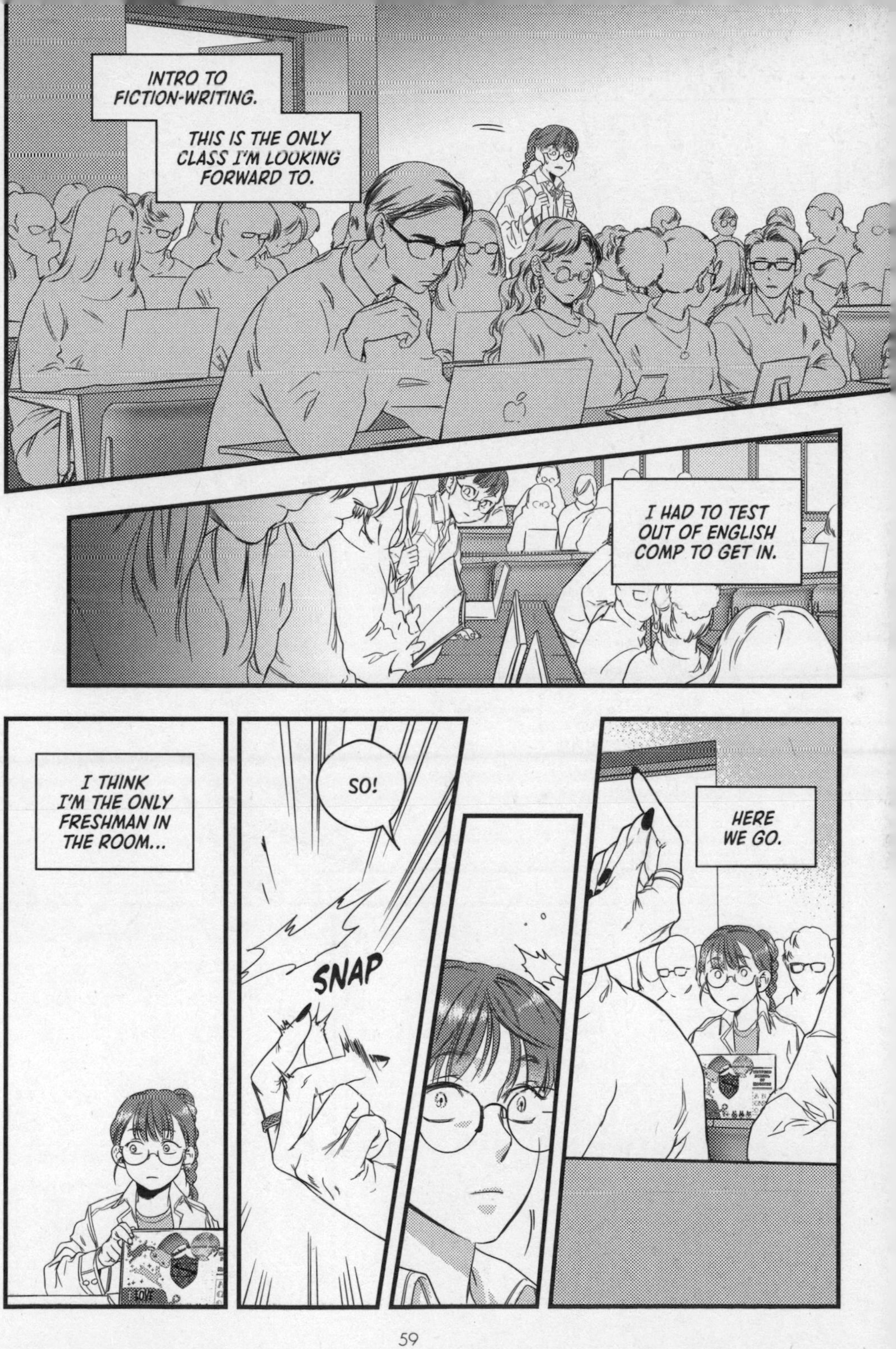
INTRO TO FICTION-WRITING.
THIS IS THE ONLY CLASS I'M LOOKING FORWARD TO.
I HAD TO TEST OUT OF ENGLISH COMP TO GET IN.
I THINK I'M THE ONLY FRESHMAN IN THE ROOM...
SO!
SNAP
HERE WE GO.

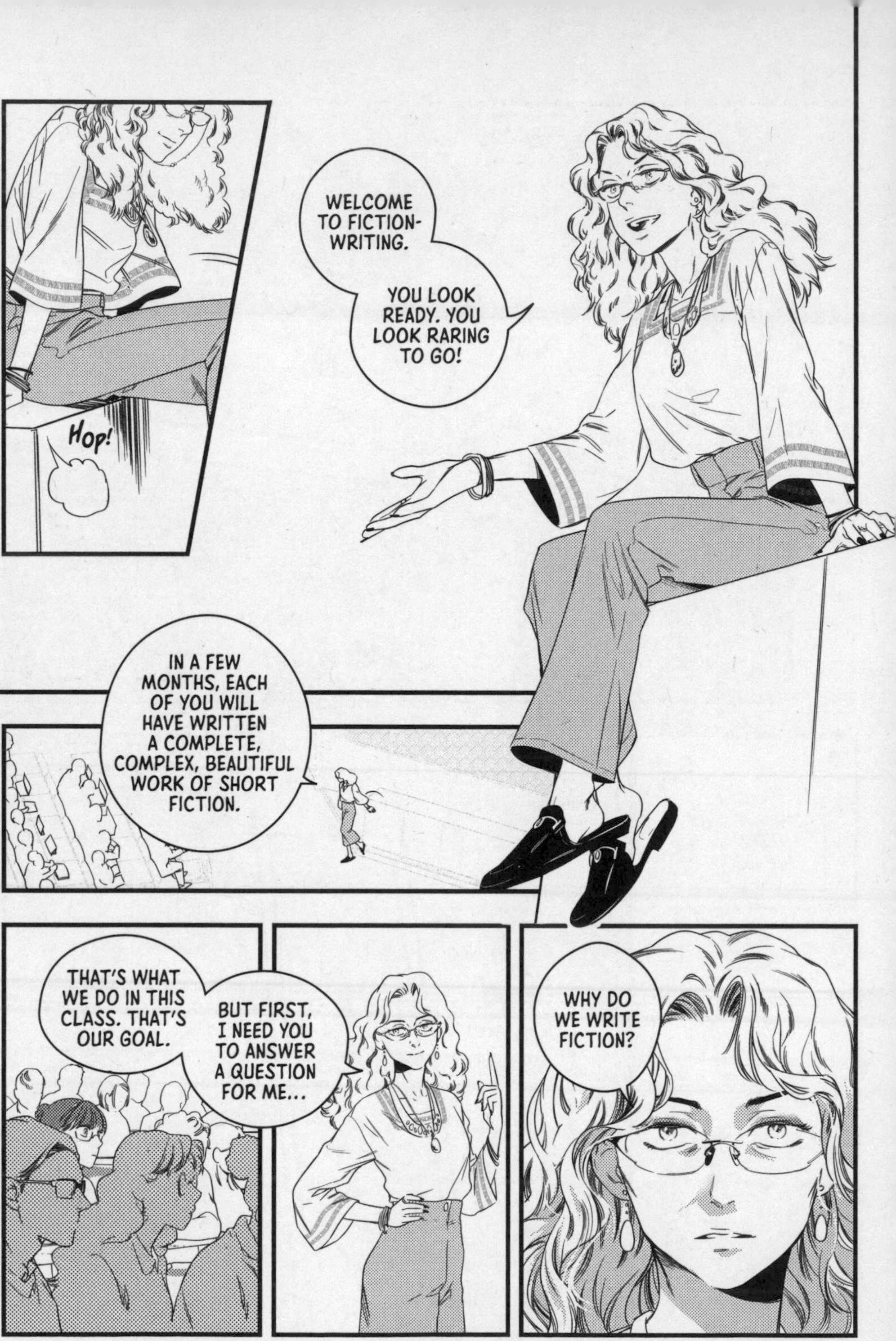
HOP!
WELCOME TO FICTION-WRITING.
YOU LOOK READY. YOU LOOK RARING TO GO!
IN A FEW MONTHS, EACH OF YOU WILL HAVE WRITTEN A COMPLETE, COMPLEX, BEAUTIFUL WORK OF SHORT FICTION.
THAT'S WHAT WE DO IN THIS CLASS. THAT'S OUR GOAL.
BUT FIRST, I NEED YOU TO ANSWER A QUESTION FOR ME...
WHY DO WE WRITE FICTION?

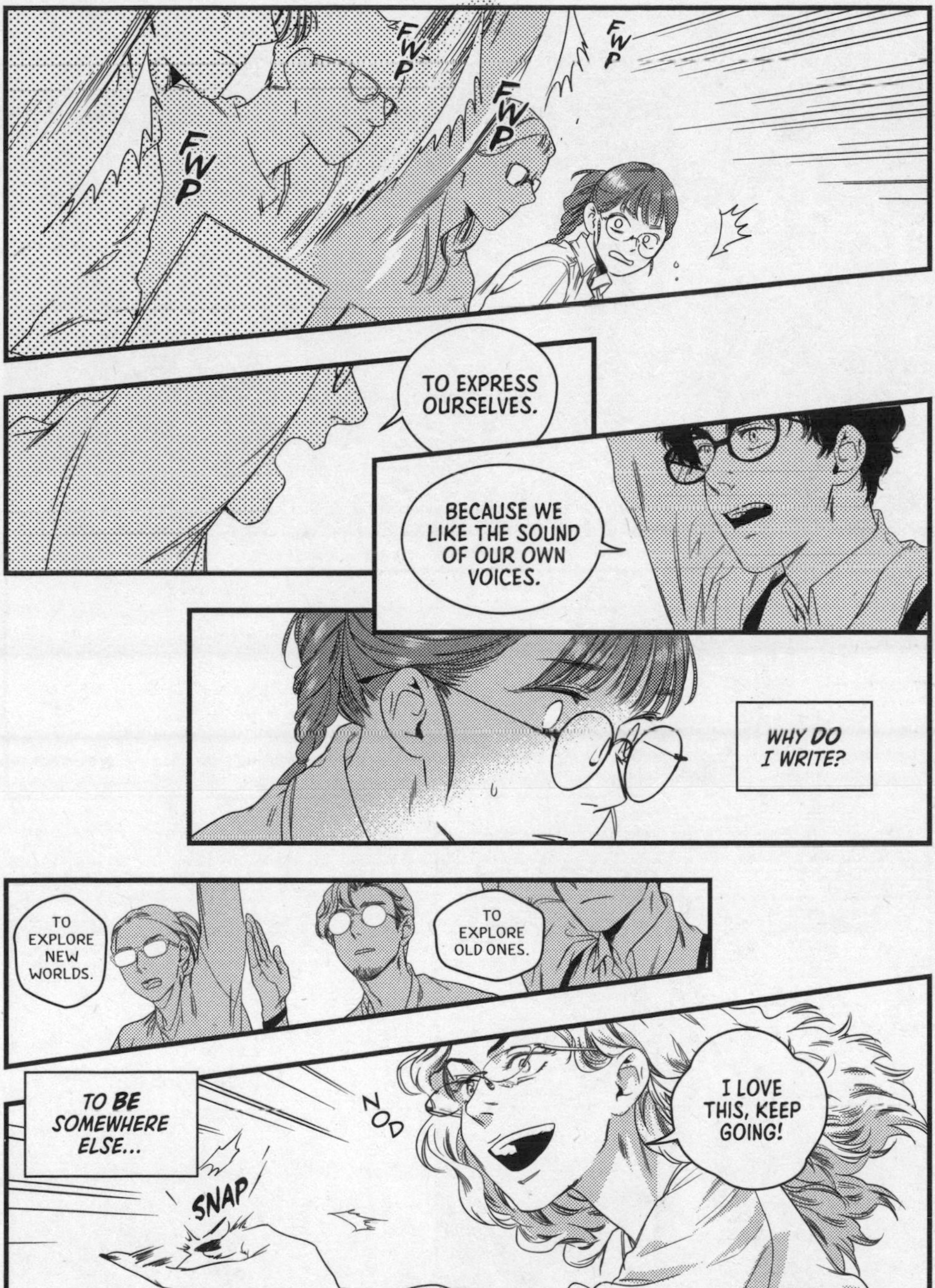
FWP
FWP
FWP
FWP
TO EXPRESS OURSELVES.
BECAUSE WE LIKE THE SOUND OF OUR OWN VOICES.
WHY *DO* I WRITE?
TO EXPLORE NEW WORLDS.
TO EXPLORE OLD ONES.
TO *BE* SOMEWHERE ELSE...
NOD
SNAP
I LOVE THIS, KEEP GOING!

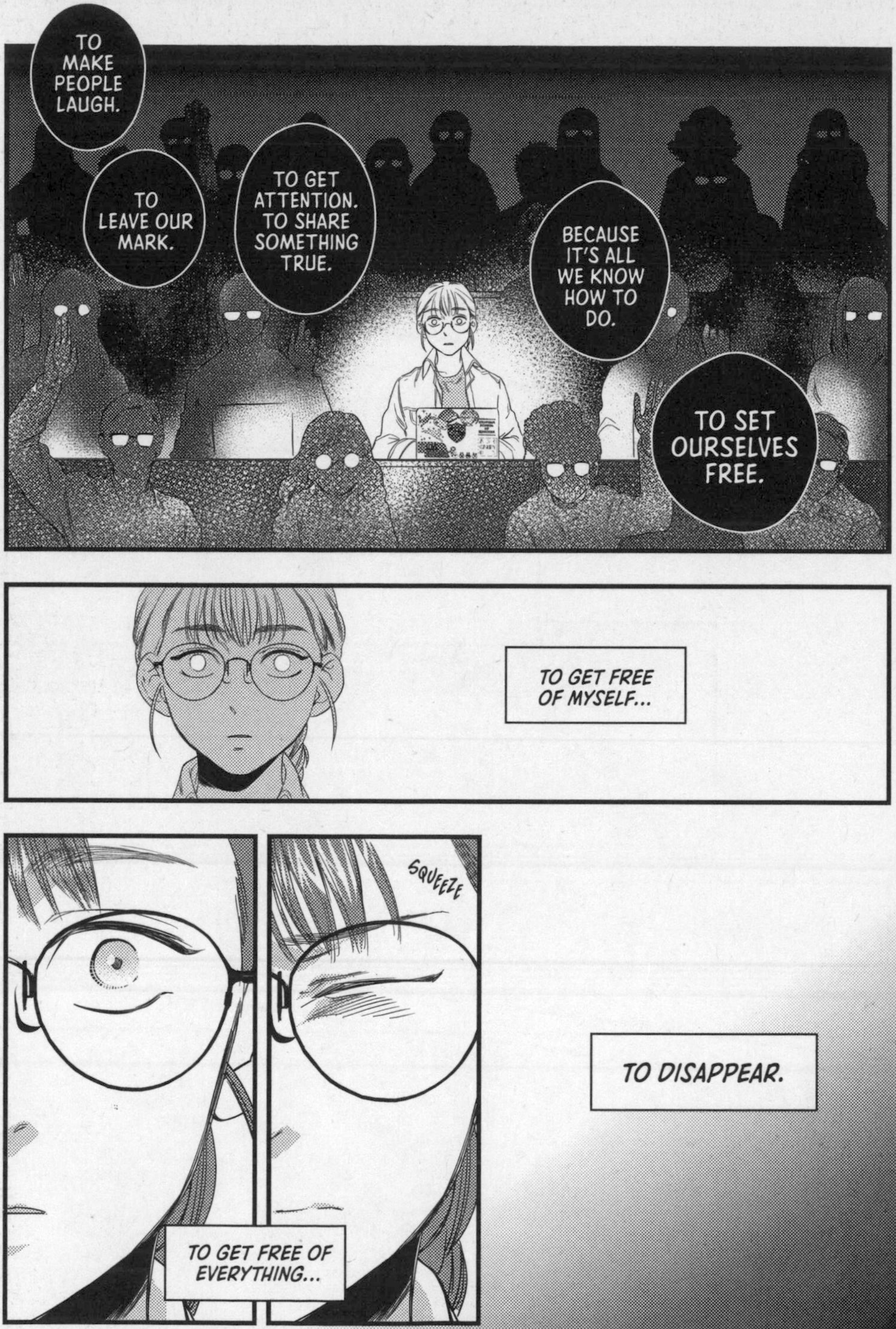
TO MAKE PEOPLE LAUGH.
TO LEAVE OUR MARK.
TO GET ATTENTION. TO SHARE SOMETHING TRUE.
BECAUSE IT'S ALL WE KNOW HOW TO DO.
TO SET OURSELVES FREE.
TO GET FREE OF MYSELF...
TO GET FREE OF EVERYTHING...
SQUEEZE
TO DISAPPEAR.

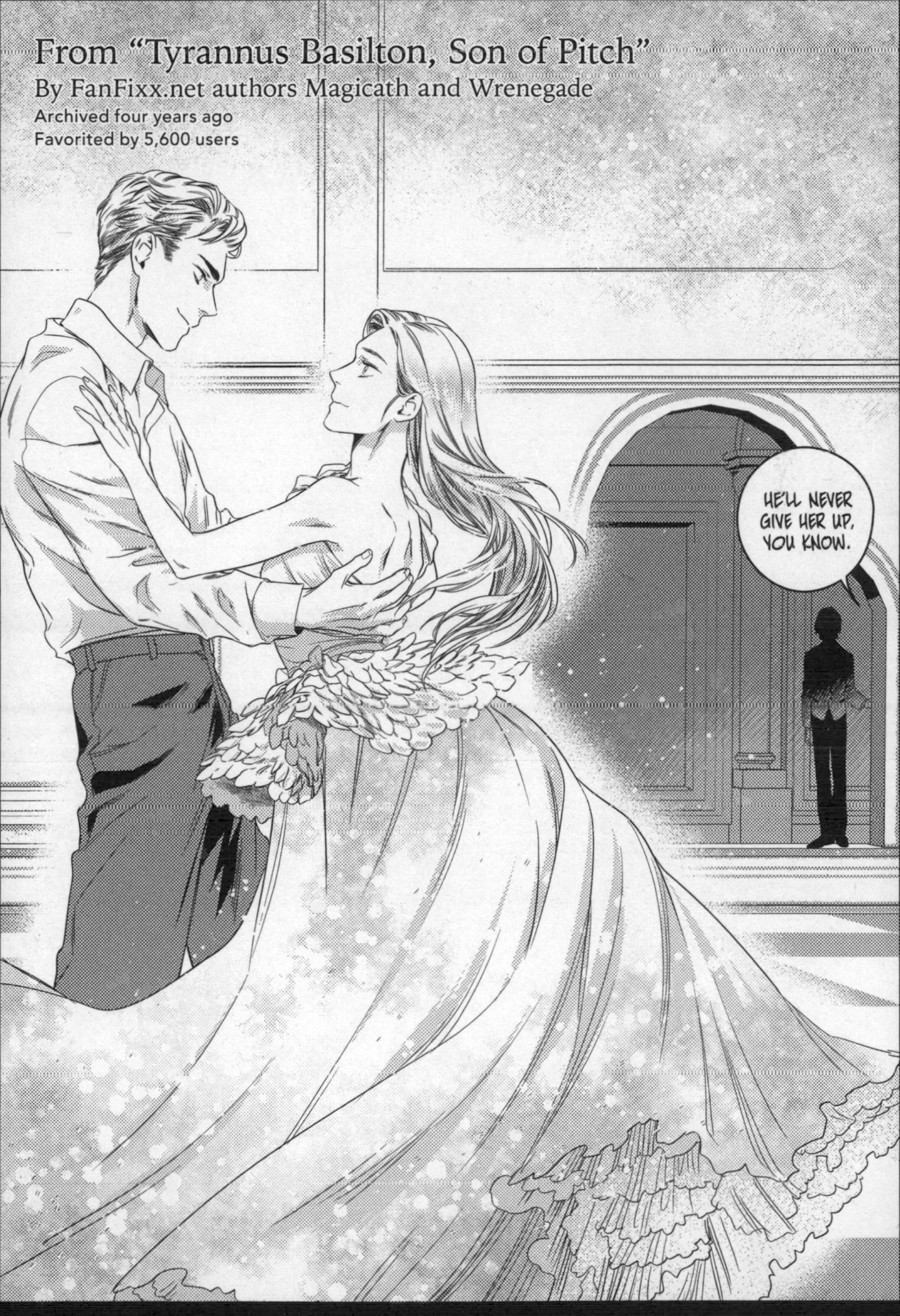
From "Tyrannus Basilton, Son of Pitch"
By FanFixx.net authors Magicath and Wrenegade
Archived four years ago
Favorited by 5,600 users
HE'LL NEVER GIVE HER UP, YOU KNOW.

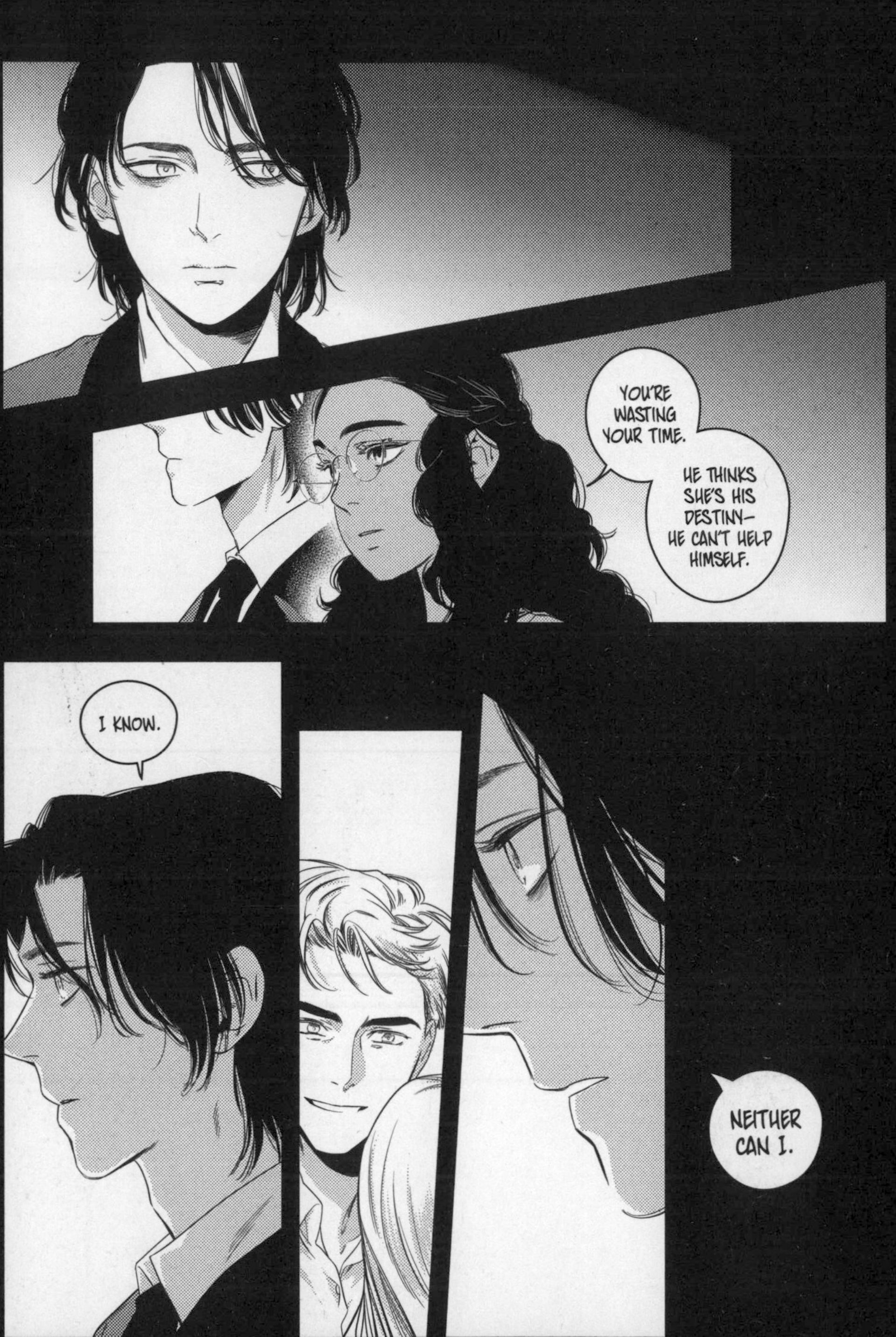
YOU'RE WASTING YOUR TIME.
HE THINKS SHE'S HIS DESTINY— HE CAN'T HELP HIMSELF.
I KNOW.
NEITHER CAN I.

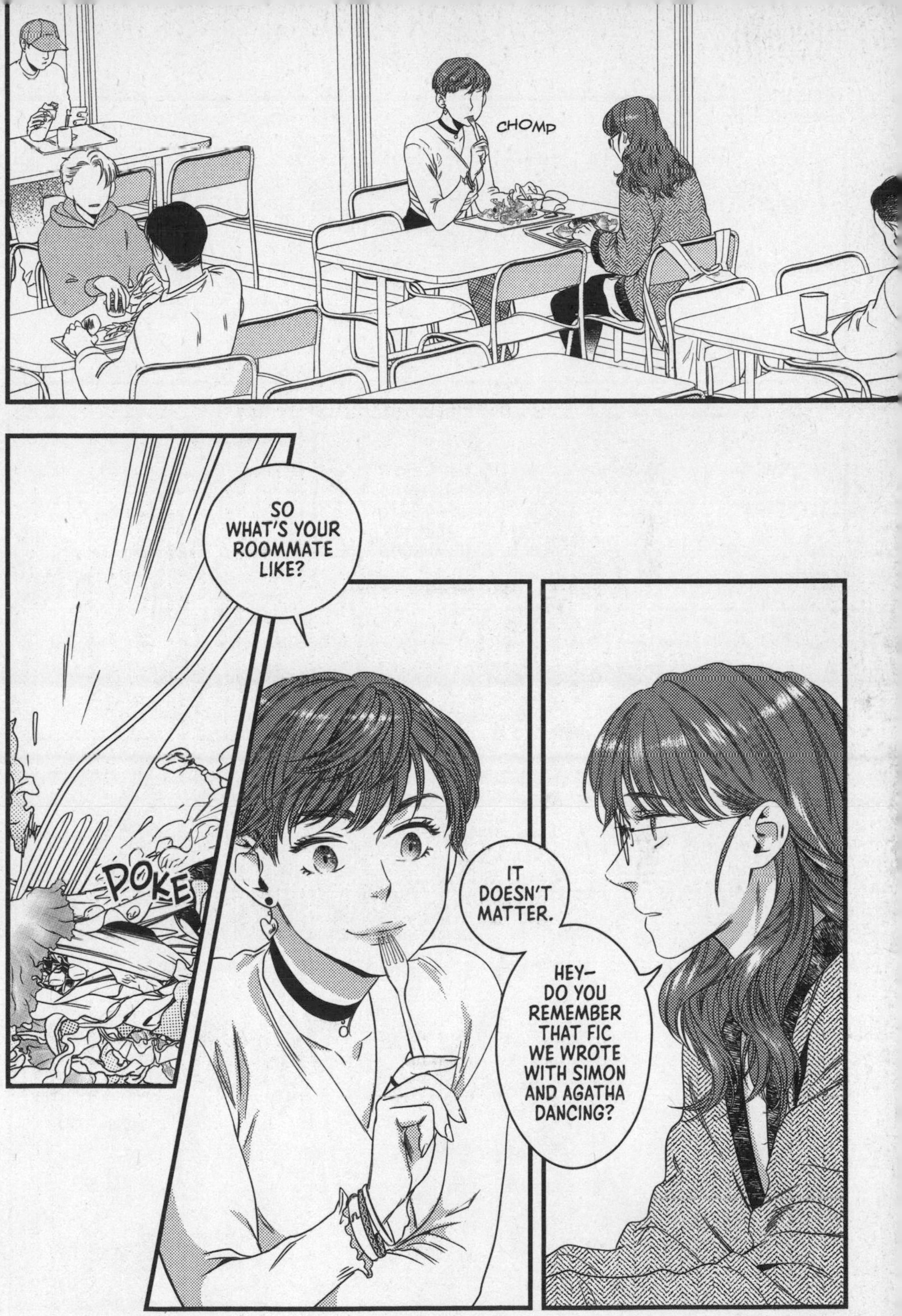
CHOMP
SO WHAT'S YOUR ROOMMATE LIKE?
POKE
IT DOESN'T MATTER.
HEY— DO YOU REMEMBER THAT FIC WE WROTE WITH SIMON AND AGATHA DANCING?

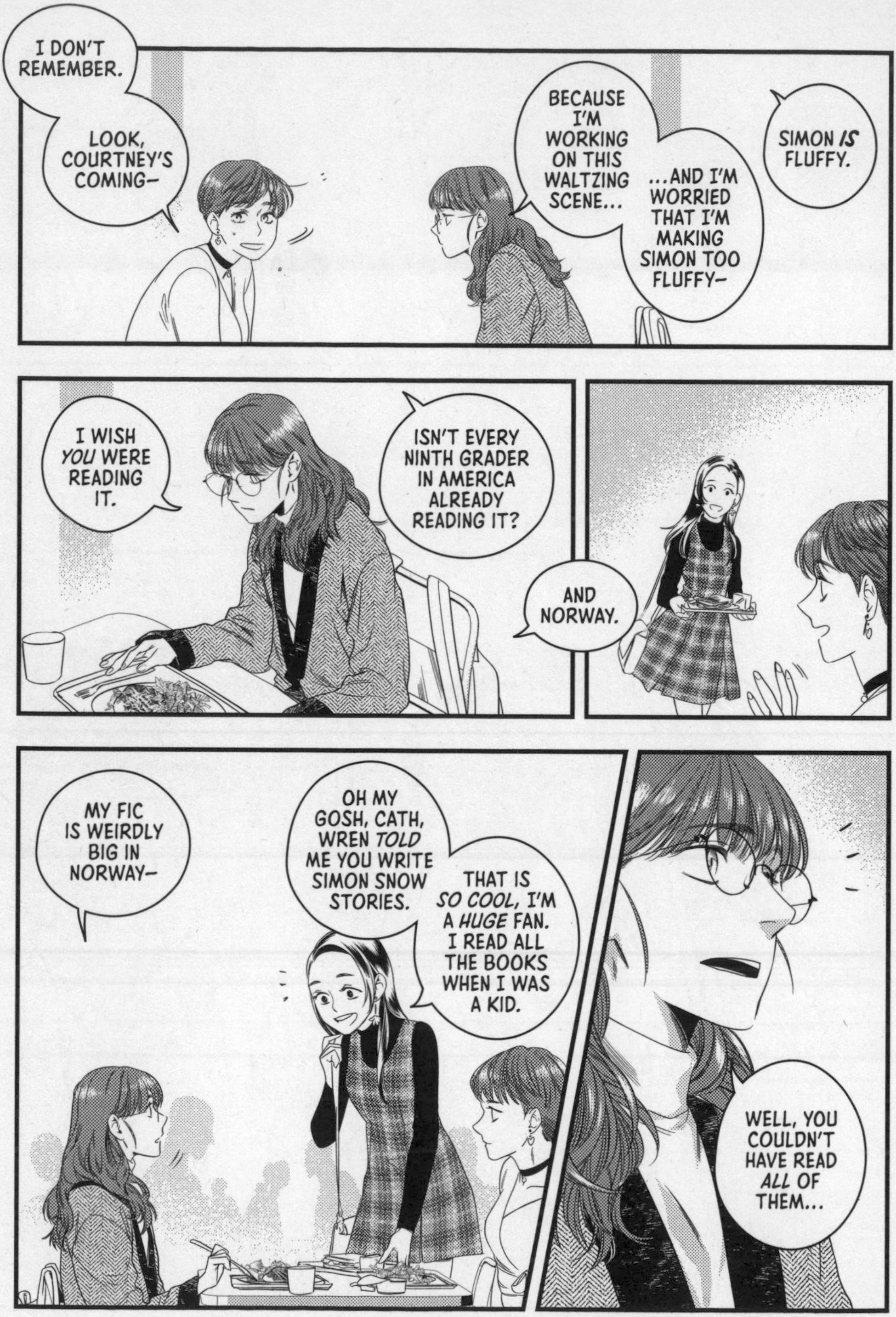
I DON'T REMEMBER.
LOOK, COURTNEY'S COMING—
BECAUSE I'M WORKING ON THIS WALTZING SCENE...
...AND I'M WORRIED THAT I'M MAKING SIMON TOO FLUFFY—
SIMON *IS* FLUFFY.
I WISH *YOU* WERE READING IT.
ISN'T EVERY NINTH GRADER IN AMERICA ALREADY READING IT?
AND NORWAY.
MY FIC IS WEIRDLY BIG IN NORWAY—
OH MY GOSH, CATH, WREN *TOLD* ME YOU WRITE SIMON SNOW STORIES.
THAT IS *SO COOL*, I'M A *HUGE* FAN. I READ ALL THE BOOKS WHEN I WAS A KID.
WELL, YOU COULDN'T HAVE READ *ALL* OF THEM...

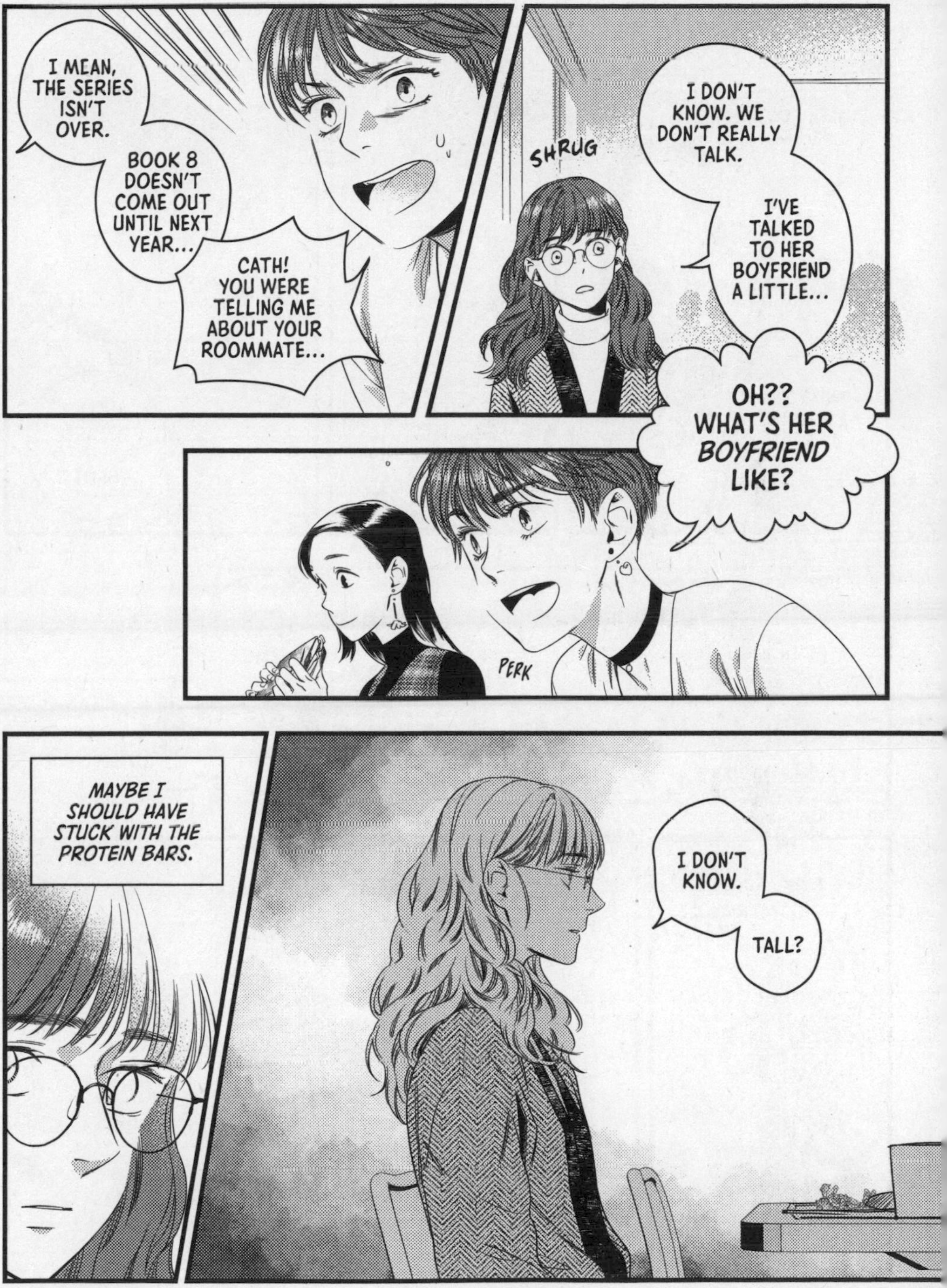
I MEAN, THE SERIES ISN'T OVER.
BOOK 8 DOESN'T COME OUT UNTIL NEXT YEAR...
CATH! YOU WERE TELLING ME ABOUT YOUR ROOMMATE...
SHRUG
I DON'T KNOW. WE DON'T REALLY TALK.
I'VE TALKED TO HER BOYFRIEND A LITTLE...
OH?? WHAT'S HER *BOYFRIEND* LIKE?
PERK
MAYBE I SHOULD HAVE STUCK WITH THE PROTEIN BARS.
I DON'T KNOW.
TALL?

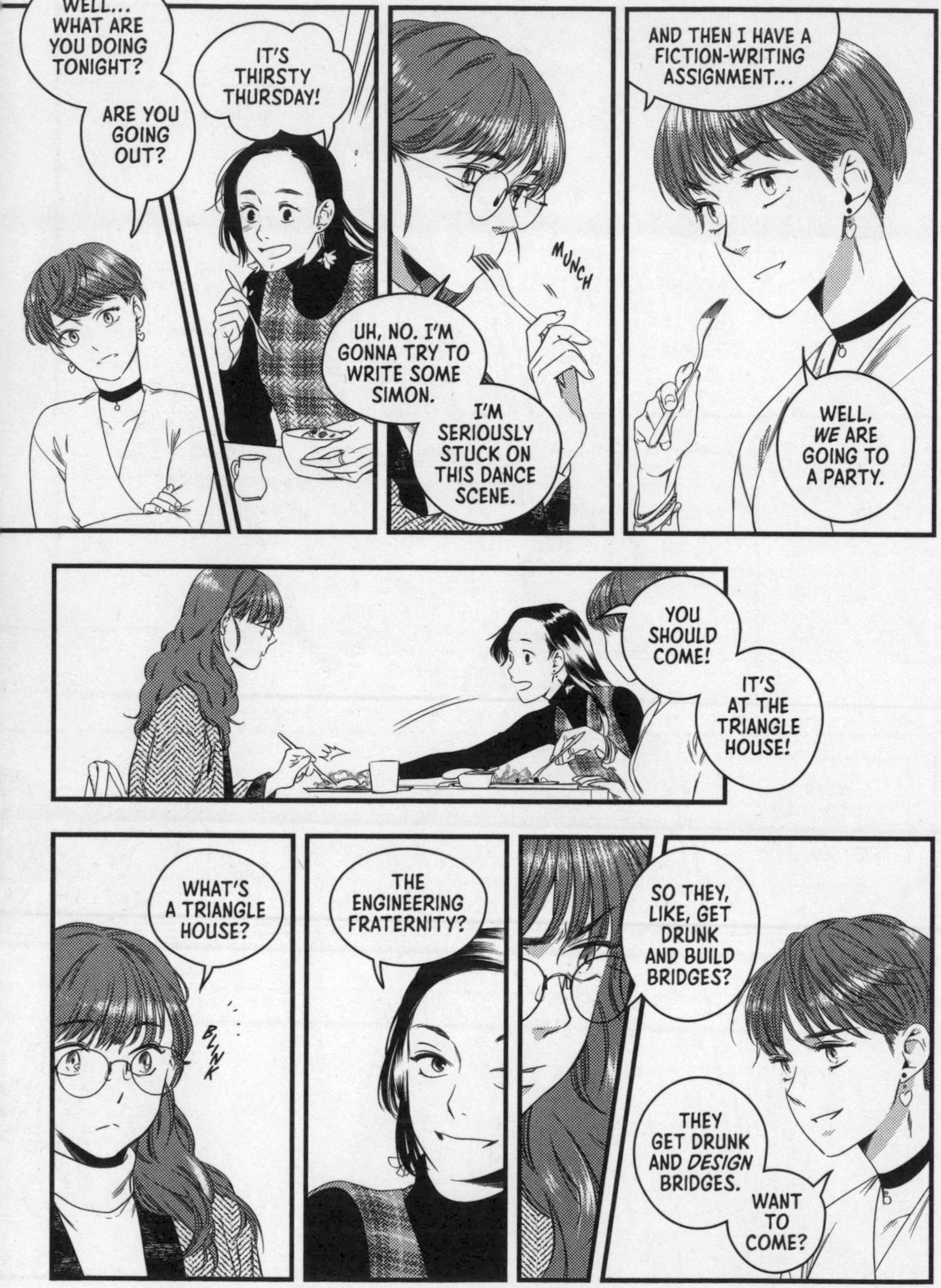
WELL... WHAT ARE YOU DOING TONIGHT?
ARE YOU GOING OUT?
IT'S THIRSTY THURSDAY!
UH, NO. I'M GONNA TRY TO WRITE SOME SIMON.
I'M SERIOUSLY STUCK ON THIS DANCE SCENE.
MUNCH
AND THEN I HAVE A FICTION-WRITING ASSIGNMENT...
WELL, *WE* ARE GOING TO A PARTY.
YOU SHOULD COME!
IT'S AT THE TRIANGLE HOUSE!
WHAT'S A TRIANGLE HOUSE?
BLINK
THE ENGINEERING FRATERNITY?
SO THEY, LIKE, GET DRUNK AND BUILD BRIDGES?
THEY GET DRUNK AND *DESIGN* BRIDGES.
WANT TO COME?

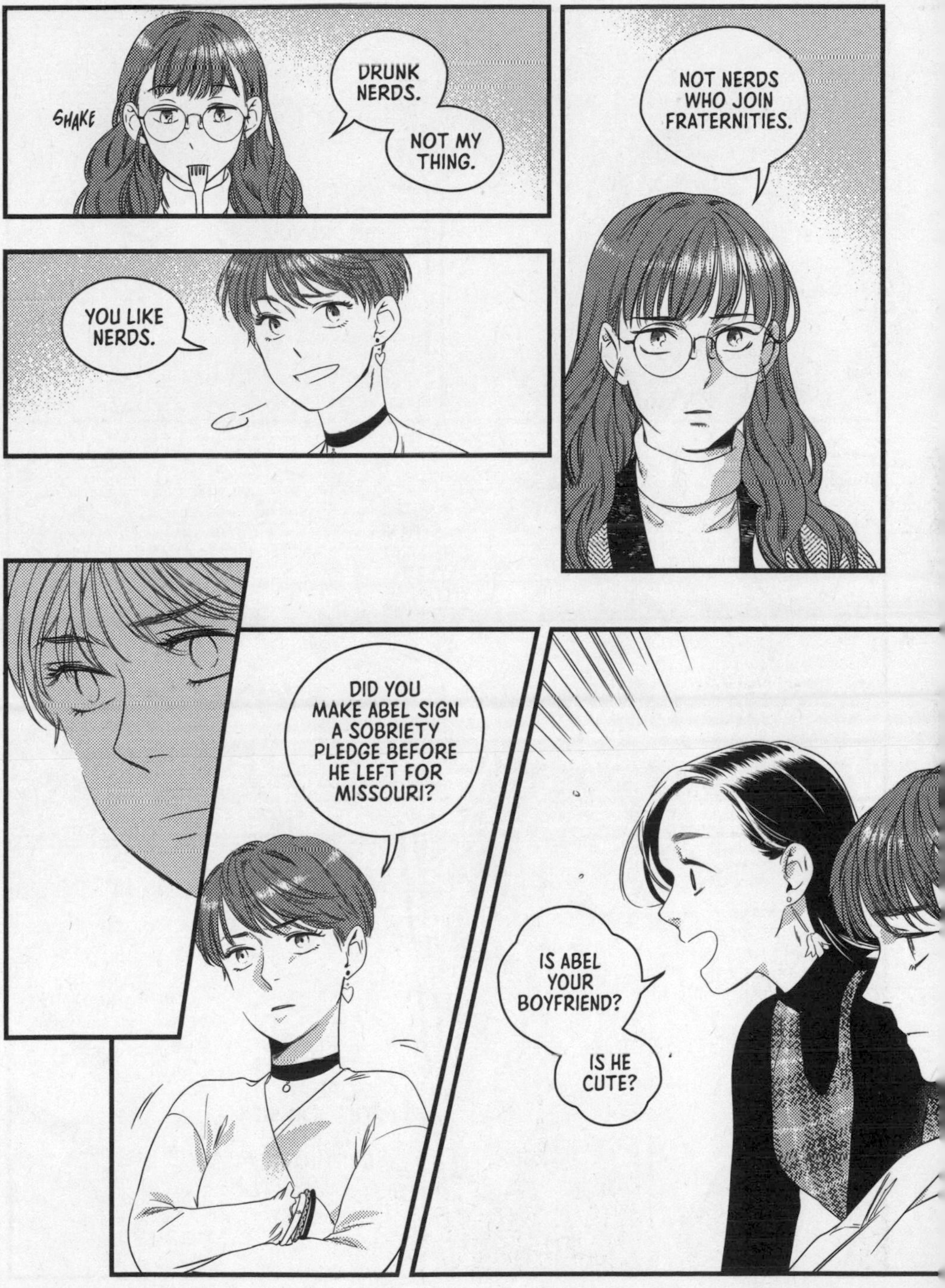
SHAKE
DRUNK NERDS.
NOT MY THING.
NOT NERDS WHO JOIN FRATERNITIES.
YOU LIKE NERDS.
DID YOU MAKE ABEL SIGN A SOBRIETY PLEDGE BEFORE HE LEFT FOR MISSOURI?
IS ABEL YOUR BOYFRIEND?
IS HE CUTE?

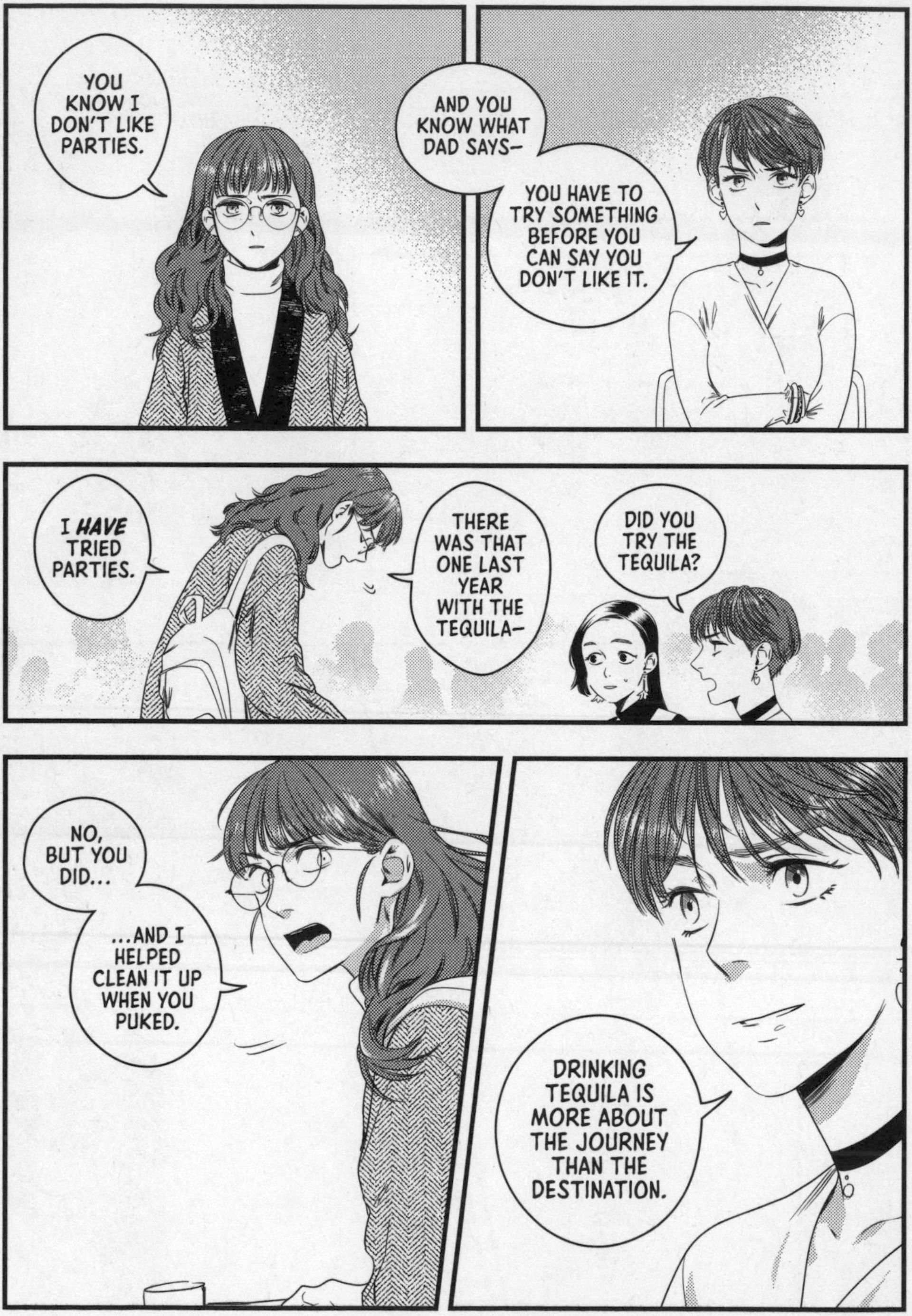
YOU KNOW I DON'T LIKE PARTIES.
AND YOU KNOW WHAT DAD SAYS–
YOU HAVE TO TRY SOMETHING BEFORE YOU CAN SAY YOU DON'T LIKE IT.
I *HAVE* TRIED PARTIES.
THERE WAS THAT ONE LAST YEAR WITH THE TEQUILA–
DID YOU TRY THE TEQUILA?
NO, BUT YOU DID...
...AND I HELPED CLEAN IT UP WHEN YOU PUKED.
DRINKING TEQUILA IS MORE ABOUT THE JOURNEY THAN THE DESTINATION.

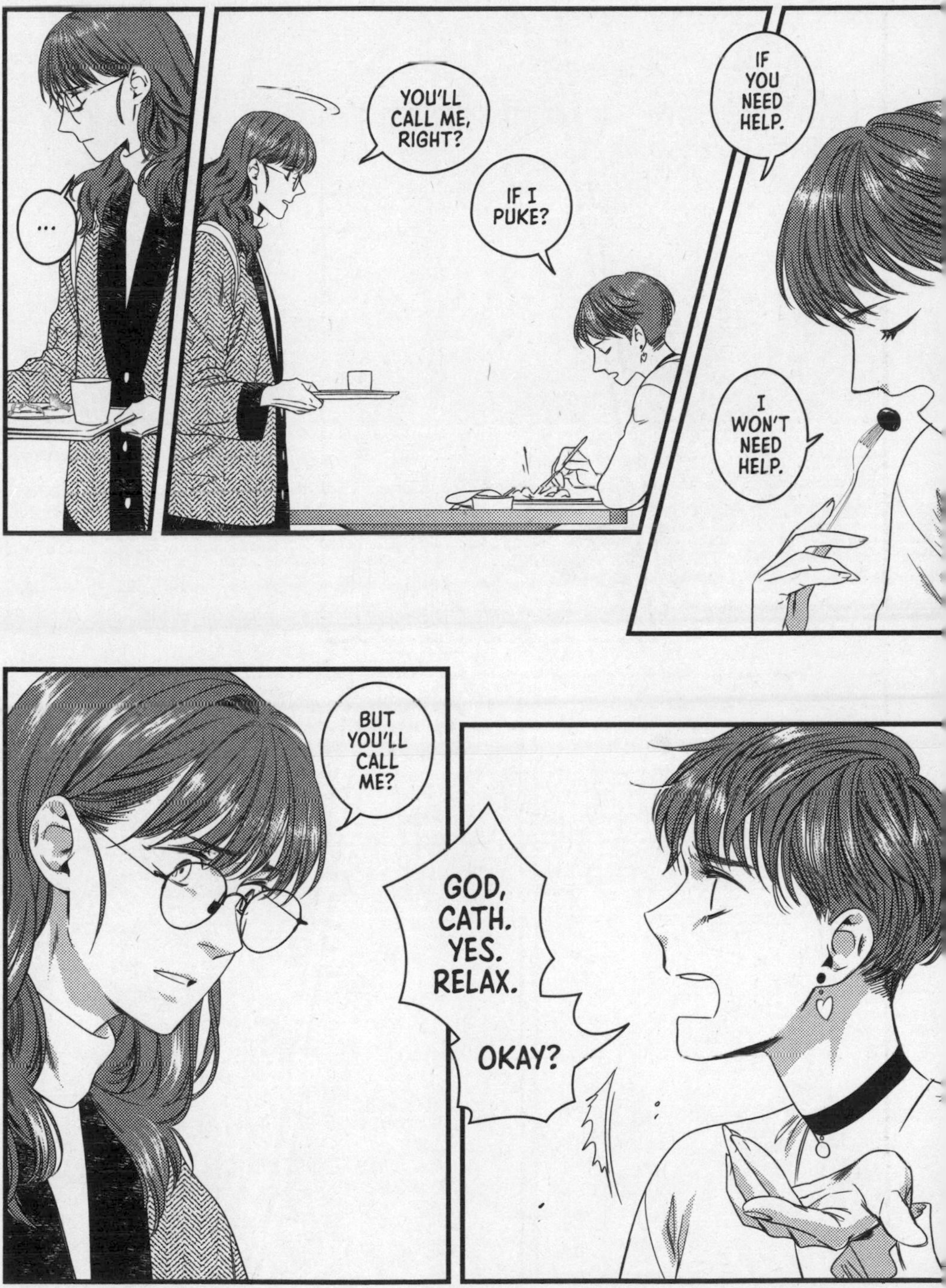
...
YOU'LL CALL ME, RIGHT?
IF I PUKE?
IF YOU NEED HELP.
I WON'T NEED HELP.
BUT YOU'LL CALL ME?
GOD, CATH. YES. RELAX.
OKAY?

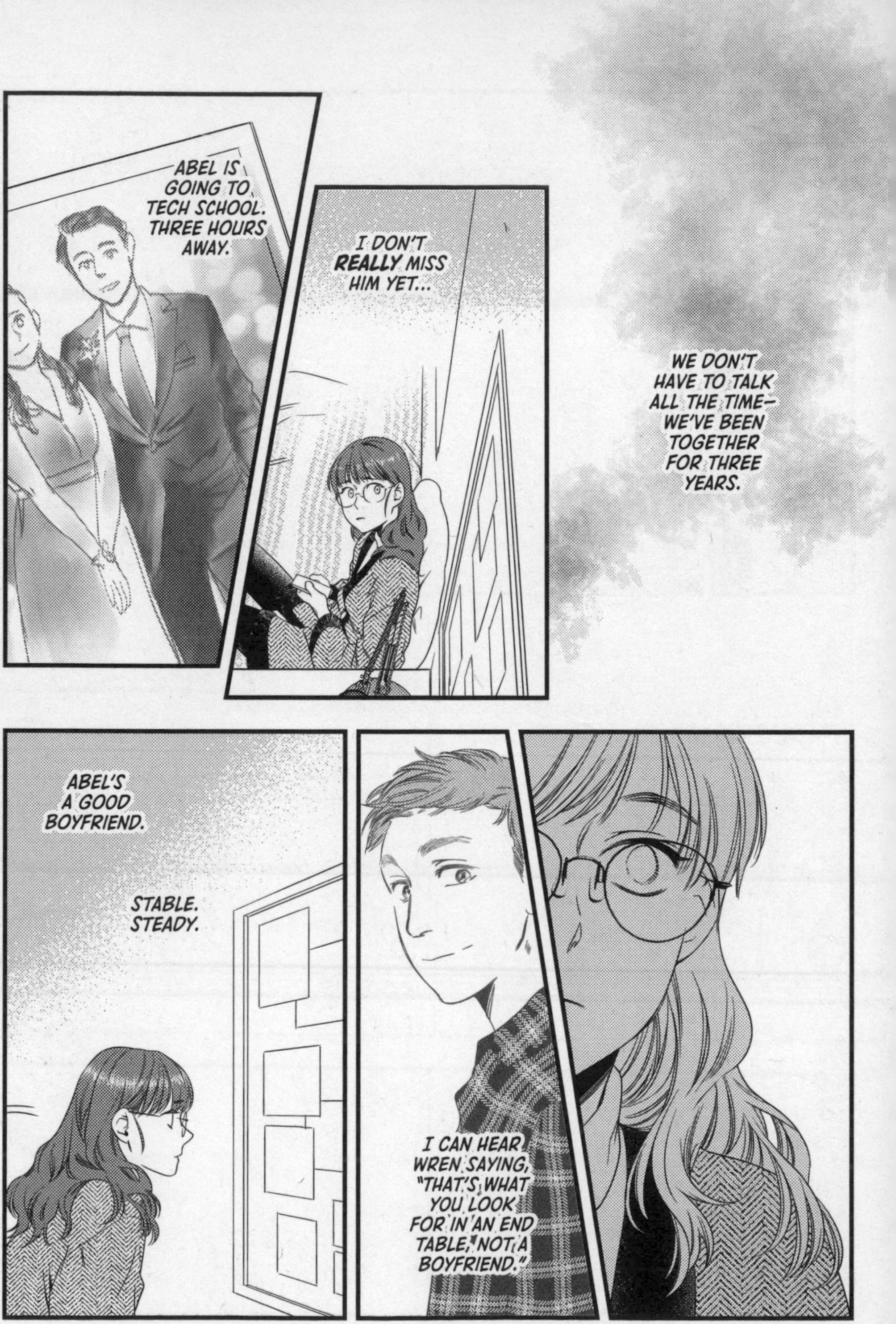

ABEL IS GOING TO TECH SCHOOL. THREE HOURS AWAY.
I DON'T **REALLY** MISS HIM YET...
WE DON'T HAVE TO TALK ALL THE TIME—WE'VE BEEN TOGETHER FOR THREE YEARS.
ABEL'S A GOOD BOYFRIEND.
STABLE. STEADY.
I CAN HEAR WREN SAYING, "THAT'S WHAT YOU LOOK FOR IN AN END TABLE, NOT A BOYFRIEND."

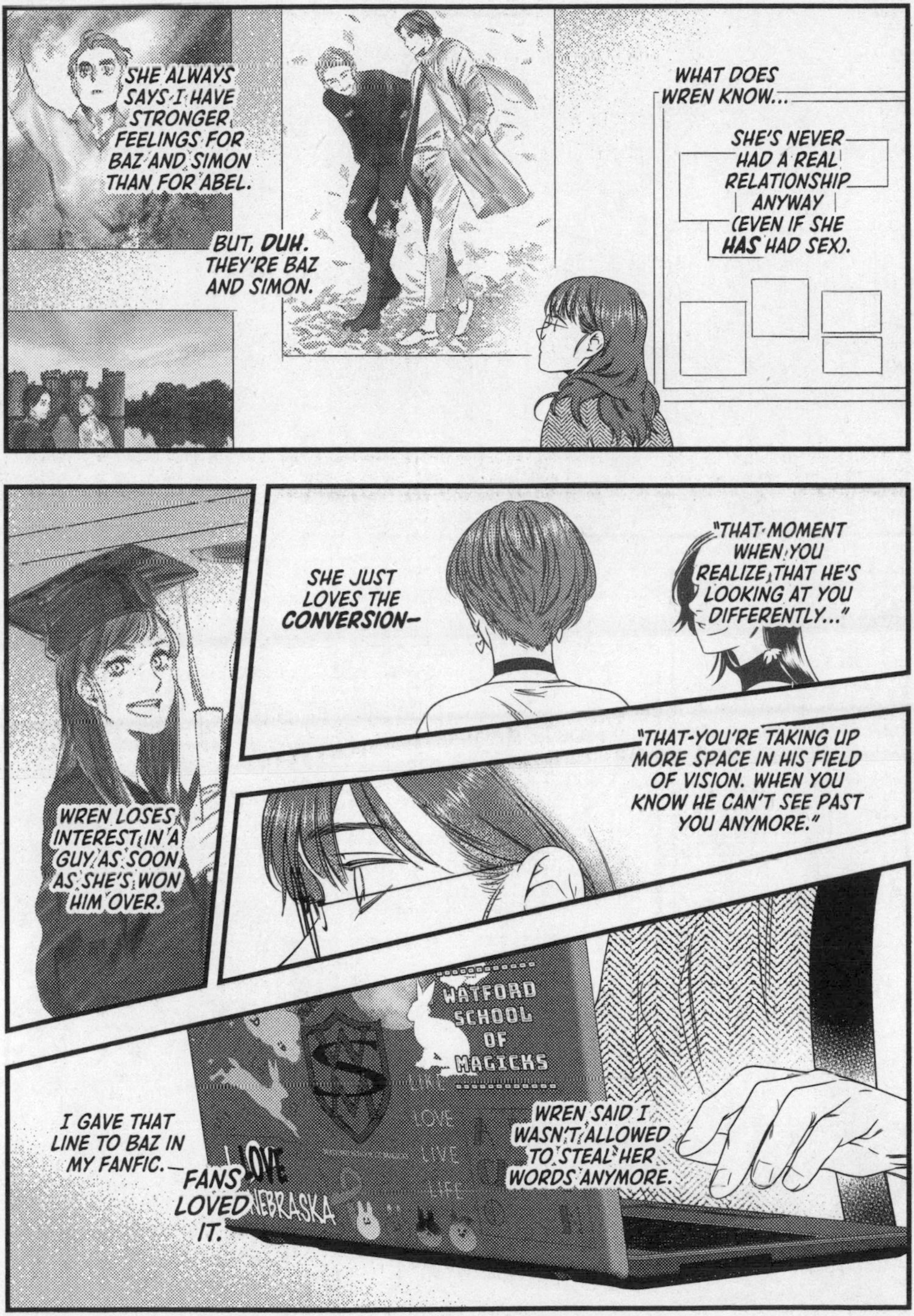
SHE ALWAYS SAYS I HAVE STRONGER FEELINGS FOR BAZ AND SIMON THAN FOR ABEL.
BUT, **DUH.** THEY'RE BAZ AND SIMON.
WHAT DOES WREN KNOW...
SHE'S NEVER HAD A REAL RELATIONSHIP ANYWAY (EVEN IF SHE **HAS** HAD SEX).
WREN LOSES INTEREST IN A GUY AS SOON AS SHE'S WON HIM OVER.
SHE JUST LOVES THE **CONVERSION**—
"THAT MOMENT WHEN YOU REALIZE THAT HE'S LOOKING AT YOU DIFFERENTLY..."
"THAT-YOU'RE TAKING UP MORE SPACE IN HIS FIELD OF VISION. WHEN YOU KNOW HE CAN'T SEE PAST YOU ANYMORE."
WATFORD SCHOOL OF MAGICKS
I GAVE THAT LINE TO BAZ IN MY FANFIC.—
FANS LOVED IT.
I LOVE NEBRASKA
LOVE LIVE LIFE
WREN SAID I WASN'T ALLOWED TO STEAL HER WORDS ANYMORE.

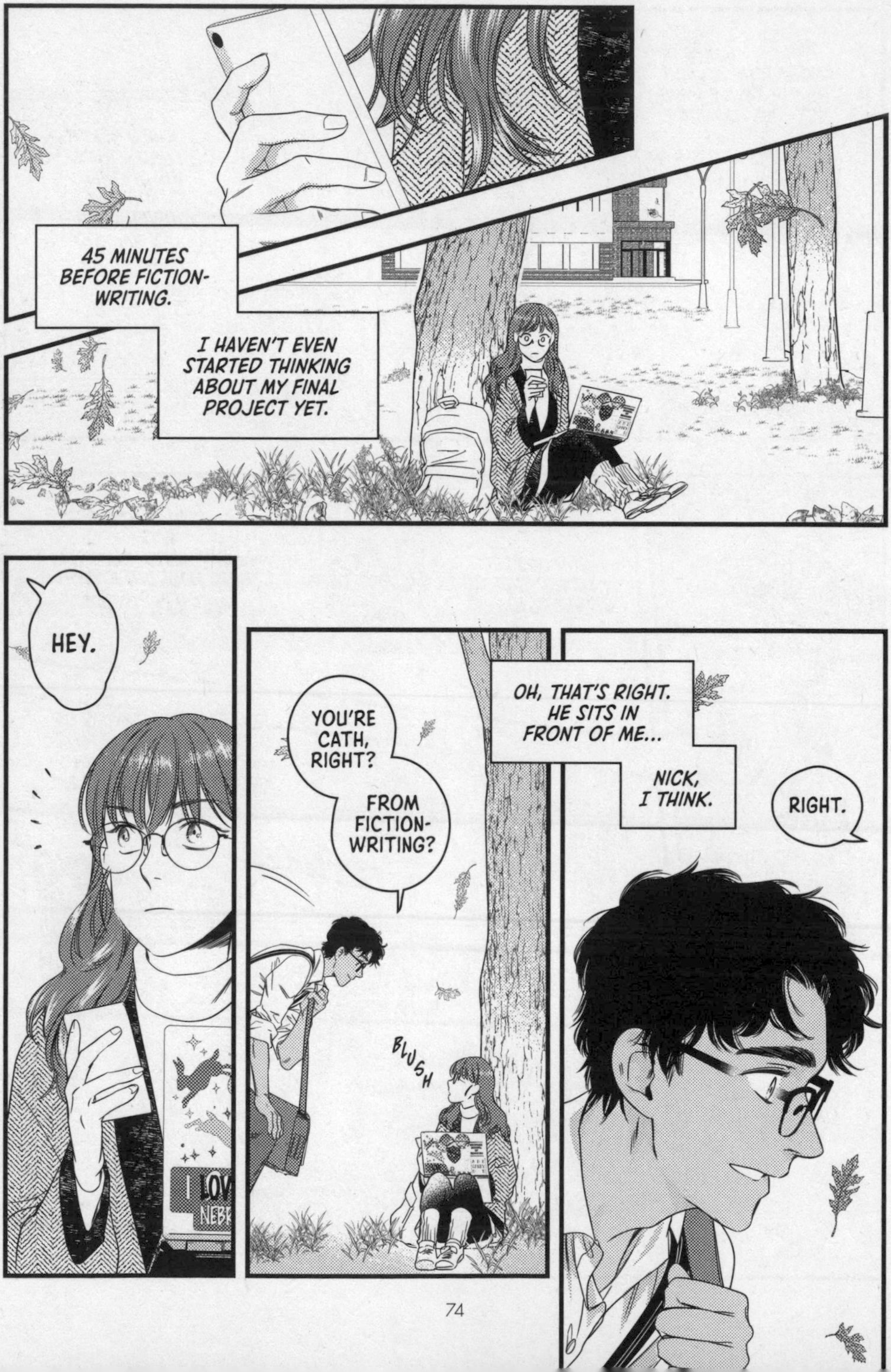
45 MINUTES BEFORE FICTION-WRITING.
I HAVEN'T EVEN STARTED THINKING ABOUT MY FINAL PROJECT YET.
HEY.
YOU'RE CATH, RIGHT?
FROM FICTION-WRITING?
BLUSH
OH, THAT'S RIGHT. HE SITS IN FRONT OF ME...
NICK, I THINK.
RIGHT.

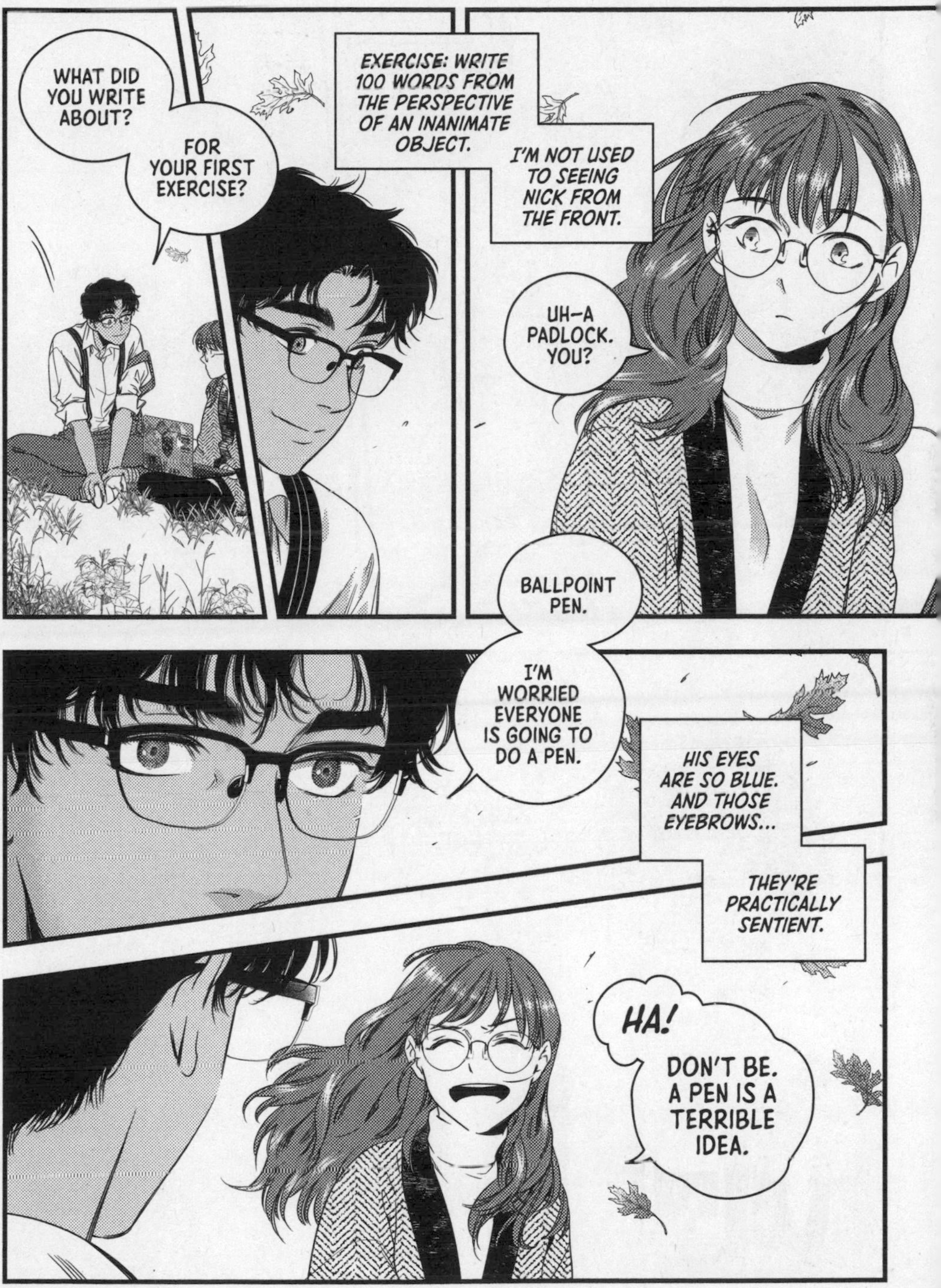
WHAT DID YOU WRITE ABOUT?
FOR YOUR FIRST EXERCISE?
EXERCISE: WRITE 100 WORDS FROM THE PERSPECTIVE OF AN INANIMATE OBJECT.
I'M NOT USED TO SEEING NICK FROM THE FRONT.
UH—A PADLOCK. YOU?
BALLPOINT PEN.
I'M WORRIED EVERYONE IS GOING TO DO A PEN.
HIS EYES ARE SO BLUE. AND THOSE EYEBROWS...
THEY'RE PRACTICALLY SENTIENT.
HA!
DON'T BE. A PEN IS A TERRIBLE IDEA.

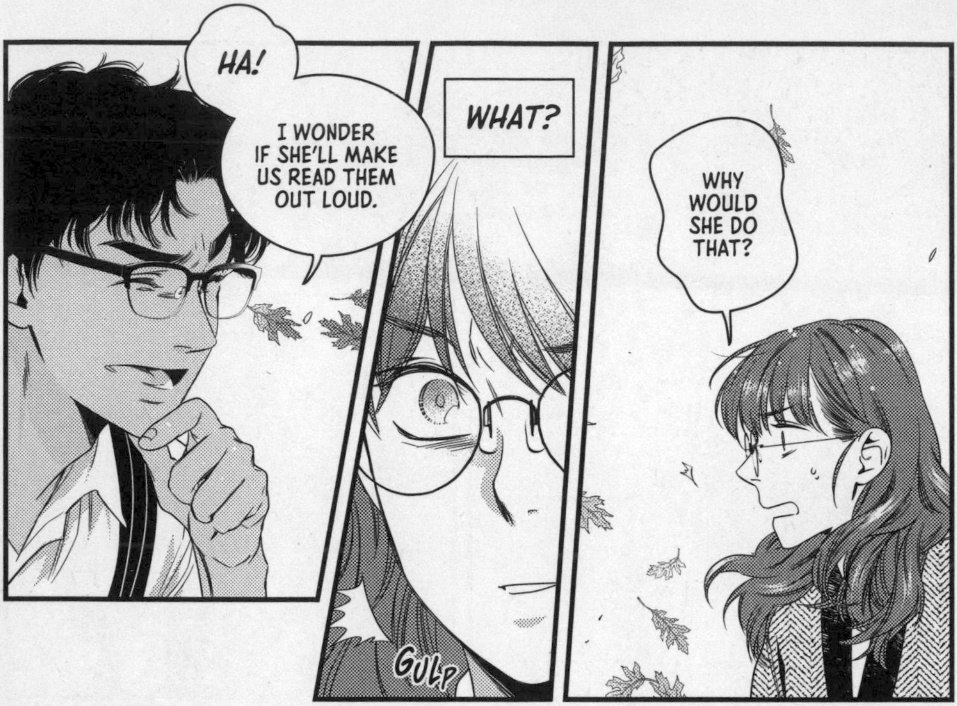
HA!
I WONDER IF SHE'LL MAKE US READ THEM OUT LOUD.
WHAT?
GULP
WHY WOULD SHE DO THAT?
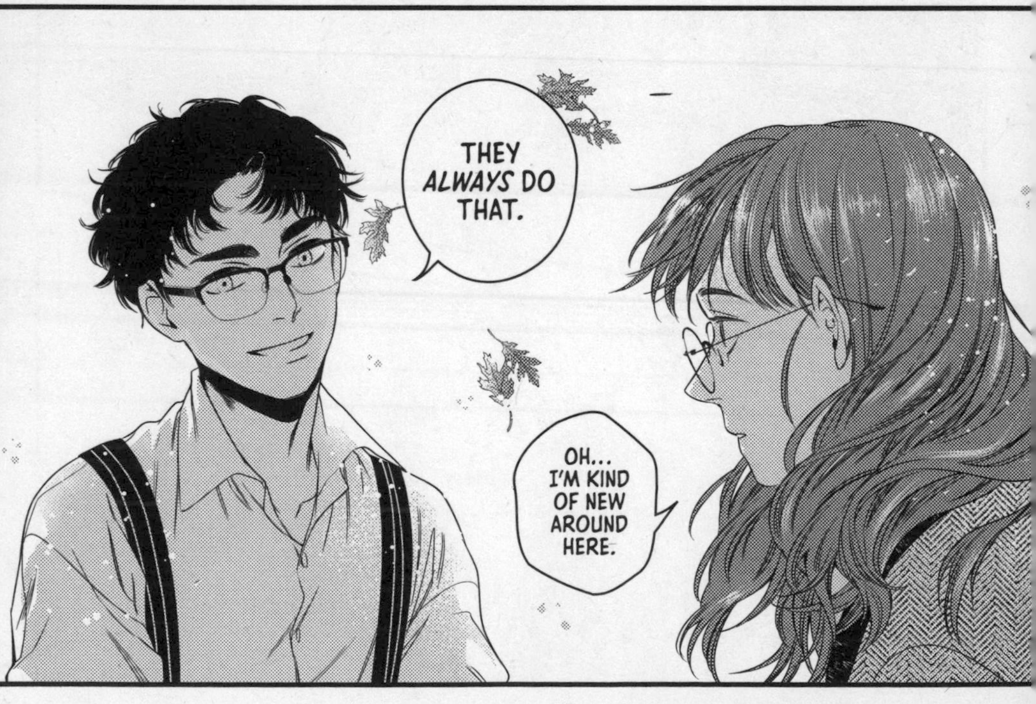
THEY *ALWAYS* DO THAT.
OH... I'M KIND OF NEW AROUND HERE.

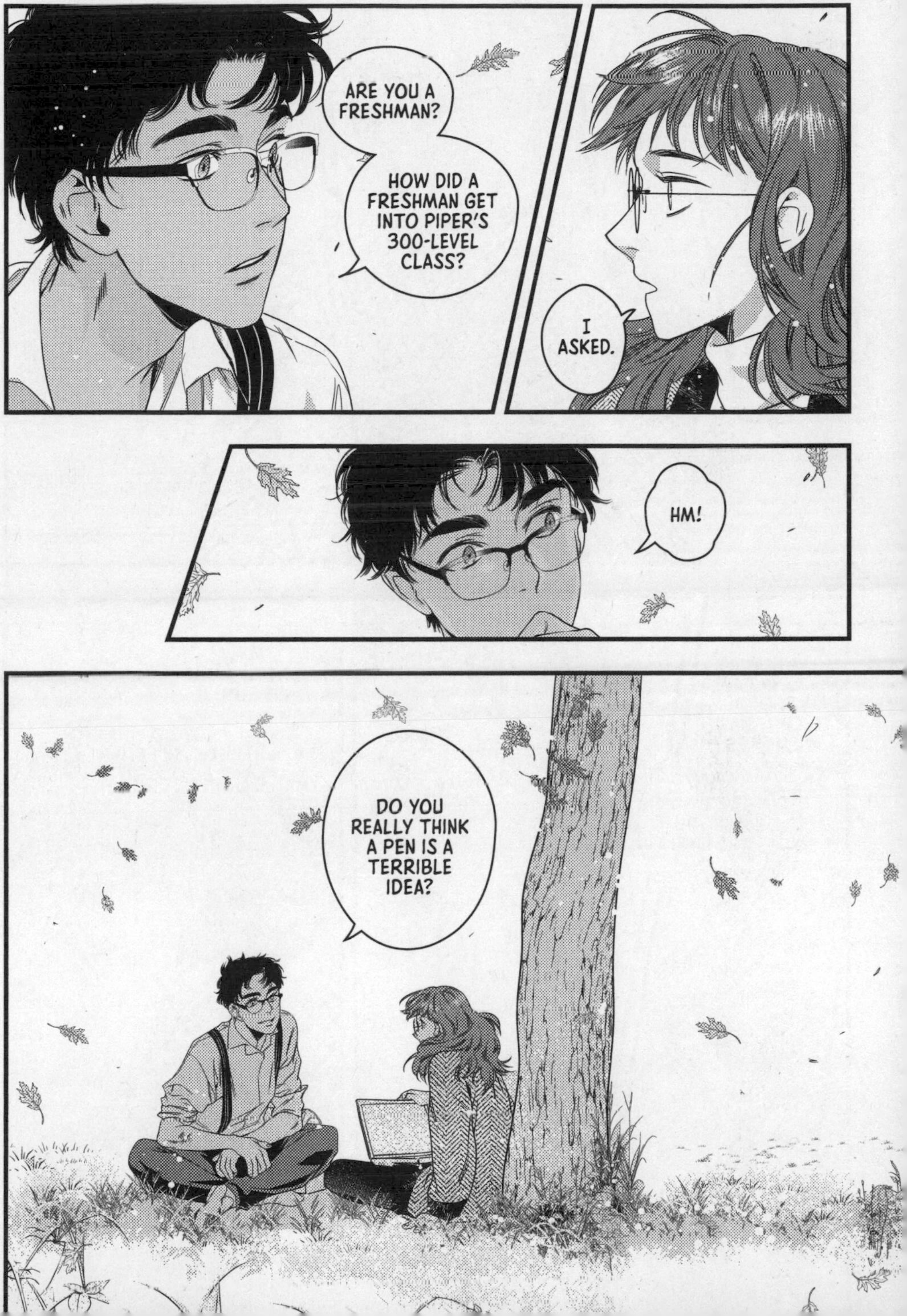
ARE YOU A FRESHMAN?
HOW DID A FRESHMAN GET INTO PIPER'S 300-LEVEL CLASS?
I ASKED.
HM!
DO YOU REALLY THINK A PEN IS A TERRIBLE IDEA?

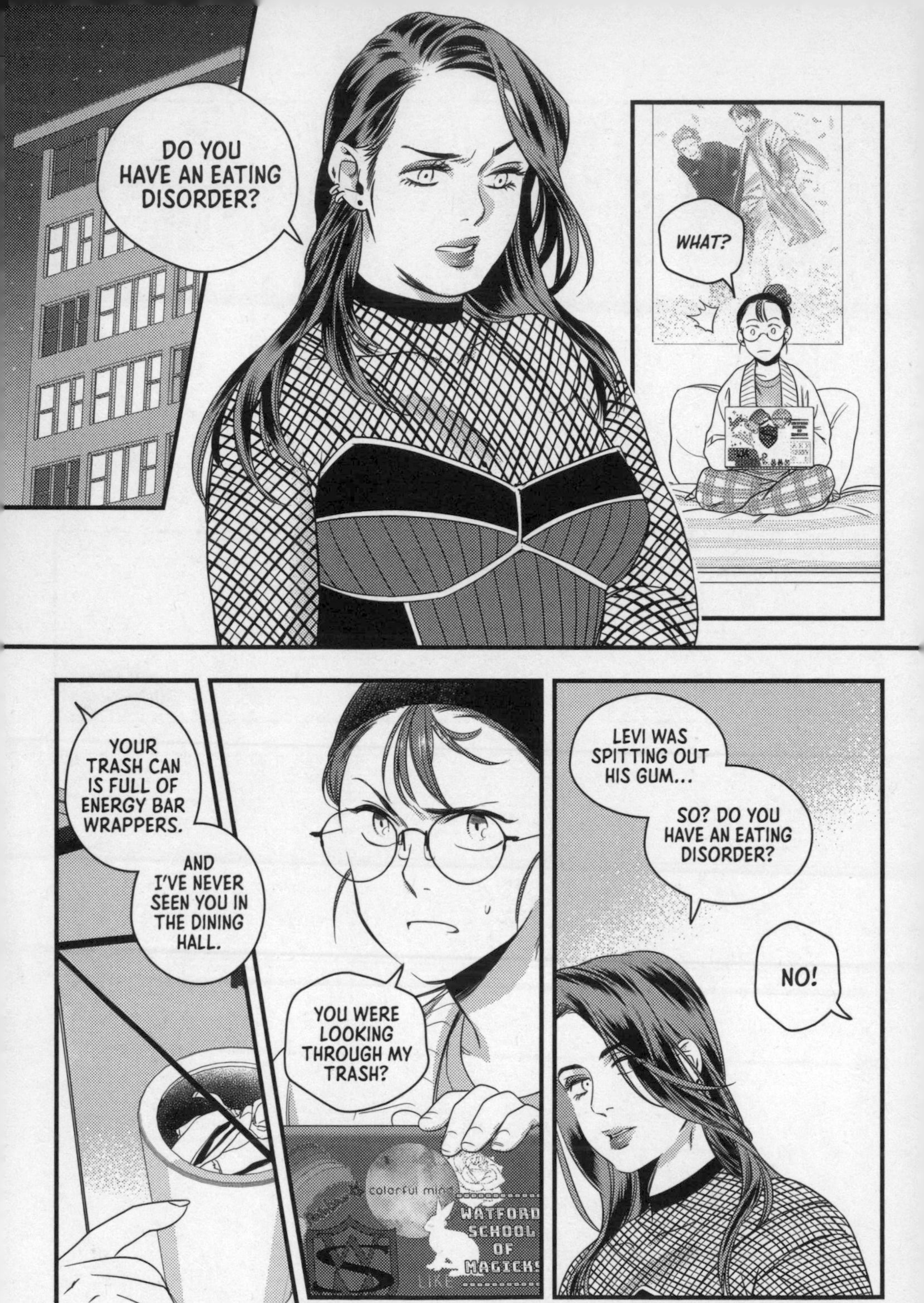
DO YOU HAVE AN EATING DISORDER?
WHAT?
YOUR TRASH CAN IS FULL OF ENERGY BAR WRAPPERS.
AND I'VE NEVER SEEN YOU IN THE DINING HALL.
YOU WERE LOOKING THROUGH MY TRASH?
colorful mind
WATFORD SCHOOL OF MAGICKS
LEVI WAS SPITTING OUT HIS GUM...
SO? DO YOU HAVE AN EATING DISORDER?
NO!

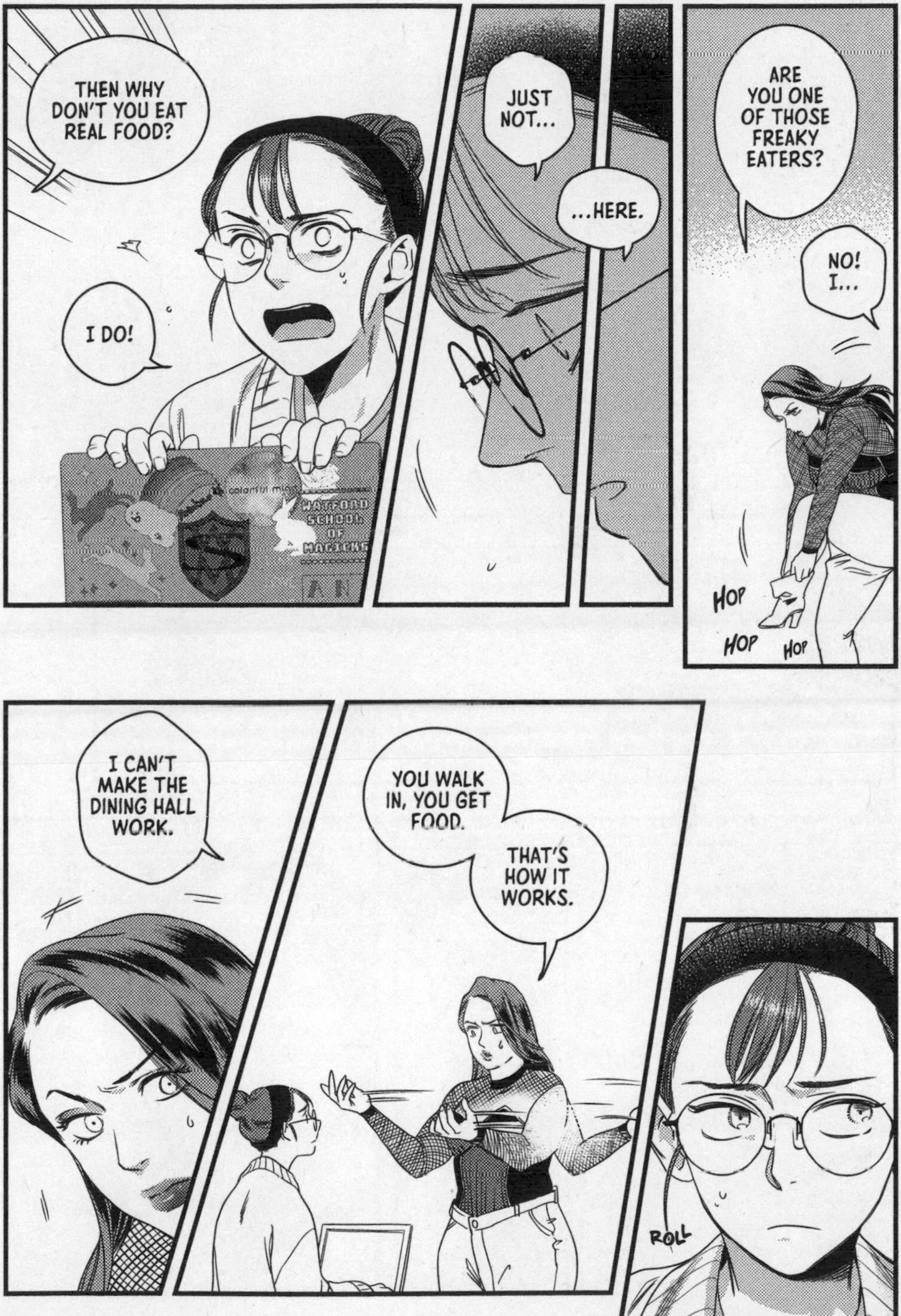
THEN WHY DON'T YOU EAT REAL FOOD?
I DO!
JUST NOT...
...HERE.
ARE YOU ONE OF THOSE FREAKY EATERS?
NO! I...
HOP
HOP
HOP
I CAN'T MAKE THE DINING HALL WORK.
YOU WALK IN, YOU GET FOOD.
THAT'S HOW IT WORKS.
ROLL

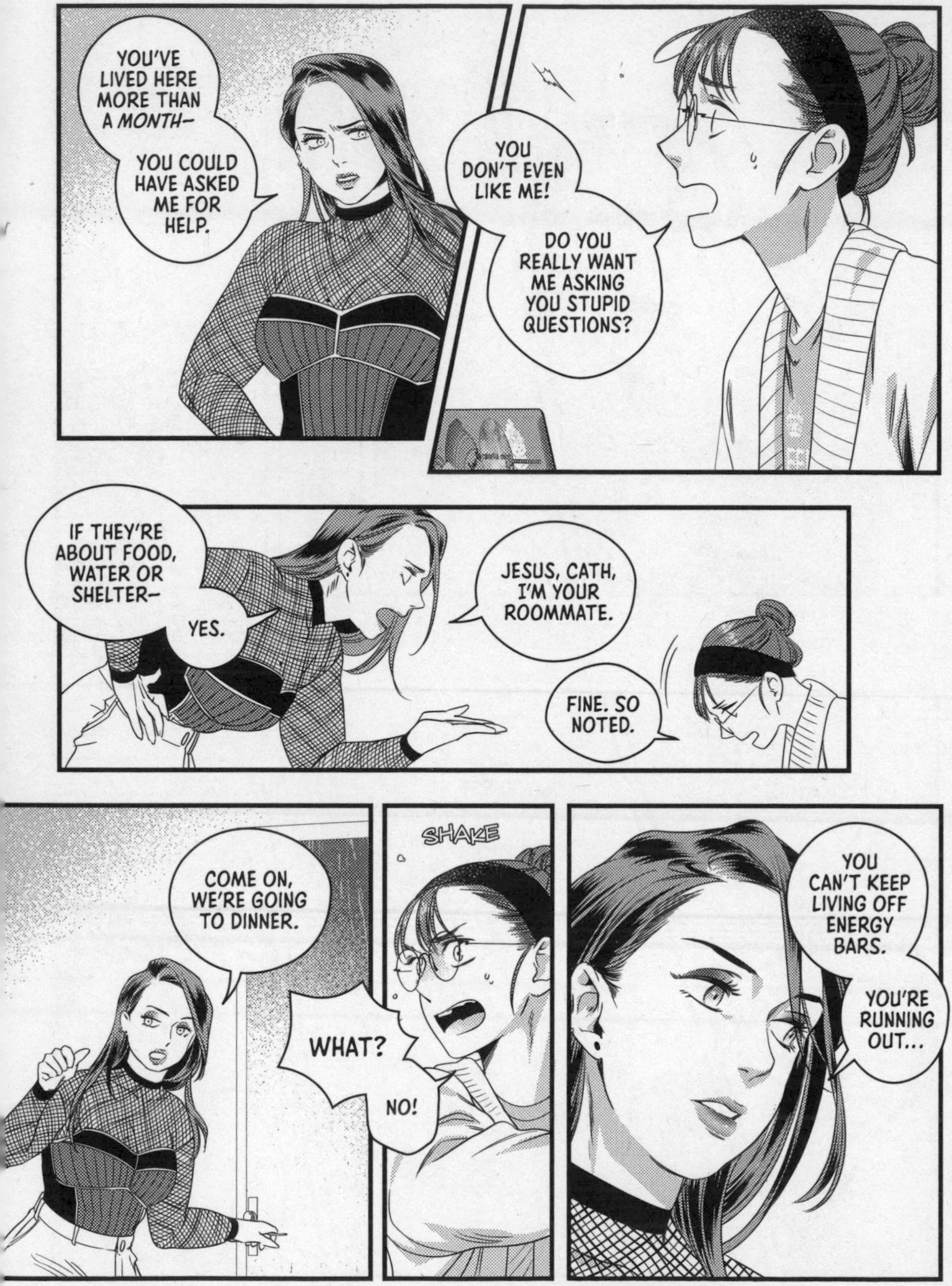
YOU'VE LIVED HERE MORE THAN A *MONTH*–
YOU COULD HAVE ASKED ME FOR HELP.
YOU DON'T EVEN LIKE ME!
DO YOU REALLY WANT ME ASKING YOU STUPID QUESTIONS?
IF THEY'RE ABOUT FOOD, WATER OR SHELTER–
YES.
JESUS, CATH, I'M YOUR ROOMMATE.
FINE. SO NOTED.
COME ON, WE'RE GOING TO DINNER.
SHAKE
WHAT?
NO!
YOU CAN'T KEEP LIVING OFF ENERGY BARS.
YOU'RE RUNNING OUT...

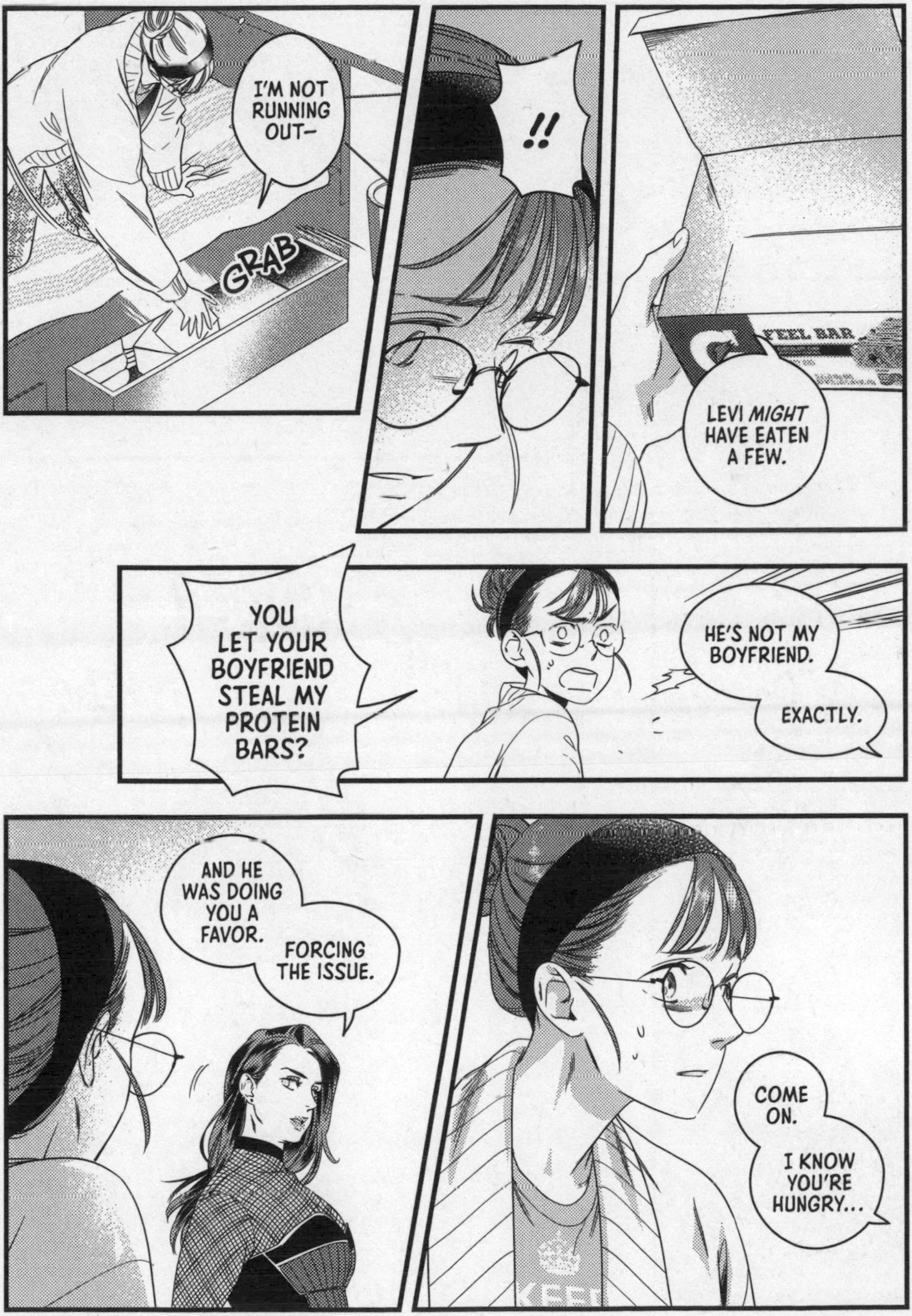
I'M NOT RUNNING OUT–
GRAB
!!
FEEL BAR
LEVI *MIGHT* HAVE EATEN A FEW.
YOU LET YOUR BOYFRIEND STEAL MY PROTEIN BARS?
HE'S NOT MY BOYFRIEND.
EXACTLY.
AND HE WAS DOING YOU A FAVOR.
FORCING THE ISSUE.
COME ON.
I KNOW YOU'RE HUNGRY...

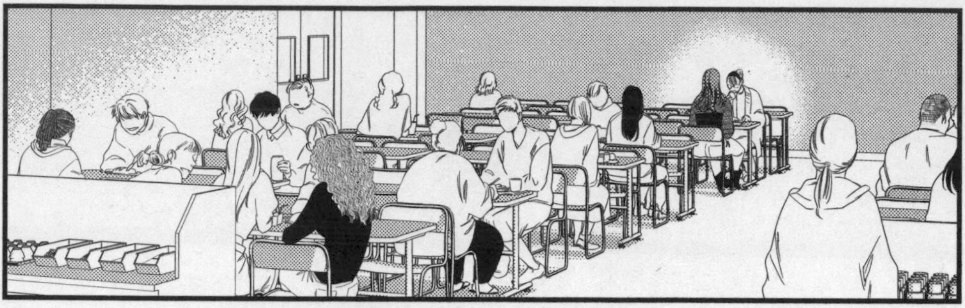

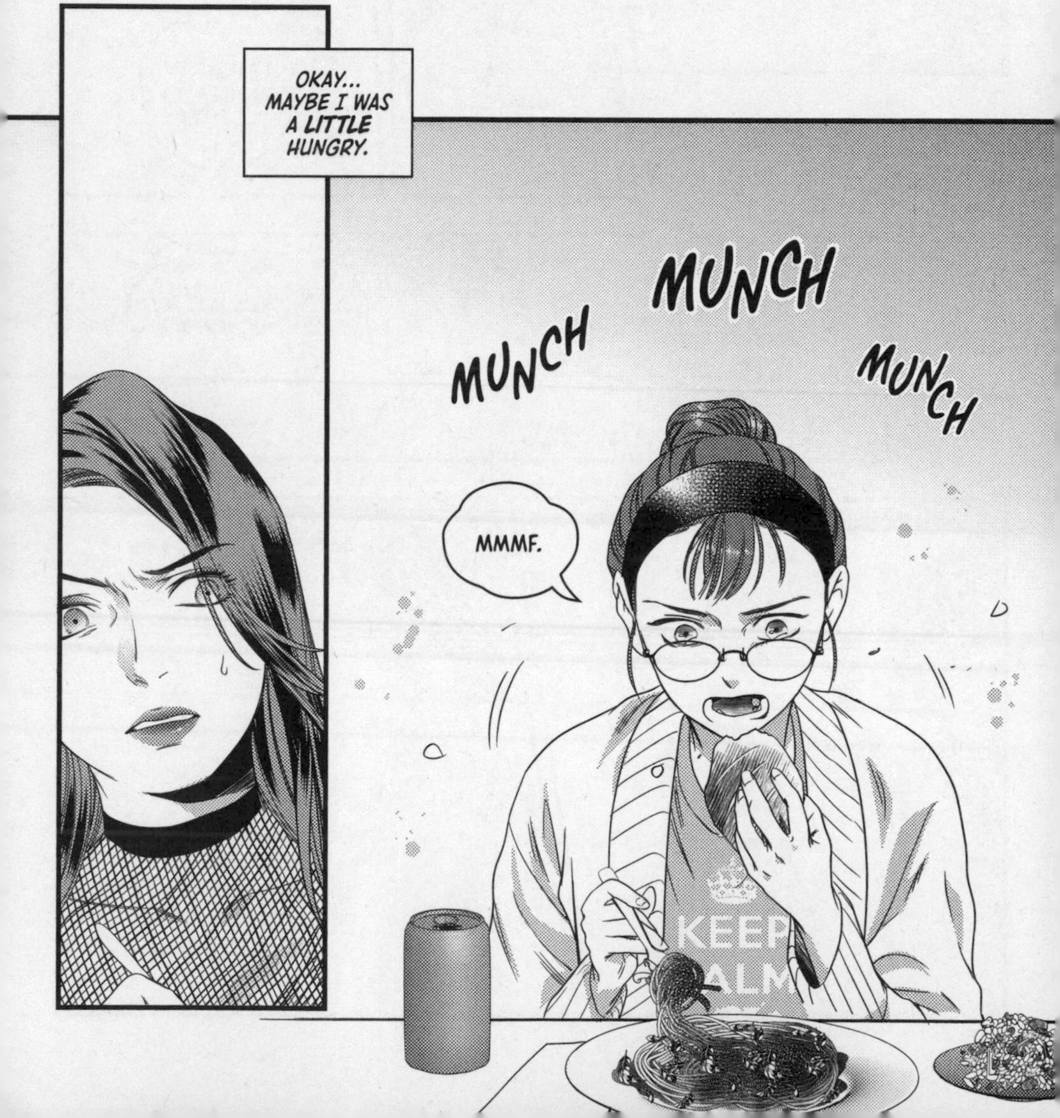
OKAY... MAYBE I WAS A LITTLE HUNGRY.
MUNCH
MUNCH
MUNCH
MMMF.

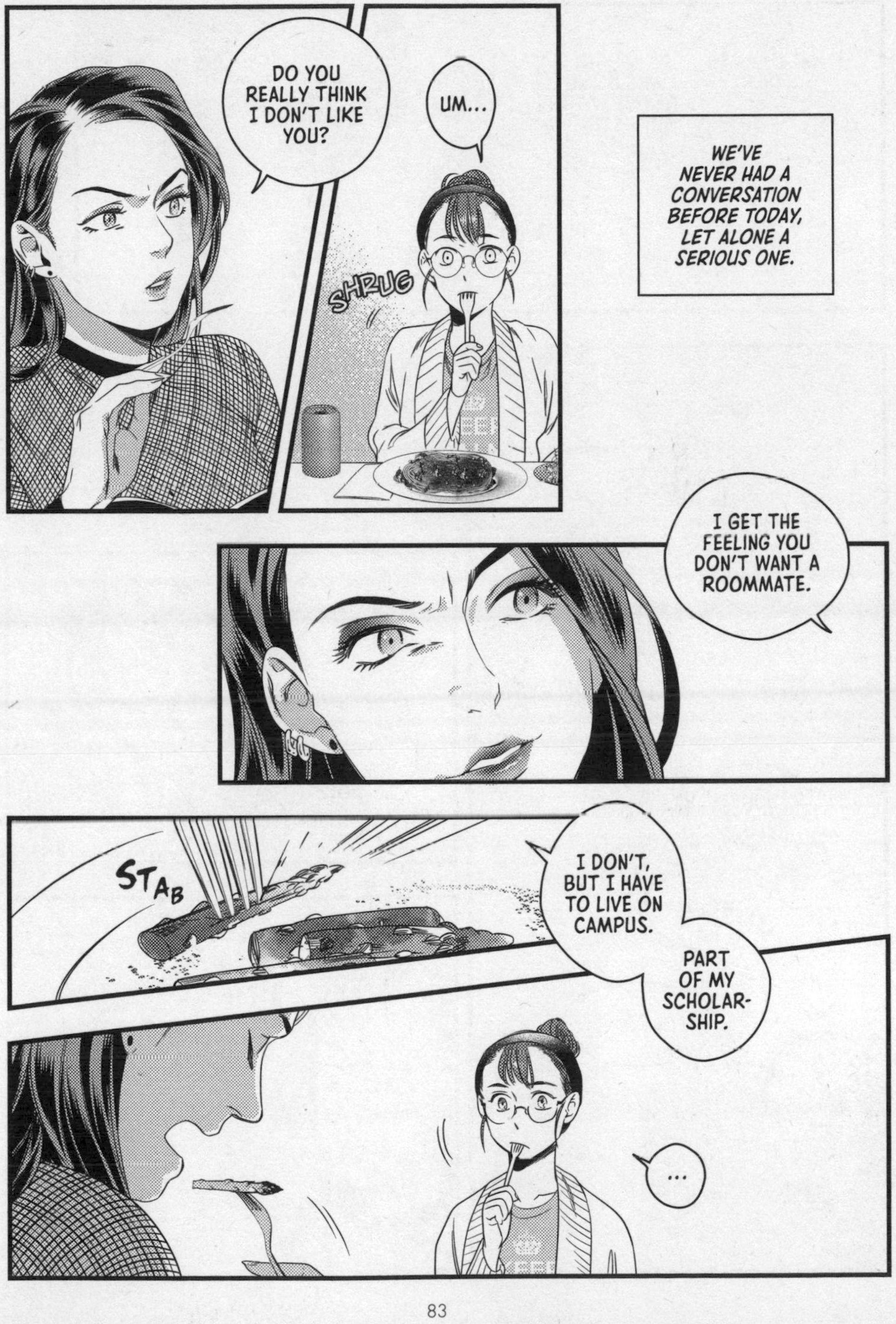
DO YOU REALLY THINK I DON'T LIKE YOU?
UM...
SHRUG
WE'VE NEVER HAD A CONVERSATION BEFORE TODAY, LET ALONE A SERIOUS ONE.
I GET THE FEELING YOU DON'T WANT A ROOMMATE.
STAB
I DON'T, BUT I HAVE TO LIVE ON CAMPUS.
PART OF MY SCHOLAR-SHIP.
...

I DIDN'T WANT A ROOMMATE EITHER...
I THOUGHT I WAS GOING TO LIVE WITH MY SISTER.
YOU HAVE A SISTER WHO GOES HERE?
NOD
TWIN.
EW.
WEIRD.
WHY IS THAT WEIRD?
IT JUST IS. IT'S CREEPY.
IDENTICAL?
TECHNICALLY.
EW!
HA!
IT'S NOT CREEPY, WHAT IS WRONG WITH YOU?
SO WHY AREN'T YOU LIVING WITH HER?

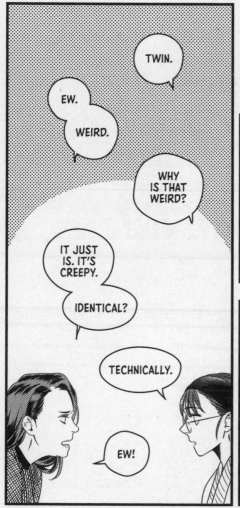

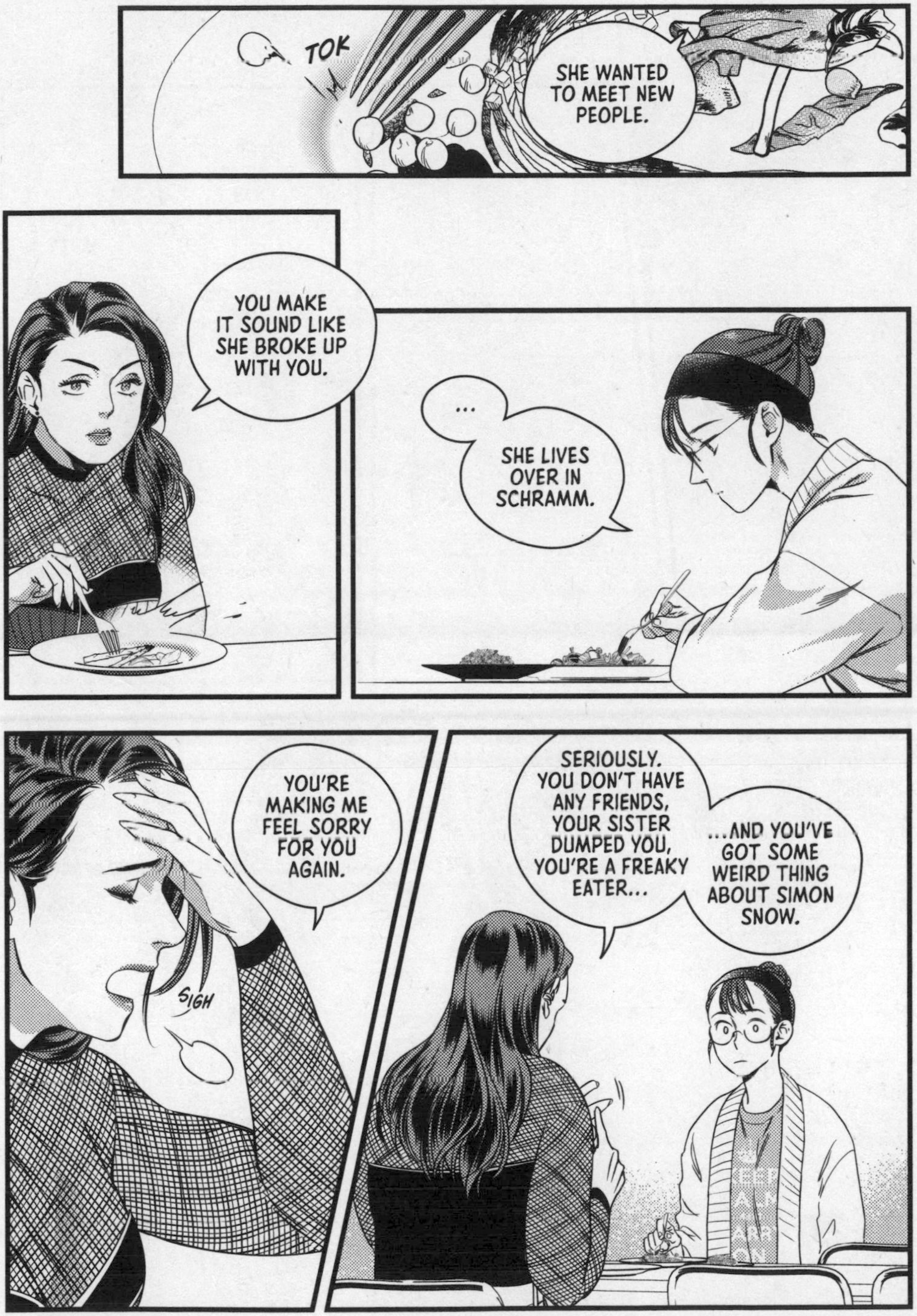
TOK
SHE WANTED TO MEET NEW PEOPLE.
YOU MAKE IT SOUND LIKE SHE BROKE UP WITH YOU.
...
SHE LIVES OVER IN SCHRAMM.
YOU'RE MAKING ME FEEL SORRY FOR YOU AGAIN.
SIGH
SERIOUSLY. YOU DON'T HAVE ANY FRIENDS, YOUR SISTER DUMPED YOU, YOU'RE A FREAKY EATER...
...AND YOU'VE GOT SOME WEIRD THING ABOUT SIMON SNOW.

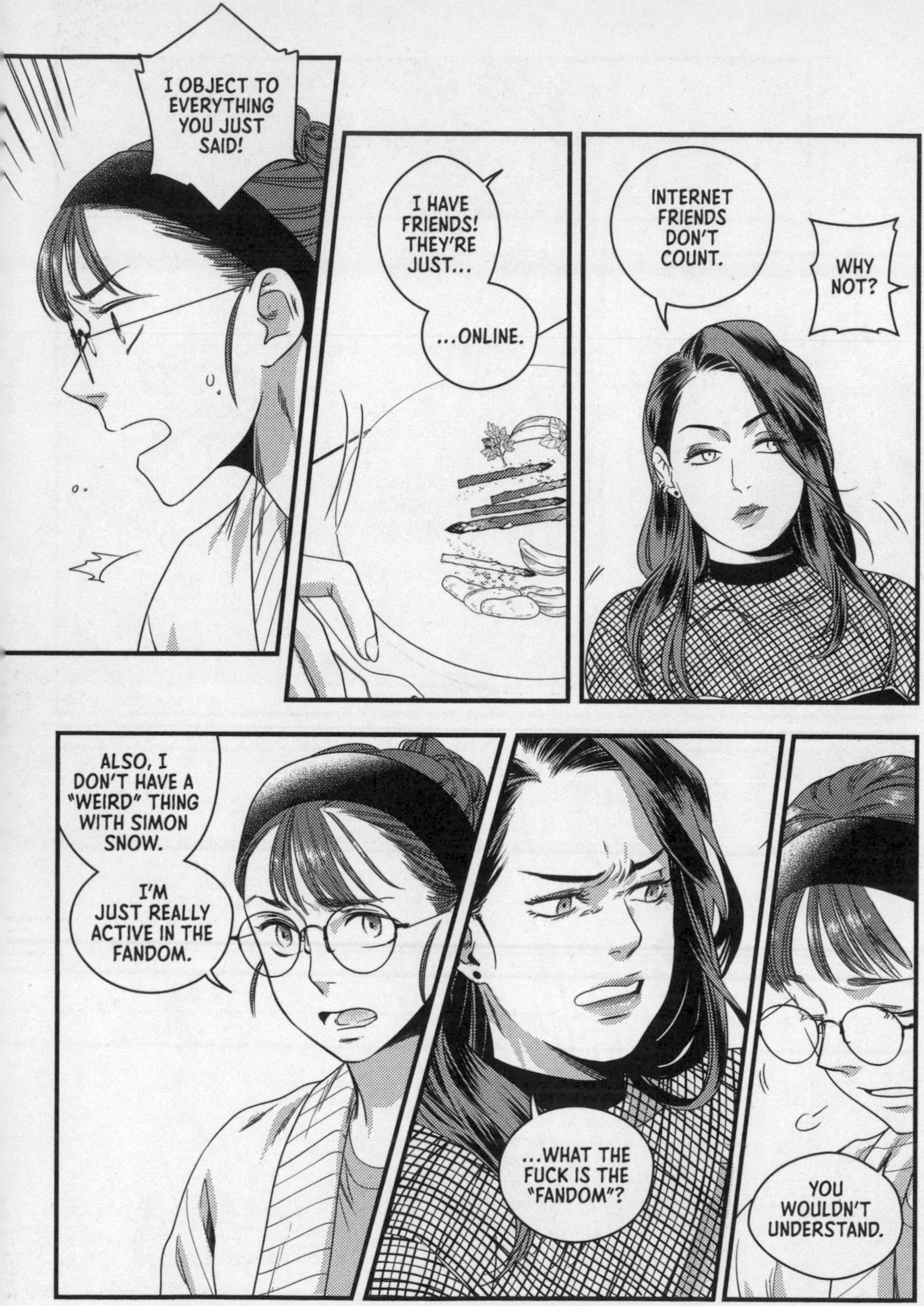
I OBJECT TO EVERYTHING YOU JUST SAID!
I HAVE FRIENDS! THEY'RE JUST...
...ONLINE.
INTERNET FRIENDS DON'T COUNT.
WHY NOT?
ALSO, I DON'T HAVE A "WEIRD" THING WITH SIMON SNOW.
I'M JUST REALLY ACTIVE IN THE FANDOM.
...WHAT THE FUCK IS THE "FANDOM"?
YOU WOULDN'T UNDERSTAND.

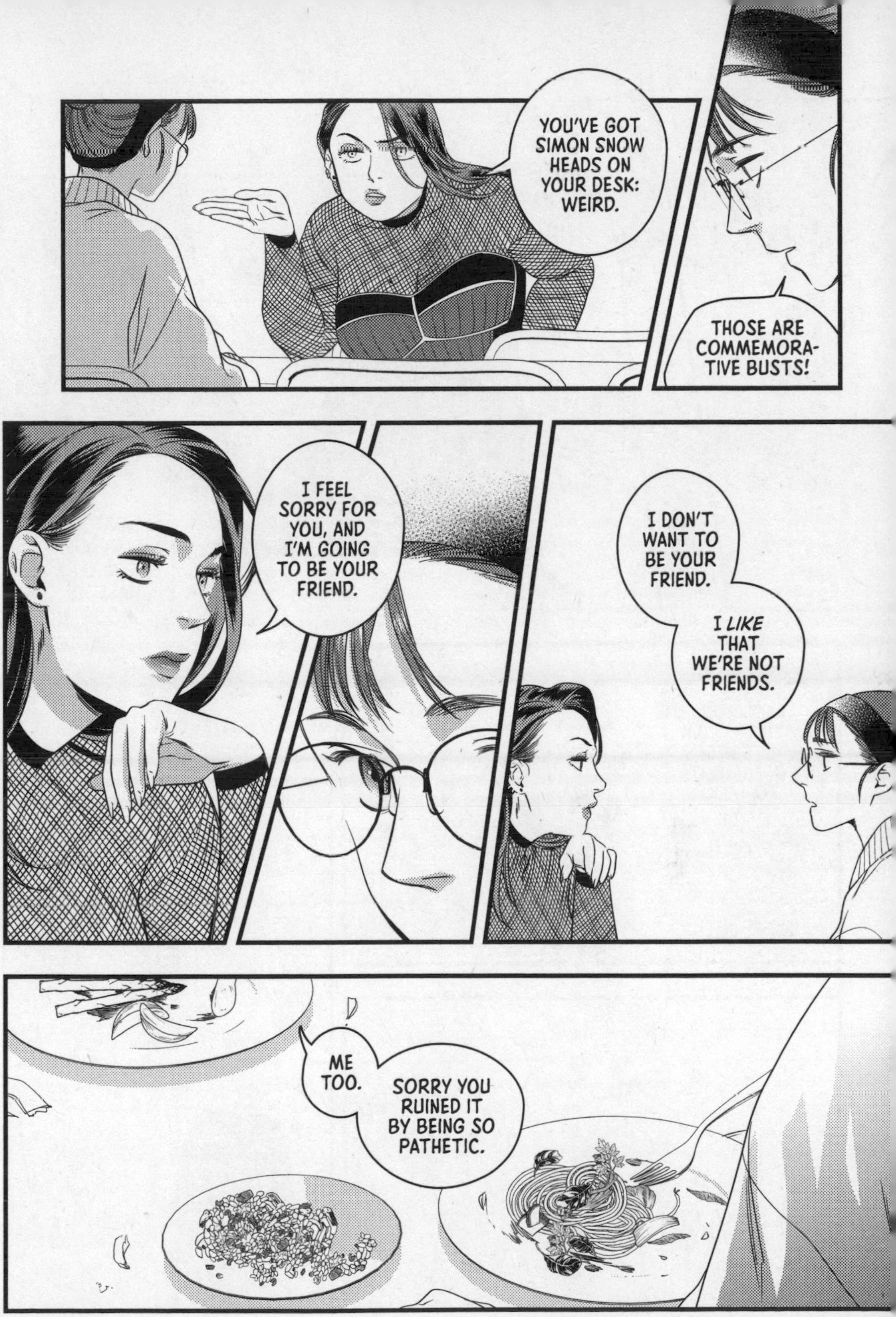
YOU'VE GOT SIMON SNOW HEADS ON YOUR DESK: WEIRD.
THOSE ARE COMMEMORATIVE BUSTS!
I FEEL SORRY FOR YOU, AND I'M GOING TO BE YOUR FRIEND.
I DON'T WANT TO BE YOUR FRIEND.
I *LIKE* THAT WE'RE NOT FRIENDS.
ME TOO.
SORRY YOU RUINED IT BY BEING SO PATHETIC.

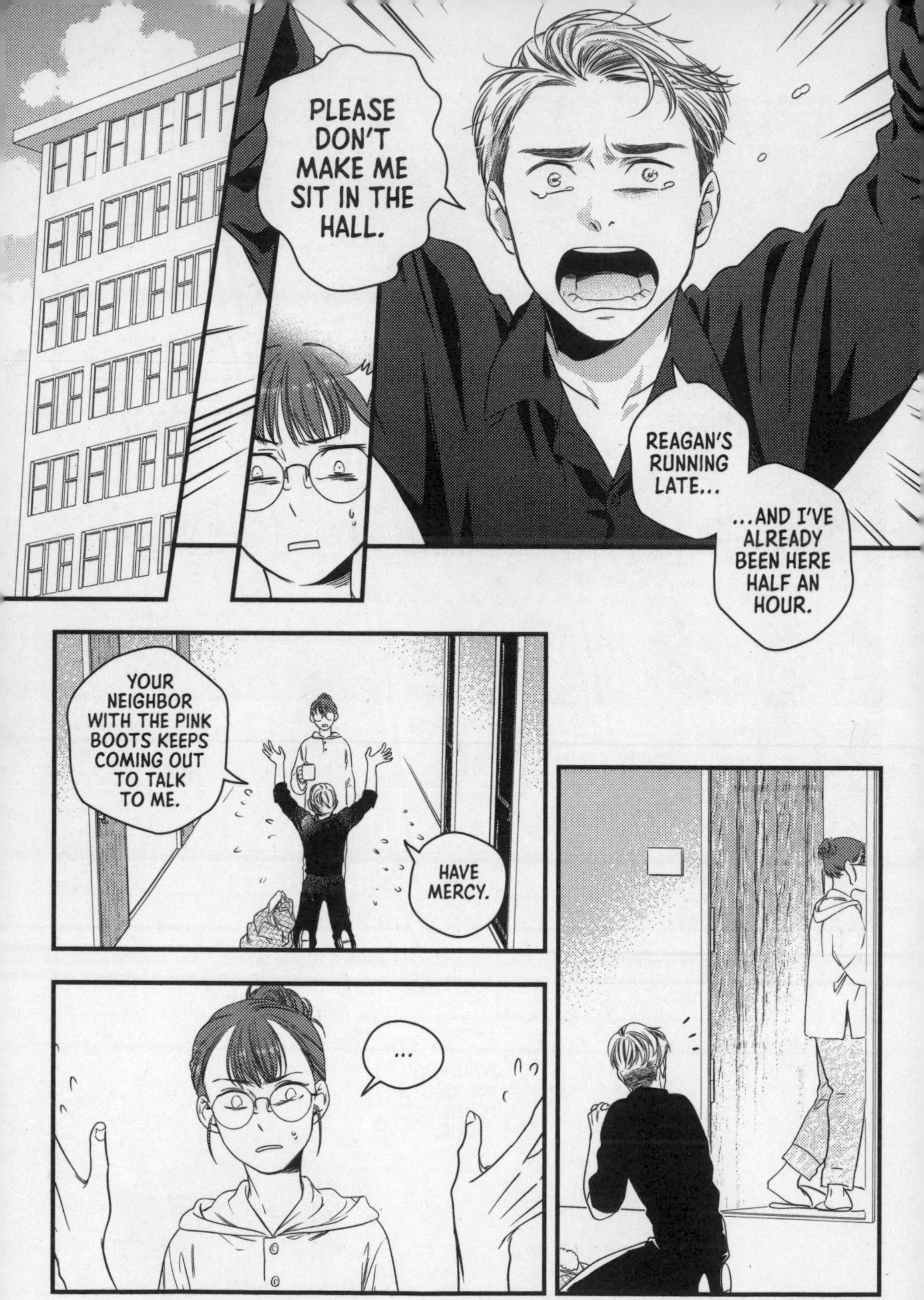
PLEASE DON'T MAKE ME SIT IN THE HALL.
REAGAN'S RUNNING LATE...
...AND I'VE ALREADY BEEN HERE HALF AN HOUR.
YOUR NEIGHBOR WITH THE PINK BOOTS KEEPS COMING OUT TO TALK TO ME.
HAVE MERCY.
...

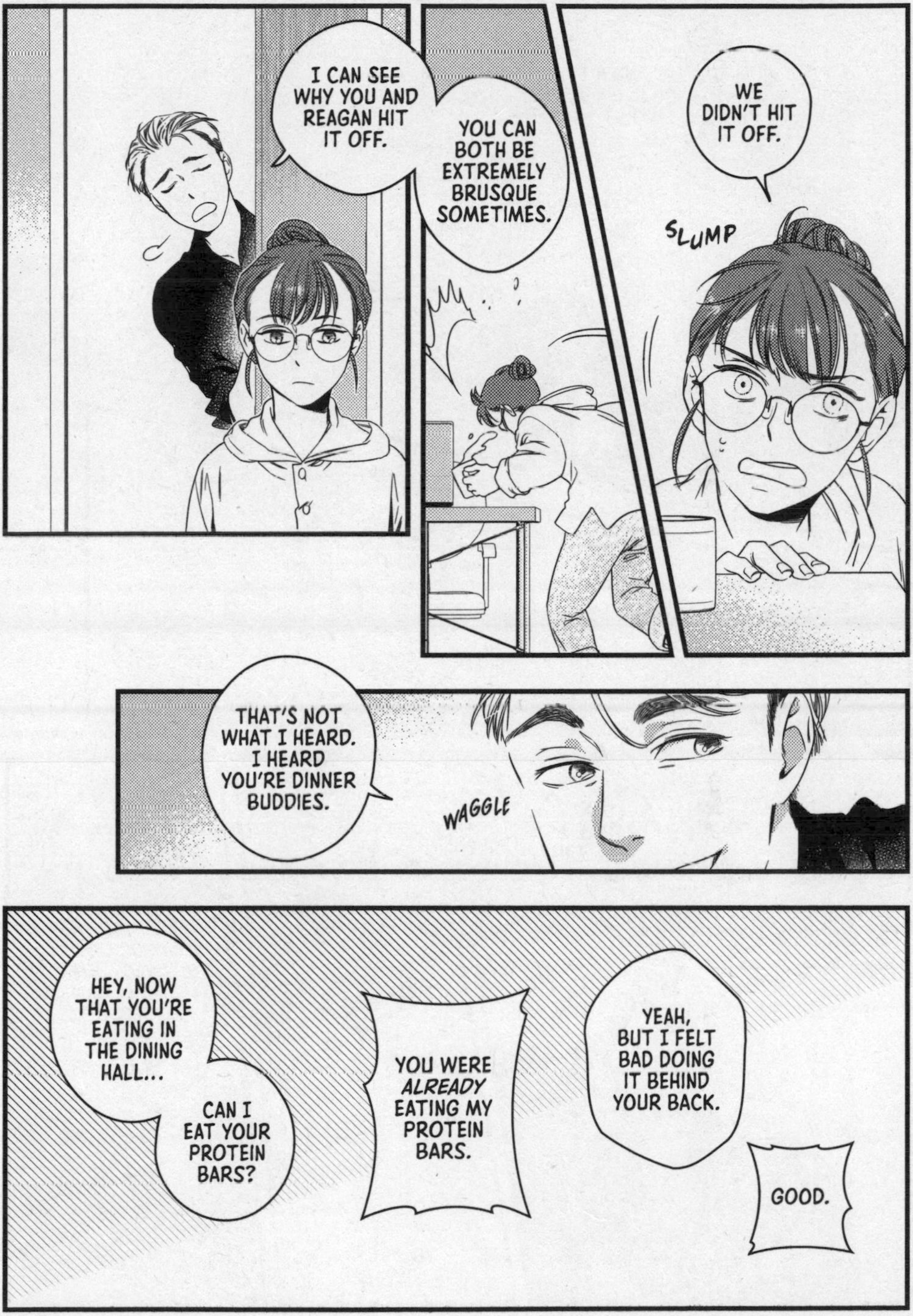
I CAN SEE WHY YOU AND REAGAN HIT IT OFF.
YOU CAN BOTH BE EXTREMELY BRUSQUE SOMETIMES.
SLUMP
WE DIDN'T HIT IT OFF.
THAT'S NOT WHAT I HEARD. I HEARD YOU'RE DINNER BUDDIES.
WAGGLE
HEY, NOW THAT YOU'RE EATING IN THE DINING HALL...
CAN I EAT YOUR PROTEIN BARS?
YOU WERE *ALREADY* EATING MY PROTEIN BARS.
YEAH, BUT I FELT BAD DOING IT BEHIND YOUR BACK.
GOOD.

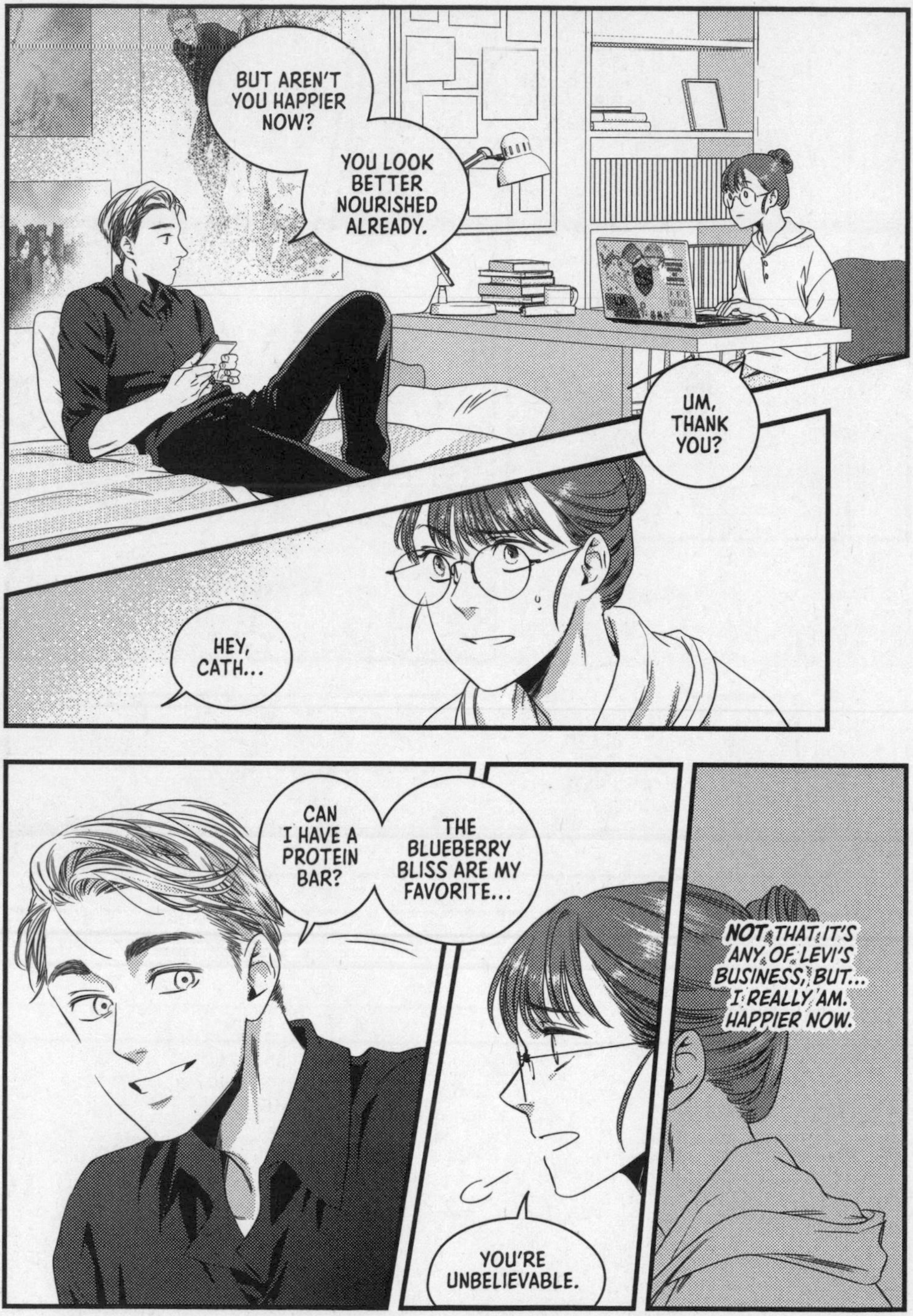
BUT AREN'T YOU HAPPIER NOW?
YOU LOOK BETTER NOURISHED ALREADY.
UM, THANK YOU?
HEY, CATH...
CAN I HAVE A PROTEIN BAR?
THE BLUEBERRY BLISS ARE MY FAVORITE...
YOU'RE UNBELIEVABLE.
NOT THAT IT'S ANY OF LEVI'S BUSINESS, BUT... I REALLY AM. HAPPIER NOW.

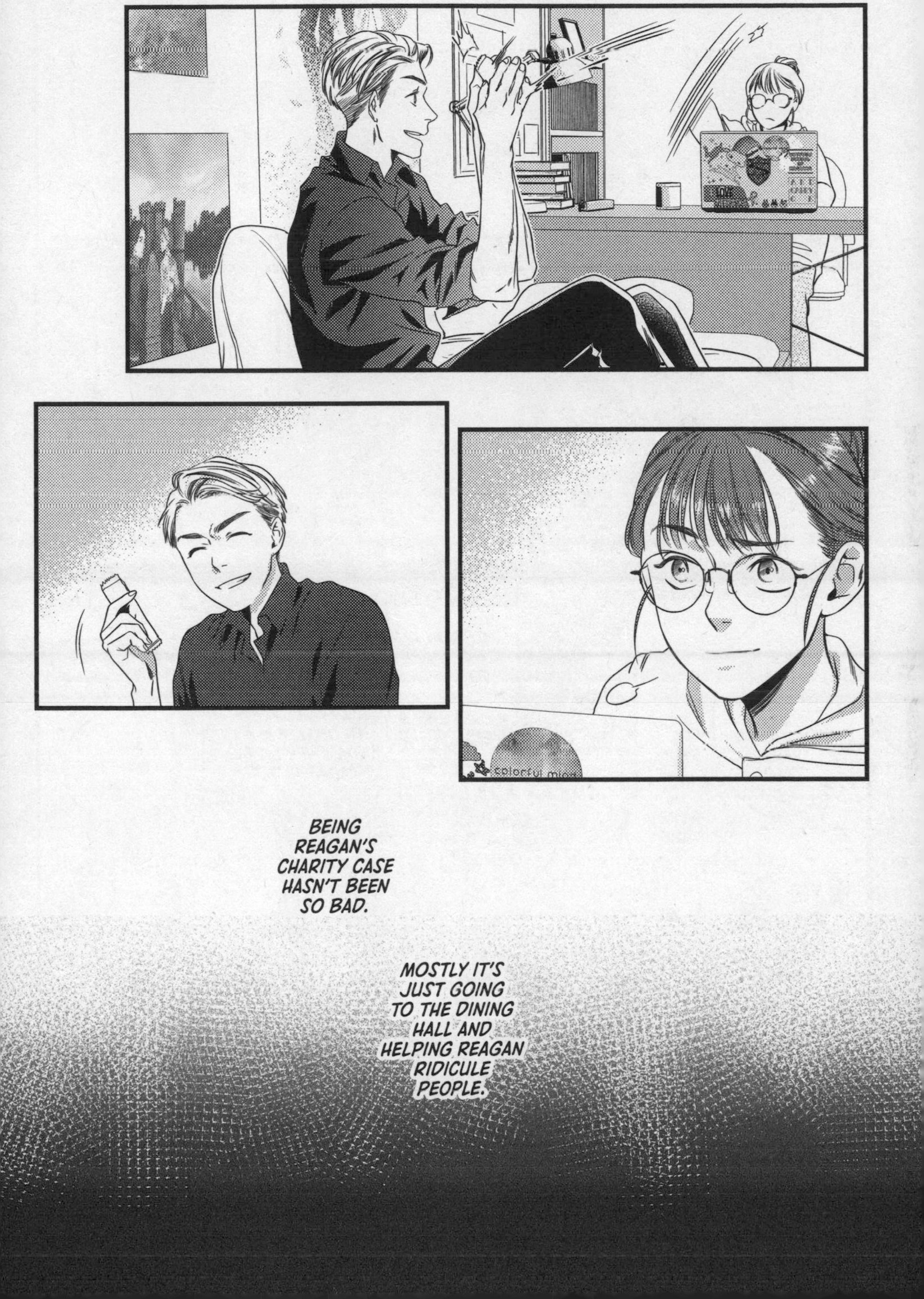
BEING REAGAN'S CHARITY CASE HASN'T BEEN SO BAD.
MOSTLY IT'S JUST GOING TO THE DINING HALL AND HELPING REAGAN RIDICULE PEOPLE.

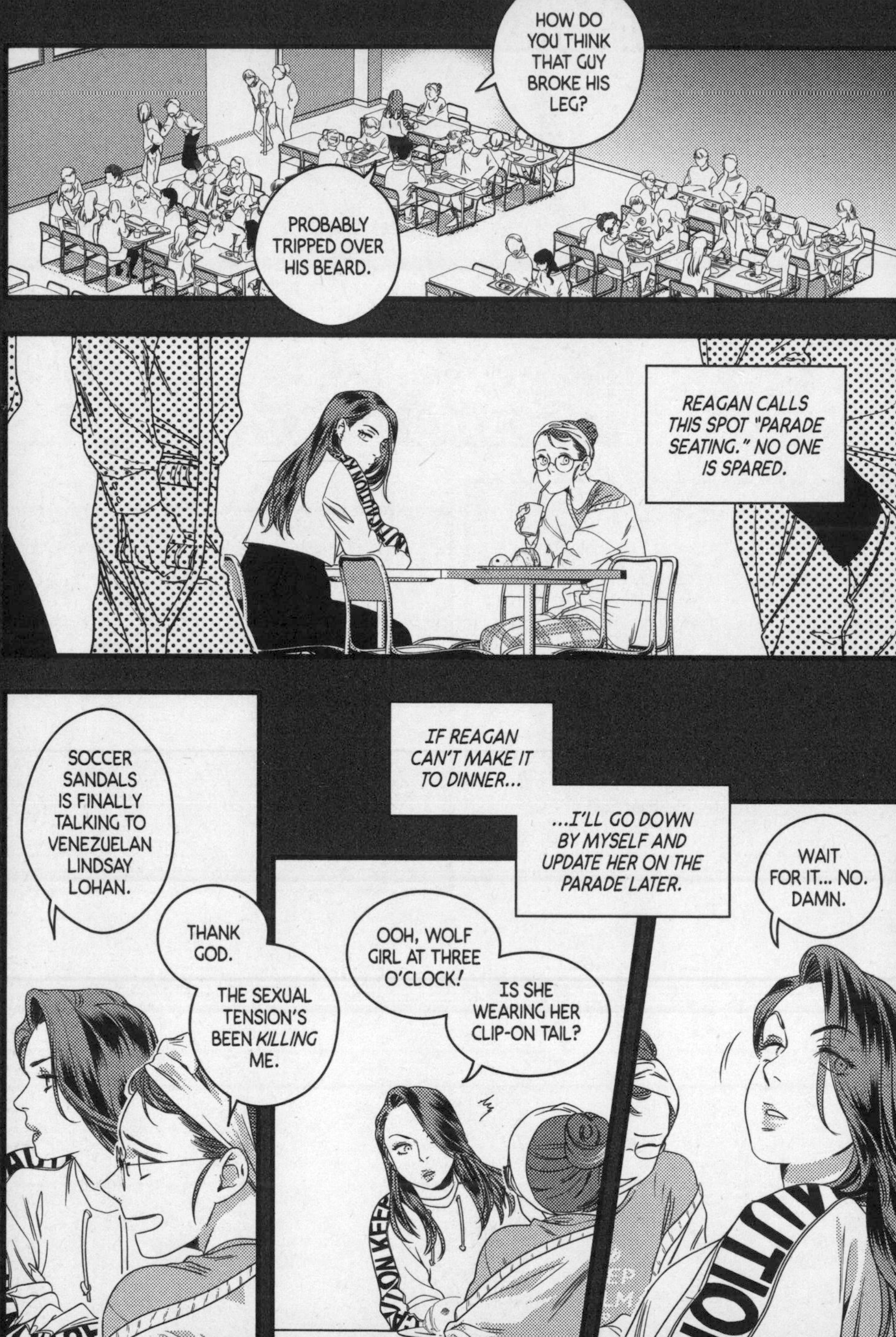
HOW DO YOU THINK THAT GUY BROKE HIS LEG?
PROBABLY TRIPPED OVER HIS BEARD.
REAGAN CALLS THIS SPOT "PARADE SEATING." NO ONE IS SPARED.
SOCCER SANDALS IS FINALLY TALKING TO VENEZUELAN LINDSAY LOHAN.
THANK GOD.
THE SEXUAL TENSION'S BEEN *KILLING* ME.
IF REAGAN CAN'T MAKE IT TO DINNER...
...I'LL GO DOWN BY MYSELF AND UPDATE HER ON THE PARADE LATER.
OOH, WOLF GIRL AT THREE O'CLOCK!
IS SHE WEARING HER CLIP-ON TAIL?
WAIT FOR IT... NO. DAMN.

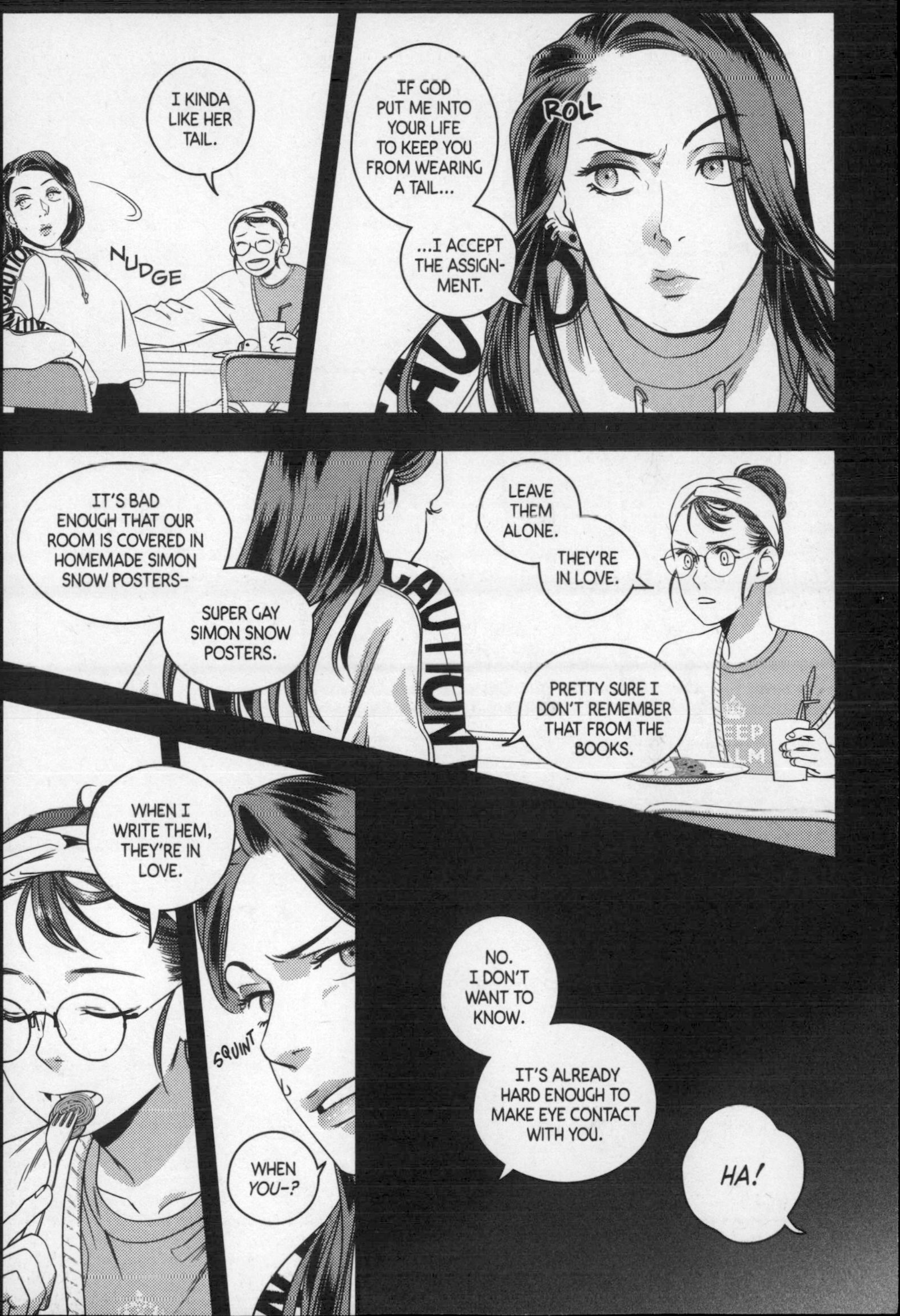
I KINDA LIKE HER TAIL.
NUDGE
IF GOD PUT ME INTO YOUR LIFE TO KEEP YOU FROM WEARING A TAIL...
...I ACCEPT THE ASSIGN-MENT.
ROLL
IT'S BAD ENOUGH THAT OUR ROOM IS COVERED IN HOMEMADE SIMON SNOW POSTERS–
SUPER GAY SIMON SNOW POSTERS.
LEAVE THEM ALONE.
THEY'RE IN LOVE.
PRETTY SURE I DON'T REMEMBER THAT FROM THE BOOKS.
WHEN I WRITE THEM, THEY'RE IN LOVE.
SQUINT
WHEN *YOU*–?
NO. I DON'T WANT TO KNOW.
IT'S ALREADY HARD ENOUGH TO MAKE EYE CONTACT WITH YOU.
HA!

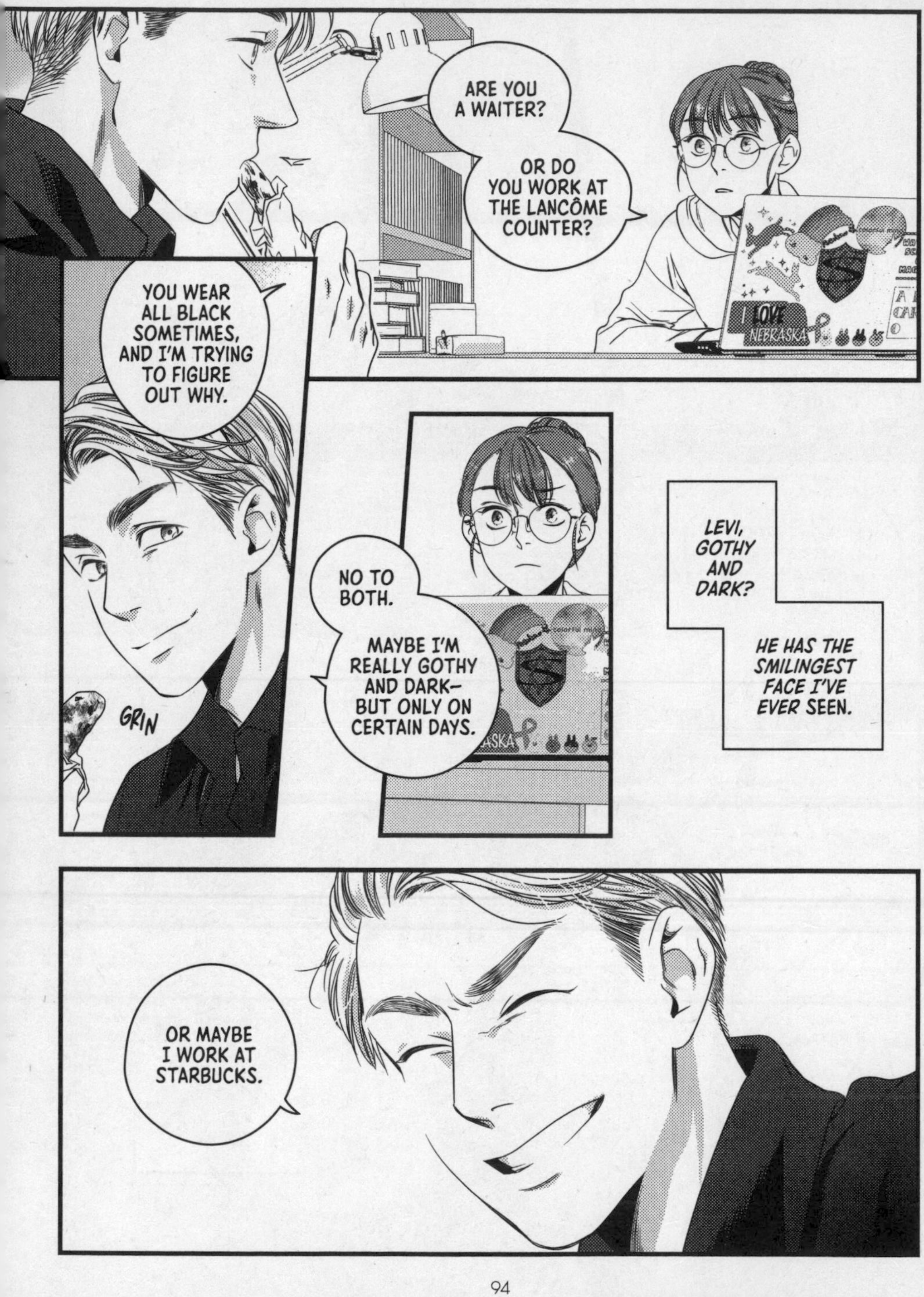
ARE YOU A WAITER?
OR DO YOU WORK AT THE LANCÔME COUNTER?
I LOVE NEBRASKA
YOU WEAR ALL BLACK SOMETIMES, AND I'M TRYING TO FIGURE OUT WHY.
GRIN
NO TO BOTH.
MAYBE I'M REALLY GOTHY AND DARK— BUT ONLY ON CERTAIN DAYS.
LEVI, GOTHY AND DARK?
HE HAS THE SMILINGEST FACE I'VE EVER SEEN.
OR MAYBE I WORK AT STARBUCKS.

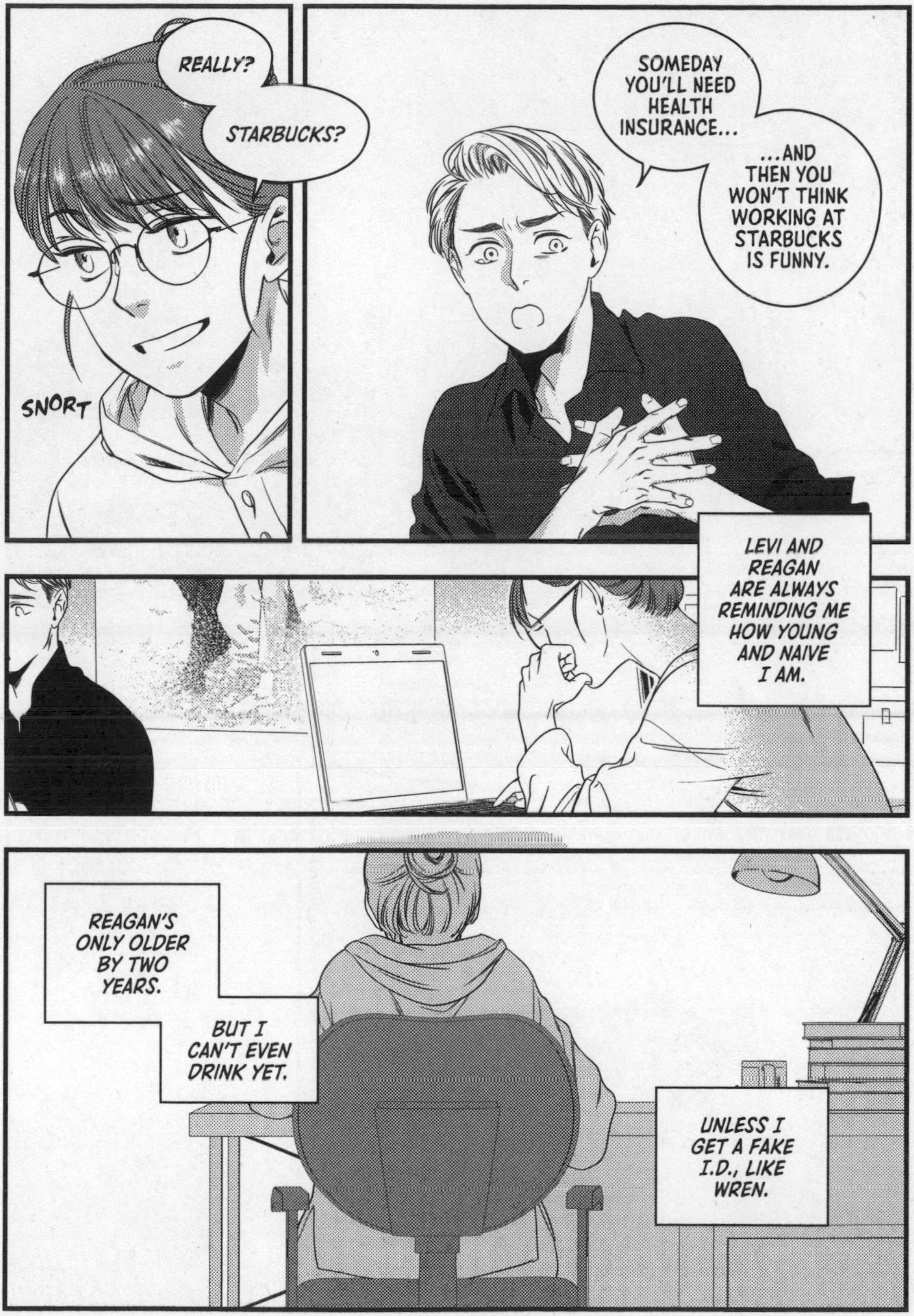
REALLY?
STARBUCKS?
SNORT
SOMEDAY YOU'LL NEED HEALTH INSURANCE...
...AND THEN YOU WON'T THINK WORKING AT STARBUCKS IS FUNNY.
LEVI AND REAGAN ARE ALWAYS REMINDING ME HOW YOUNG AND NAIVE I AM.
REAGAN'S ONLY OLDER BY TWO YEARS.
BUT I CAN'T EVEN DRINK YET.
UNLESS I GET A FAKE I.D., LIKE WREN.

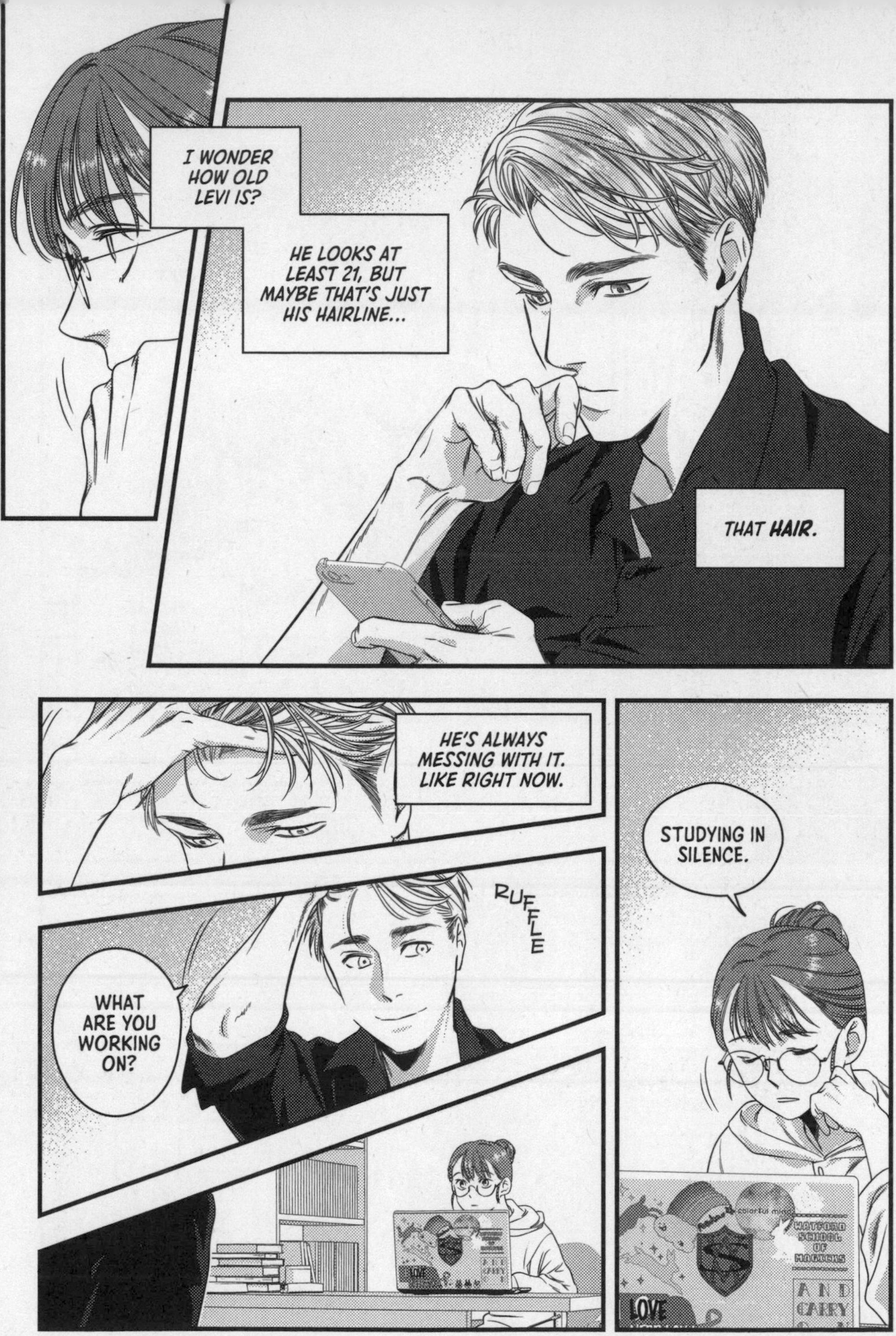
I WONDER HOW OLD LEVI IS?
HE LOOKS AT LEAST 21, BUT MAYBE THAT'S JUST HIS HAIRLINE...
THAT HAIR.
HE'S ALWAYS MESSING WITH IT. LIKE RIGHT NOW.
RUFFLE
WHAT ARE YOU WORKING ON?
STUDYING IN SILENCE.
WATFORD SCHOOL OF MAGICKS
LOVE

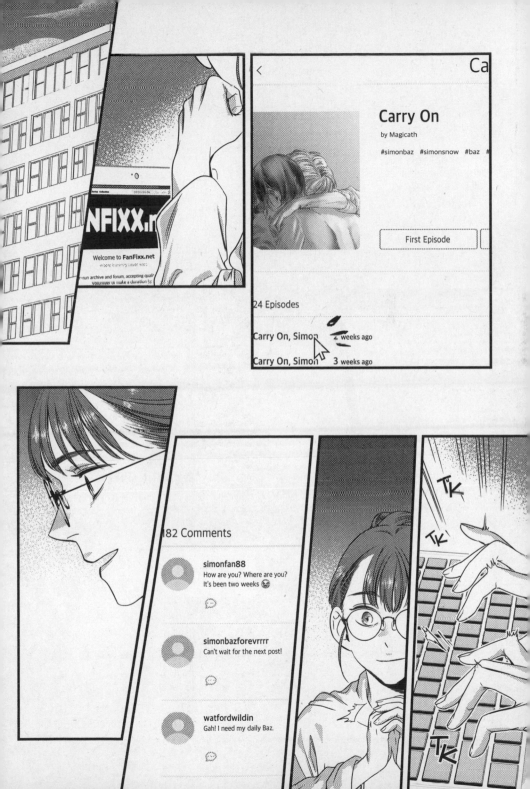

NFIXX.n

Welcome to FanFixx.net

~run archive and forum, accepting qual~
volunteer or make a donation to

<

Ca

Carry On

by Magicath

#simonbaz #simonsnow #baz #

First Episode

24 Episodes

Carry On, Simon   2 weeks ago

Carry On, Simon   3 weeks ago

82 Comments

simonfan88
How are you? Where are you?
It's been two weeks 😭

simonbazforevrrrr
Can't wait for the next post!

watfordwildin
Gah! I need my daily Baz.

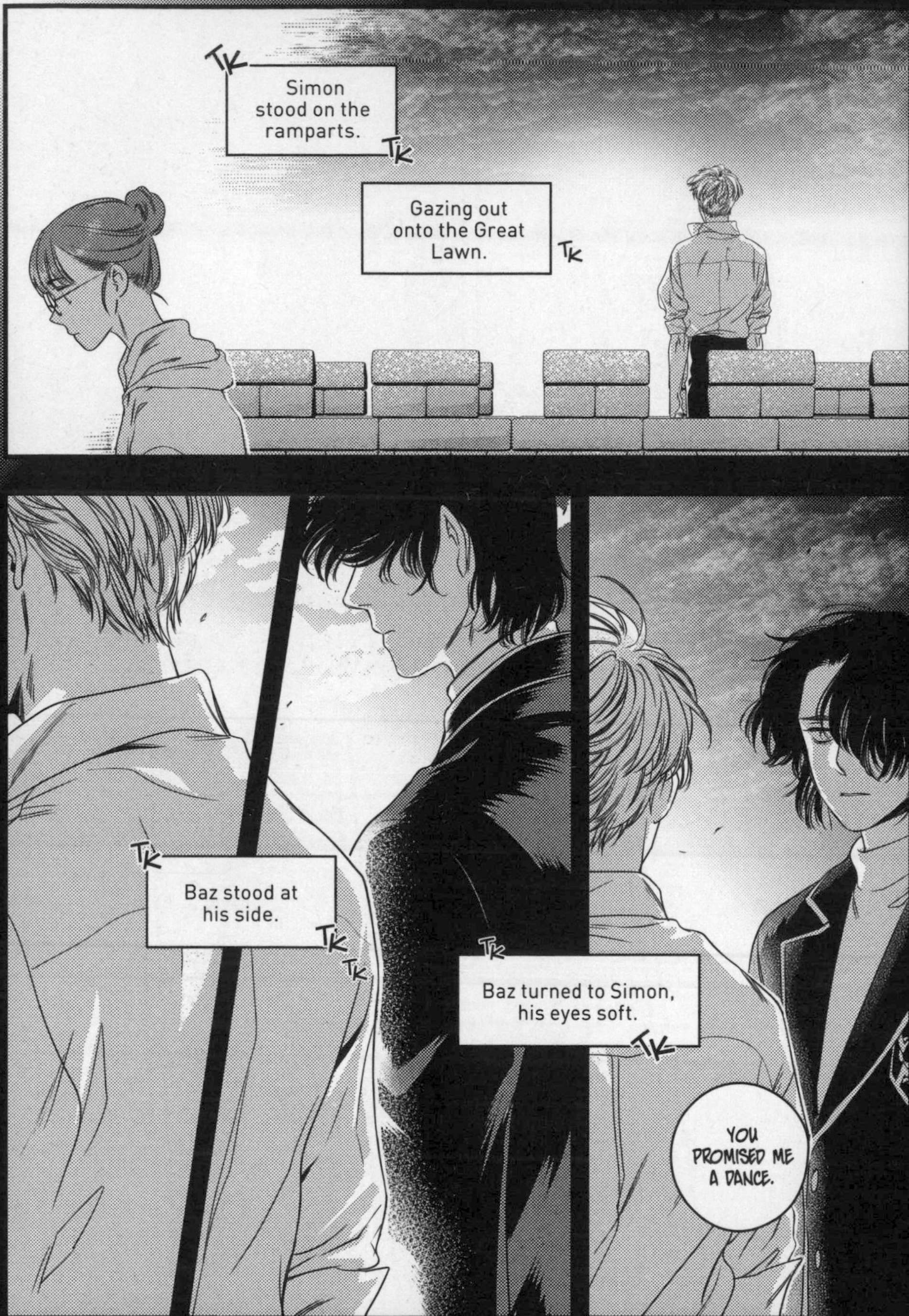
TK
Simon stood on the ramparts.
TK
Gazing out onto the Great Lawn.
TK
TK
Baz stood at his side.
TK
TK
TK
Baz turned to Simon, his eyes soft.
TK
YOU PROMISED ME A DANCE.

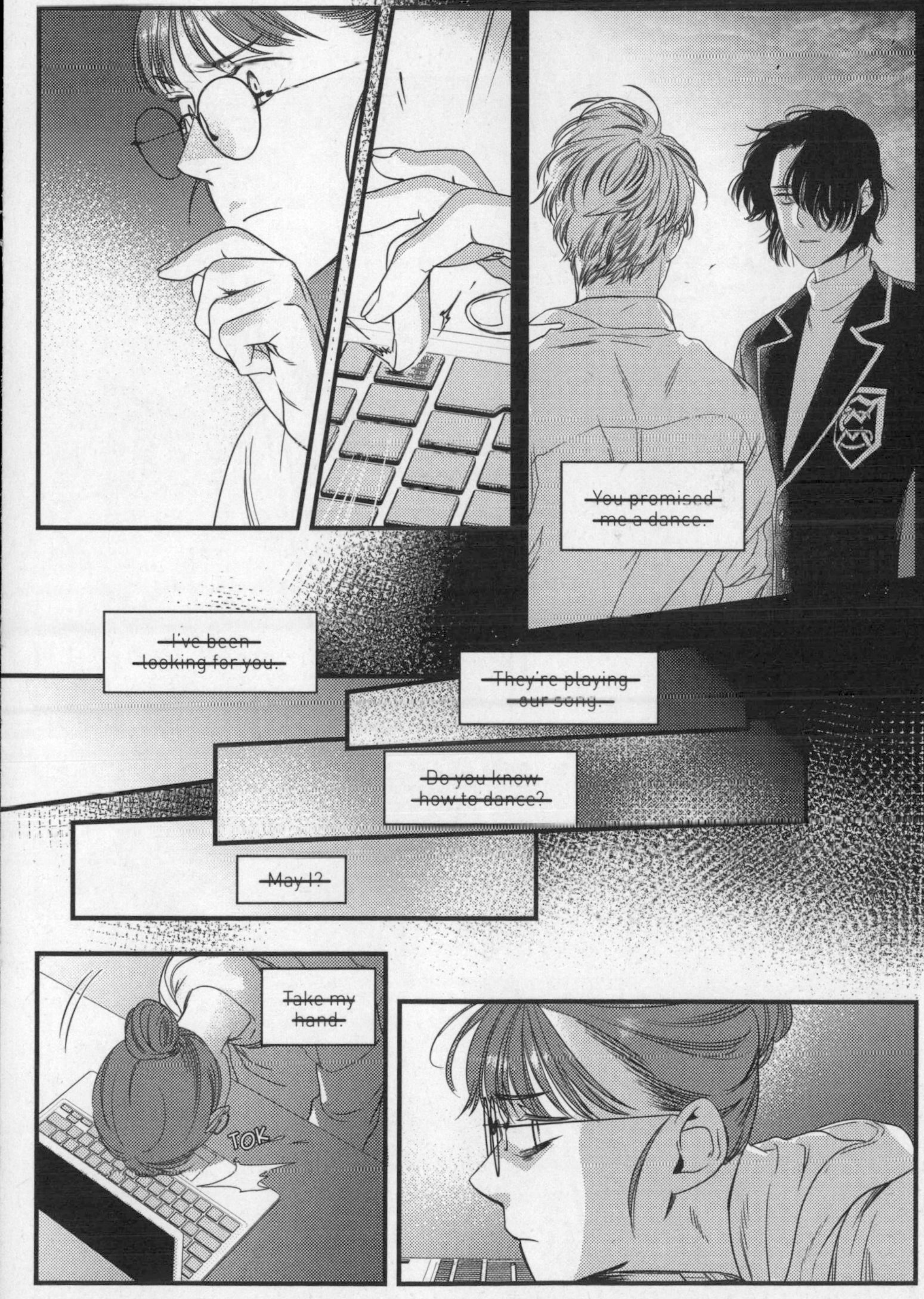
~~You promised me a dance.~~
~~I've been looking for you.~~
~~They're playing our song.~~
~~Do you know how to dance?~~
~~May I?~~
~~Take my hand.~~
TOK

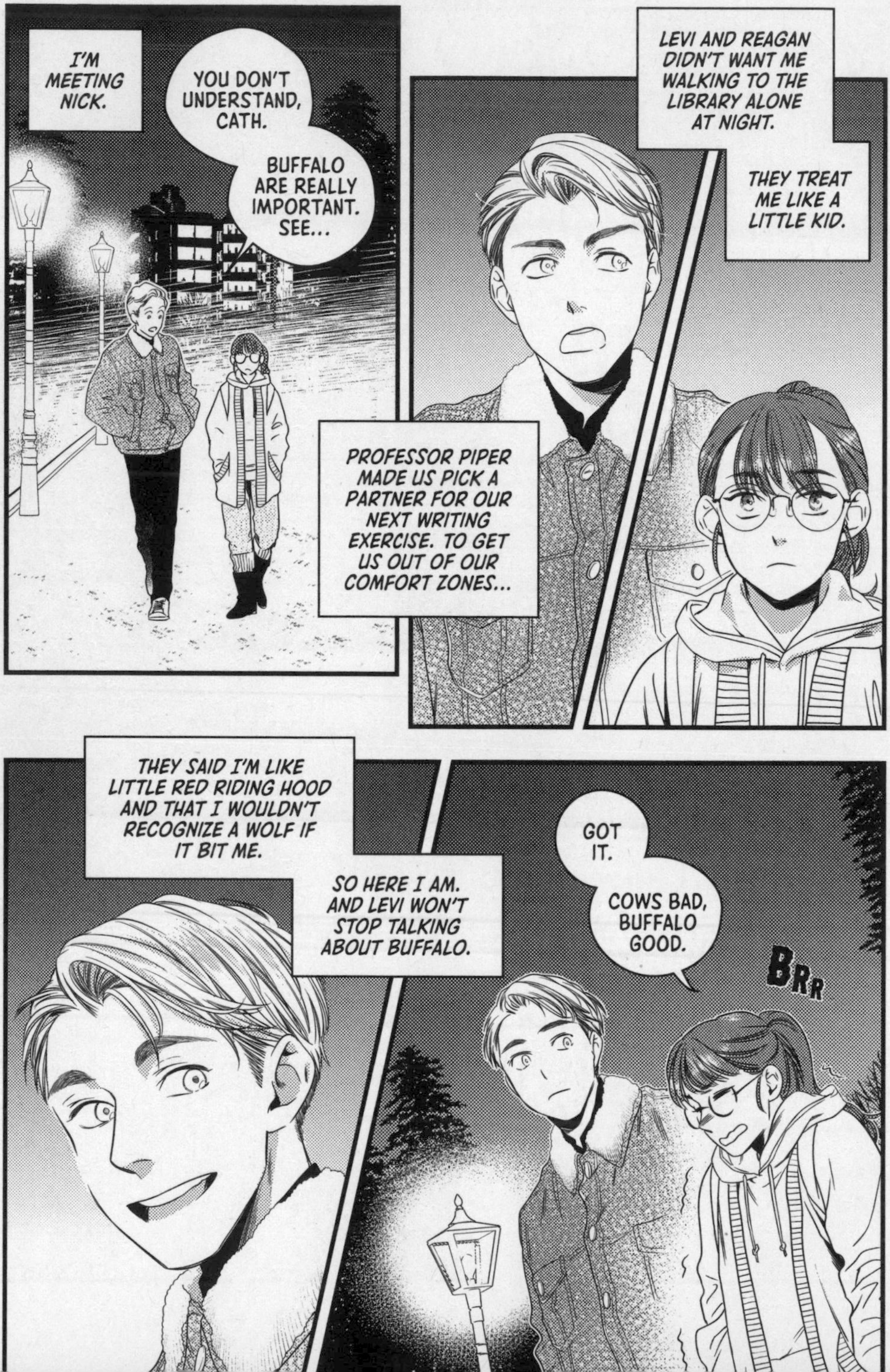
I'M MEETING NICK.
YOU DON'T UNDERSTAND, CATH.
BUFFALO ARE REALLY IMPORTANT. SEE...
PROFESSOR PIPER MADE US PICK A PARTNER FOR OUR NEXT WRITING EXERCISE. TO GET US OUT OF OUR COMFORT ZONES...
LEVI AND REAGAN DIDN'T WANT ME WALKING TO THE LIBRARY ALONE AT NIGHT.
THEY TREAT ME LIKE A LITTLE KID.
THEY SAID I'M LIKE LITTLE RED RIDING HOOD AND THAT I WOULDN'T RECOGNIZE A WOLF IF IT BIT ME.
SO HERE I AM. AND LEVI WON'T STOP TALKING ABOUT BUFFALO.
GOT IT.
COWS BAD, BUFFALO GOOD.
BRR

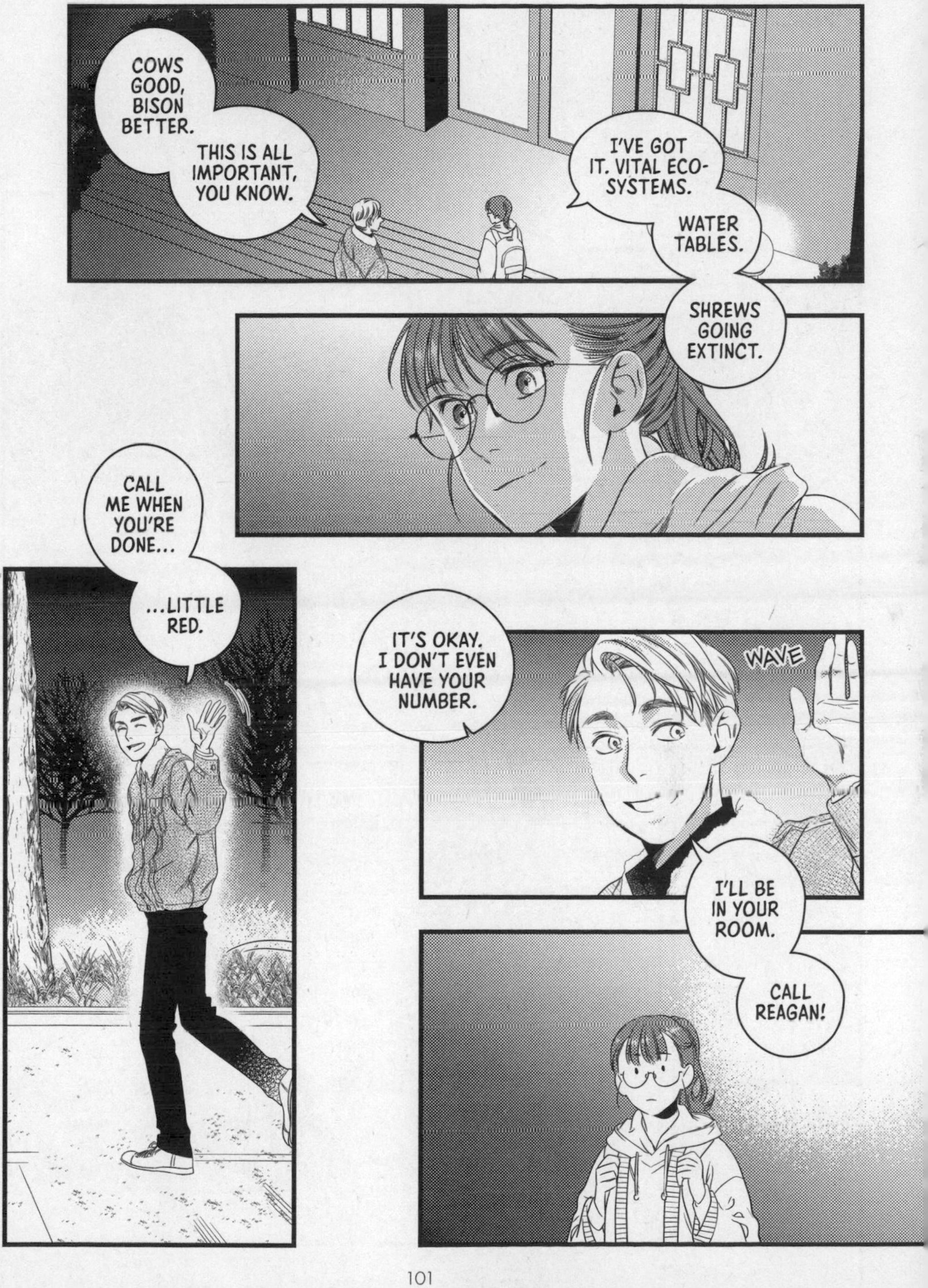
COWS GOOD, BISON BETTER.
THIS IS ALL IMPORTANT, YOU KNOW.
I'VE GOT IT. VITAL ECO-SYSTEMS.
WATER TABLES.
SHREWS GOING EXTINCT.
CALL ME WHEN YOU'RE DONE...
...LITTLE RED.
IT'S OKAY. I DON'T EVEN HAVE YOUR NUMBER.
WAVE
I'LL BE IN YOUR ROOM.
CALL REAGAN!

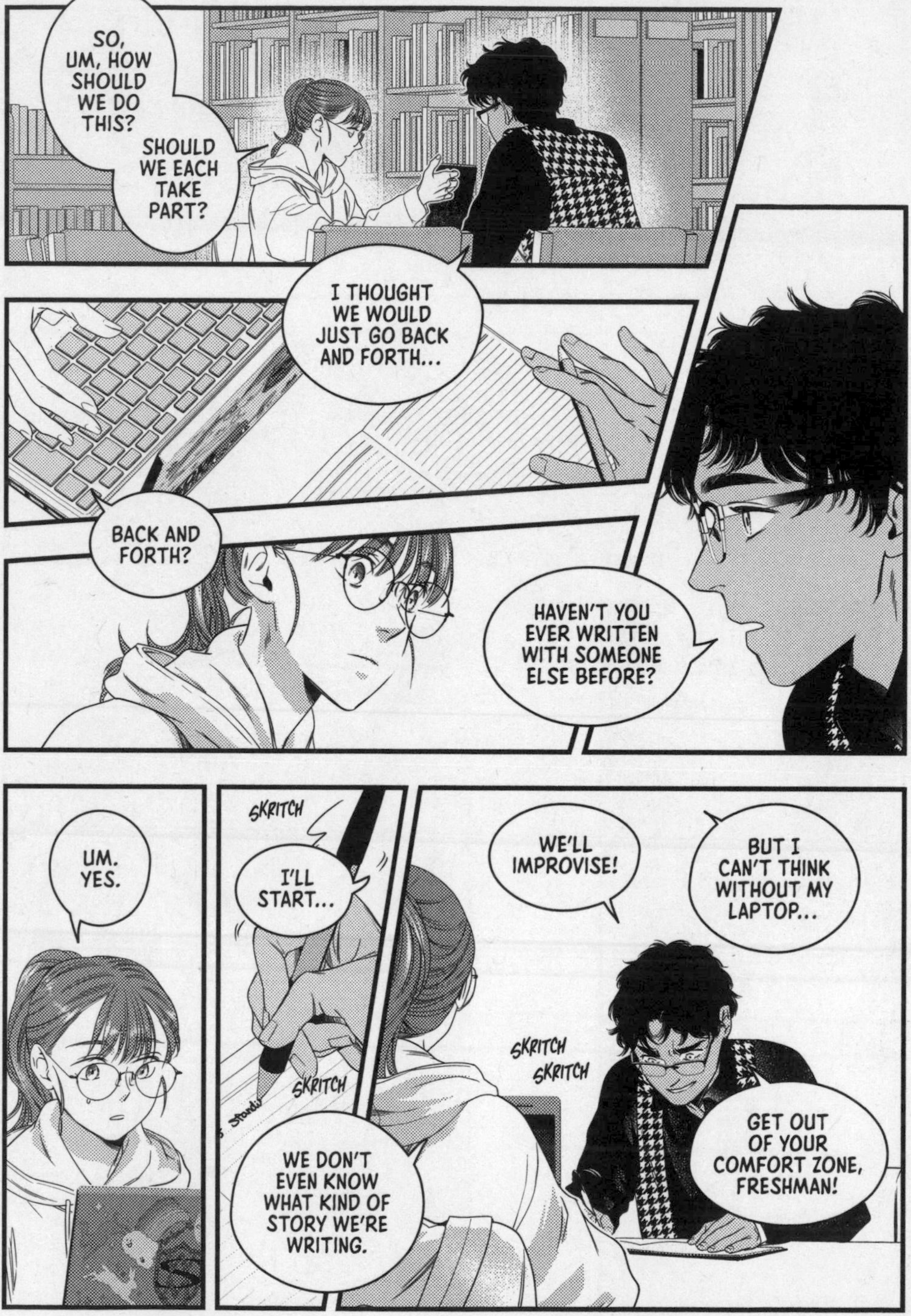
SO, UM, HOW SHOULD WE DO THIS?
SHOULD WE EACH TAKE PART?
I THOUGHT WE WOULD JUST GO BACK AND FORTH...
BACK AND FORTH?
HAVEN'T YOU EVER WRITTEN WITH SOMEONE ELSE BEFORE?
UM. YES.
SKRITCH
I'LL START...
SKRITCH
WE DON'T EVEN KNOW WHAT KIND OF STORY WE'RE WRITING.
WE'LL IMPROVISE!
BUT I CAN'T THINK WITHOUT MY LAPTOP...
SKRITCH SKRITCH
GET OUT OF YOUR COMFORT ZONE, FRESHMAN!

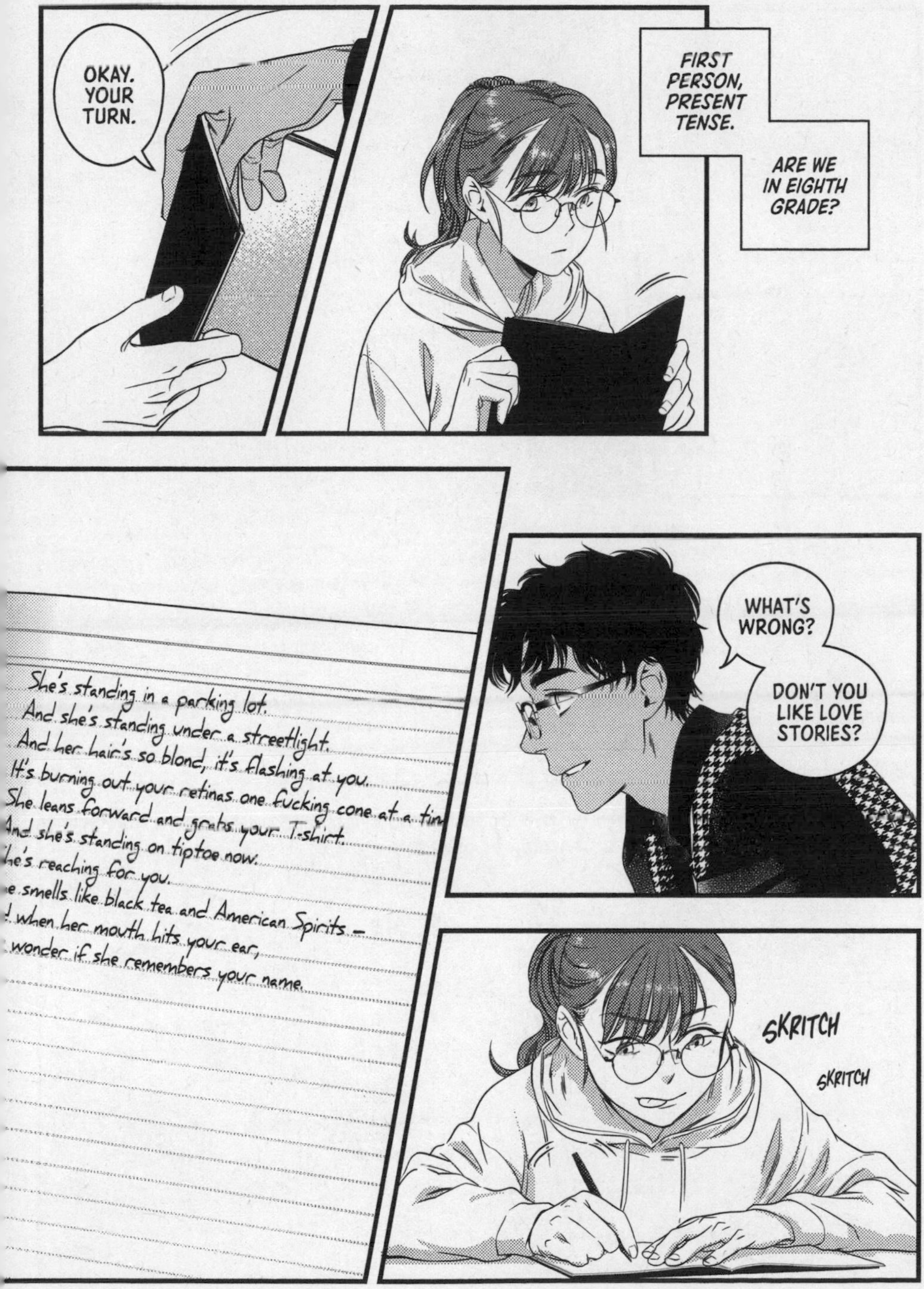
OKAY. YOUR TURN.
FIRST PERSON, PRESENT TENSE.
ARE WE IN EIGHTH GRADE?
She's standing in a parking lot.
And she's standing under a streetlight.
And her hair's so blond, it's flashing at you.
It's burning out your retinas one fucking cone at a tim
She leans forward and grabs your T-shirt.
And she's standing on tiptoe now.
he's reaching for you.
e smells like black tea and American Spirits —
when her mouth hits your ear,
wonder if she remembers your name.
WHAT'S WRONG?
DON'T YOU LIKE LOVE STORIES?
SKRITCH
SKRITCH

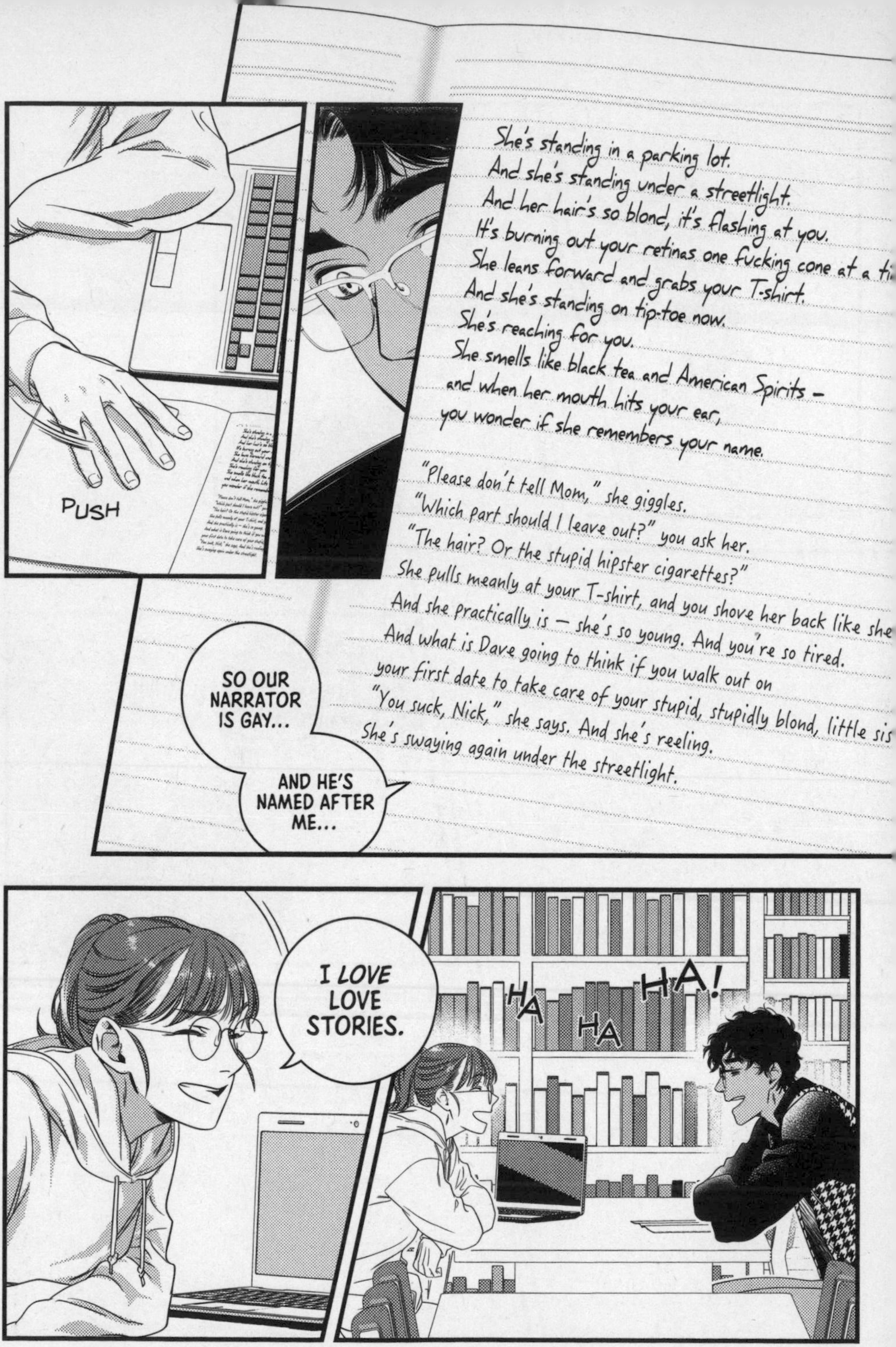
PUSH
She's standing in a parking lot.
And she's standing under a streetlight.
And her hair's so blond, it's flashing at you.
It's burning out your retinas one fucking cone at a ti
She leans forward and grabs your T-shirt.
And she's standing on tip-toe now.
She's reaching for you.
She smells like black tea and American Spirits –
and when her mouth hits your ear,
you wonder if she remembers your name.
"Please don't tell Mom," she giggles.
"Which part should I leave out?" you ask her.
"The hair? Or the stupid hipster cigarettes?"
She pulls meanly at your T-shirt, and you shove her back like she
And she practically is – she's so young. And you're so tired.
And what is Dave going to think if you walk out on
your first date to take care of your stupid, stupidly blond, little sis
"You suck, Nick," she says. And she's reeling.
She's swaying again under the streetlight.
SO OUR NARRATOR IS GAY...
AND HE'S NAMED AFTER ME...
I *LOVE* LOVE STORIES.
HA
HA
HA!

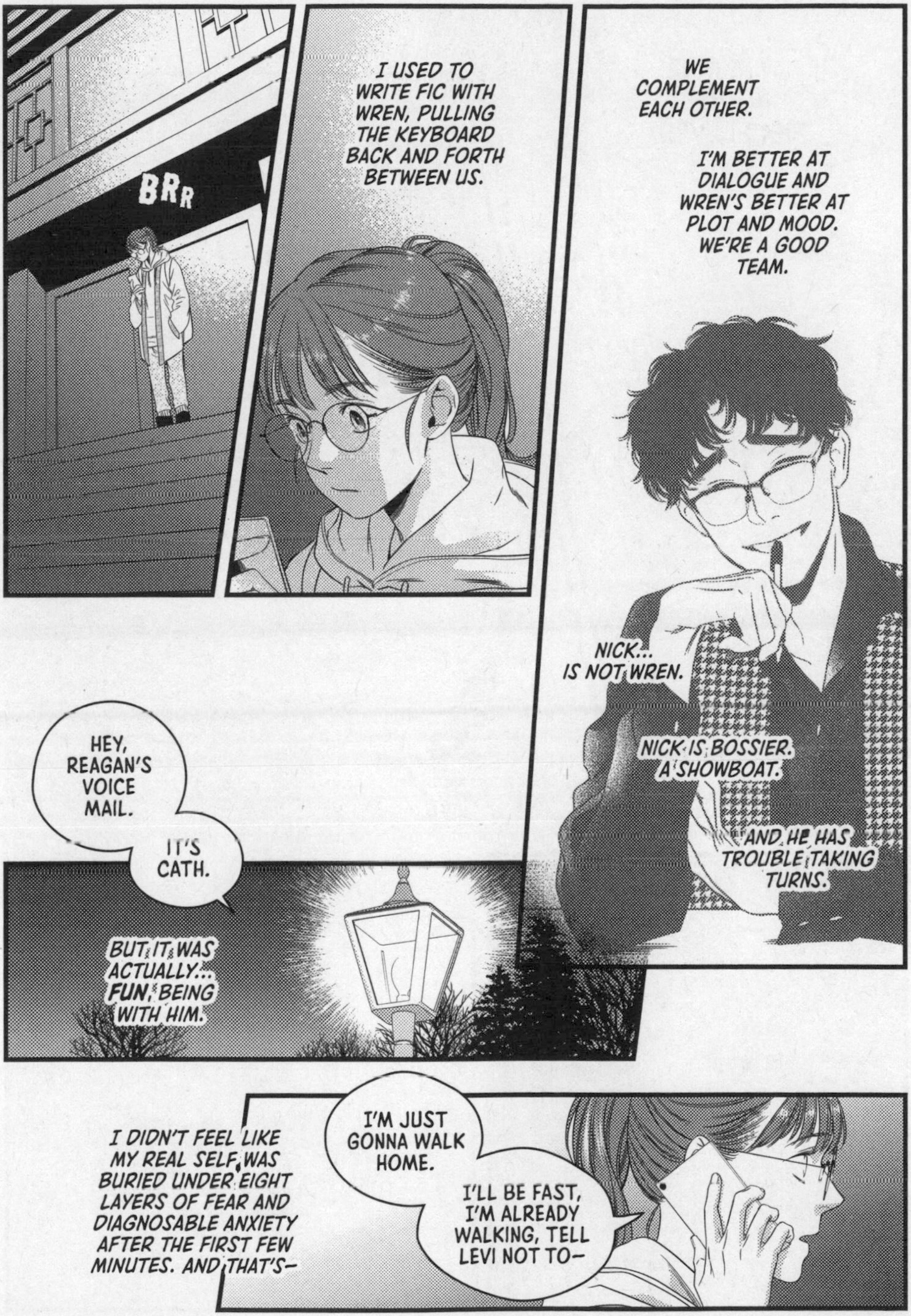
BRR
I USED TO WRITE FIC WITH WREN, PULLING THE KEYBOARD BACK AND FORTH BETWEEN US.
WE COMPLEMENT EACH OTHER.
I'M BETTER AT DIALOGUE AND WREN'S BETTER AT PLOT AND MOOD. WE'RE A GOOD TEAM.
NICK... IS NOT WREN.
NICK IS BOSSIER. A SHOWBOAT.
AND HE HAS TROUBLE TAKING TURNS.
HEY, REAGAN'S VOICE MAIL.
IT'S CATH.
BUT IT WAS ACTUALLY... FUN, BEING WITH HIM.
I DIDN'T FEEL LIKE MY REAL SELF WAS BURIED UNDER EIGHT LAYERS OF FEAR AND DIAGNOSABLE ANXIETY AFTER THE FIRST FEW MINUTES. AND THAT'S—
I'M JUST GONNA WALK HOME.
I'LL BE FAST, I'M ALREADY WALKING, TELL LEVI NOT TO—

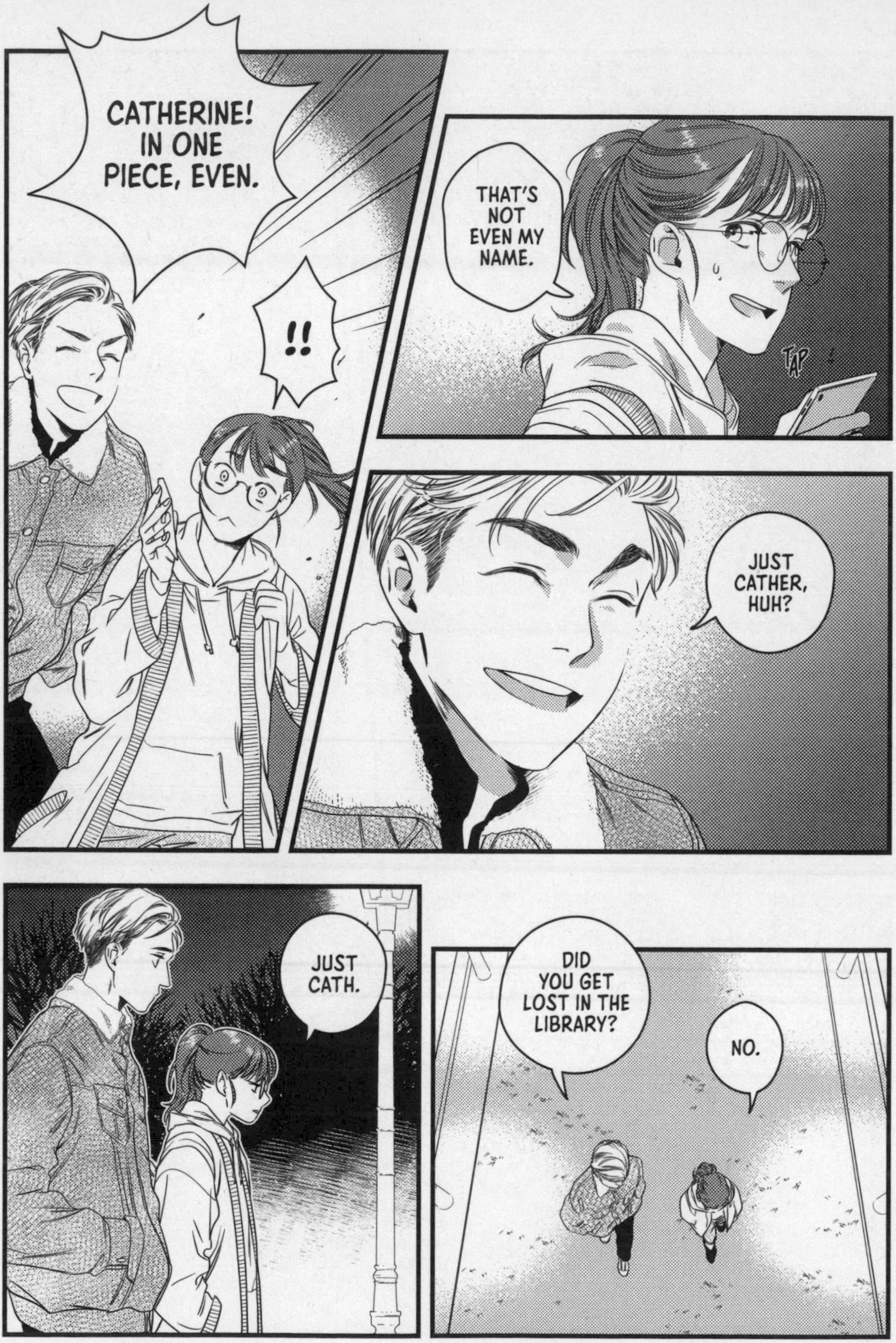
CATHERINE! IN ONE PIECE, EVEN.
!!
THAT'S NOT EVEN MY NAME.
TAP
JUST CATHER, HUH?
JUST CATH.
DID YOU GET LOST IN THE LIBRARY?
NO.

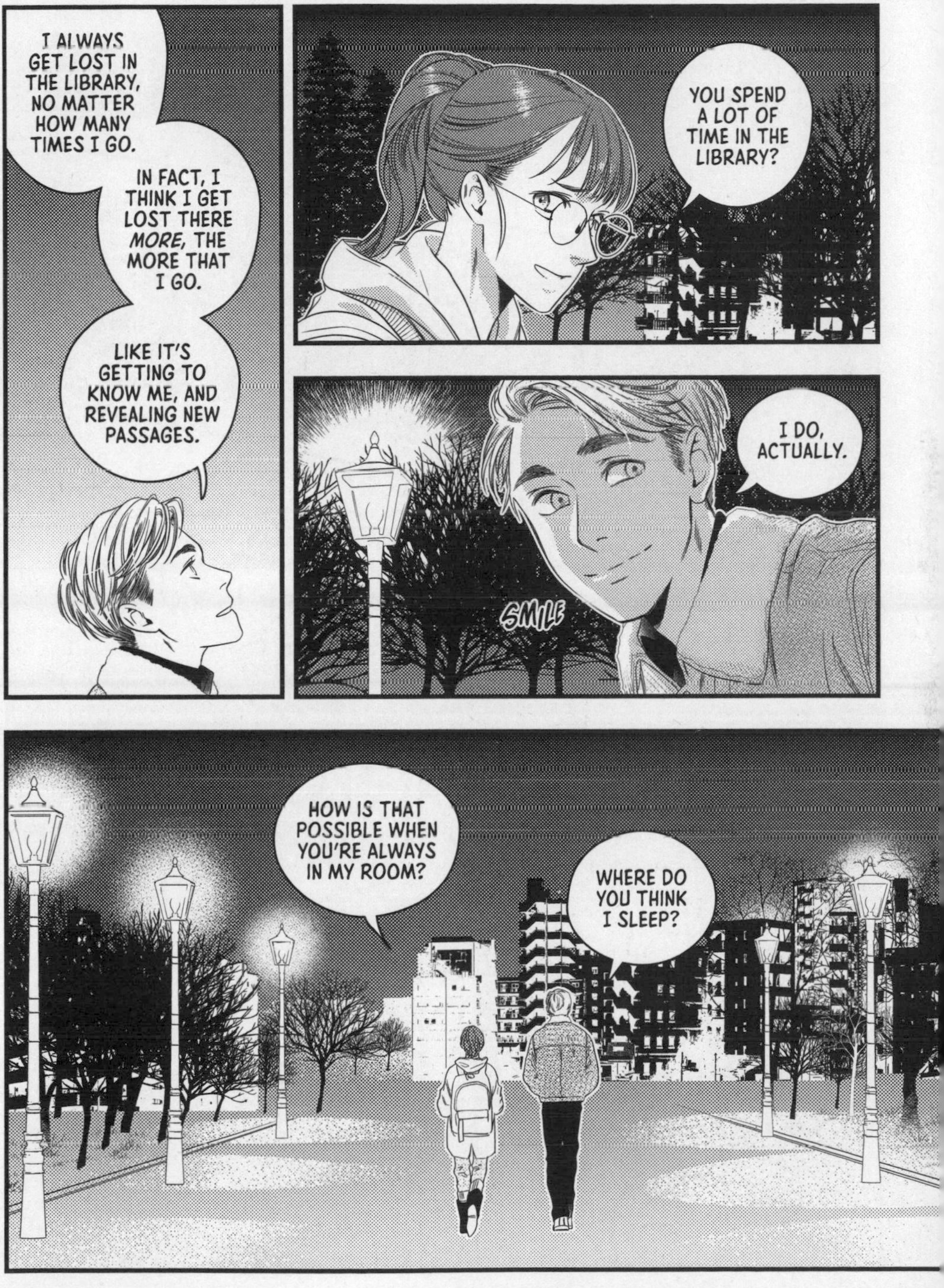
I ALWAYS GET LOST IN THE LIBRARY, NO MATTER HOW MANY TIMES I GO.
IN FACT, I THINK I GET LOST THERE *MORE*, THE MORE THAT I GO.
LIKE IT'S GETTING TO KNOW ME, AND REVEALING NEW PASSAGES.
YOU SPEND A LOT OF TIME IN THE LIBRARY?
I DO, ACTUALLY.
SMILE
HOW IS THAT POSSIBLE WHEN YOU'RE ALWAYS IN MY ROOM?
WHERE DO YOU THINK I SLEEP?

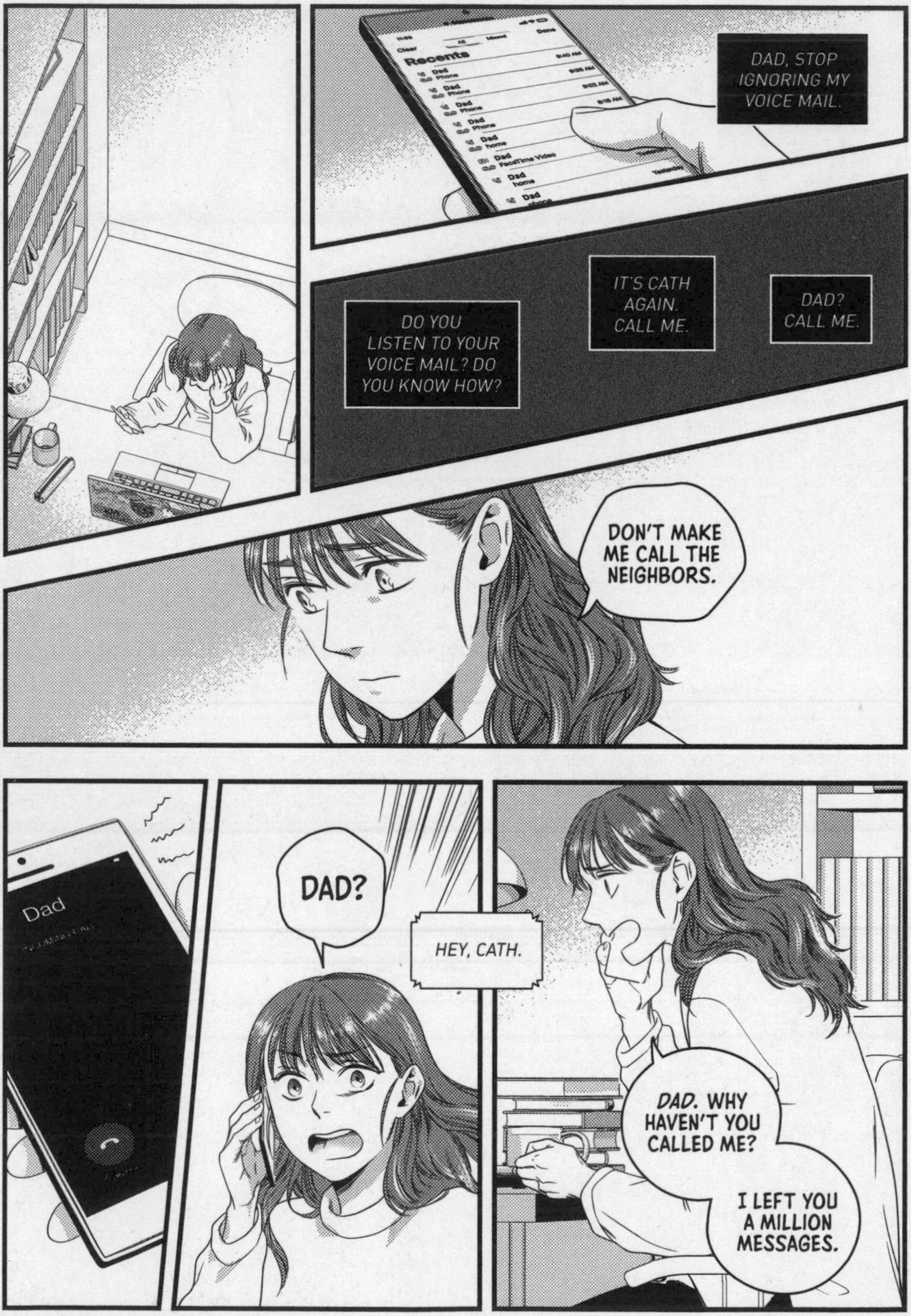
Recents
DAD, STOP IGNORING MY VOICE MAIL.
DO YOU LISTEN TO YOUR VOICE MAIL? DO YOU KNOW HOW?
IT'S CATH AGAIN. CALL ME.
DAD? CALL ME.
DON'T MAKE ME CALL THE NEIGHBORS.
Dad
DAD?
HEY, CATH.
DAD. WHY HAVEN'T YOU CALLED ME?
I LEFT YOU A MILLION MESSAGES.

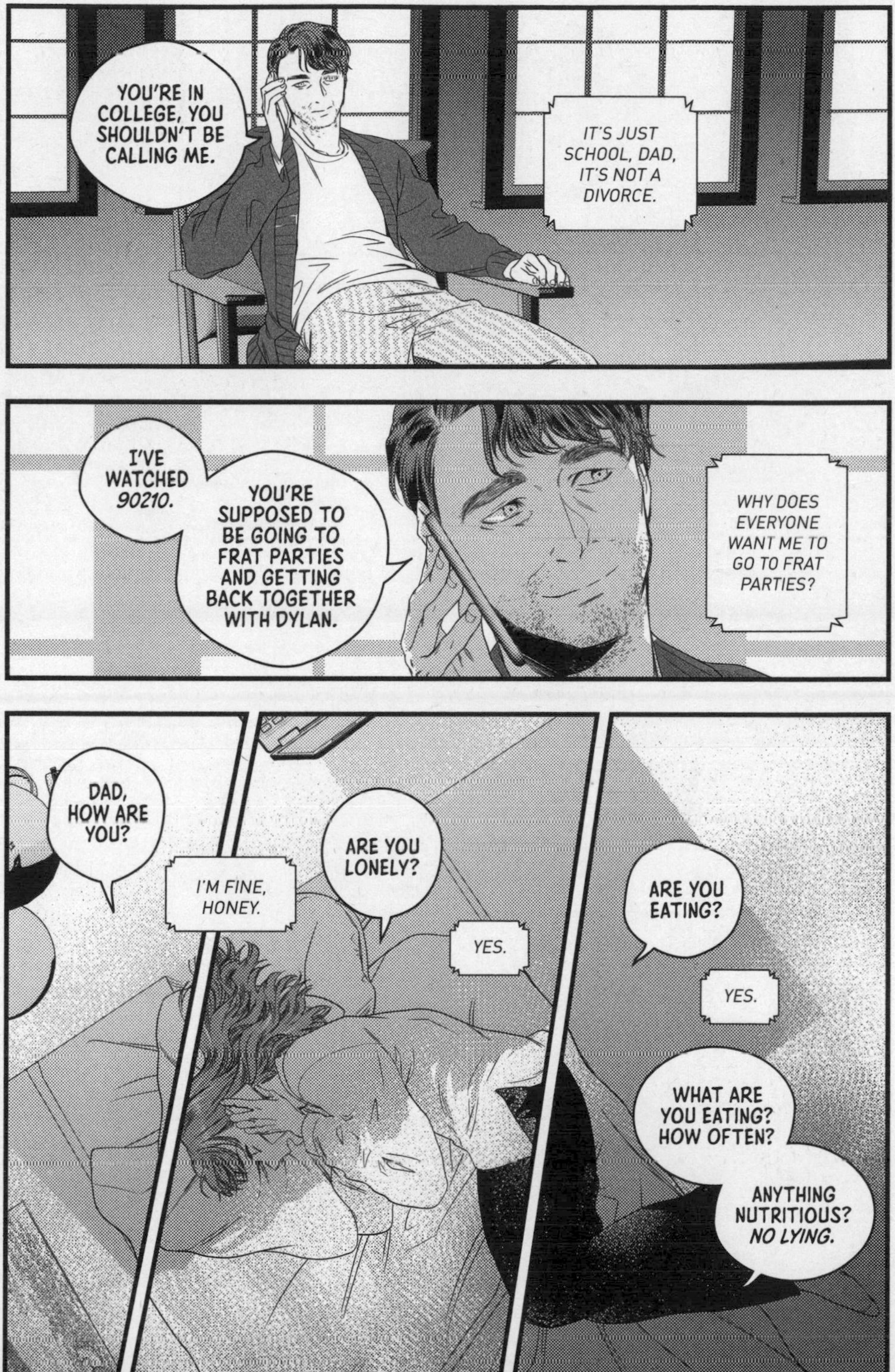
YOU'RE IN COLLEGE, YOU SHOULDN'T BE CALLING ME.
IT'S JUST SCHOOL, DAD, IT'S NOT A DIVORCE.
I'VE WATCHED *90210.*
YOU'RE SUPPOSED TO BE GOING TO FRAT PARTIES AND GETTING BACK TOGETHER WITH DYLAN.
WHY DOES EVERYONE WANT ME TO GO TO FRAT PARTIES?
DAD, HOW ARE YOU?
I'M FINE, HONEY.
ARE YOU LONELY?
YES.
ARE YOU EATING?
YES.
WHAT ARE YOU EATING? HOW OFTEN?
ANYTHING NUTRITIOUS? *NO LYING.*

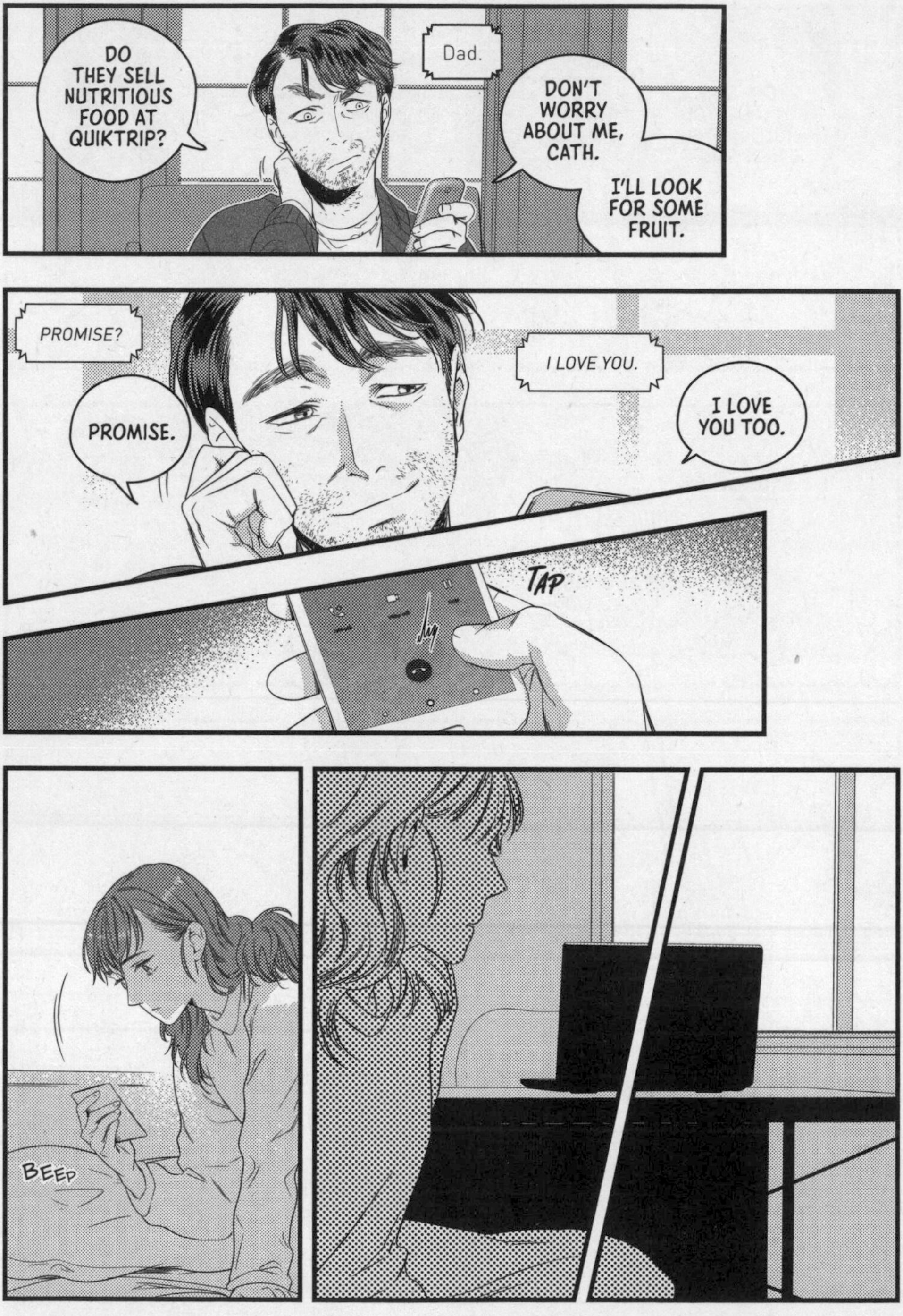
DO THEY SELL NUTRITIOUS FOOD AT QUIKTRIP?
Dad.
DON'T WORRY ABOUT ME, CATH.
I'LL LOOK FOR SOME FRUIT.
PROMISE?
PROMISE.
I LOVE YOU.
I LOVE YOU TOO.
TAP
BEEP

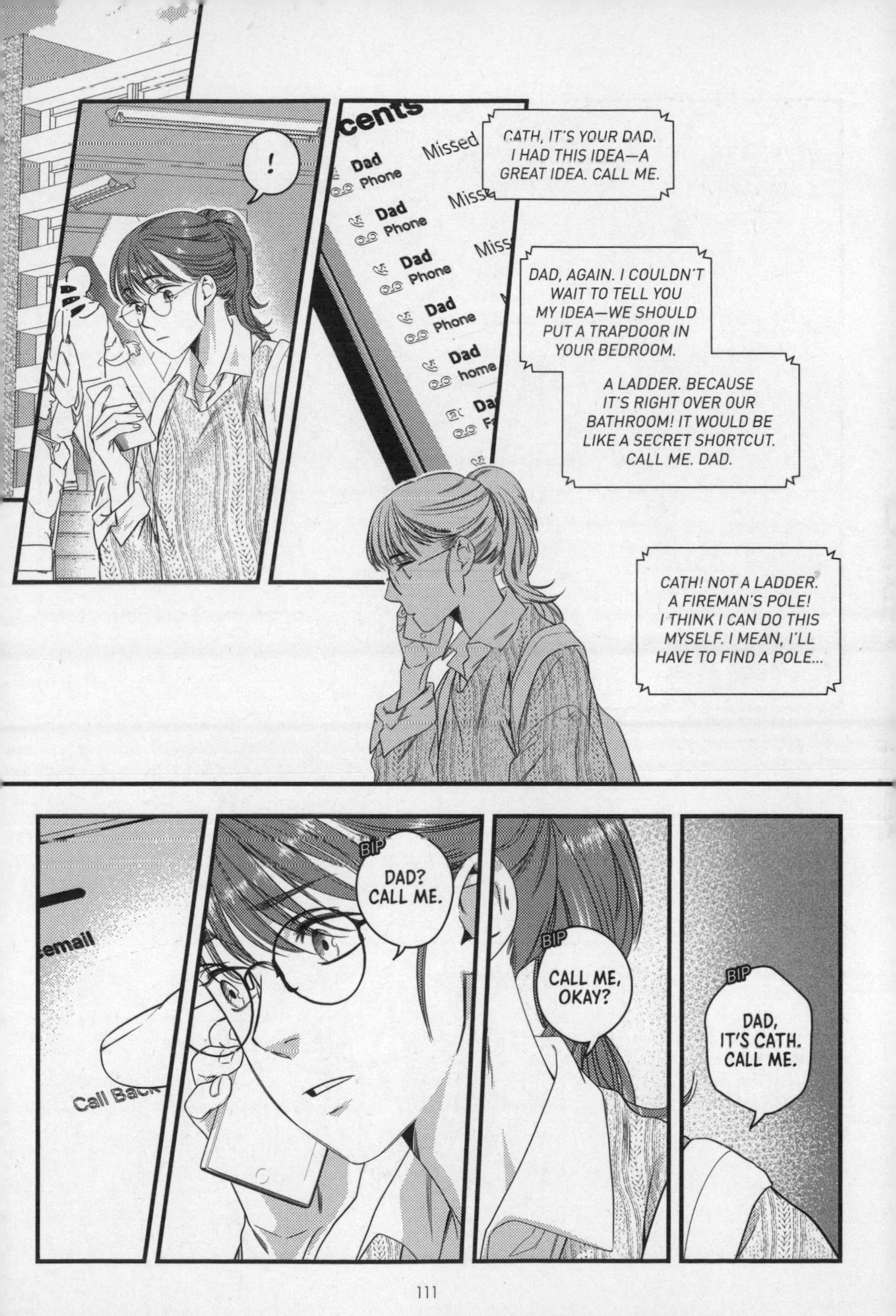
!
cents
Dad
Phone
Missed
Dad
Phone
Dad
Phone
Dad
Phone
Dad
home
CATH, IT'S YOUR DAD. I HAD THIS IDEA—A GREAT IDEA. CALL ME.
DAD, AGAIN. I COULDN'T WAIT TO TELL YOU MY IDEA—WE SHOULD PUT A TRAPDOOR IN YOUR BEDROOM.
A LADDER. BECAUSE IT'S RIGHT OVER OUR BATHROOM! IT WOULD BE LIKE A SECRET SHORTCUT. CALL ME. DAD.
CATH! NOT A LADDER. A FIREMAN'S POLE! I THINK I CAN DO THIS MYSELF. I MEAN, I'LL HAVE TO FIND A POLE...
email
Call Back
BIP
DAD? CALL ME.
BIP
CALL ME, OKAY?
BIP
DAD, IT'S CATH. CALL ME.

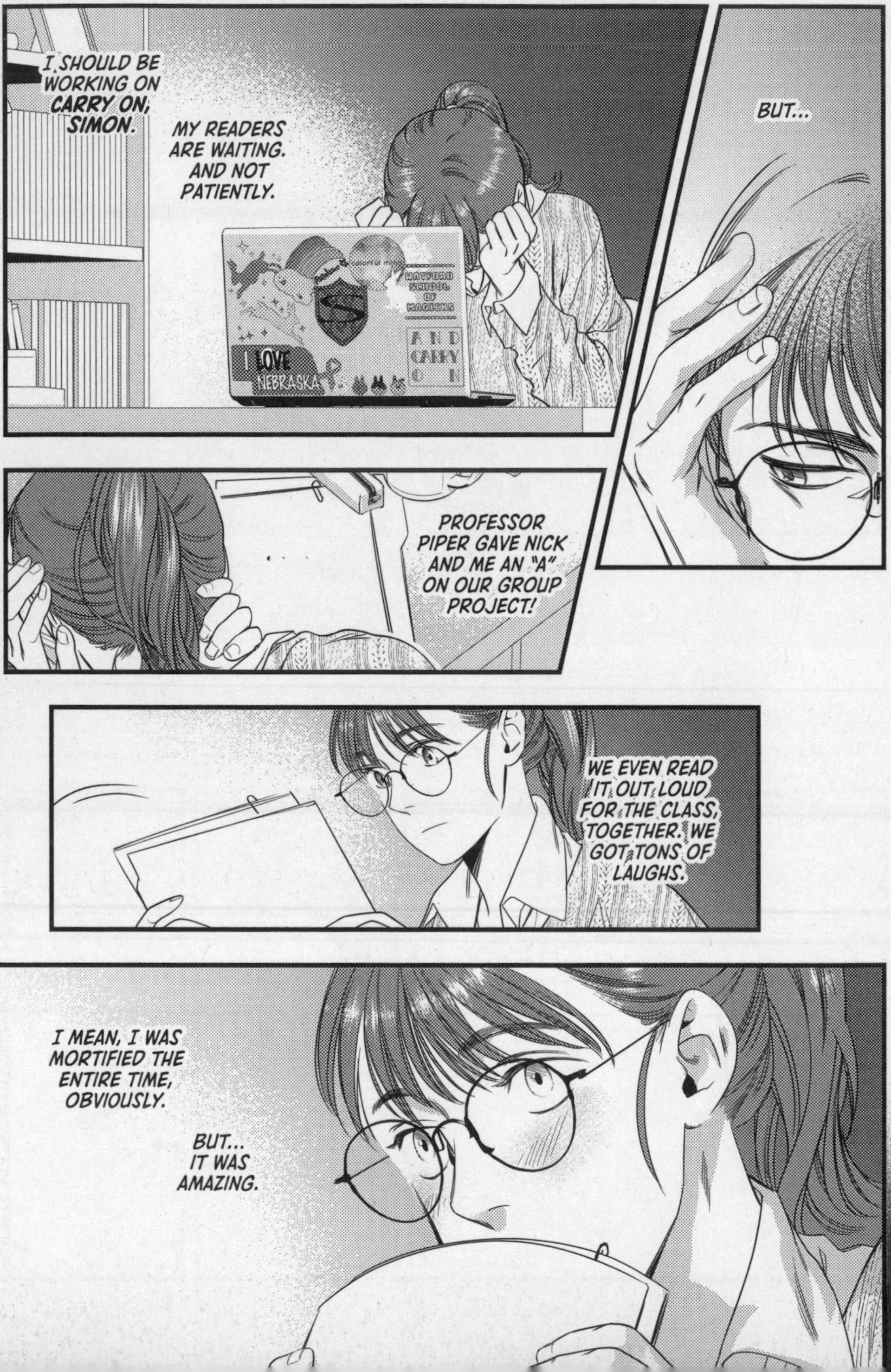
I SHOULD BE WORKING ON CARRY ON, SIMON.
MY READERS ARE WAITING. AND NOT PATIENTLY.
WATFORD SCHOOL OF MAGICKS
I LOVE NEBRASKA
AND CARRY ON
PROFESSOR PIPER GAVE NICK AND ME AN "A" ON OUR GROUP PROJECT!
BUT...
WE EVEN READ IT OUT LOUD FOR THE CLASS, TOGETHER. WE GOT TONS OF LAUGHS.
I MEAN, I WAS MORTIFIED THE ENTIRE TIME, OBVIOUSLY.
BUT... IT WAS AMAZING.

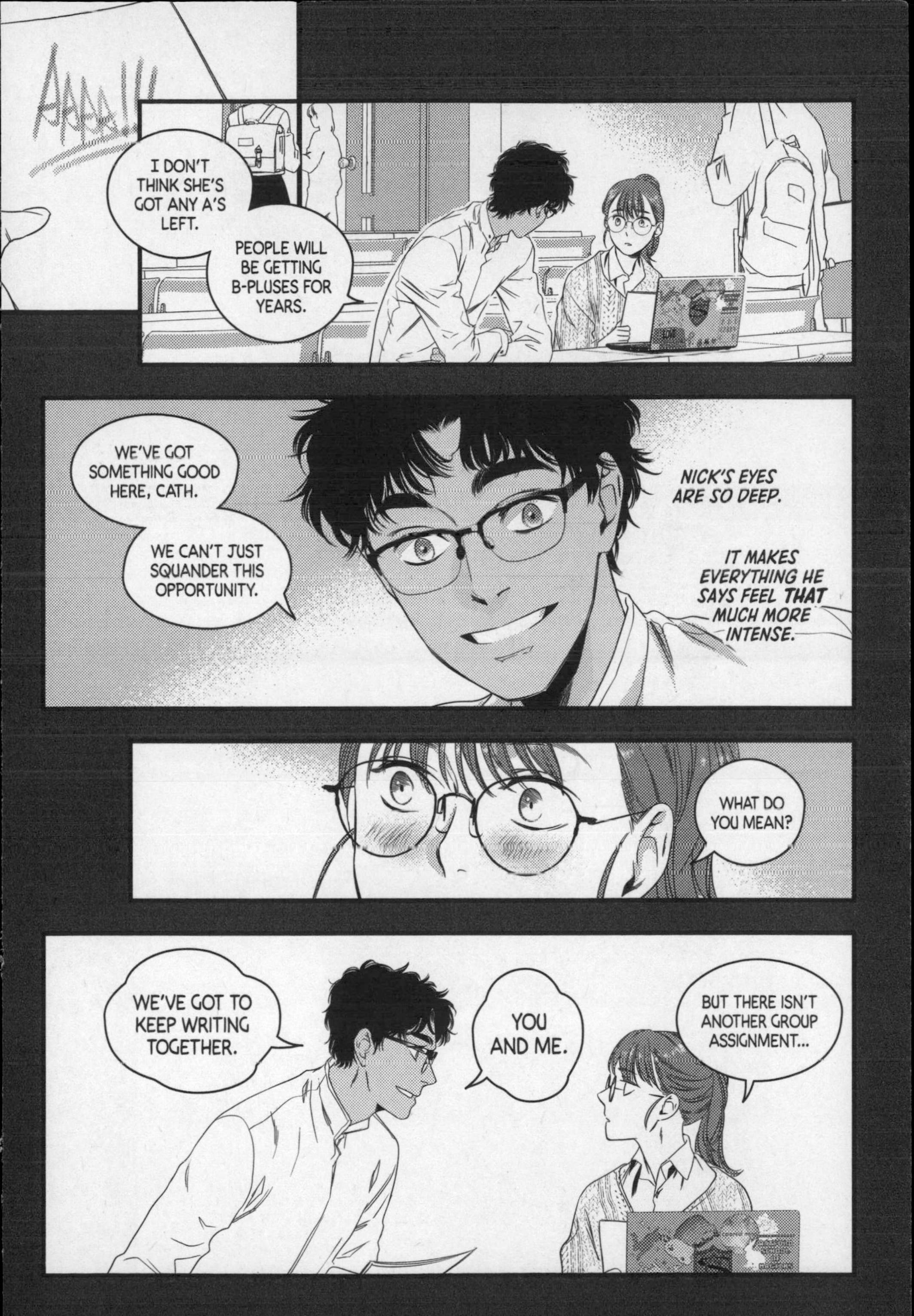
I DON'T THINK SHE'S GOT ANY A'S LEFT.
PEOPLE WILL BE GETTING B-PLUSES FOR YEARS.
WE'VE GOT SOMETHING GOOD HERE, CATH.
WE CAN'T JUST SQUANDER THIS OPPORTUNITY.
NICK'S EYES ARE SO DEEP.
IT MAKES EVERYTHING HE SAYS FEEL THAT MUCH MORE INTENSE.
WHAT DO YOU MEAN?
WE'VE GOT TO KEEP WRITING TOGETHER.
YOU AND ME.
BUT THERE ISN'T ANOTHER GROUP ASSIGNMENT...

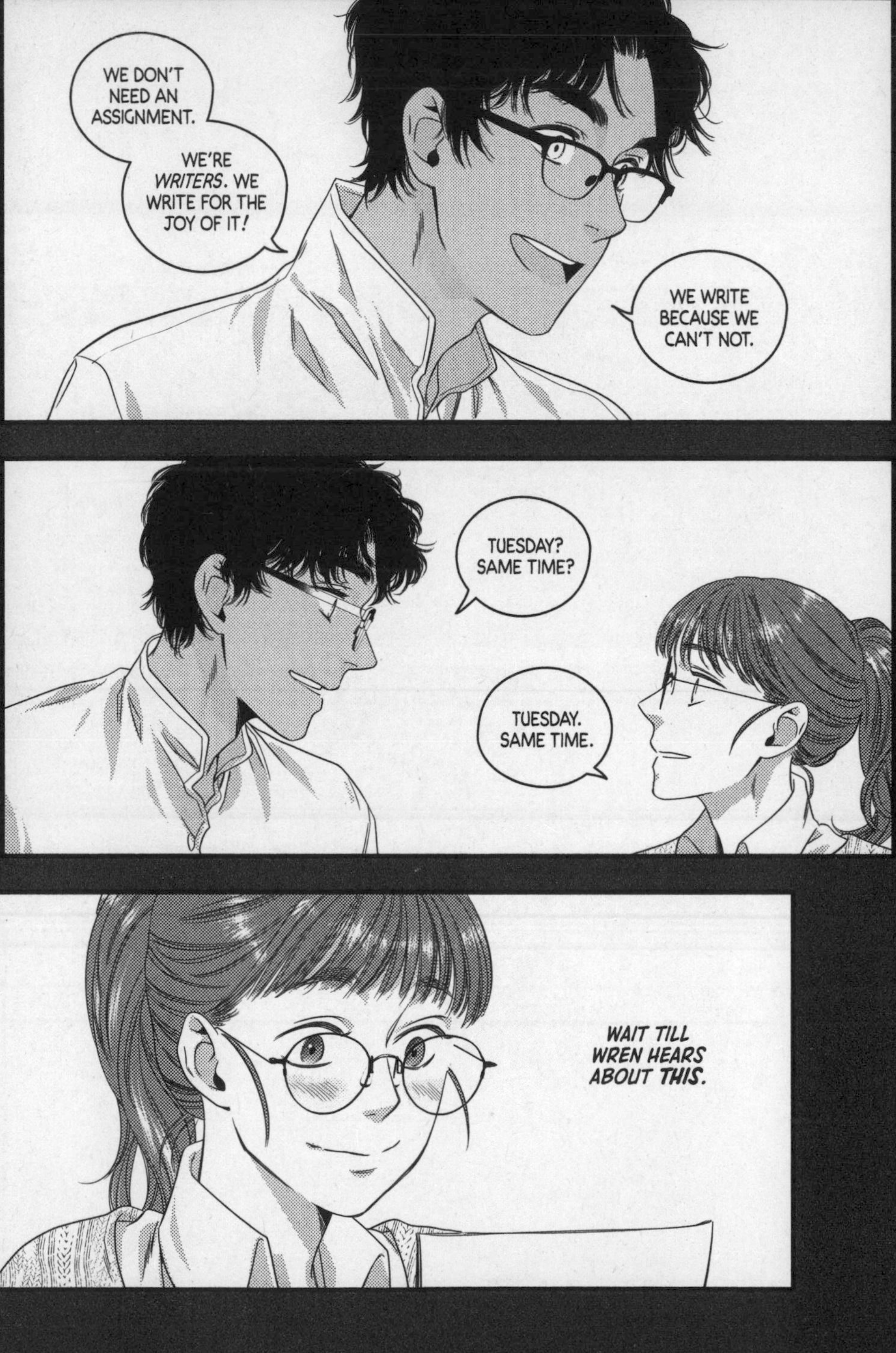
WE DON'T NEED AN ASSIGNMENT.
WE'RE *WRITERS*. WE WRITE FOR THE JOY OF IT!
WE WRITE BECAUSE WE CAN'T NOT.
TUESDAY? SAME TIME?
TUESDAY. SAME TIME.
WAIT TILL WREN HEARS ABOUT THIS.

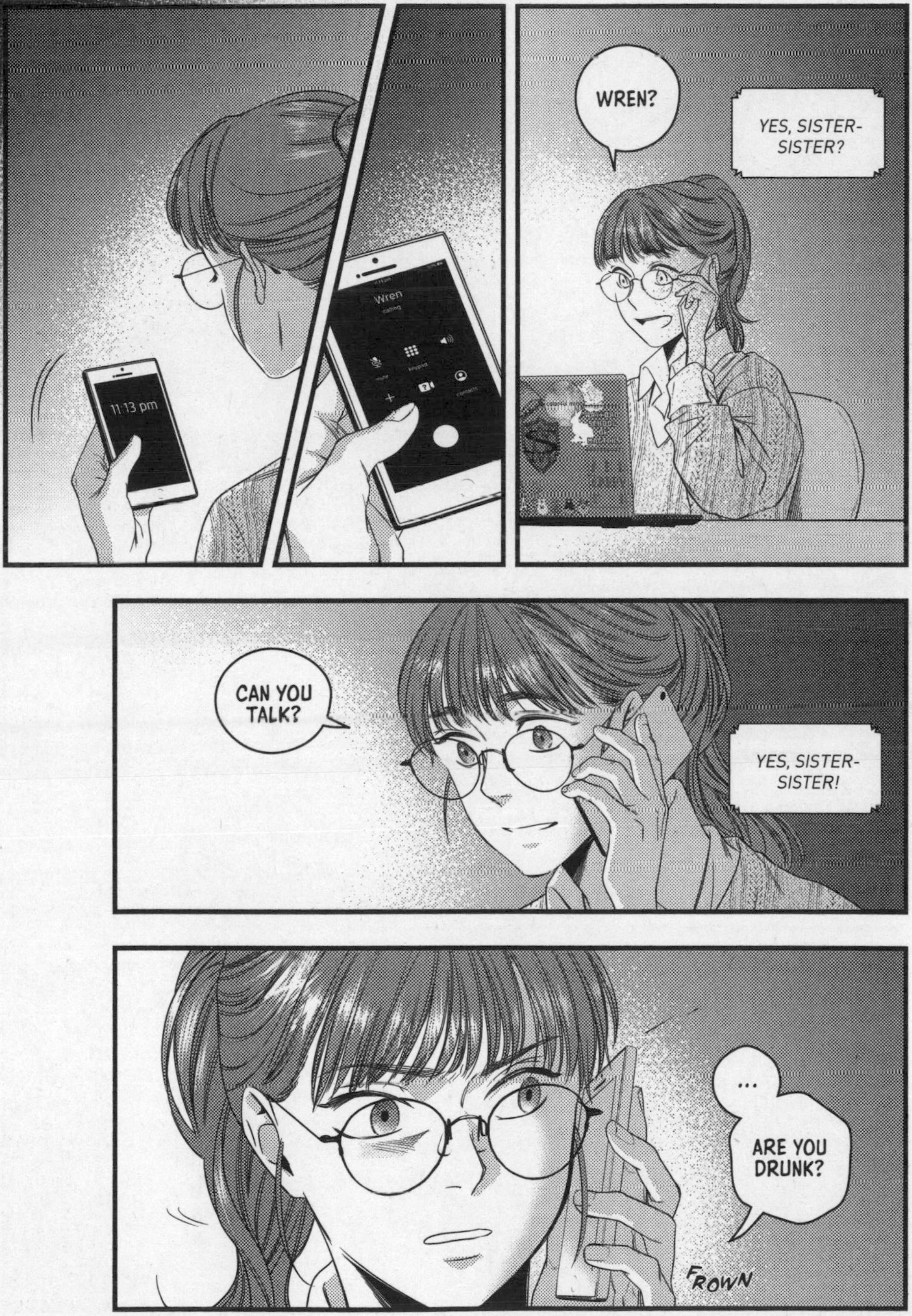
11:13 pm
Wren
WREN?
YES, SISTER-SISTER?
CAN YOU TALK?
YES, SISTER-SISTER!
...
ARE YOU DRUNK?
FROWN

I WAS DRUNK.

NOW I THINK I'M SOMETHING ELSE.

ARE YOU ALONE? WHERE'S COURTNEY?

SHE'S HERE! I MIGHT BE SITTING ON HER LEG.

ARE YOU OKAY?

YES-YES-YES, SISTER-SISTER.

THAT'S WHY I ANSWERED THE PHONE.

TO TELL YOU I WAS OKAY.

SO YOU CAN LEAVE ME ALONE FOR A WHILE.

OKAY-OKAY?

I WAS JUST CALLING TO TALK TO YOU ABOUT DAD.

I USE "JUST" SO MUCH.

IT'S MY PASSIVE-AGGRESSIVE TELL... LIKE TWITCHING WHEN LYING.

AND... BOY STUFF.

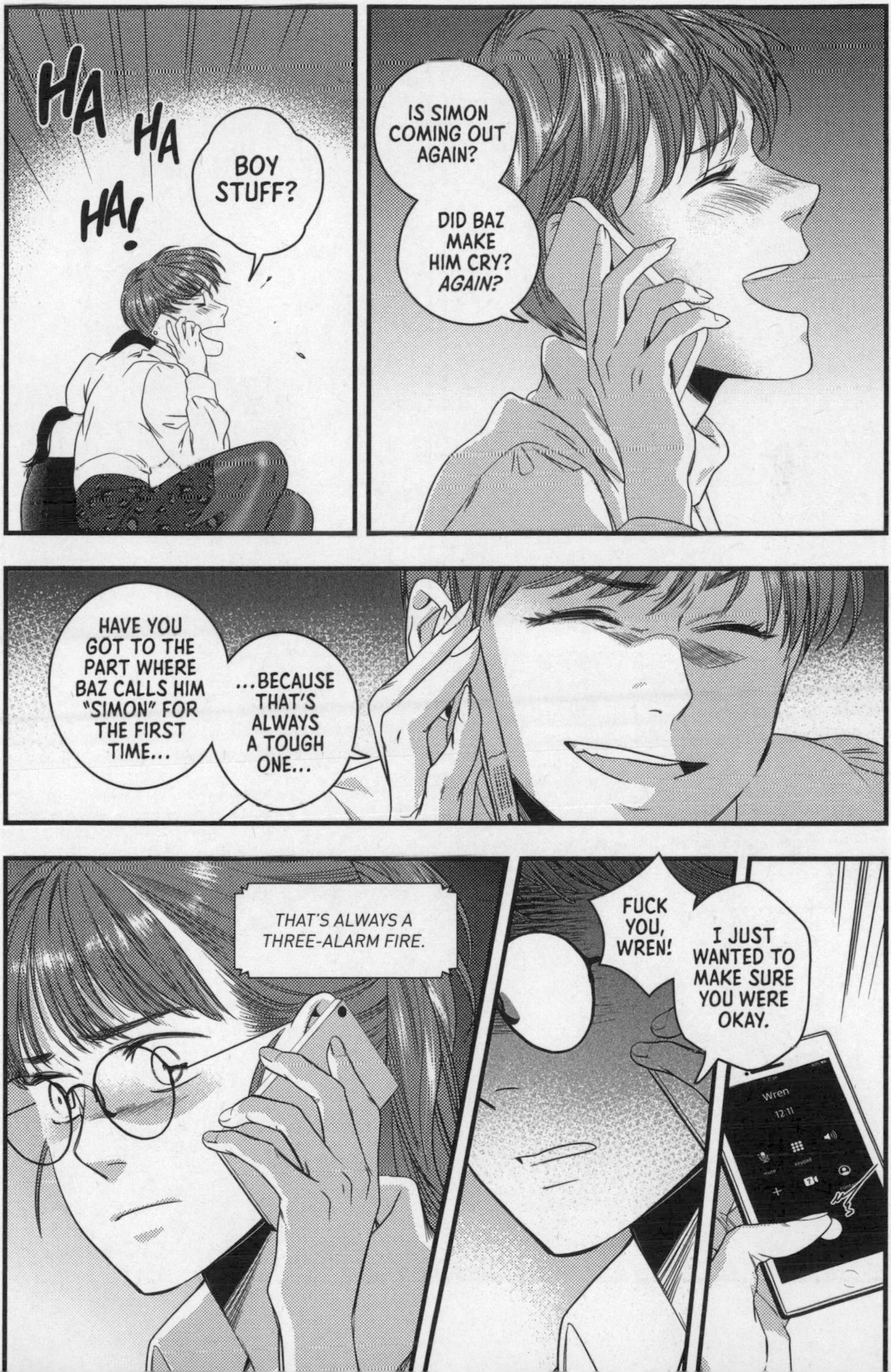
HA
HA
HA!
BOY STUFF?
IS SIMON COMING OUT AGAIN?
DID BAZ MAKE HIM CRY? *AGAIN?*
HAVE YOU GOT TO THE PART WHERE BAZ CALLS HIM "SIMON" FOR THE FIRST TIME...
...BECAUSE THAT'S ALWAYS A TOUGH ONE...
THAT'S ALWAYS A THREE-ALARM FIRE.
FUCK YOU, WREN!
I JUST WANTED TO MAKE SURE YOU WERE OKAY.
Wren
12:11

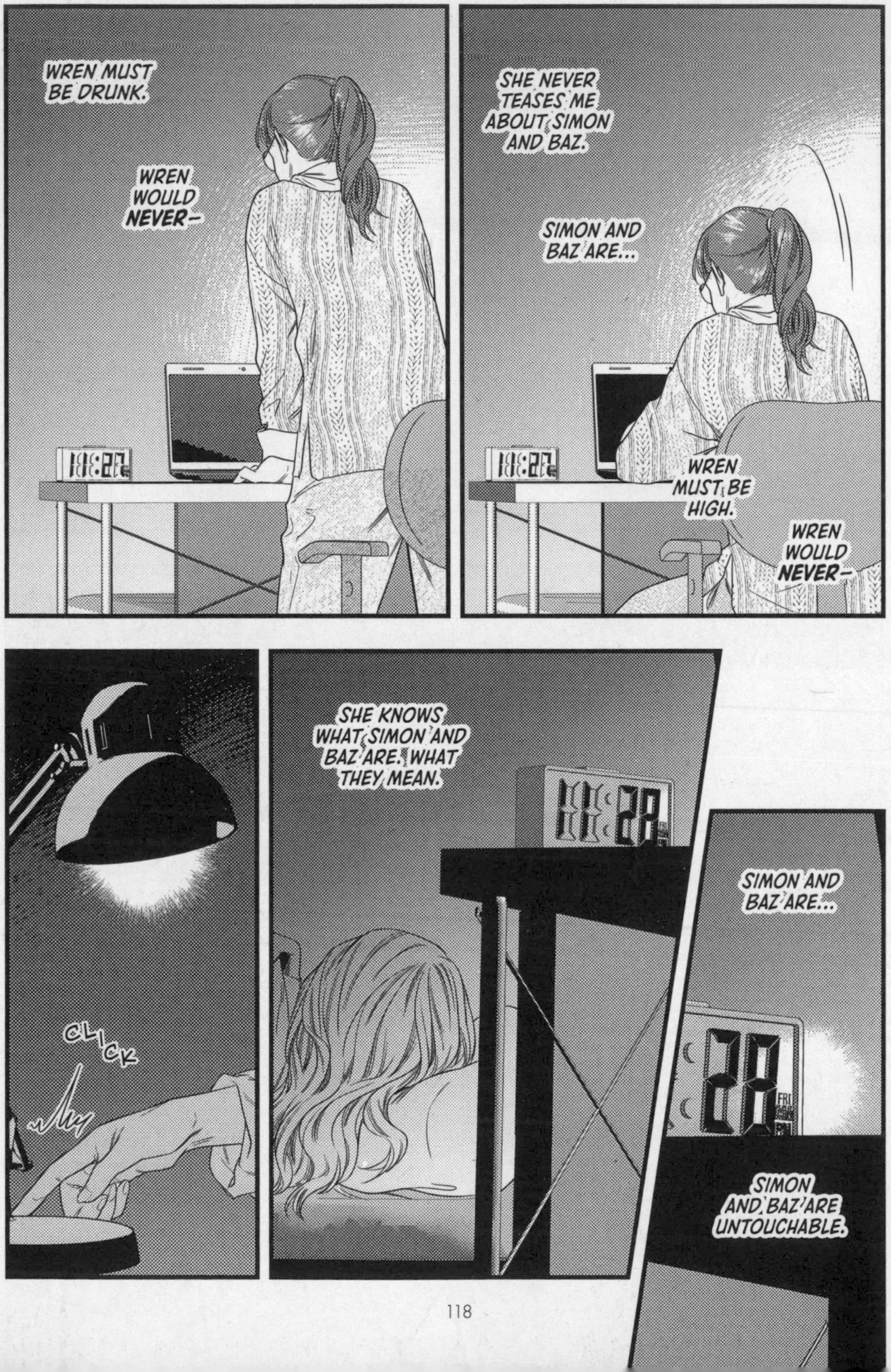
WREN MUST BE DRUNK.
WREN WOULD NEVER—
SHE NEVER TEASES ME ABOUT SIMON AND BAZ.
SIMON AND BAZ ARE...
WREN MUST BE HIGH.
WREN WOULD NEVER—
CLICK
SHE KNOWS WHAT SIMON AND BAZ ARE. WHAT THEY MEAN.
SIMON AND BAZ ARE...
SIMON AND BAZ ARE UNTOUCHABLE.

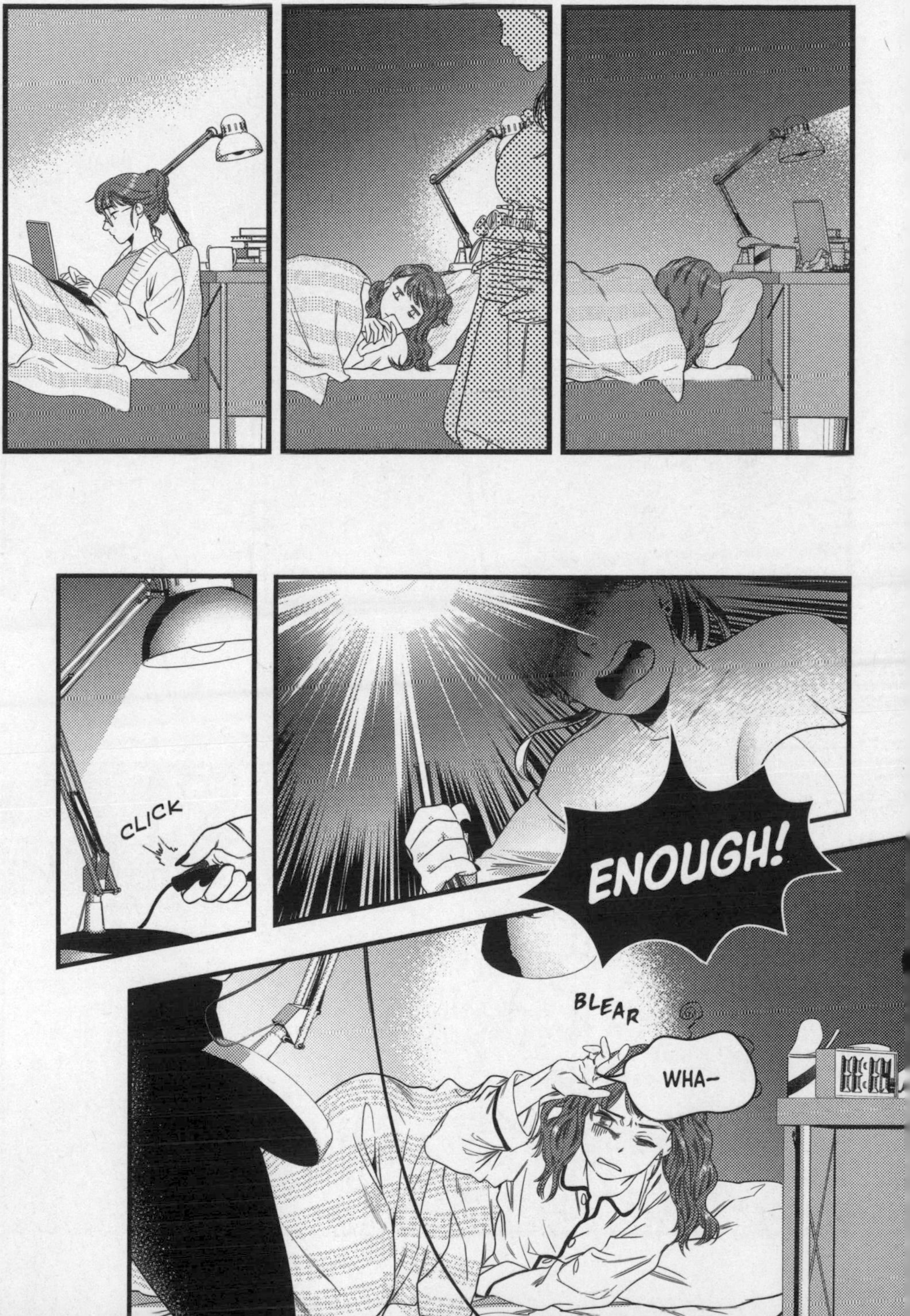
CLICK
ENOUGH!
BLEAR
WHA-

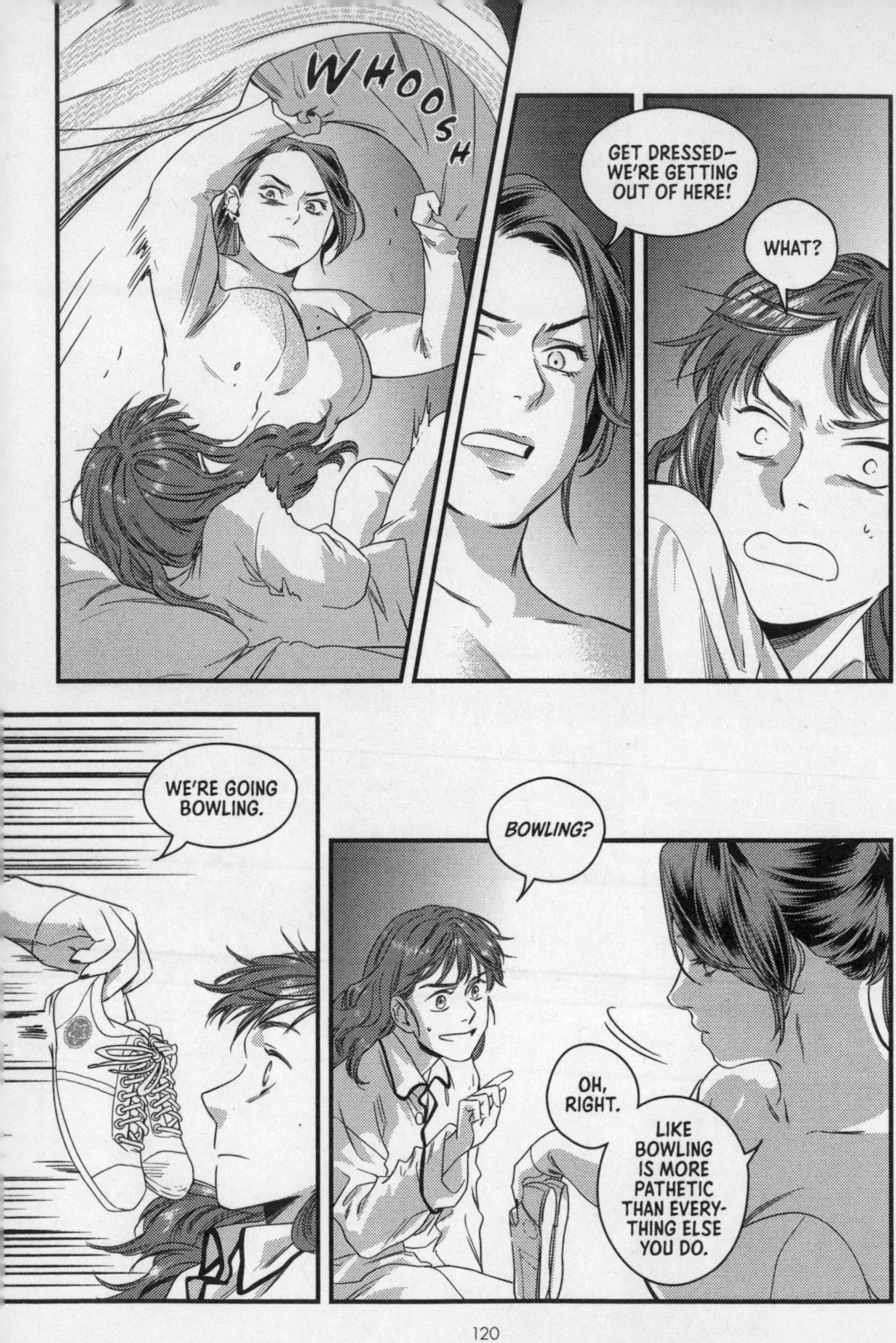
WHOOSH
GET DRESSED— WE'RE GETTING OUT OF HERE!
WHAT?
WE'RE GOING BOWLING.
BOWLING?
OH, RIGHT.
LIKE BOWLING IS MORE PATHETIC THAN EVERY-THING ELSE YOU DO.

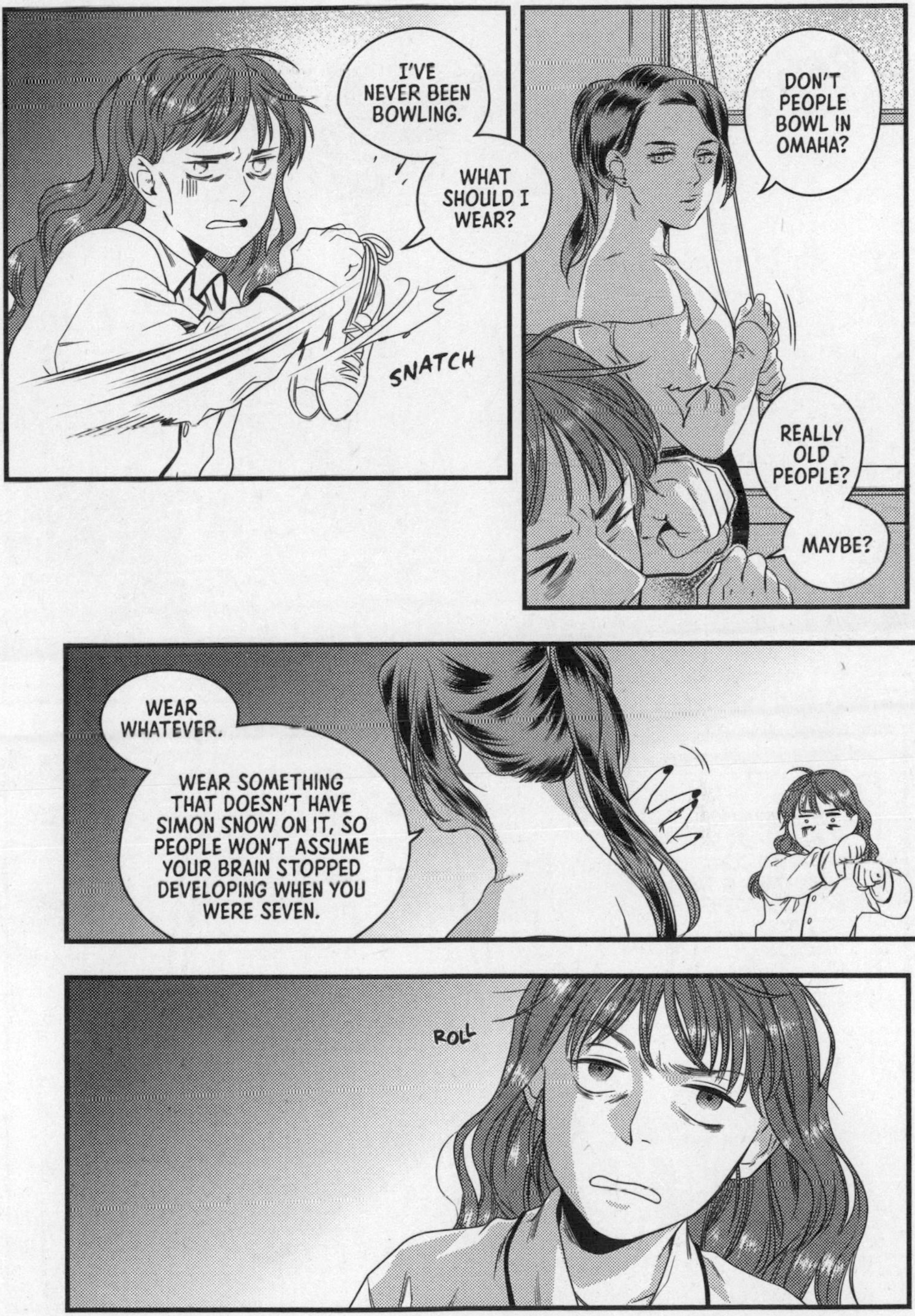

I'VE NEVER BEEN BOWLING.
WHAT SHOULD I WEAR?
SNATCH
DON'T PEOPLE BOWL IN OMAHA?
REALLY OLD PEOPLE?
MAYBE?
WEAR WHATEVER.
WEAR SOMETHING THAT DOESN'T HAVE SIMON SNOW ON IT, SO PEOPLE WON'T ASSUME YOUR BRAIN STOPPED DEVELOPING WHEN YOU WERE SEVEN.
ROLL

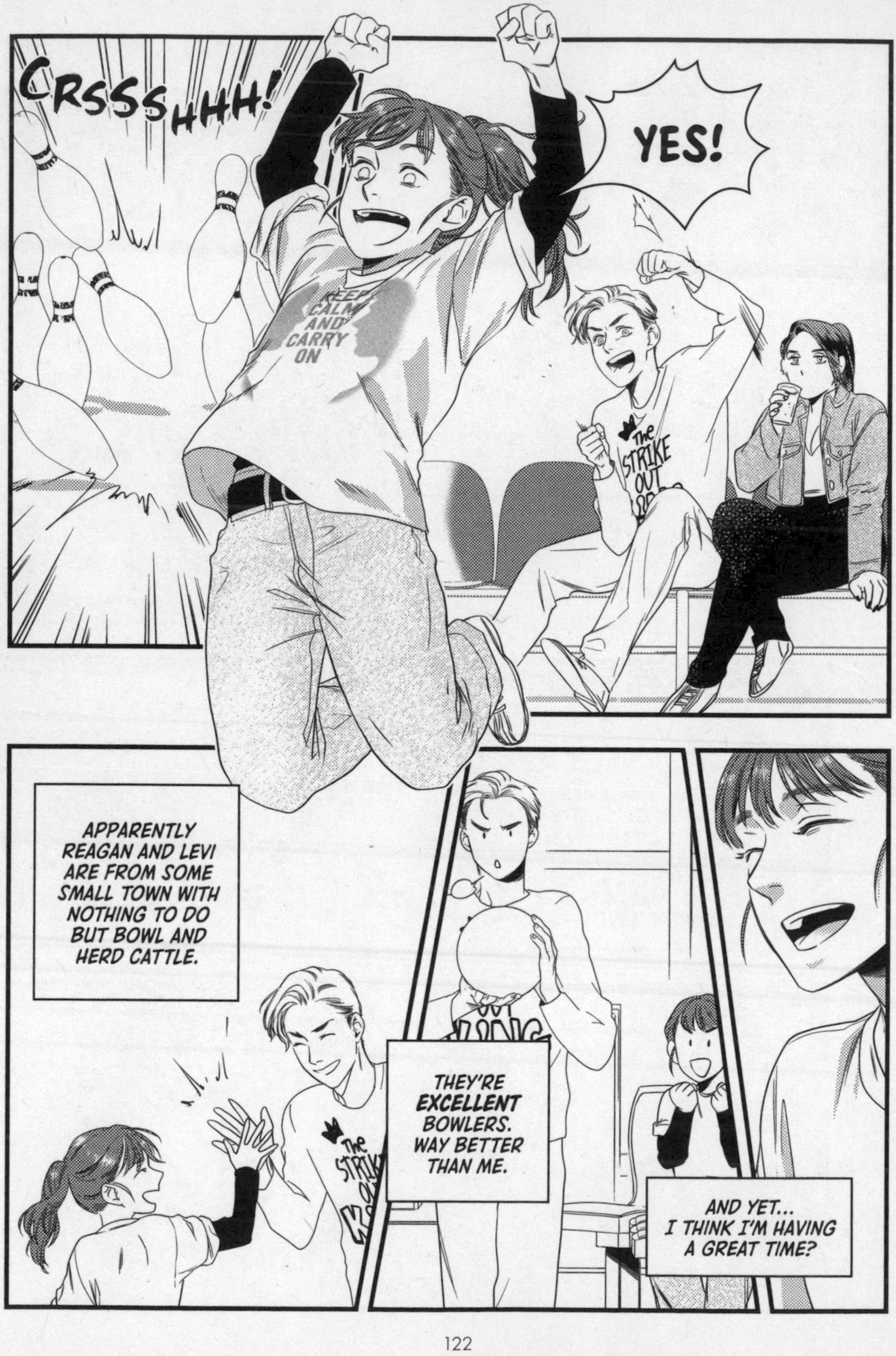
CRSSSHHH!
YES!
APPARENTLY REAGAN AND LEVI ARE FROM SOME SMALL TOWN WITH NOTHING TO DO BUT BOWL AND HERD CATTLE.
THEY'RE **EXCELLENT** BOWLERS. WAY BETTER THAN ME.
AND YET... I THINK I'M HAVING A GREAT TIME?

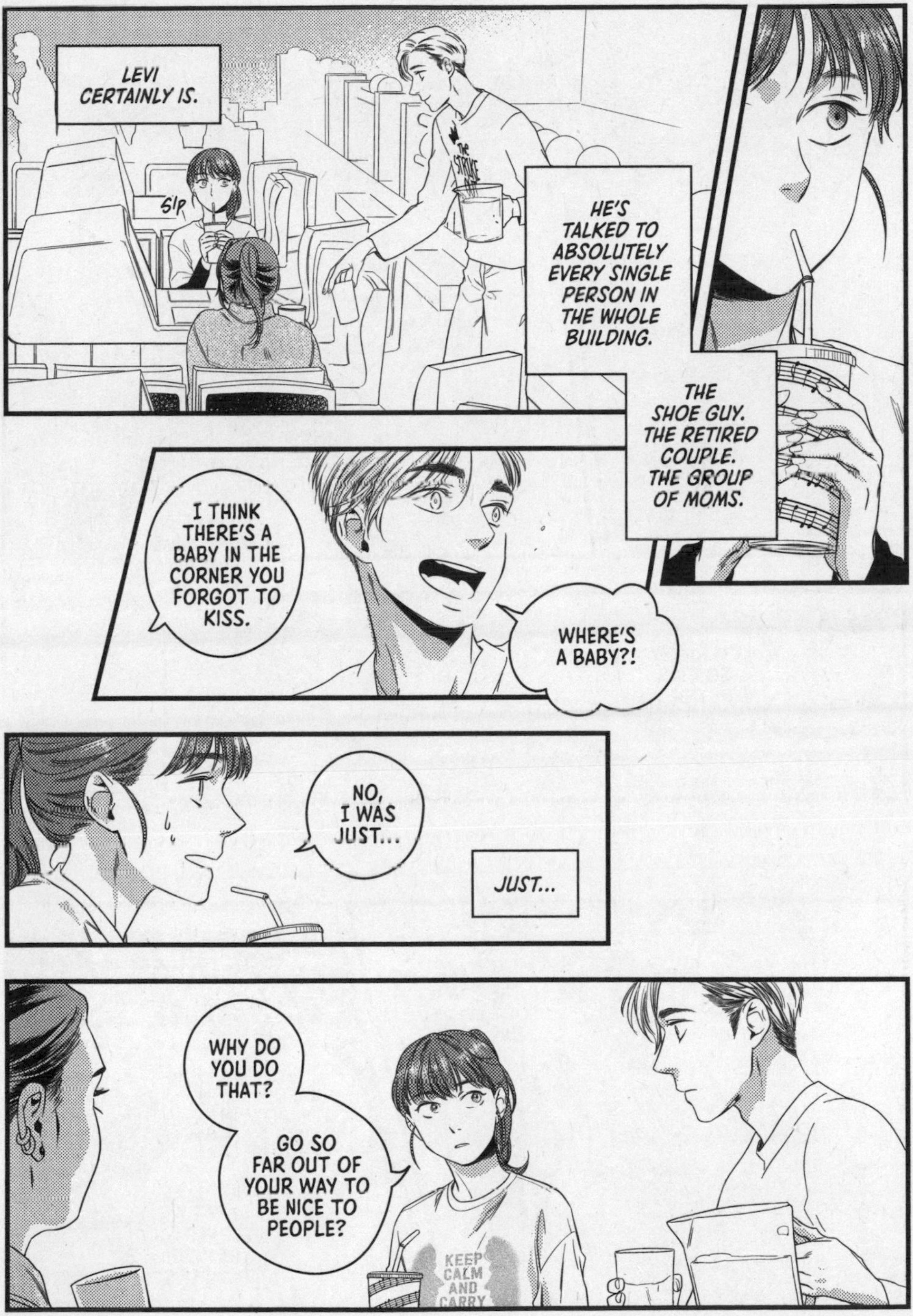
LEVI CERTAINLY IS.
SIP
HE'S TALKED TO ABSOLUTELY EVERY SINGLE PERSON IN THE WHOLE BUILDING.
THE SHOE GUY. THE RETIRED COUPLE. THE GROUP OF MOMS.
I THINK THERE'S A BABY IN THE CORNER YOU FORGOT TO KISS.
WHERE'S A BABY?!
NO, I WAS JUST...
JUST...
WHY DO YOU DO THAT?
GO SO FAR OUT OF YOUR WAY TO BE NICE TO PEOPLE?
KEEP CALM AND CARRY

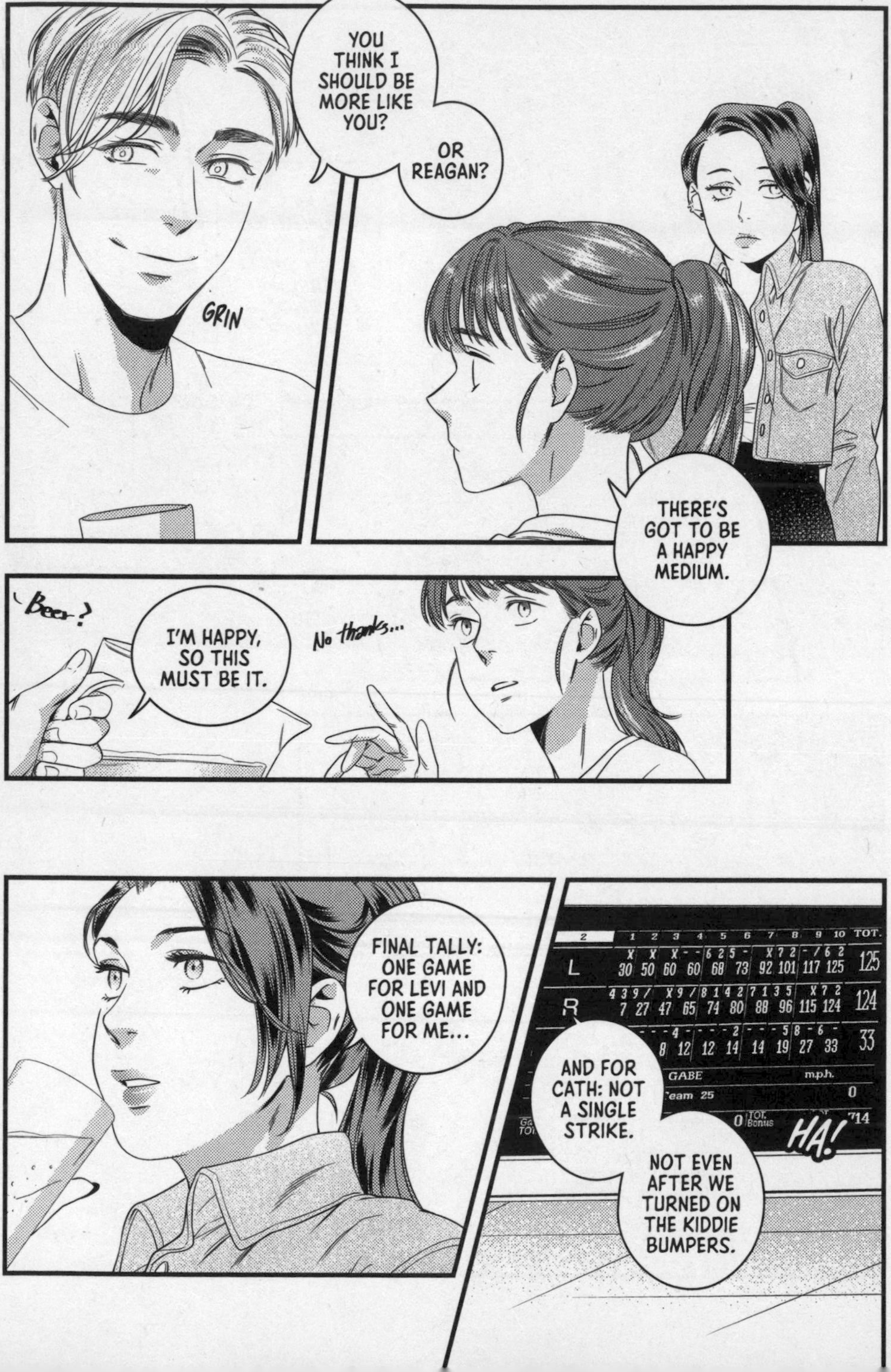
YOU THINK I SHOULD BE MORE LIKE YOU?
OR REAGAN?
GRIN
THERE'S GOT TO BE A HAPPY MEDIUM.
Beer?
I'M HAPPY, SO THIS MUST BE IT.
No thanks...
FINAL TALLY: ONE GAME FOR LEVI AND ONE GAME FOR ME...
AND FOR CATH: NOT A SINGLE STRIKE.
HA!
NOT EVEN AFTER WE TURNED ON THE KIDDIE BUMPERS.

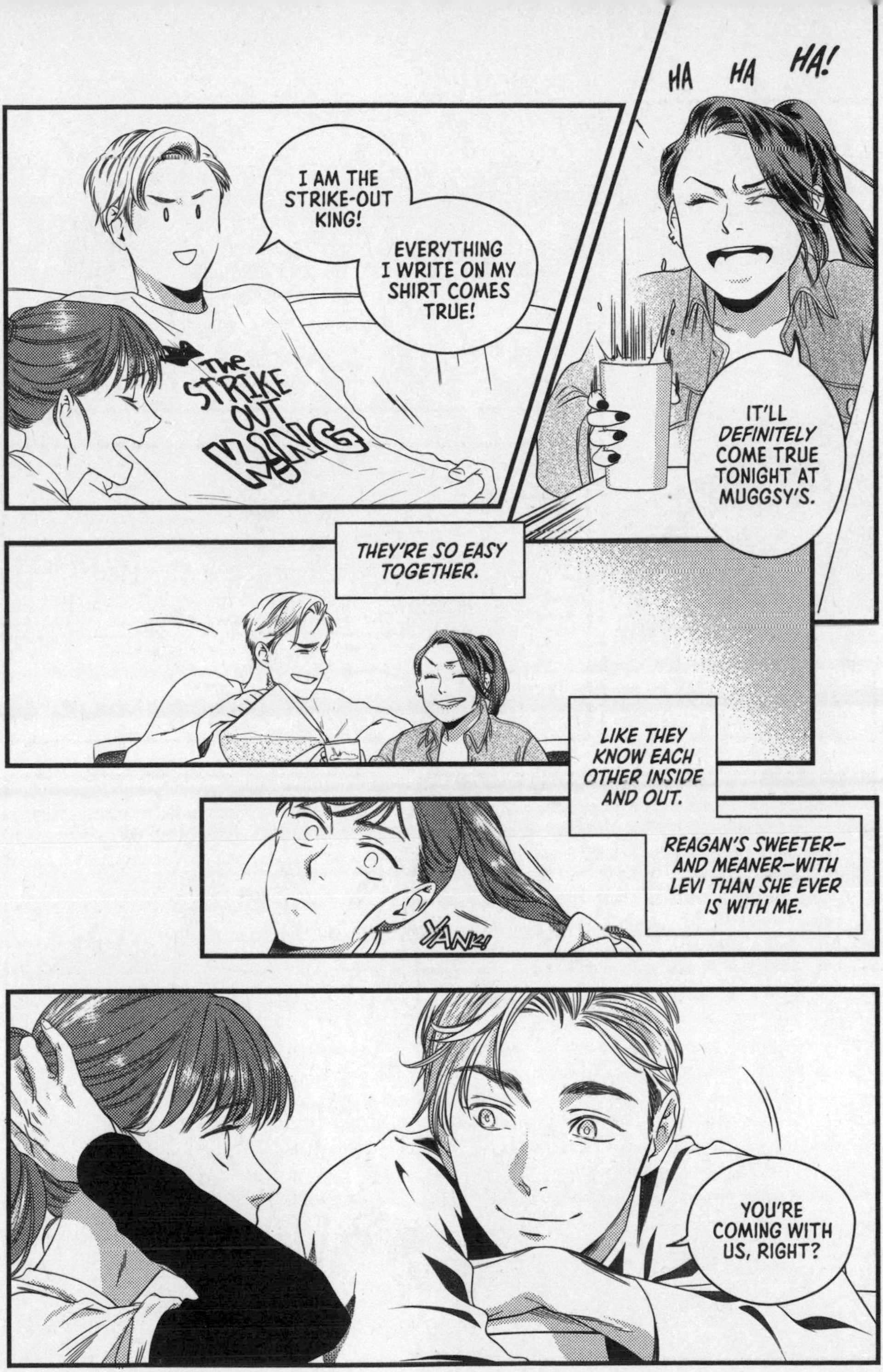

I AM THE STRIKE-OUT KING!
EVERYTHING I WRITE ON MY SHIRT COMES TRUE!
The STRIKE OUT KING
HA HA HA!
IT'LL *DEFINITELY* COME TRUE TONIGHT AT MUGGSY'S.
THEY'RE SO EASY TOGETHER.
LIKE THEY KNOW EACH OTHER INSIDE AND OUT.
REAGAN'S SWEETER—AND MEANER—WITH LEVI THAN SHE EVER IS WITH ME.
YANK!
YOU'RE COMING WITH US, RIGHT?

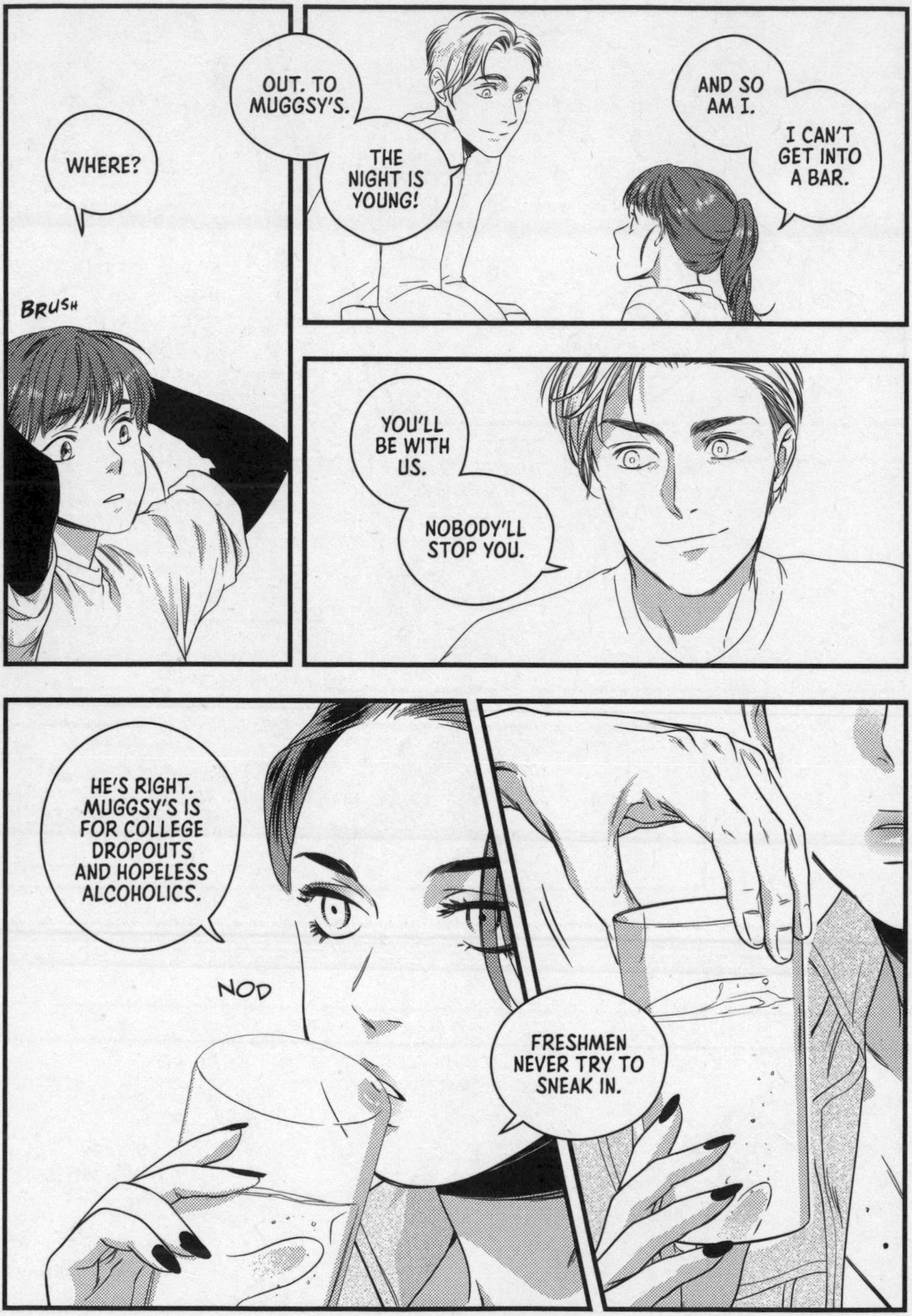
WHERE?
OUT. TO MUGGSY'S.
THE NIGHT IS YOUNG!
AND SO AM I.
I CAN'T GET INTO A BAR.
BRUSH
YOU'LL BE WITH US.
NOBODY'LL STOP YOU.
HE'S RIGHT. MUGGSY'S IS FOR COLLEGE DROPOUTS AND HOPELESS ALCOHOLICS.
NOD
FRESHMEN NEVER TRY TO SNEAK IN.

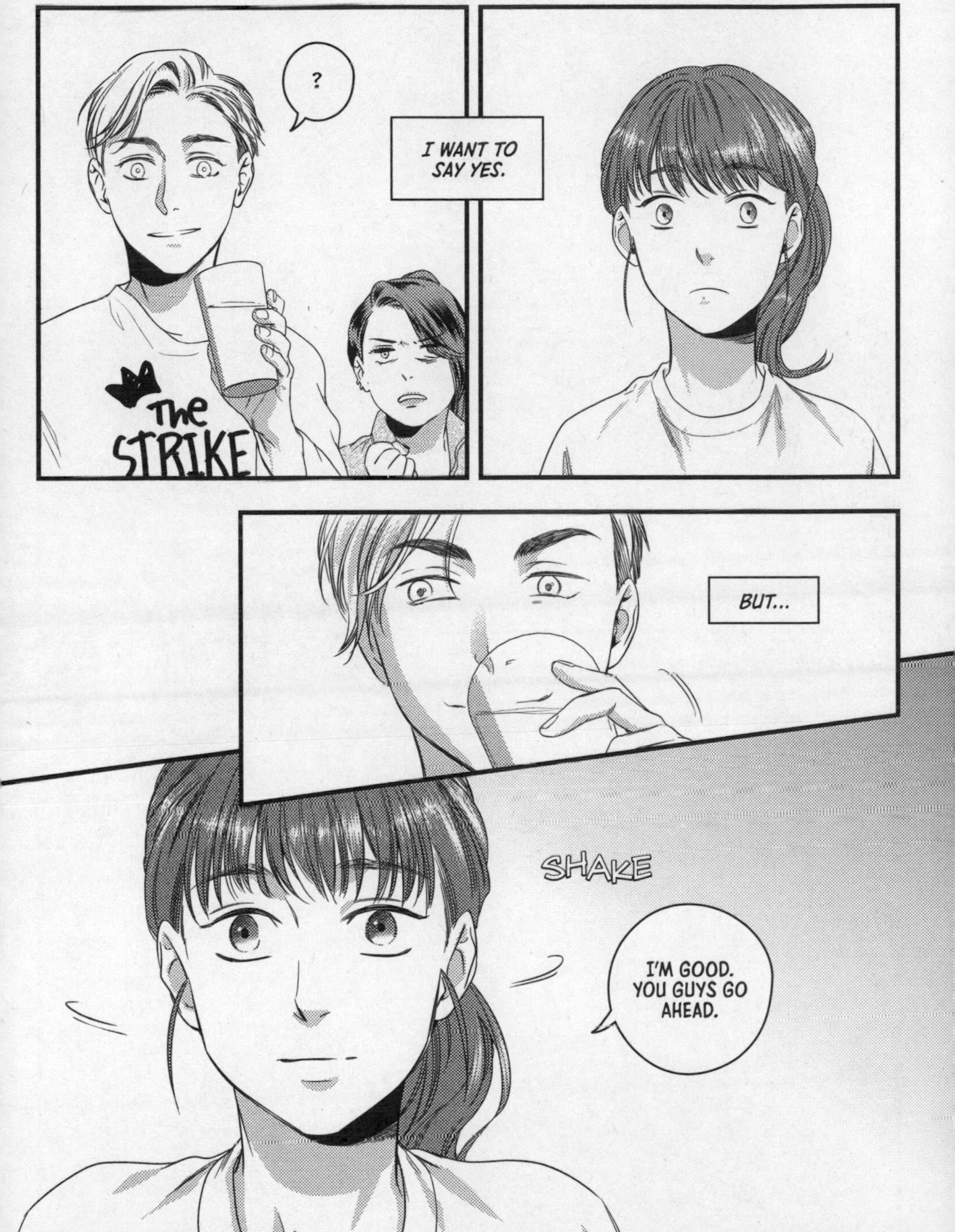
?
I WANT TO SAY YES.
BUT...
SHAKE
I'M GOOD. YOU GUYS GO AHEAD.

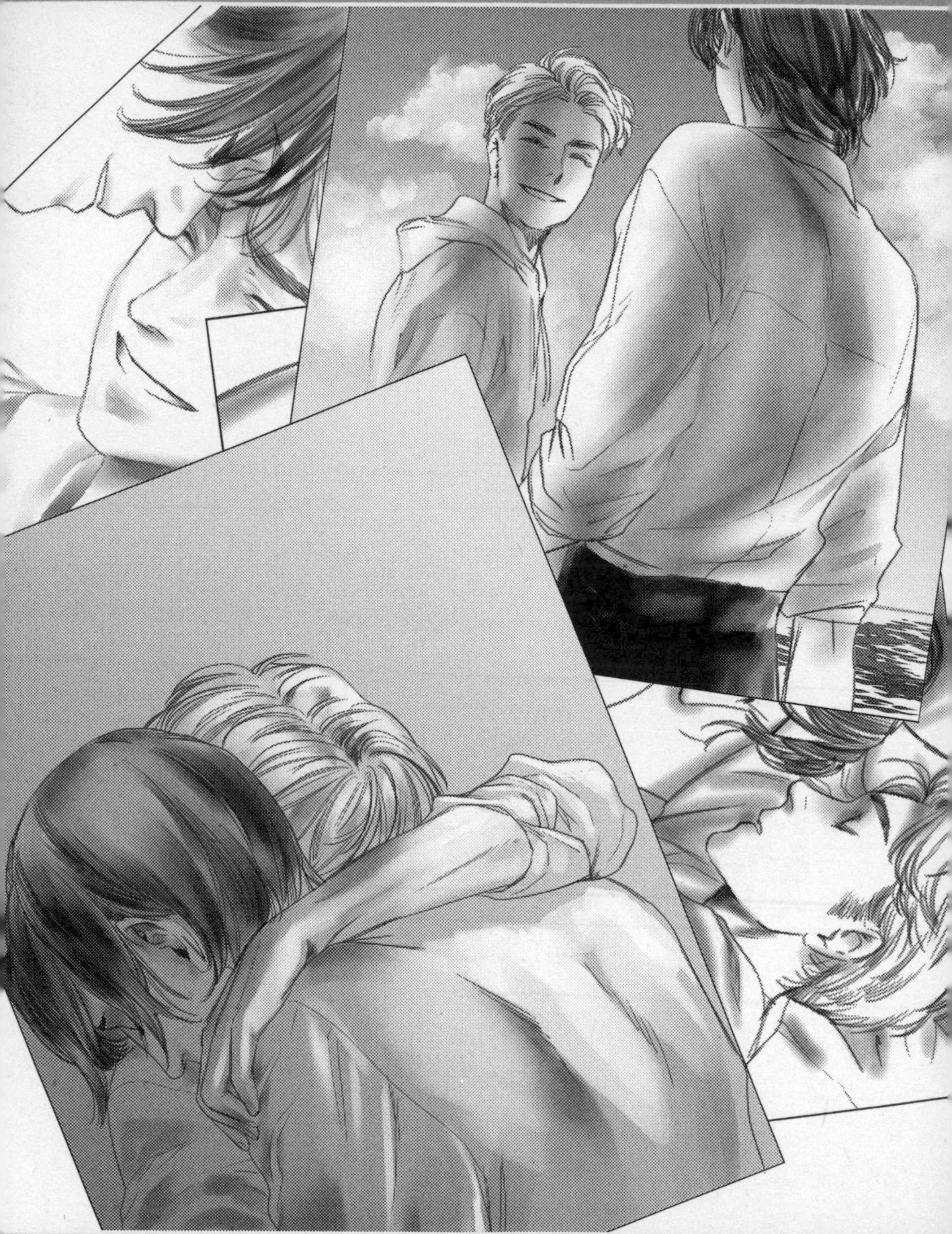

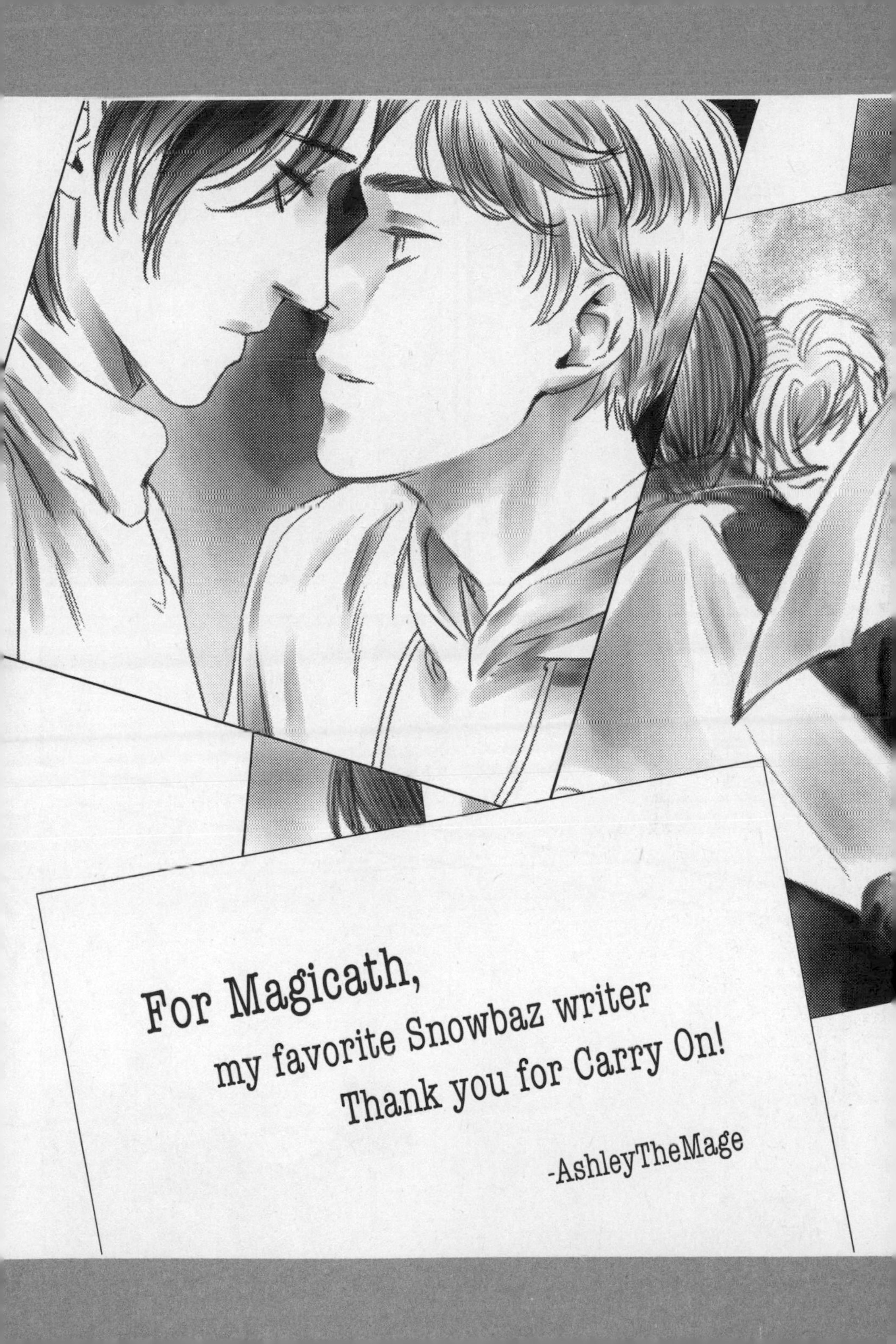
For Magicath,
my favorite Snowbaz writer
Thank you for Carry On!
-AshleyTheMage

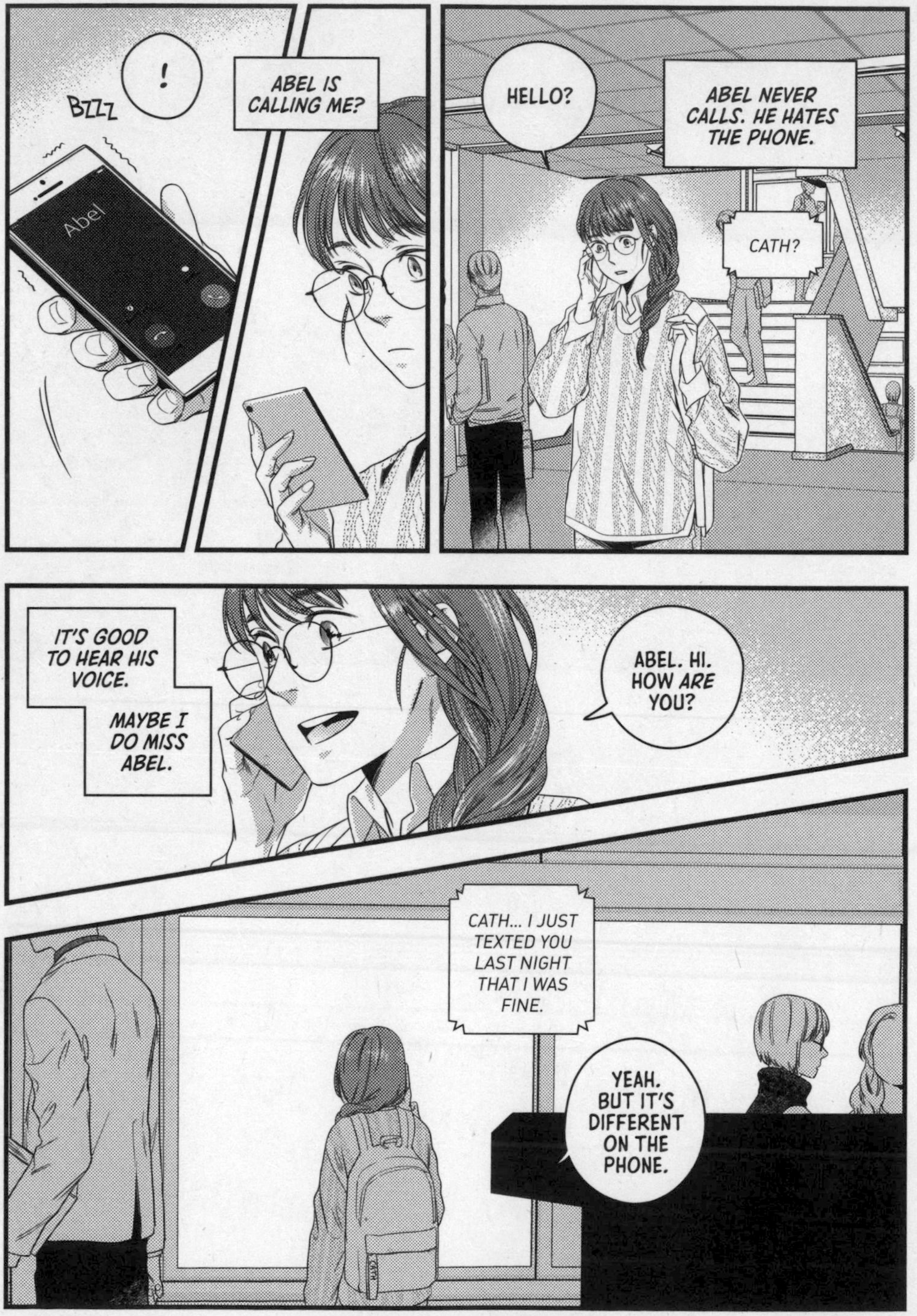
BZZZ
!
Abel
ABEL IS CALLING ME?
HELLO?
ABEL NEVER CALLS. HE HATES THE PHONE.
CATH?
IT'S GOOD TO HEAR HIS VOICE.
MAYBE I DO MISS ABEL.
ABEL. HI. HOW ARE YOU?
CATH... I JUST TEXTED YOU LAST NIGHT THAT I WAS FINE.
YEAH. BUT IT'S DIFFERENT ON THE PHONE.

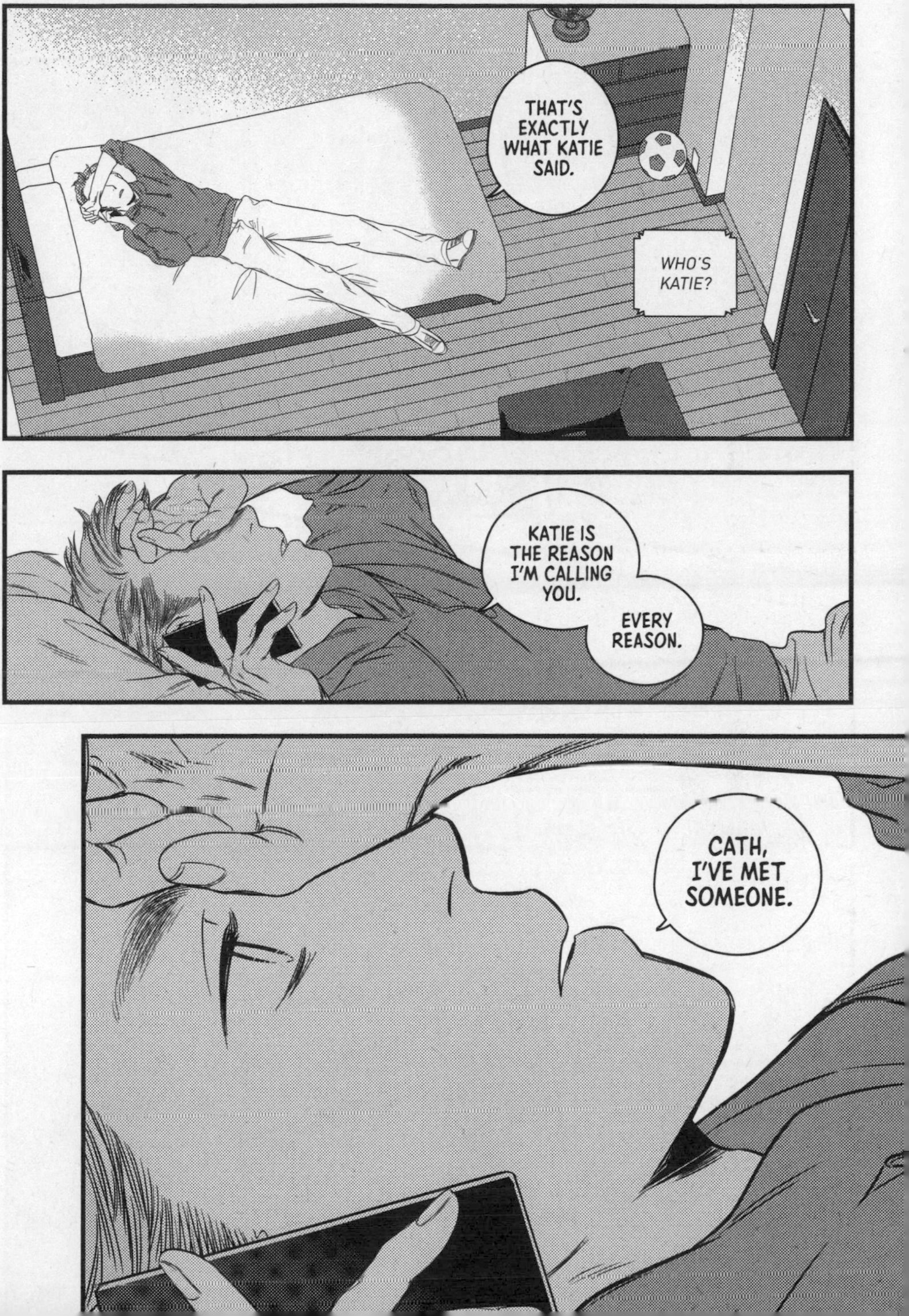
THAT'S EXACTLY WHAT KATIE SAID.
WHO'S KATIE?
KATIE IS THE REASON I'M CALLING YOU.
EVERY REASON.
CATH, I'VE MET SOMEONE.

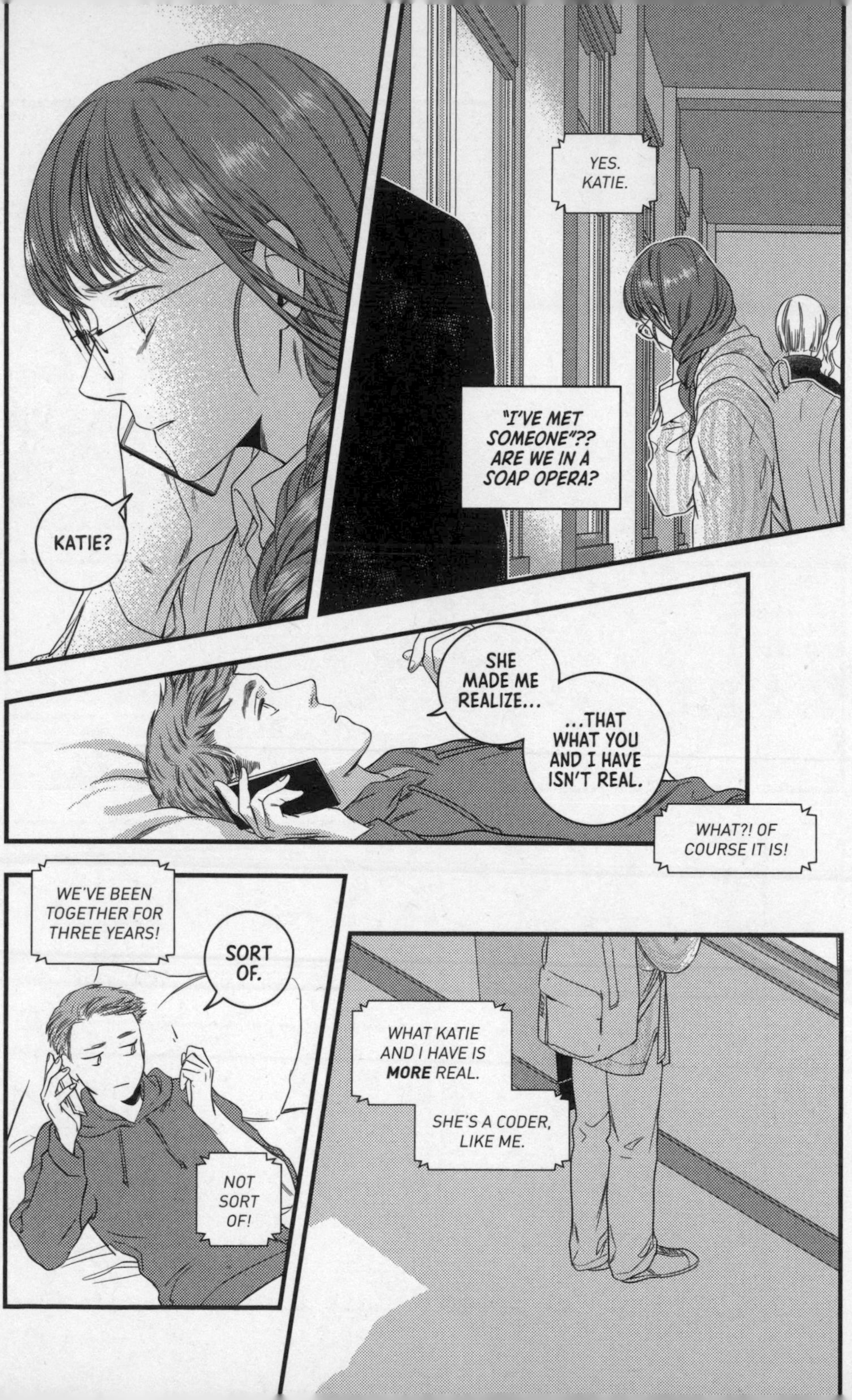
KATIE?
YES. KATIE.
"I'VE MET SOMEONE"?? ARE WE IN A SOAP OPERA?
SHE MADE ME REALIZE...
...THAT WHAT YOU AND I HAVE ISN'T REAL.
WHAT?! OF COURSE IT IS!
WE'VE BEEN TOGETHER FOR THREE YEARS!
SORT OF.
NOT SORT OF!
WHAT KATIE AND I HAVE IS **MORE** REAL.
SHE'S A CODER, LIKE ME.

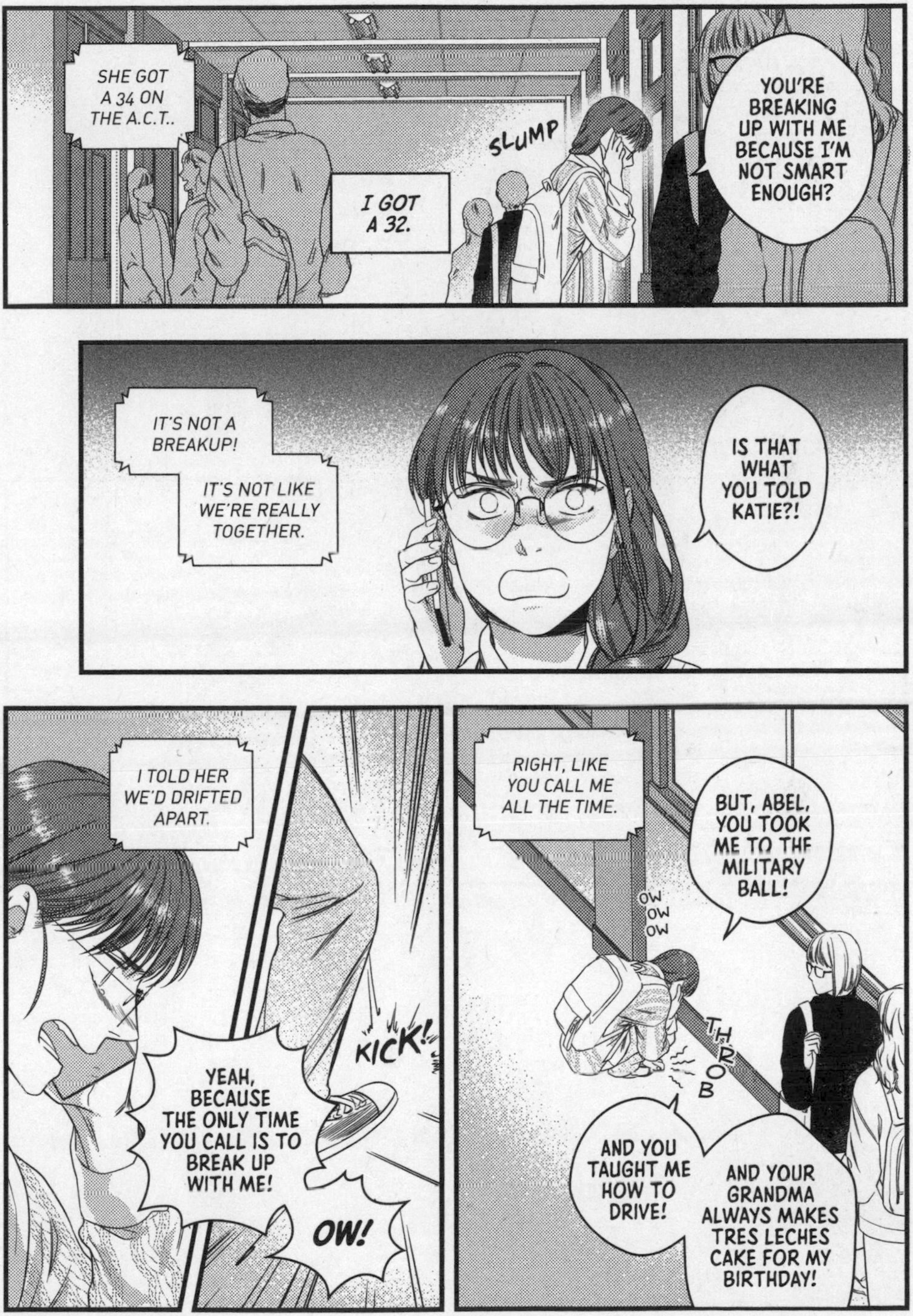
SHE GOT A 34 ON THE A.C.T..
I GOT A 32.
SLUMP
YOU'RE BREAKING UP WITH ME BECAUSE I'M NOT SMART ENOUGH?
IT'S NOT A BREAKUP!
IT'S NOT LIKE WE'RE REALLY TOGETHER.
IS THAT WHAT YOU TOLD KATIE?!
I TOLD HER WE'D DRIFTED APART.
YEAH, BECAUSE THE ONLY TIME YOU CALL IS TO BREAK UP WITH ME!
KICK!
OW!
RIGHT, LIKE YOU CALL ME ALL THE TIME.
BUT, ABEL, YOU TOOK ME TO THE MILITARY BALL!
OW OW OW
THROB
AND YOU TAUGHT ME HOW TO DRIVE!
AND YOUR GRANDMA ALWAYS MAKES TRES LECHES CAKE FOR MY BIRTHDAY!

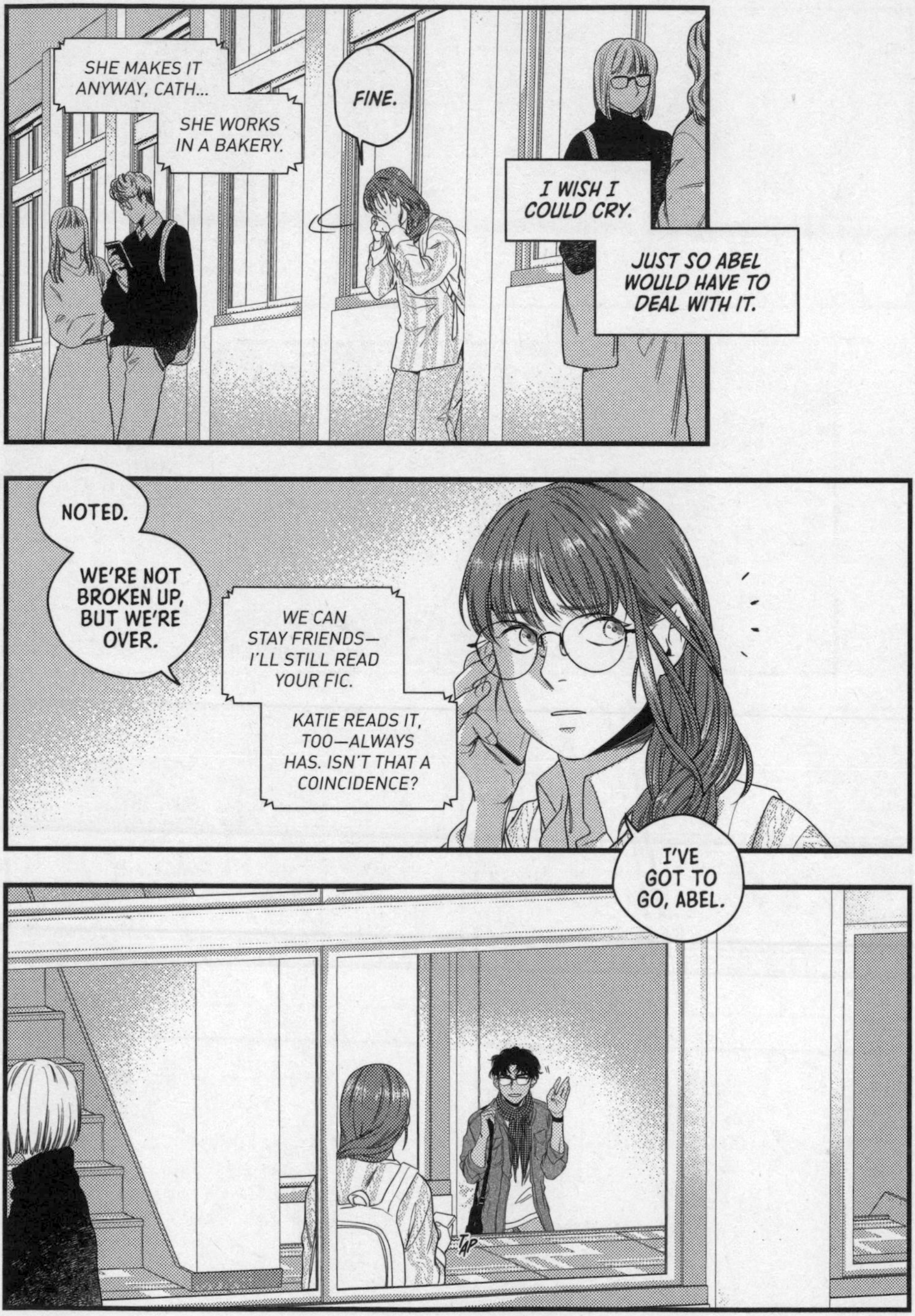
SHE MAKES IT ANYWAY, CATH...
SHE WORKS IN A BAKERY.
FINE.
I WISH I COULD CRY.
JUST SO ABEL WOULD HAVE TO DEAL WITH IT.
NOTED.
WE'RE NOT BROKEN UP, BUT WE'RE OVER.
WE CAN STAY FRIENDS— I'LL STILL READ YOUR FIC.
KATIE READS IT, TOO—ALWAYS HAS. ISN'T THAT A COINCIDENCE?
I'VE GOT TO GO, ABEL.
TAP

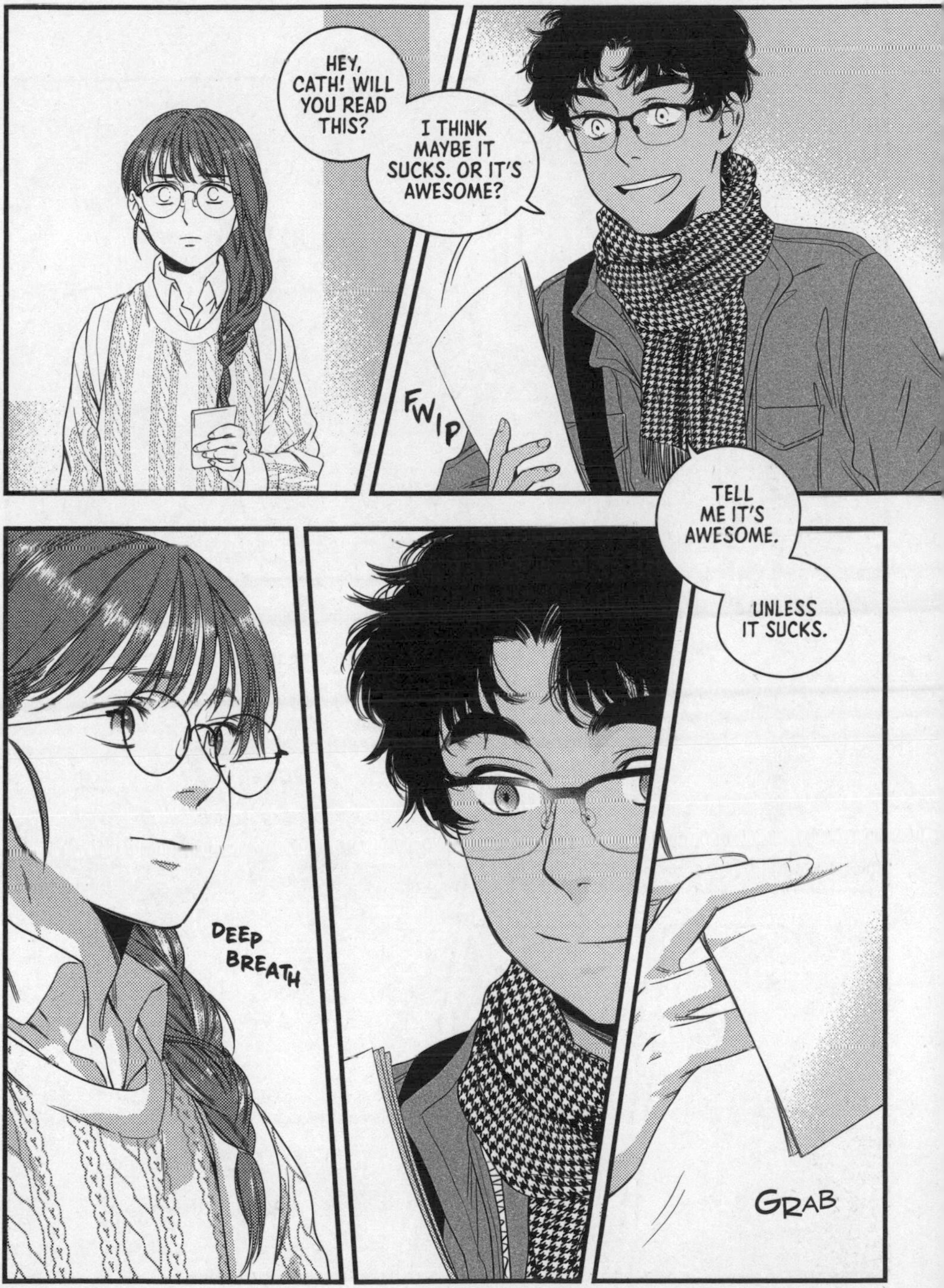
HEY, CATH! WILL YOU READ THIS?
I THINK MAYBE IT SUCKS. OR IT'S AWESOME?
FWIP
DEEP BREATH
TELL ME IT'S AWESOME.
UNLESS IT SUCKS.
GRAB

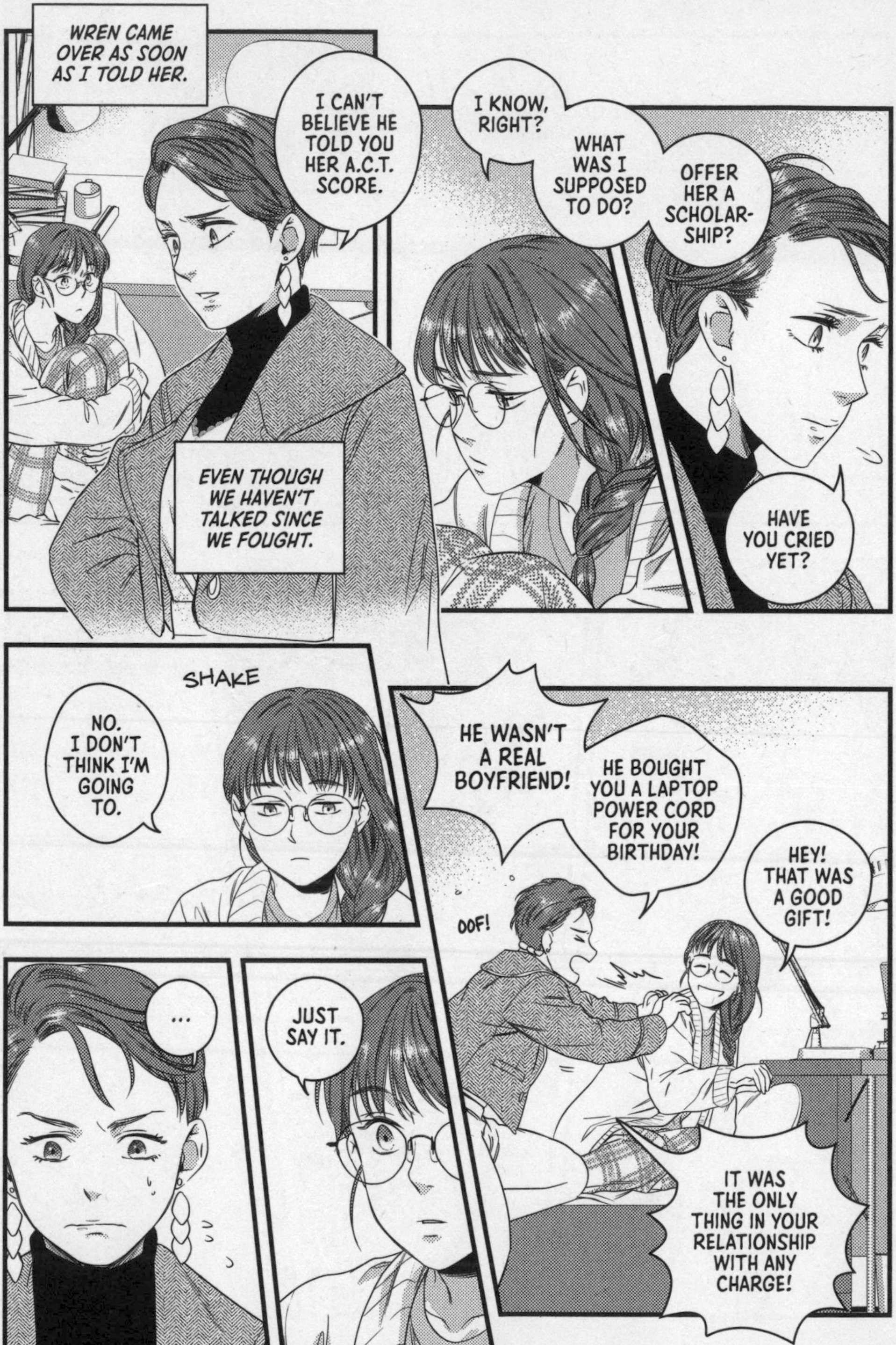
WREN CAME OVER AS SOON AS I TOLD HER.
I CAN'T BELIEVE HE TOLD YOU HER A.C.T. SCORE.
EVEN THOUGH WE HAVEN'T TALKED SINCE WE FOUGHT.
I KNOW, RIGHT?
WHAT WAS I SUPPOSED TO DO?
OFFER HER A SCHOLAR-SHIP?
HAVE YOU CRIED YET?
SHAKE
NO. I DON'T THINK I'M GOING TO.
HE WASN'T A REAL BOYFRIEND!
HE BOUGHT YOU A LAPTOP POWER CORD FOR YOUR BIRTHDAY!
OOF!
HEY! THAT WAS A GOOD GIFT!
IT WAS THE ONLY THING IN YOUR RELATIONSHIP WITH ANY CHARGE!
...
JUST SAY IT.

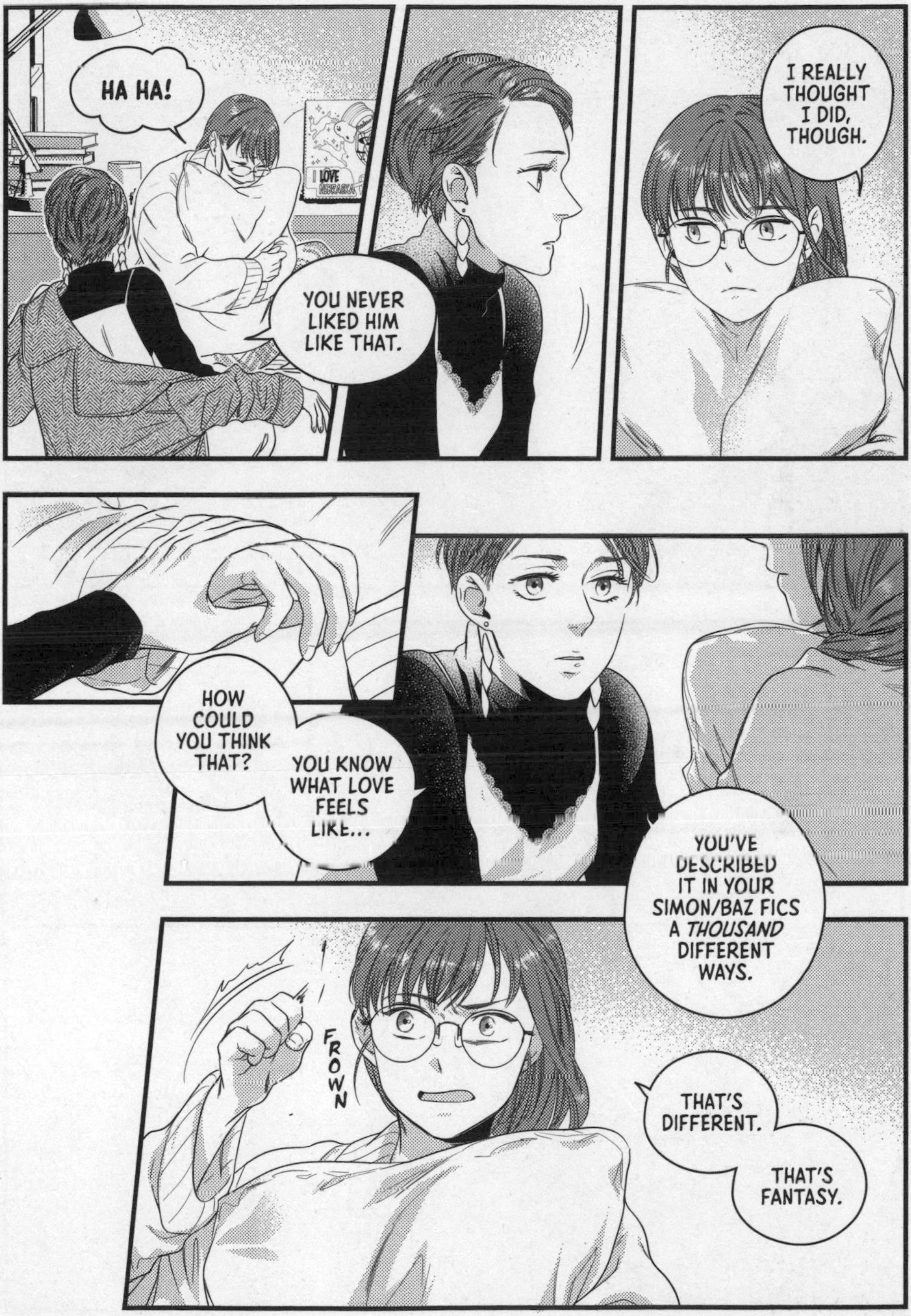
HA HA!
YOU NEVER LIKED HIM LIKE THAT.
I REALLY THOUGHT I DID, THOUGH.
HOW COULD YOU THINK THAT?
YOU KNOW WHAT LOVE FEELS LIKE...
YOU'VE DESCRIBED IT IN YOUR SIMON/BAZ FICS A *THOUSAND* DIFFERENT WAYS.
!
FROWN
THAT'S DIFFERENT.
THAT'S FANTASY.

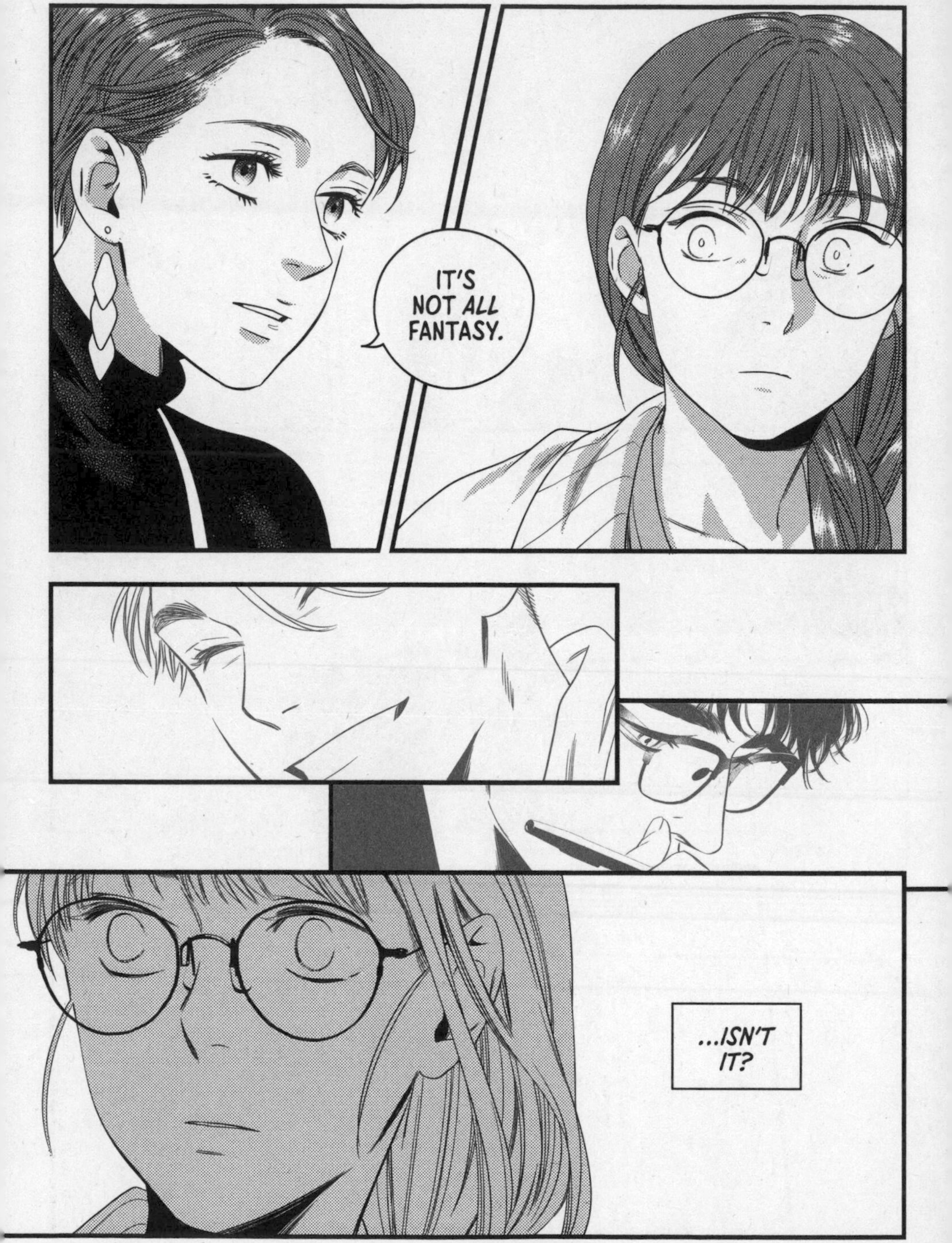
IT'S NOT ALL FANTASY.
...ISN'T IT?

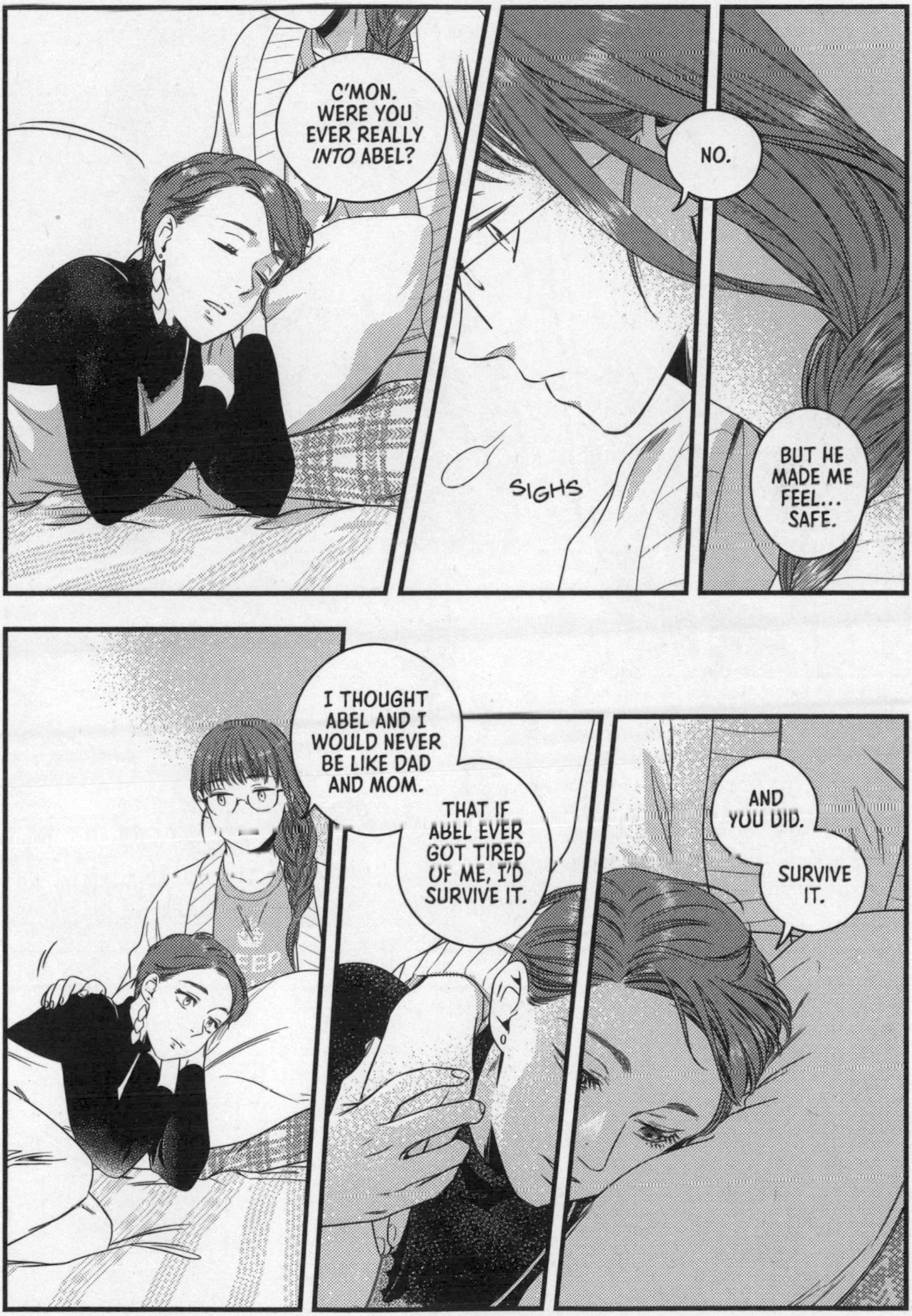
C'MON. WERE YOU EVER REALLY *INTO* ABEL?
NO.
SIGHS
BUT HE MADE ME FEEL... SAFE.
I THOUGHT ABEL AND I WOULD NEVER BE LIKE DAD AND MOM.
THAT IF ABEL EVER GOT TIRED OF ME, I'D SURVIVE IT.
AND YOU DID.
SURVIVE IT.

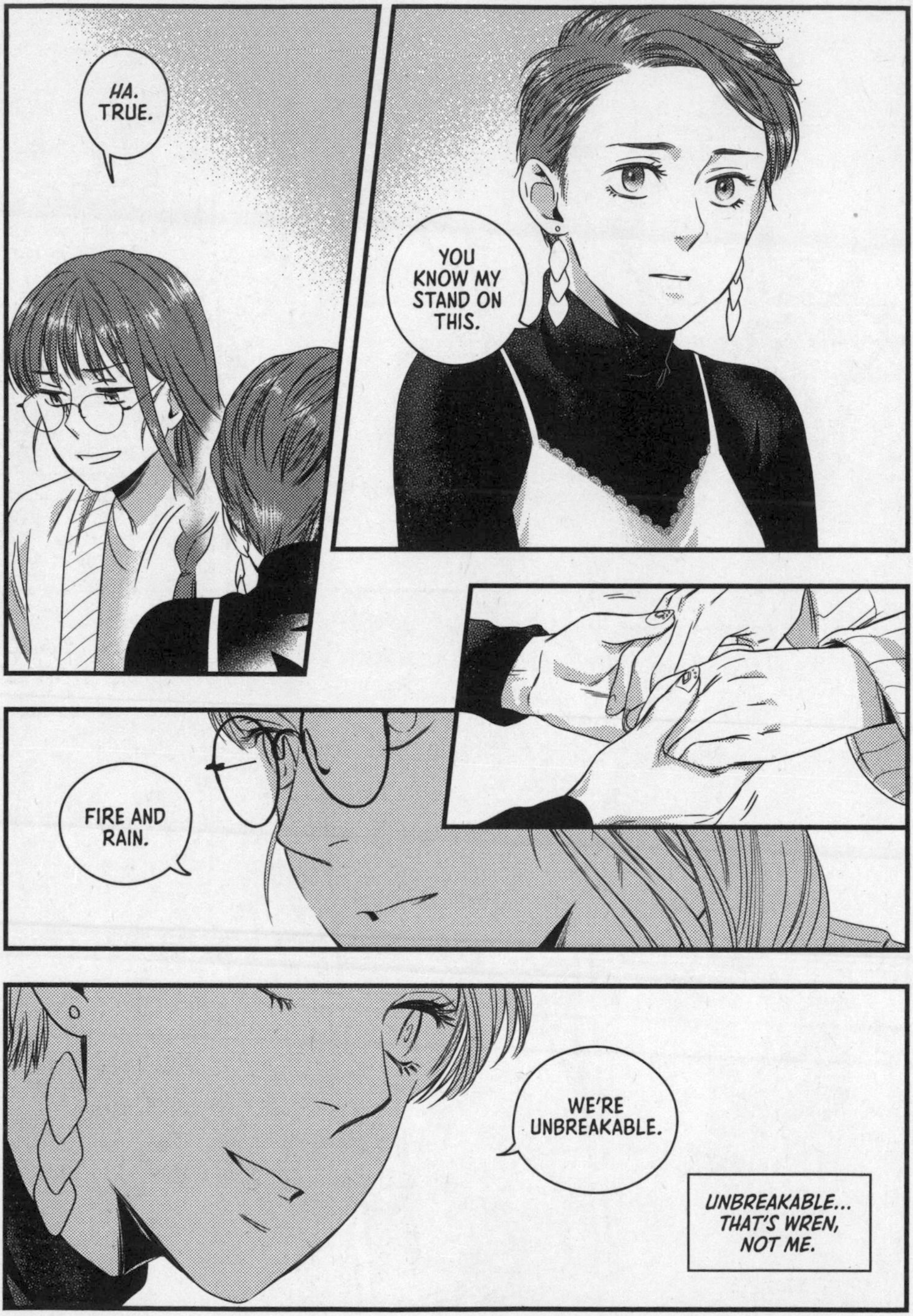
HA. TRUE.
YOU KNOW MY STAND ON THIS.
FIRE AND RAIN.
WE'RE UNBREAKABLE.
UNBREAKABLE... THAT'S WREN, NOT ME.

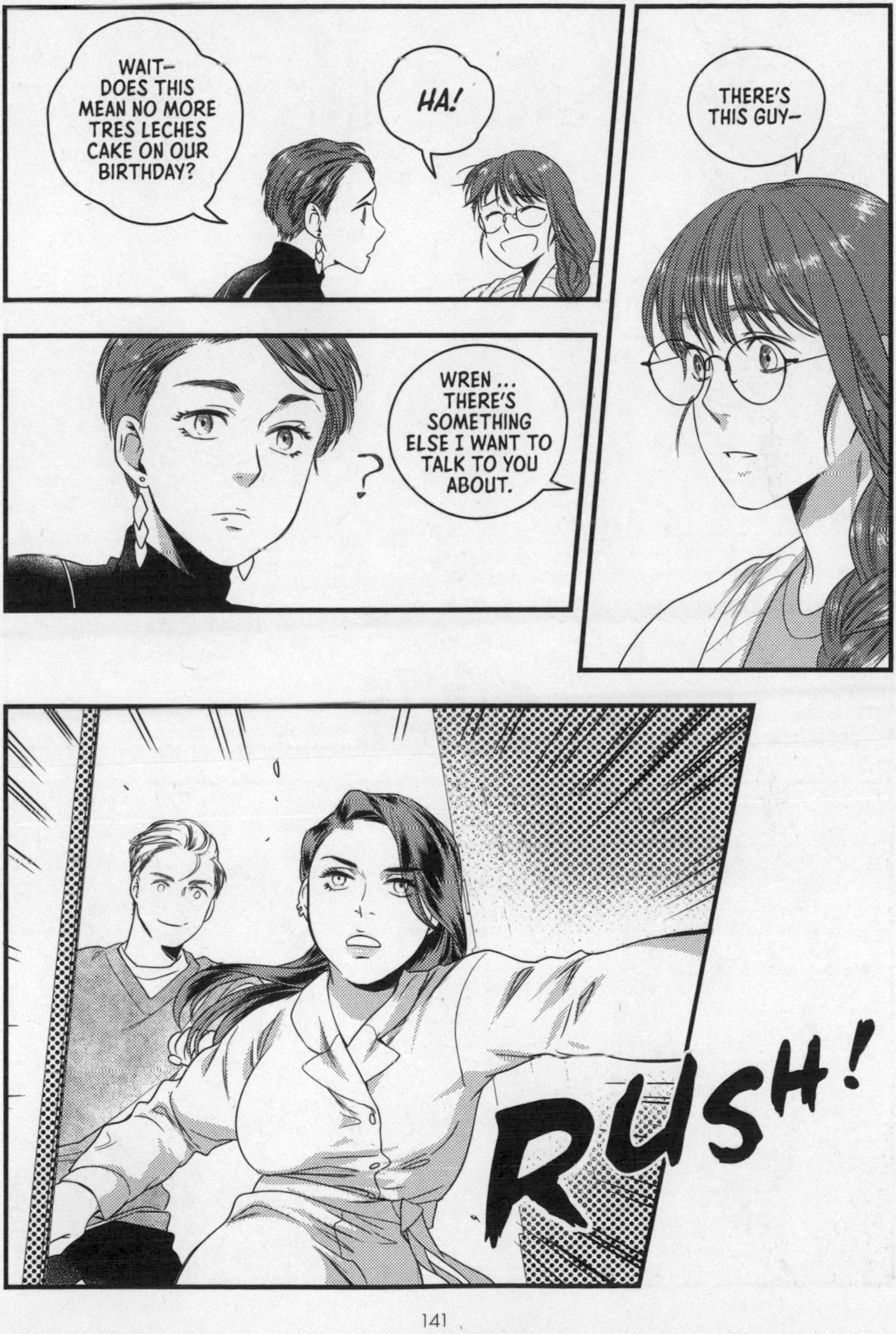
WAIT— DOES THIS MEAN NO MORE TRES LECHES CAKE ON OUR BIRTHDAY?
HA!
?
WREN ... THERE'S SOMETHING ELSE I WANT TO TALK TO YOU ABOUT.
THERE'S THIS GUY—
RUSH!

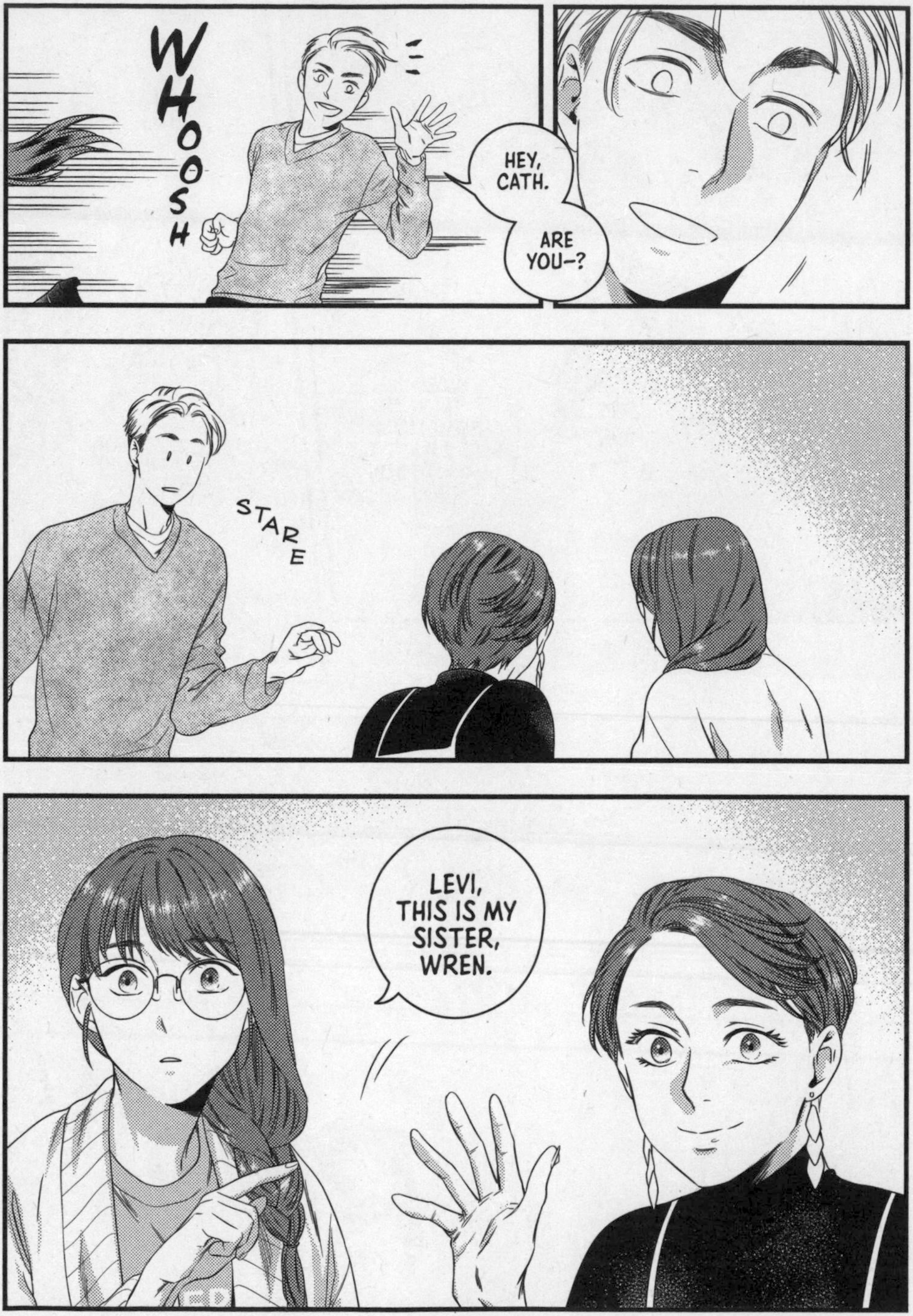
WHOOSH
HEY, CATH.
ARE YOU–?
STARE
LEVI, THIS IS MY SISTER, WREN.

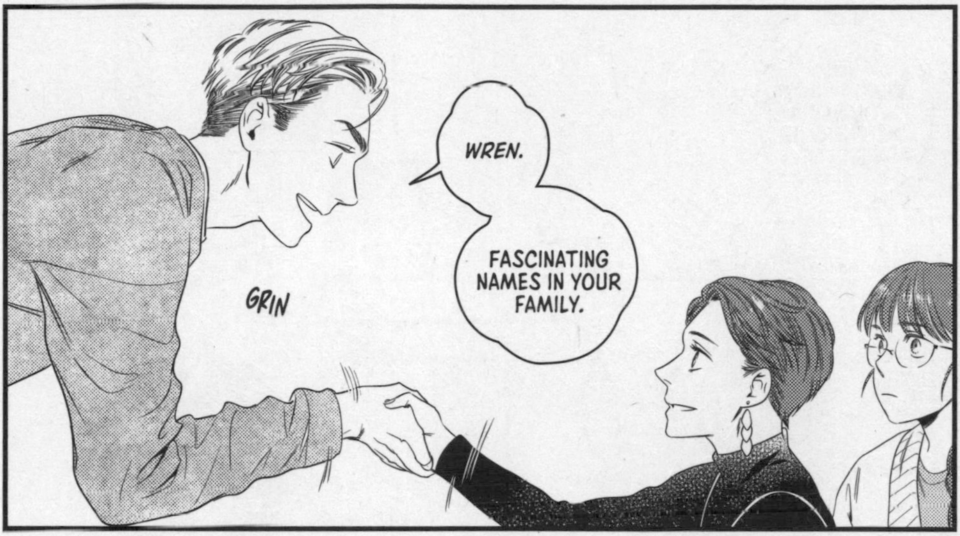
WREN.
FASCINATING NAMES IN YOUR FAMILY.
GRIN

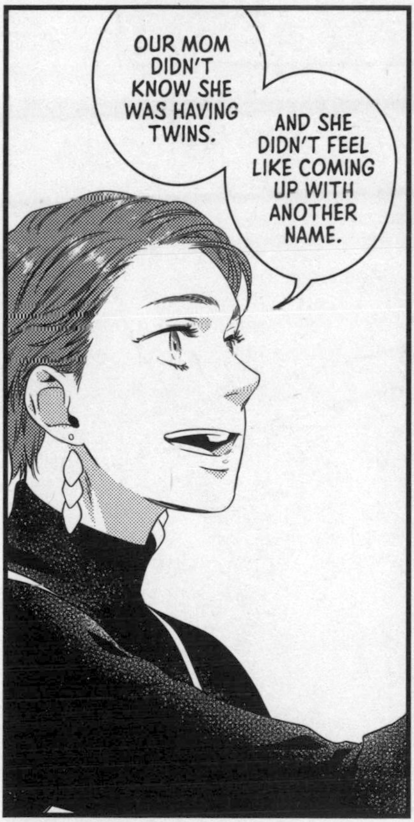
OUR MOM DIDN'T KNOW SHE WAS HAVING TWINS.
AND SHE DIDN'T FEEL LIKE COMING UP WITH ANOTHER NAME.

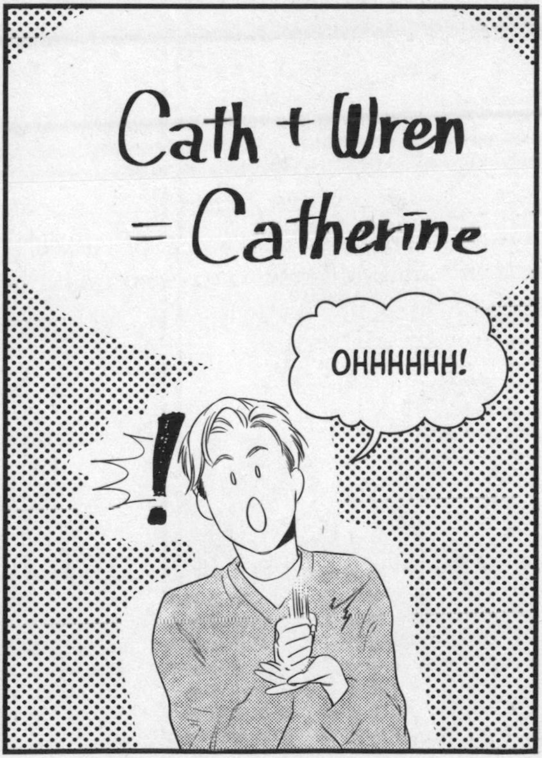
Cath + Wren
= Catherine
OHHHHHH!

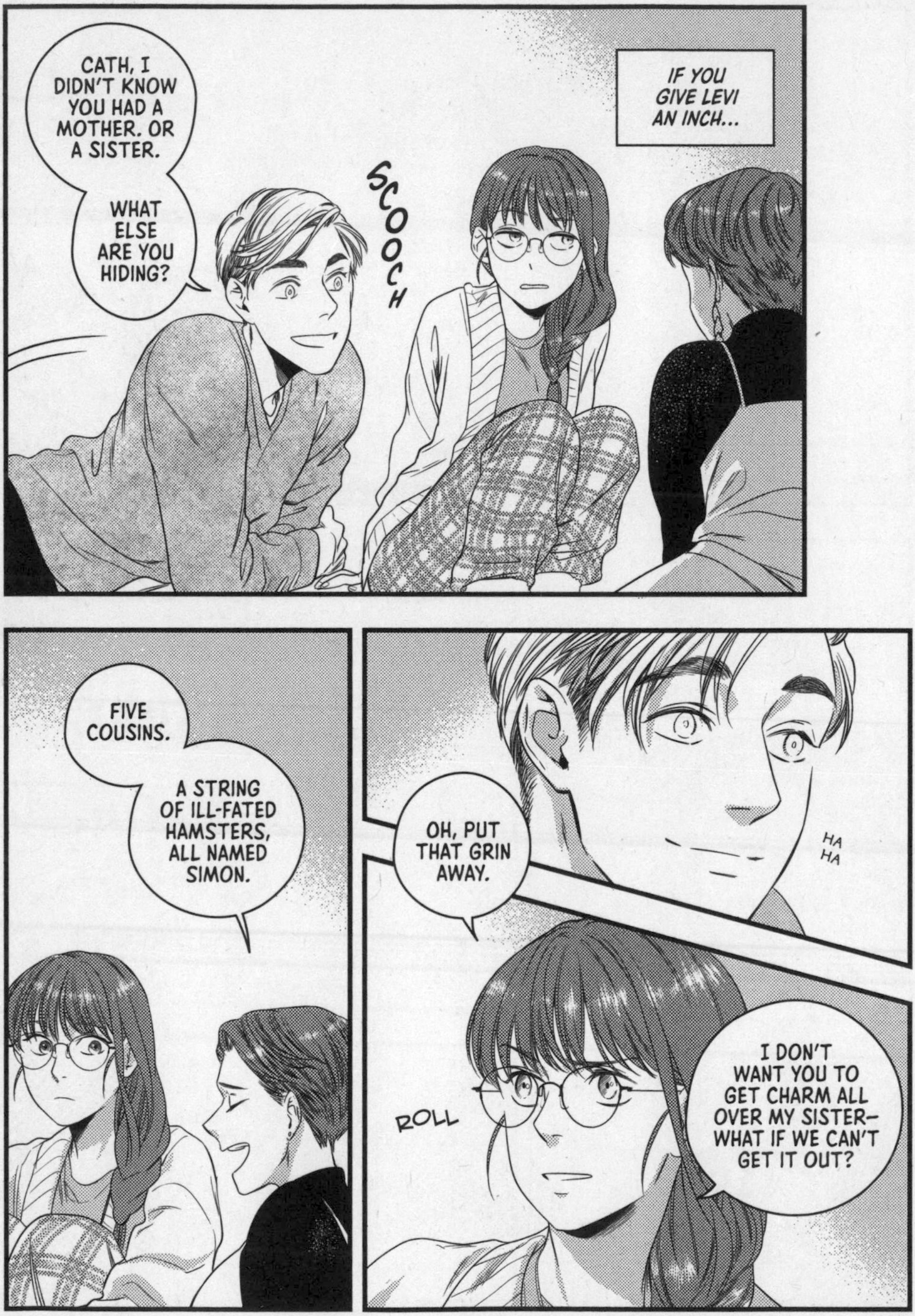
CATH, I DIDN'T KNOW YOU HAD A MOTHER. OR A SISTER.
WHAT ELSE ARE YOU HIDING?
SCOOCH
IF YOU GIVE LEVI AN INCH...
FIVE COUSINS.
A STRING OF ILL-FATED HAMSTERS, ALL NAMED SIMON.
OH, PUT THAT GRIN AWAY.
HA HA
ROLL
I DON'T WANT YOU TO GET CHARM ALL OVER MY SISTER— WHAT IF WE CAN'T GET IT OUT?

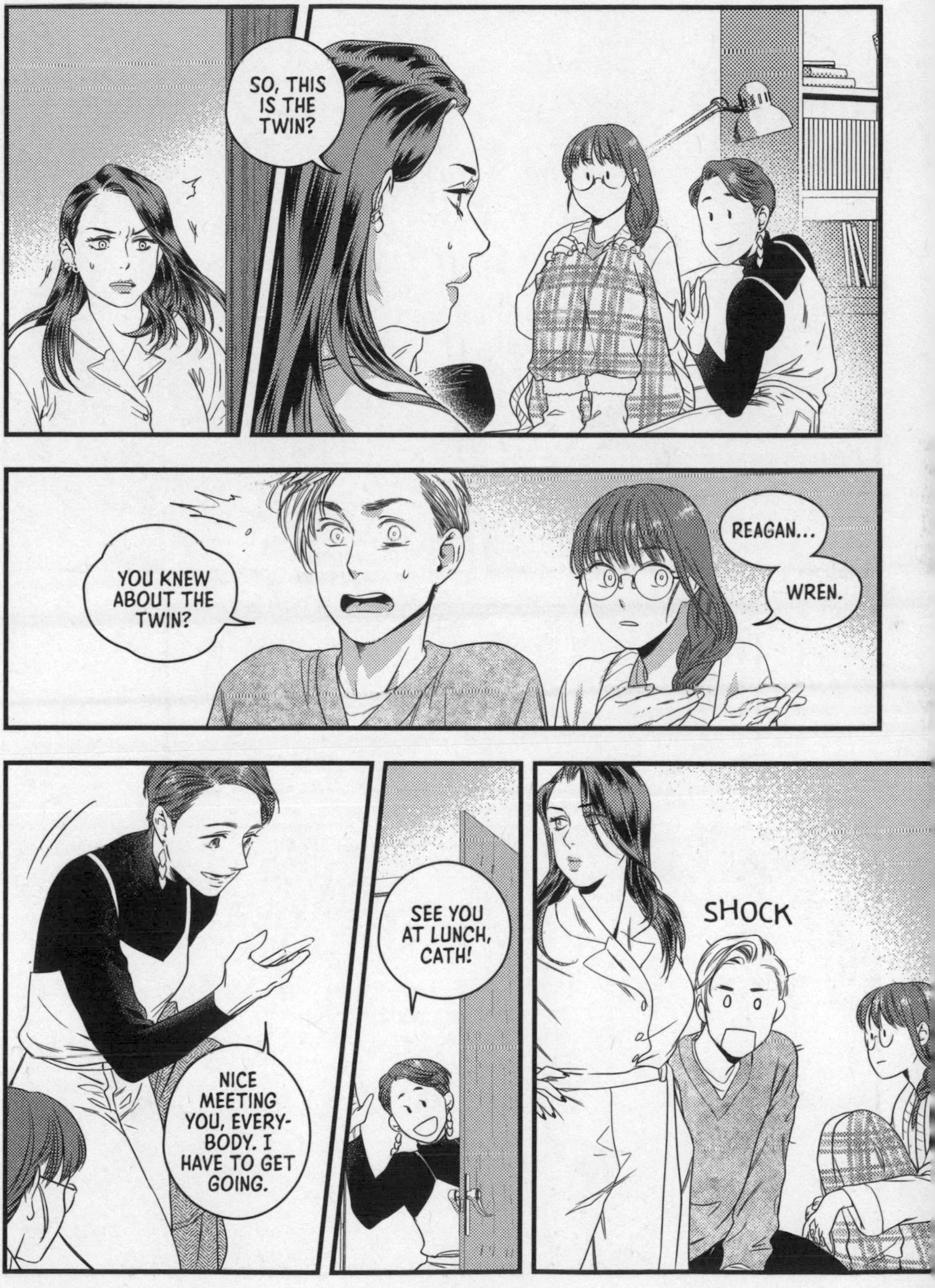
SO, THIS IS THE TWIN?
YOU KNEW ABOUT THE TWIN?
REAGAN...
WREN.
NICE MEETING YOU, EVERY-BODY. I HAVE TO GET GOING.
SEE YOU AT LUNCH, CATH!
SHOCK

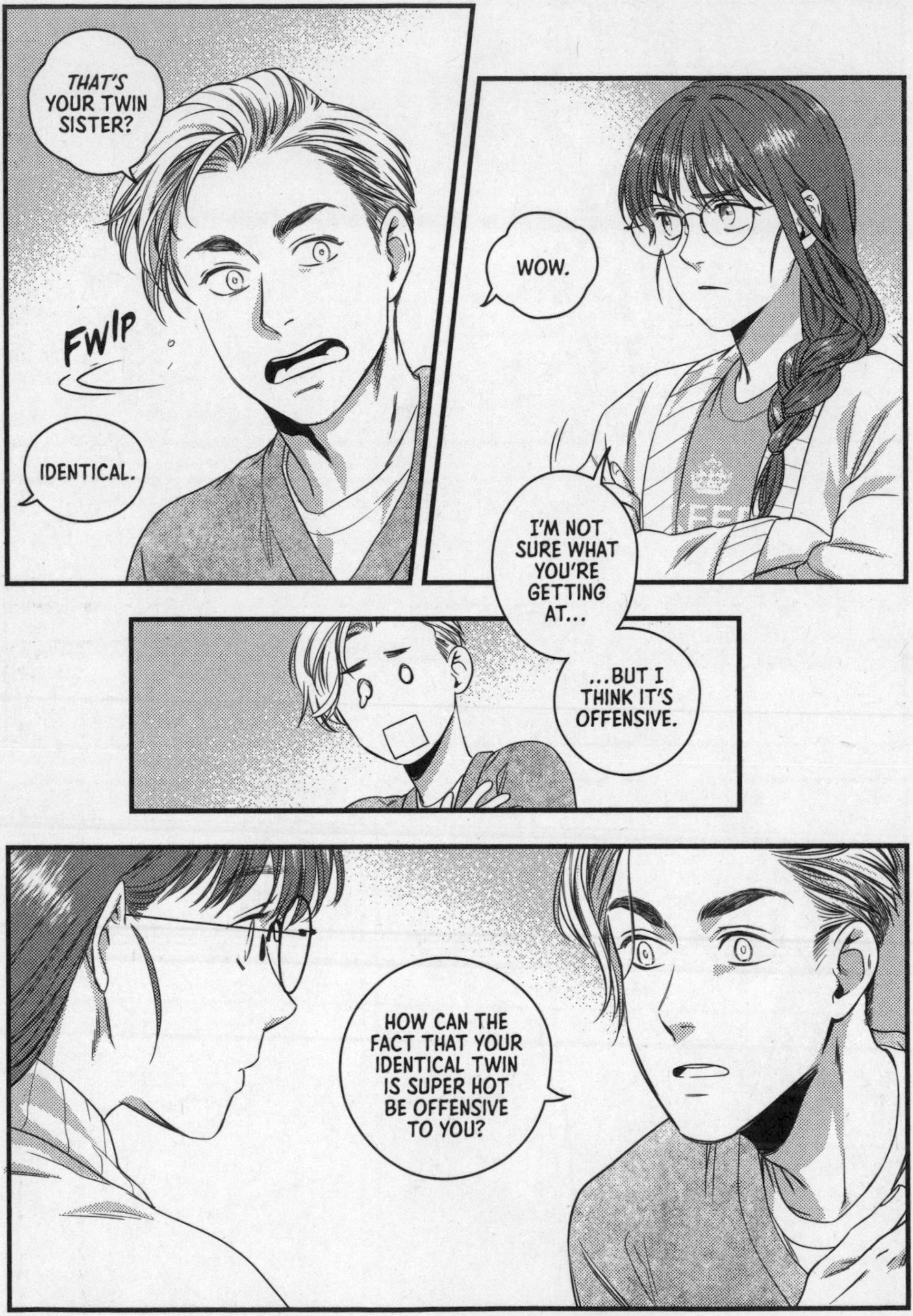
THAT'S YOUR TWIN SISTER?
FWIP
IDENTICAL.
WOW.
I'M NOT SURE WHAT YOU'RE GETTING AT...
...BUT I THINK IT'S OFFENSIVE.
HOW CAN THE FACT THAT YOUR IDENTICAL TWIN IS SUPER HOT BE OFFENSIVE TO YOU?

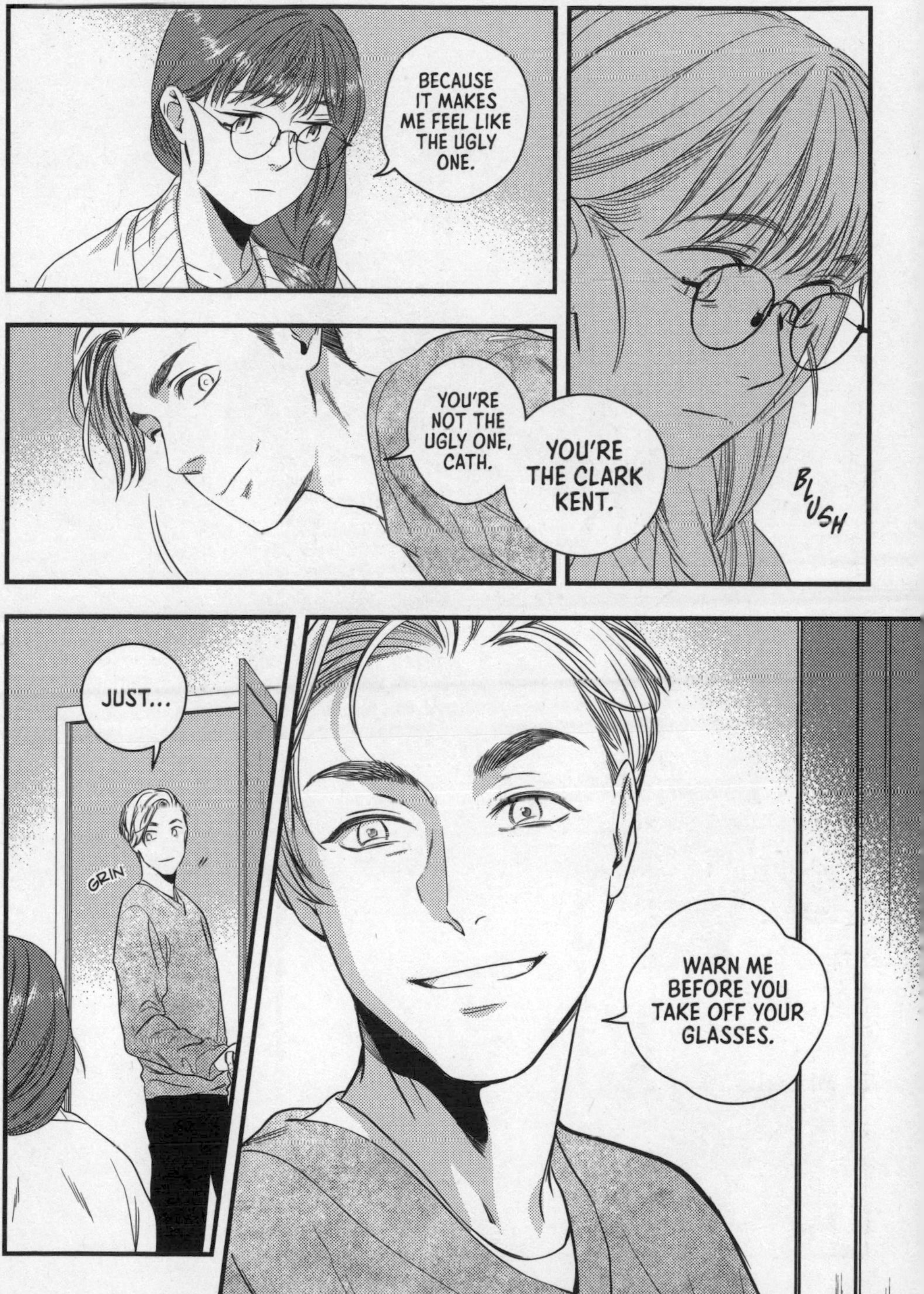
BECAUSE IT MAKES ME FEEL LIKE THE UGLY ONE.
YOU'RE NOT THE UGLY ONE, CATH.
YOU'RE THE CLARK KENT.
BLUSH
JUST...
GRIN
WARN ME BEFORE YOU TAKE OFF YOUR GLASSES.

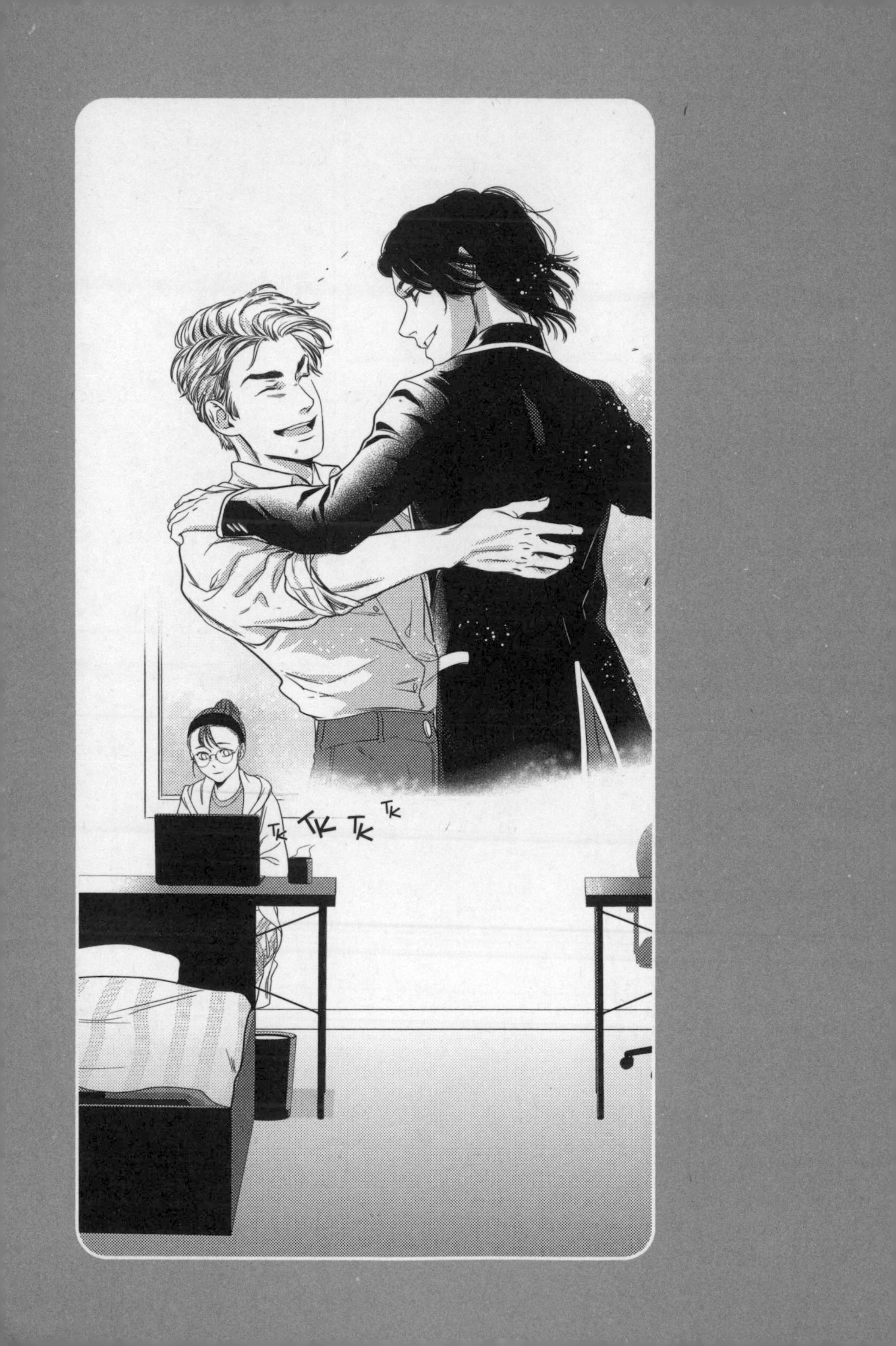
TK TK TK TK

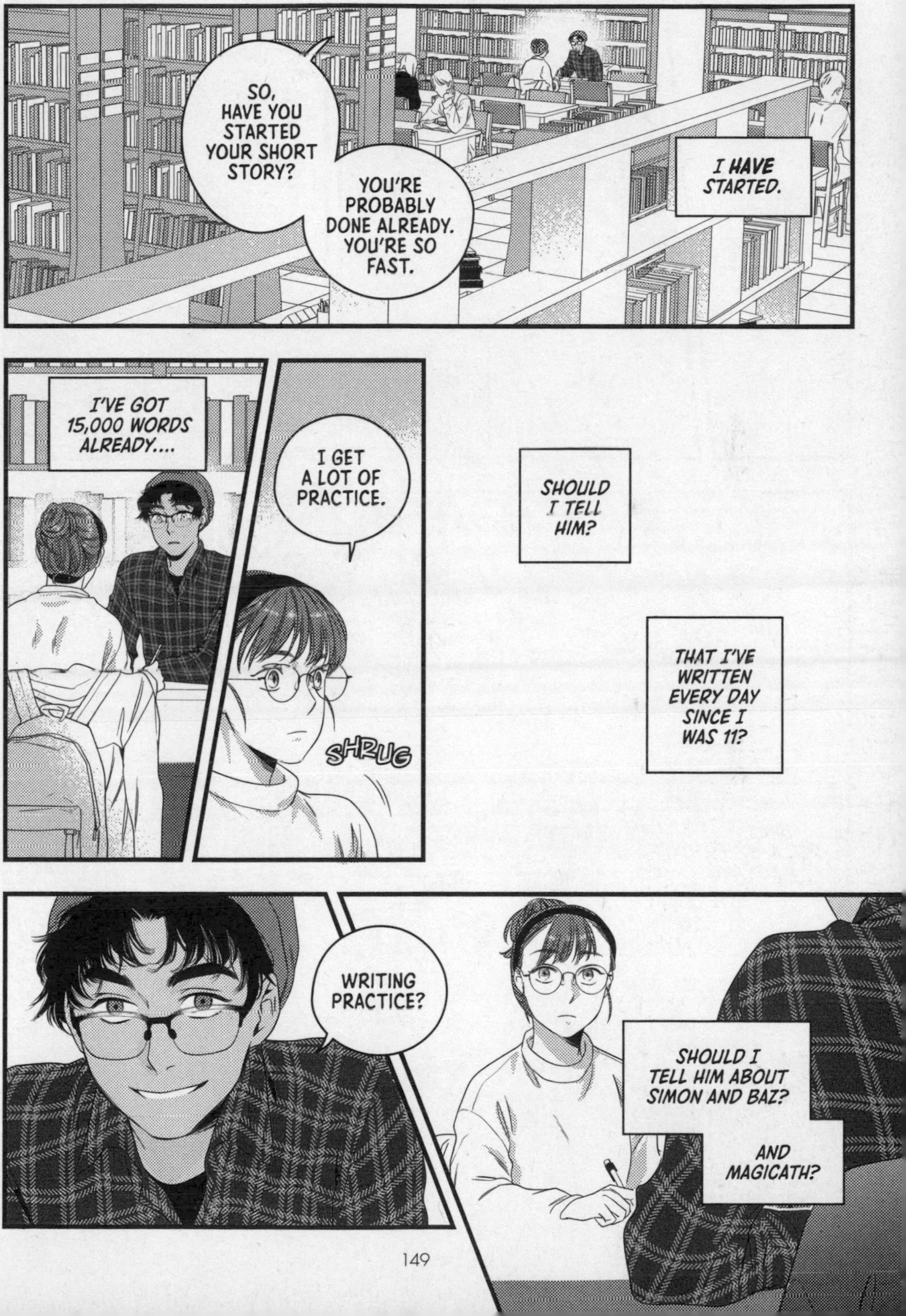
SO, HAVE YOU STARTED YOUR SHORT STORY?
YOU'RE PROBABLY DONE ALREADY. YOU'RE SO FAST.
I HAVE STARTED.
I'VE GOT 15,000 WORDS ALREADY....
I GET A LOT OF PRACTICE.
SHRUG
SHOULD I TELL HIM?
THAT I'VE WRITTEN EVERY DAY SINCE I WAS 11?
WRITING PRACTICE?
SHOULD I TELL HIM ABOUT SIMON AND BAZ?
AND MAGICATH?

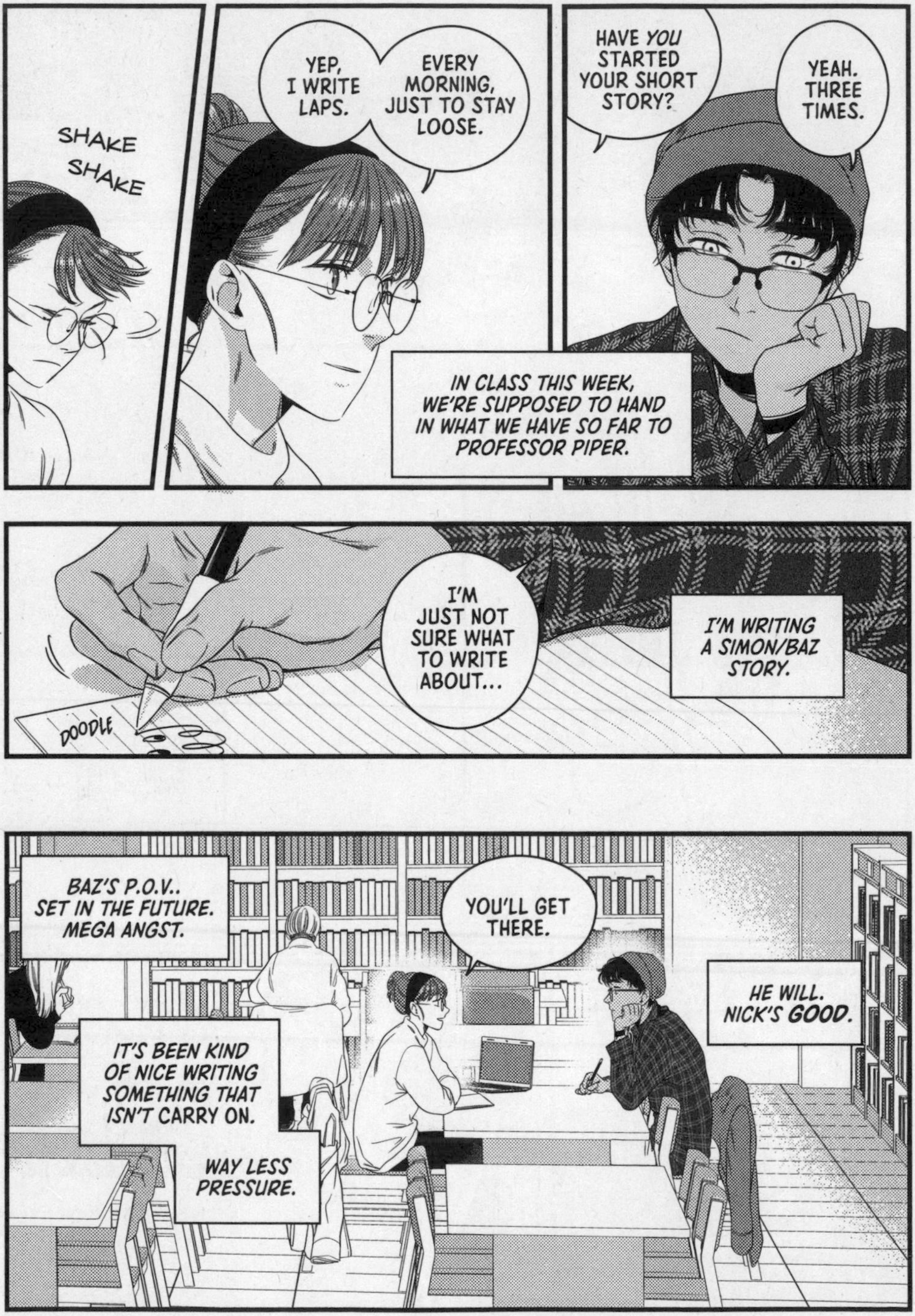
SHAKE
SHAKE
YEP, I WRITE LAPS.
EVERY MORNING, JUST TO STAY LOOSE.
HAVE *YOU* STARTED YOUR SHORT STORY?
YEAH. THREE TIMES.
IN CLASS THIS WEEK, WE'RE SUPPOSED TO HAND IN WHAT WE HAVE SO FAR TO PROFESSOR PIPER.
DOODLE
I'M JUST NOT SURE WHAT TO WRITE ABOUT...
I'M WRITING A SIMON/BAZ STORY.
BAZ'S P.O.V.. SET IN THE FUTURE. MEGA ANGST.
YOU'LL GET THERE.
IT'S BEEN KIND OF NICE WRITING SOMETHING THAT ISN'T CARRY ON.
WAY LESS PRESSURE.
HE WILL. NICK'S **GOOD**.

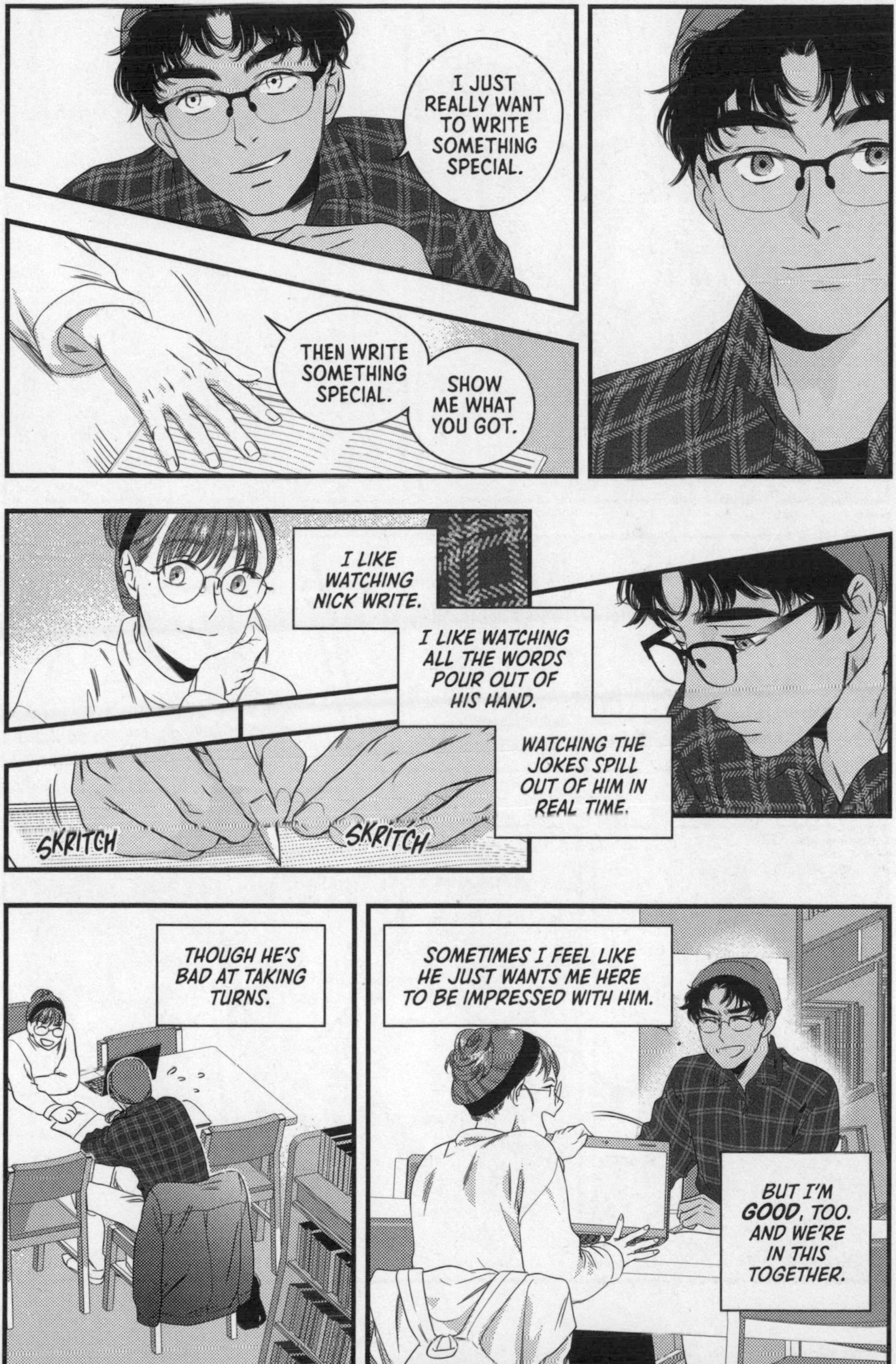
I JUST REALLY WANT TO WRITE SOMETHING SPECIAL.
THEN WRITE SOMETHING SPECIAL.
SHOW ME WHAT YOU GOT.
I LIKE WATCHING NICK WRITE.
I LIKE WATCHING ALL THE WORDS POUR OUT OF HIS HAND.
WATCHING THE JOKES SPILL OUT OF HIM IN REAL TIME.
SKRITCH
SKRITCH
THOUGH HE'S BAD AT TAKING TURNS.
SOMETIMES I FEEL LIKE HE JUST WANTS ME HERE TO BE IMPRESSED WITH HIM.
BUT I'M **GOOD**, TOO. AND WE'RE IN THIS TOGETHER.

OKAY, EVERY-BODY...

HAND IN WHAT YOU HAVE OF YOUR SHORT STORIES SO FAR—

"The Nemesis"
By Cather Avery

Fiction-Writing 300/Pages
...-Progress Ch

HEY!

SNATCH

SNATCH

PET!

THANK YOU, CATH.

I CAN HARDLY WAIT.

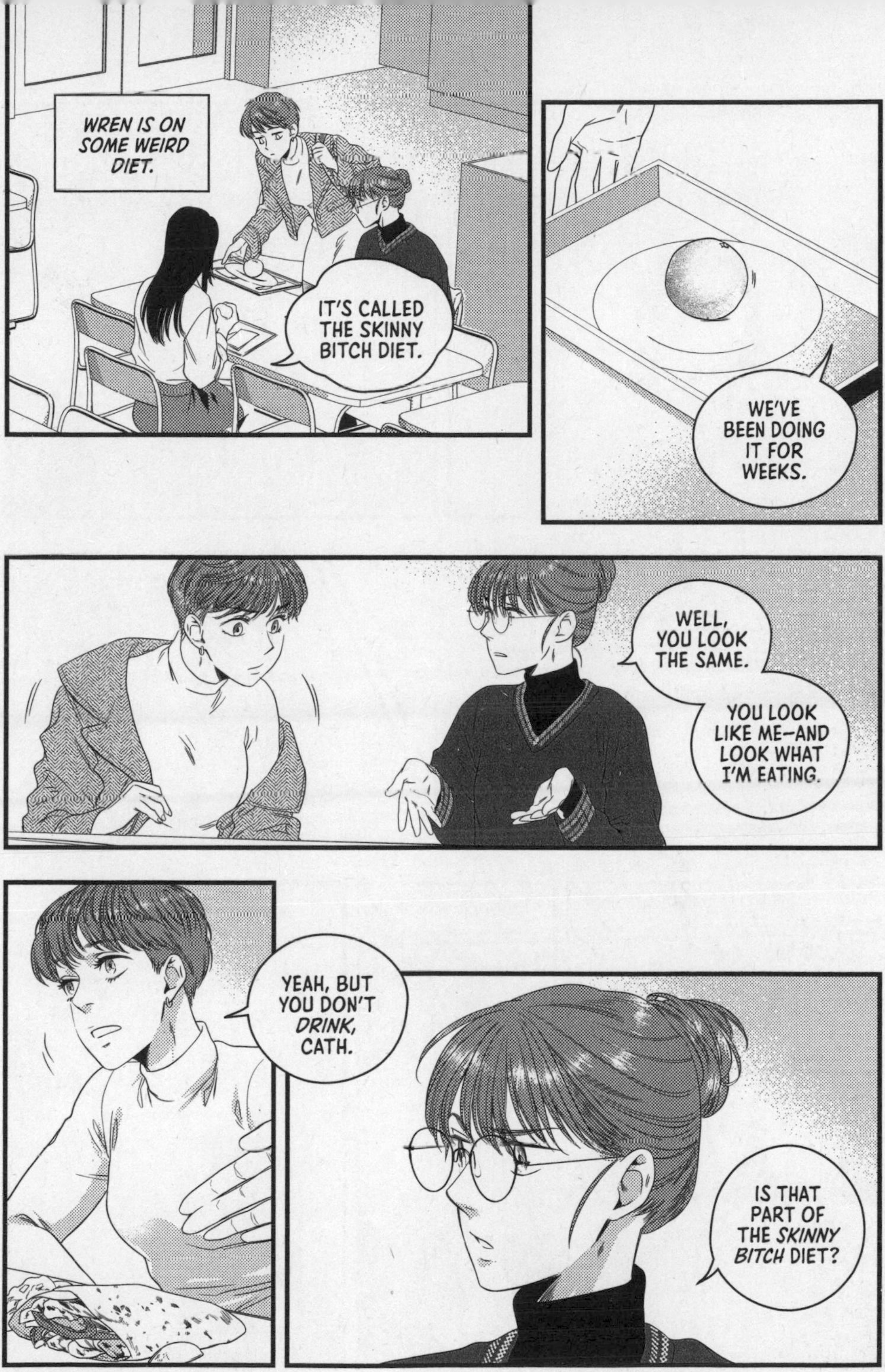
WREN IS ON SOME WEIRD DIET.
IT'S CALLED THE SKINNY BITCH DIET.
WE'VE BEEN DOING IT FOR WEEKS.
WELL, YOU LOOK THE SAME.
YOU LOOK LIKE ME—AND LOOK WHAT I'M EATING.
YEAH, BUT YOU DON'T *DRINK*, CATH.
IS THAT PART OF THE *SKINNY BITCH* DIET?

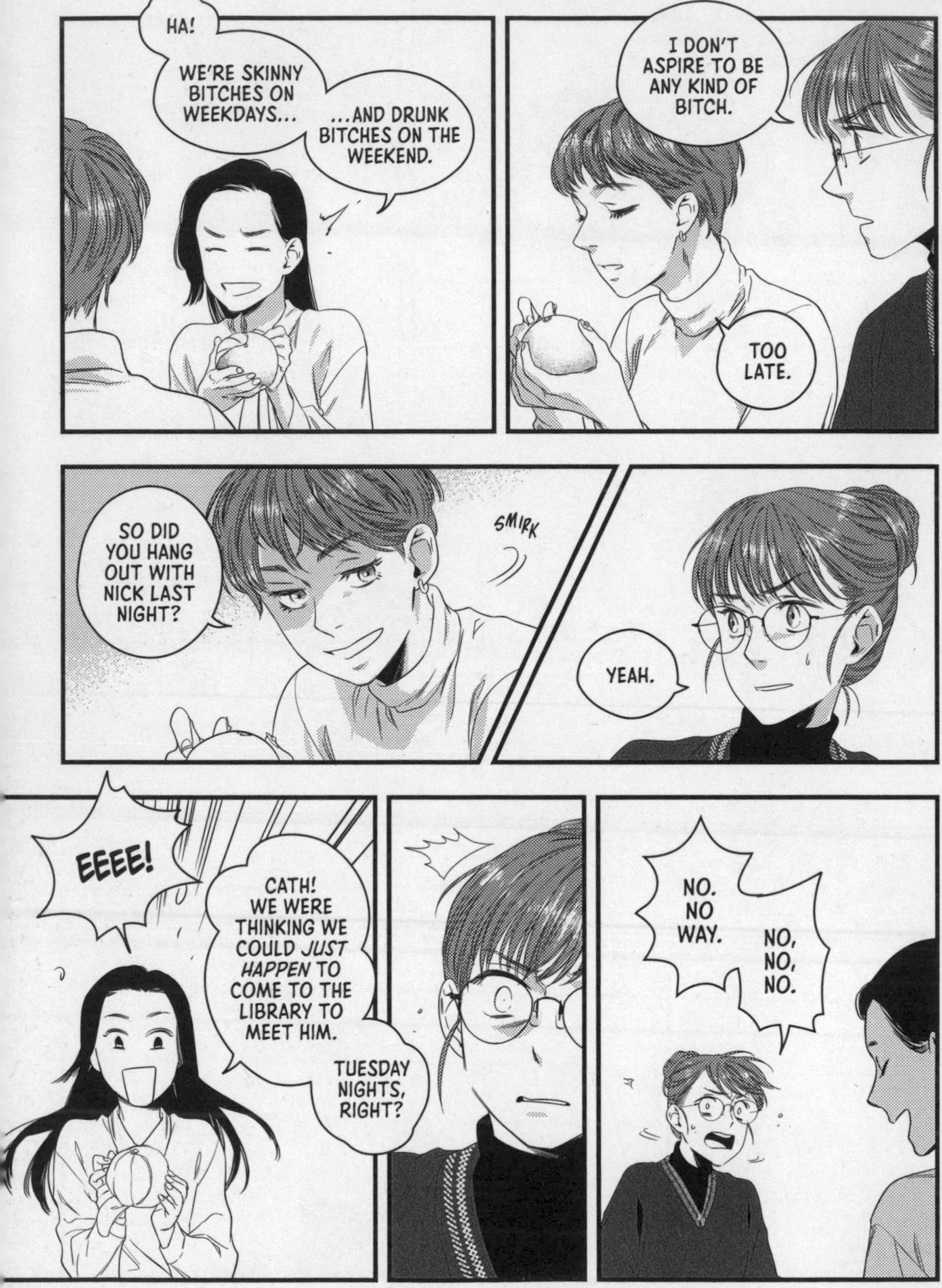
HA!
WE'RE SKINNY BITCHES ON WEEKDAYS...
...AND DRUNK BITCHES ON THE WEEKEND.
I DON'T ASPIRE TO BE ANY KIND OF BITCH.
TOO LATE.
SO DID YOU HANG OUT WITH NICK LAST NIGHT?
SMIRK
YEAH.
EEEE!
CATH! WE WERE THINKING WE COULD *JUST HAPPEN* TO COME TO THE LIBRARY TO MEET HIM.
TUESDAY NIGHTS, RIGHT?
NO. NO WAY.
NO, NO, NO.

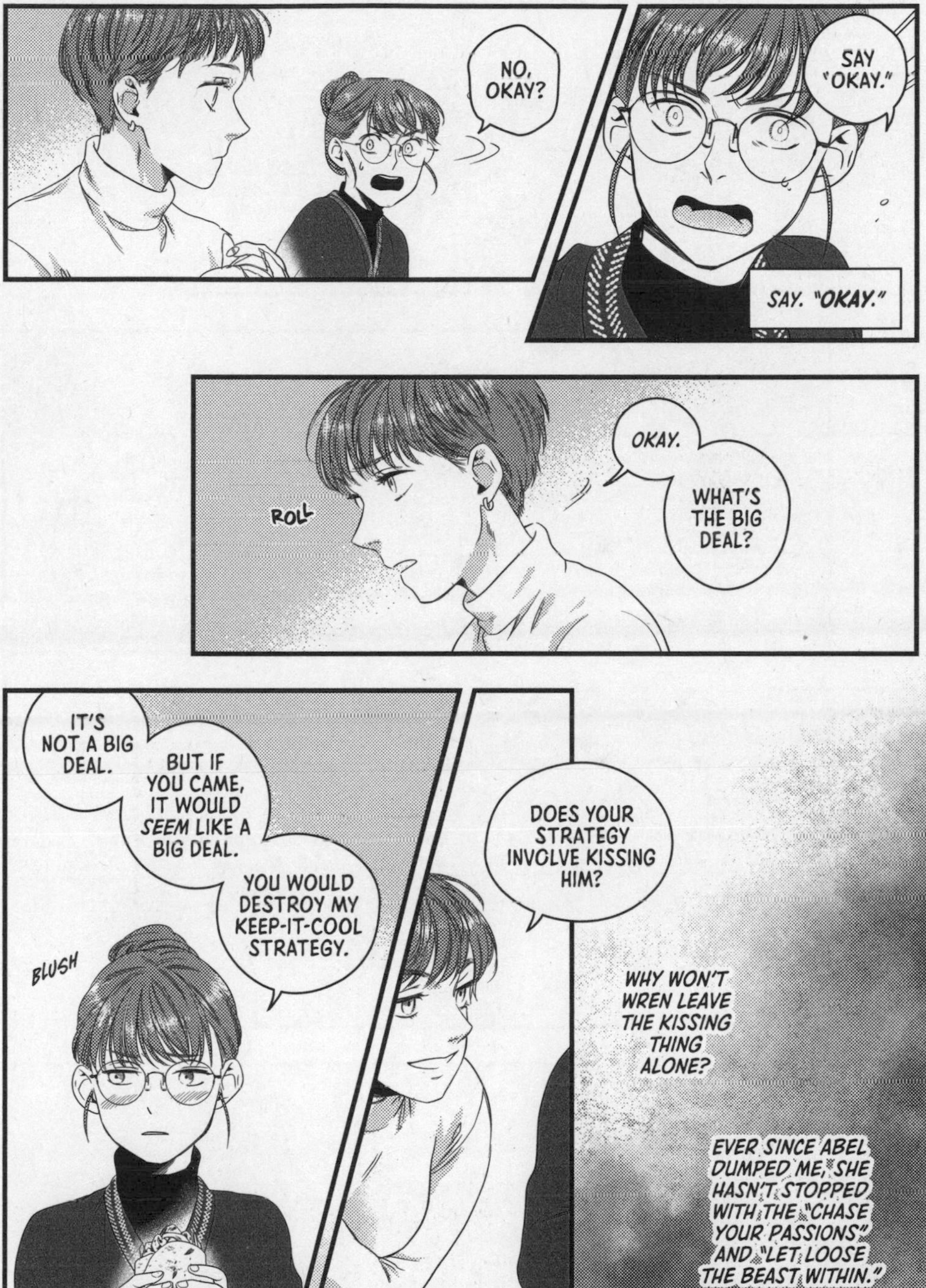
NO, OKAY?
SAY "OKAY."
SAY. "OKAY."
ROLL
OKAY.
WHAT'S THE BIG DEAL?
IT'S NOT A BIG DEAL.
BUT IF YOU CAME, IT WOULD *SEEM* LIKE A BIG DEAL.
YOU WOULD DESTROY MY KEEP-IT-COOL STRATEGY.
BLUSH
DOES YOUR STRATEGY INVOLVE KISSING HIM?
WHY WON'T WREN LEAVE THE KISSING THING ALONE?
EVER SINCE ABEL DUMPED ME, SHE HASN'T STOPPED WITH THE "CHASE YOUR PASSIONS" AND "LET LOOSE THE BEAST WITHIN."

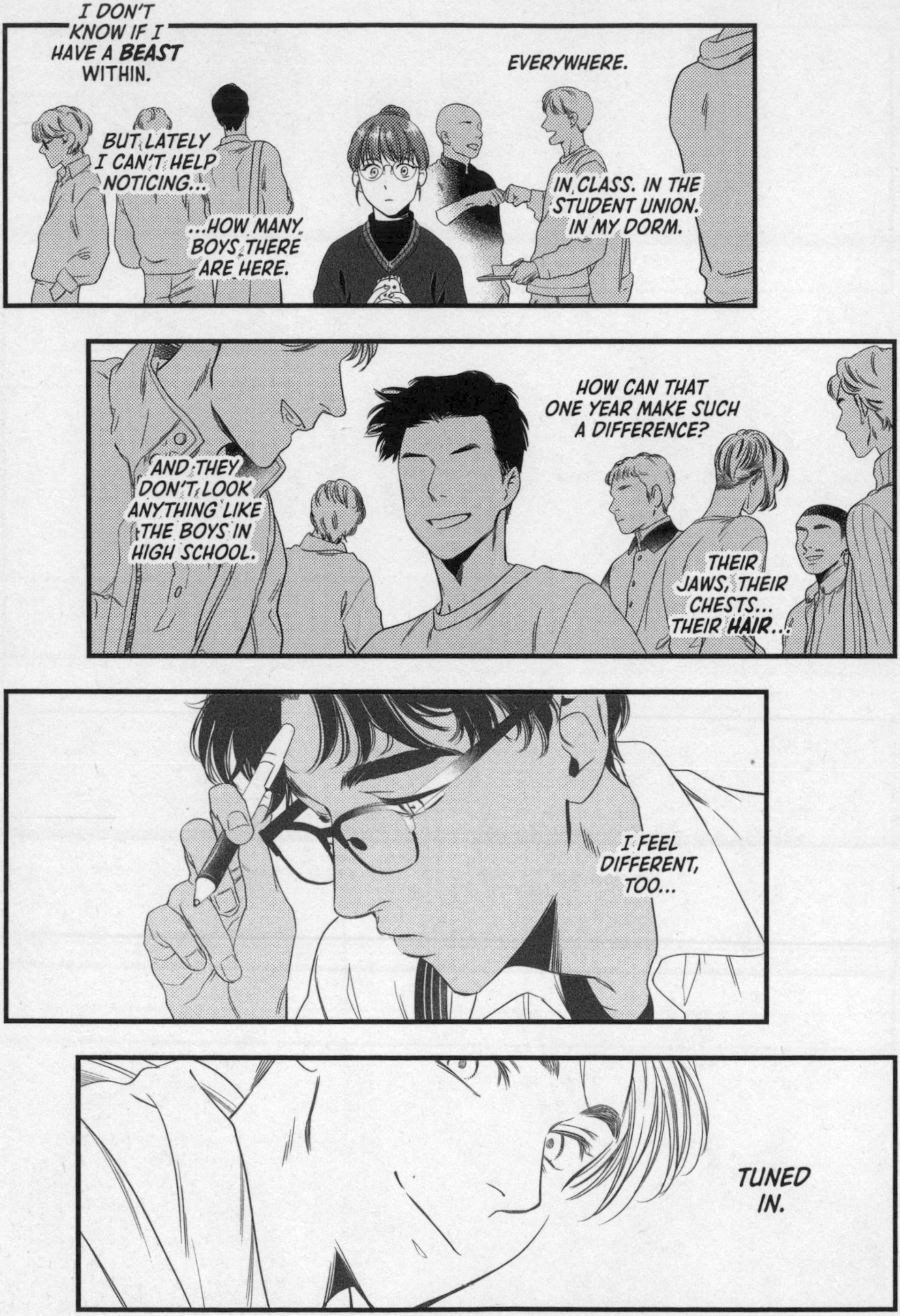
I DON'T KNOW IF I HAVE A **BEAST** WITHIN.
BUT LATELY I CAN'T HELP NOTICING...
...HOW MANY BOYS THERE ARE HERE.
EVERYWHERE.
IN CLASS. IN THE STUDENT UNION. IN MY DORM.
AND THEY DON'T LOOK ANYTHING LIKE THE BOYS IN HIGH SCHOOL.
HOW CAN THAT ONE YEAR MAKE SUCH A DIFFERENCE?
THEIR JAWS, THEIR CHESTS... THEIR **HAIR**...
I FEEL DIFFERENT, TOO...
TUNED IN.

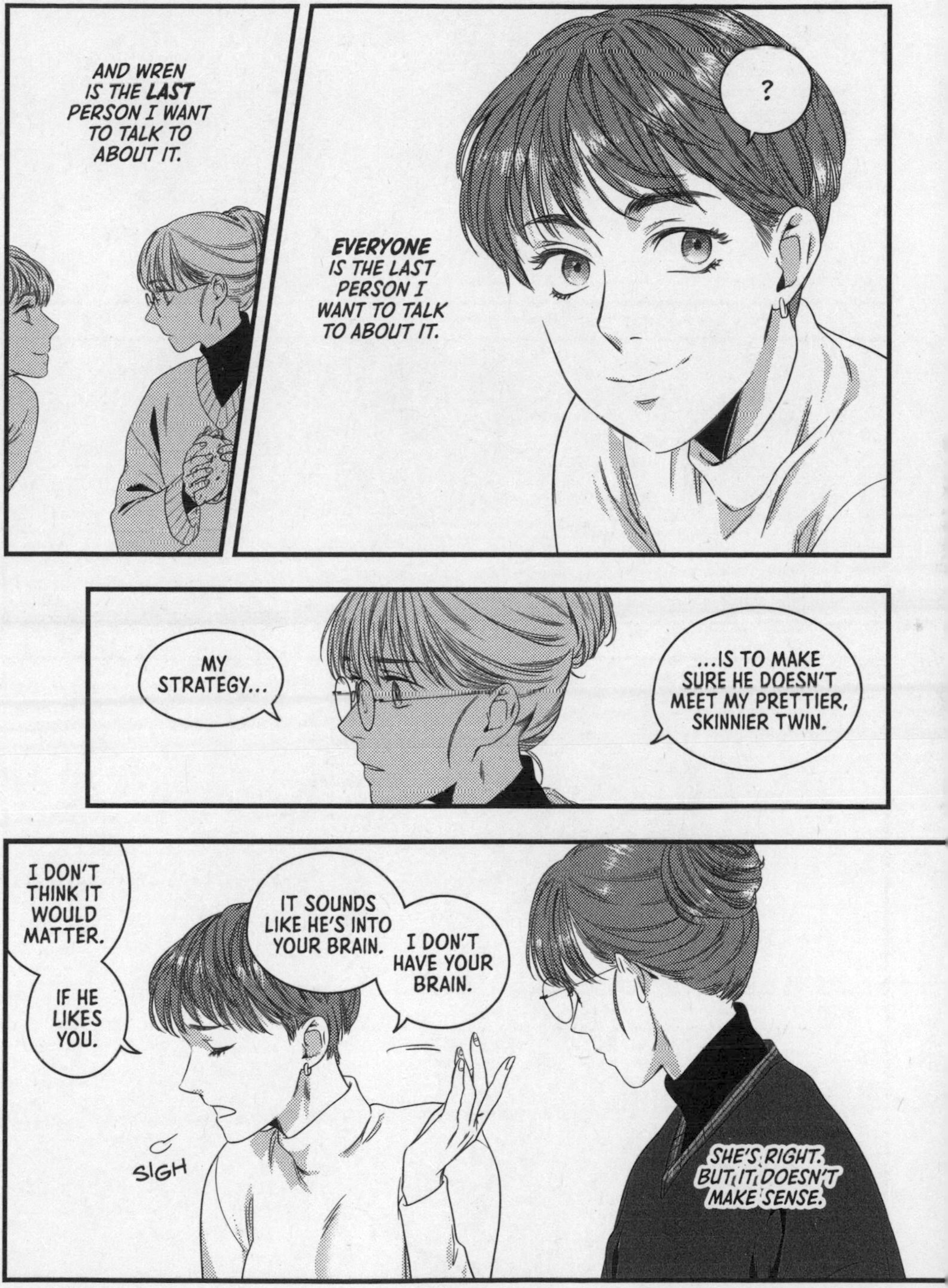
AND WREN IS THE LAST PERSON I WANT TO TALK TO ABOUT IT.
?
EVERYONE IS THE LAST PERSON I WANT TO TALK TO ABOUT IT.
MY STRATEGY...
...IS TO MAKE SURE HE DOESN'T MEET MY PRETTIER, SKINNIER TWIN.
I DON'T THINK IT WOULD MATTER.
IF HE LIKES YOU.
IT SOUNDS LIKE HE'S INTO YOUR BRAIN.
I DON'T HAVE YOUR BRAIN.
SIGH
SHE'S RIGHT. BUT IT DOESN'T MAKE SENSE.

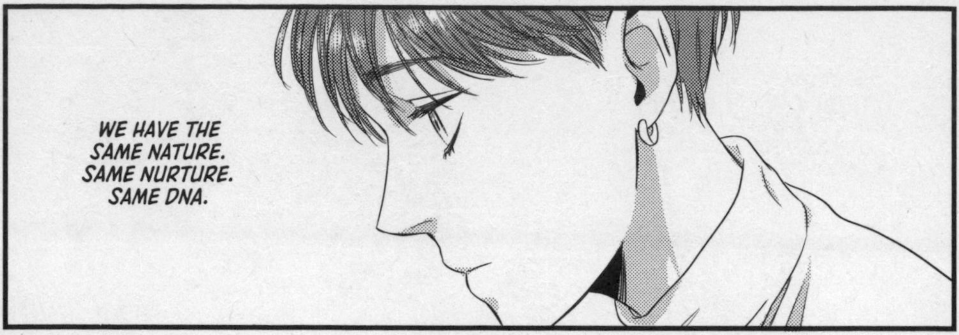
WE HAVE THE SAME NATURE. SAME NURTURE. SAME DNA.
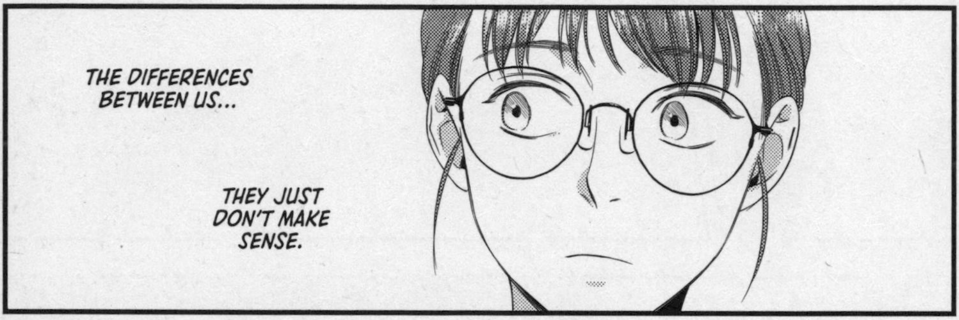
THE DIFFERENCES BETWEEN US...
THEY JUST DON'T MAKE SENSE.
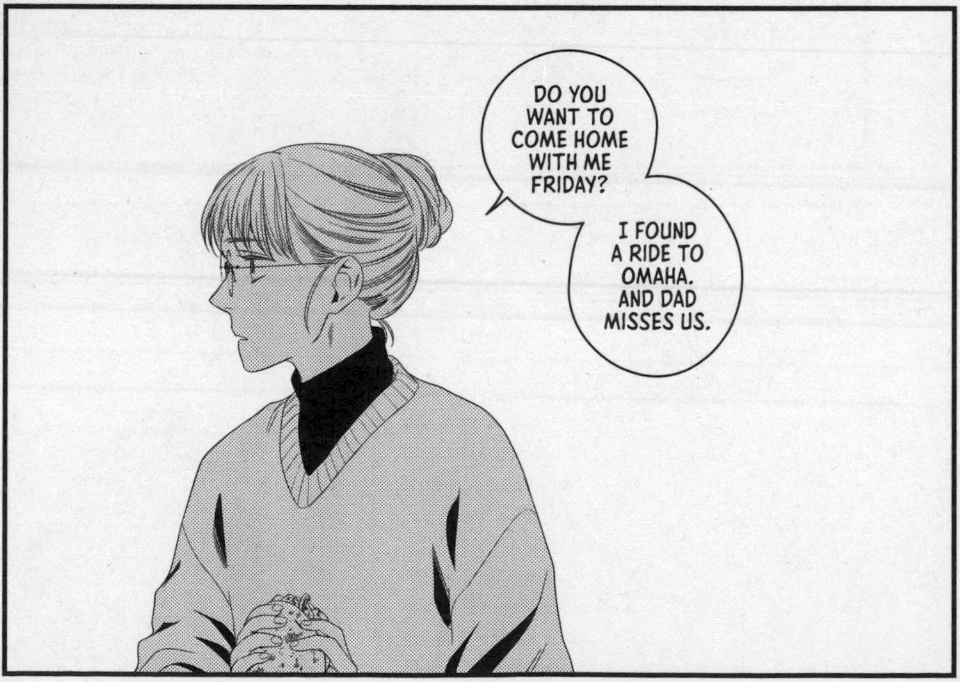
DO YOU WANT TO COME HOME WITH ME FRIDAY?
I FOUND A RIDE TO OMAHA. AND DAD MISSES US.

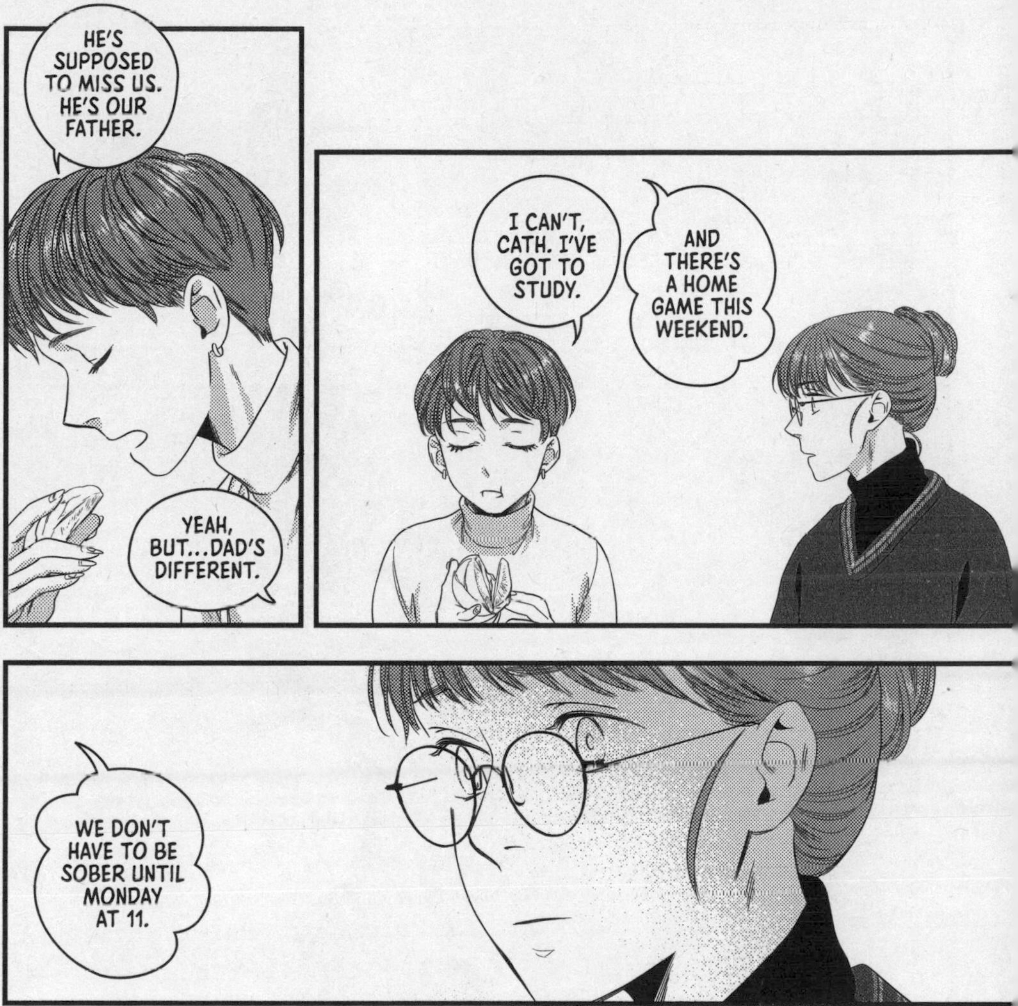
HE'S SUPPOSED TO MISS US. HE'S OUR FATHER.
YEAH, BUT...DAD'S DIFFERENT.
I CAN'T, CATH. I'VE GOT TO STUDY.
AND THERE'S A HOME GAME THIS WEEKEND.
WE DON'T HAVE TO BE SOBER UNTIL MONDAY AT 11.

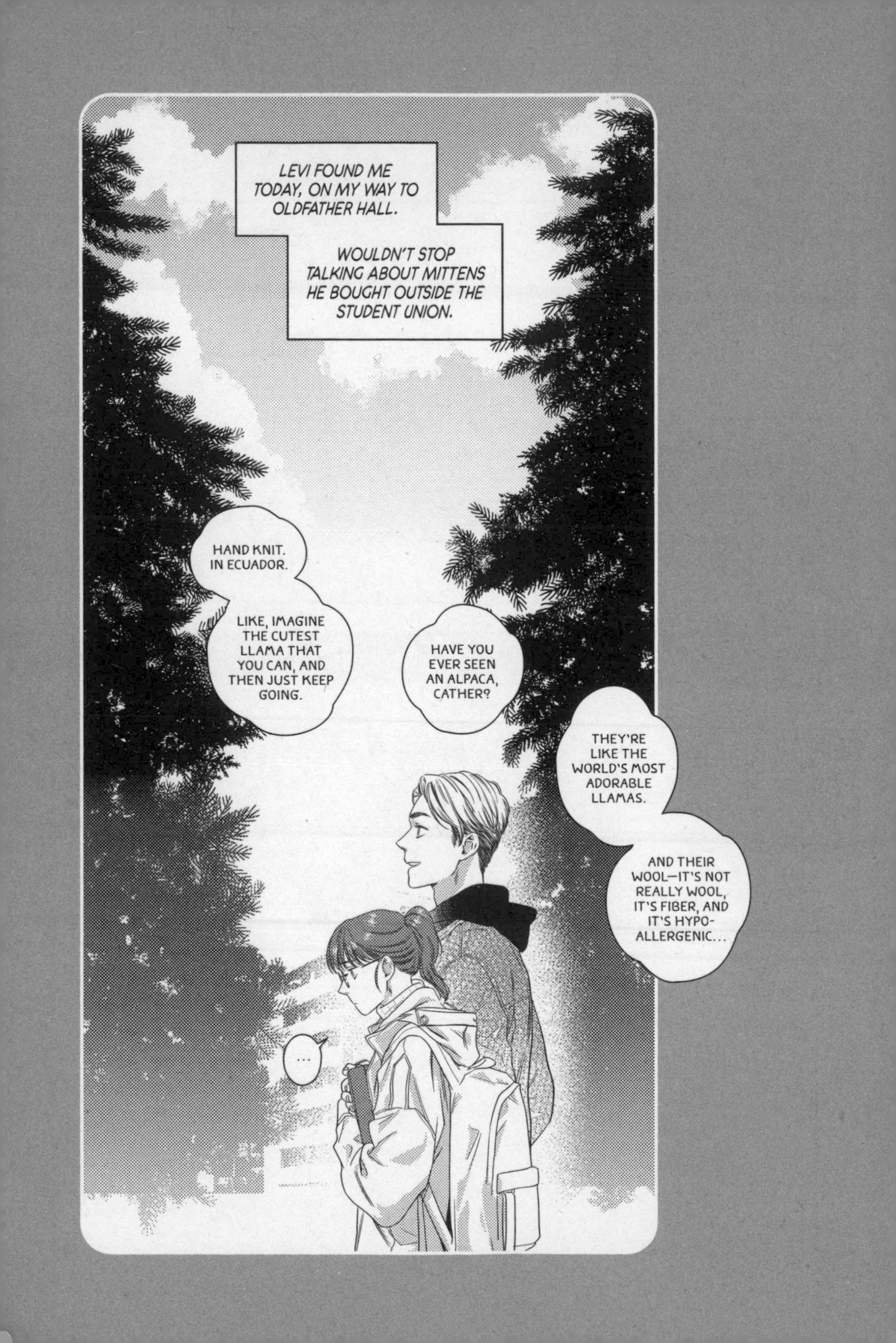
LEVI FOUND ME TODAY, ON MY WAY TO OLDFATHER HALL.
WOULDN'T STOP TALKING ABOUT MITTENS HE BOUGHT OUTSIDE THE STUDENT UNION.
HAND KNIT. IN ECUADOR.
LIKE, IMAGINE THE CUTEST LLAMA THAT YOU CAN, AND THEN JUST KEEP GOING.
HAVE YOU EVER SEEN AN ALPACA, CATHER?
THEY'RE LIKE THE WORLD'S MOST ADORABLE LLAMAS.
AND THEIR WOOL—IT'S NOT REALLY WOOL, IT'S FIBER, AND IT'S HYPO-ALLERGENIC...
...

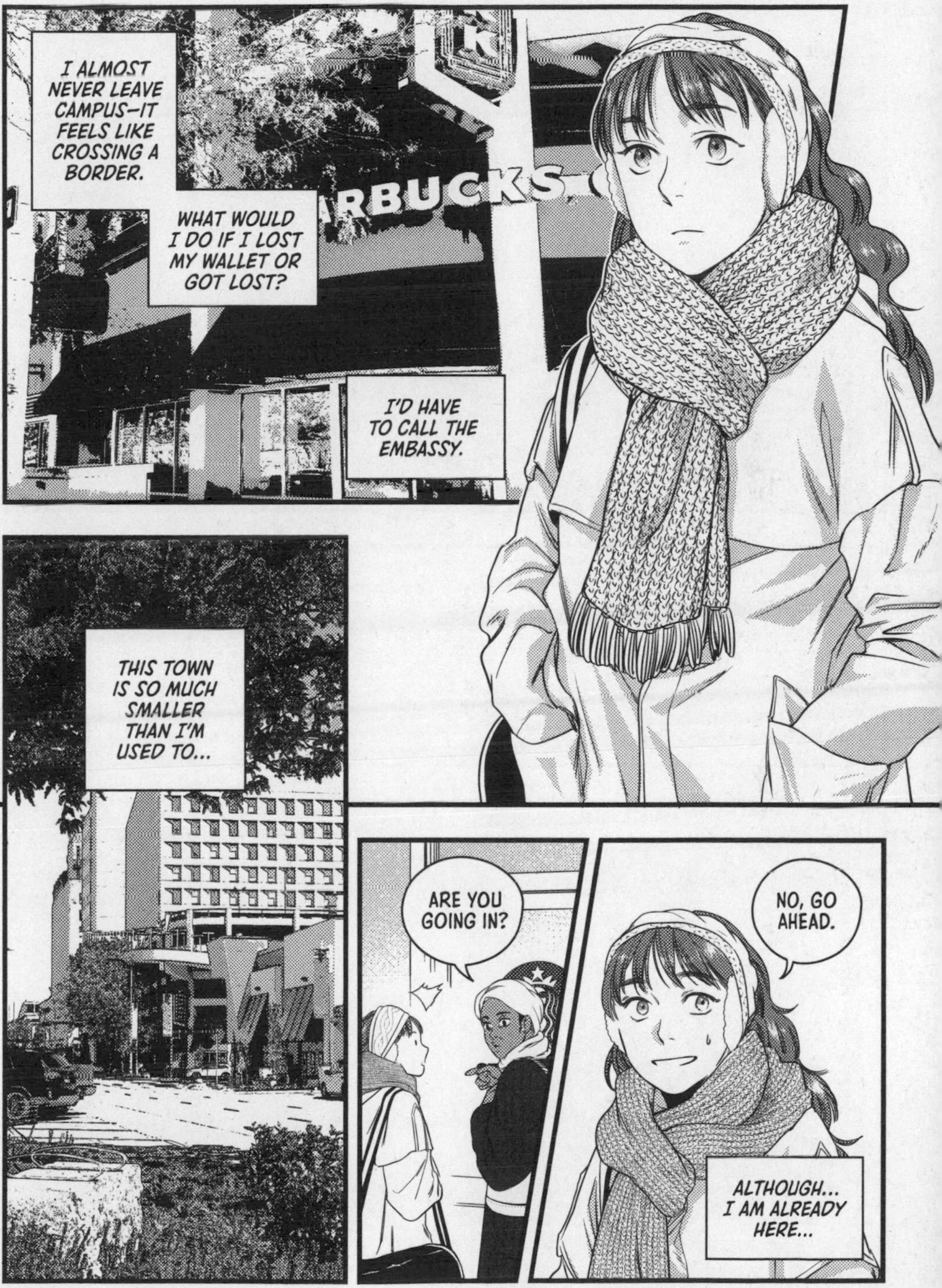
I ALMOST NEVER LEAVE CAMPUS—IT FEELS LIKE CROSSING A BORDER.
WHAT WOULD I DO IF I LOST MY WALLET OR GOT LOST?
I'D HAVE TO CALL THE EMBASSY.
THIS TOWN IS SO MUCH SMALLER THAN I'M USED TO...
ARE YOU GOING IN?
NO, GO AHEAD.
ALTHOUGH... I AM ALREADY HERE...

AND WHAT ARE THE ODDS THIS WOULD BE...

...LEVI'S STARBUCKS?

GRANDE PSL FOR BLAIR?

CAN I HELP YOU?

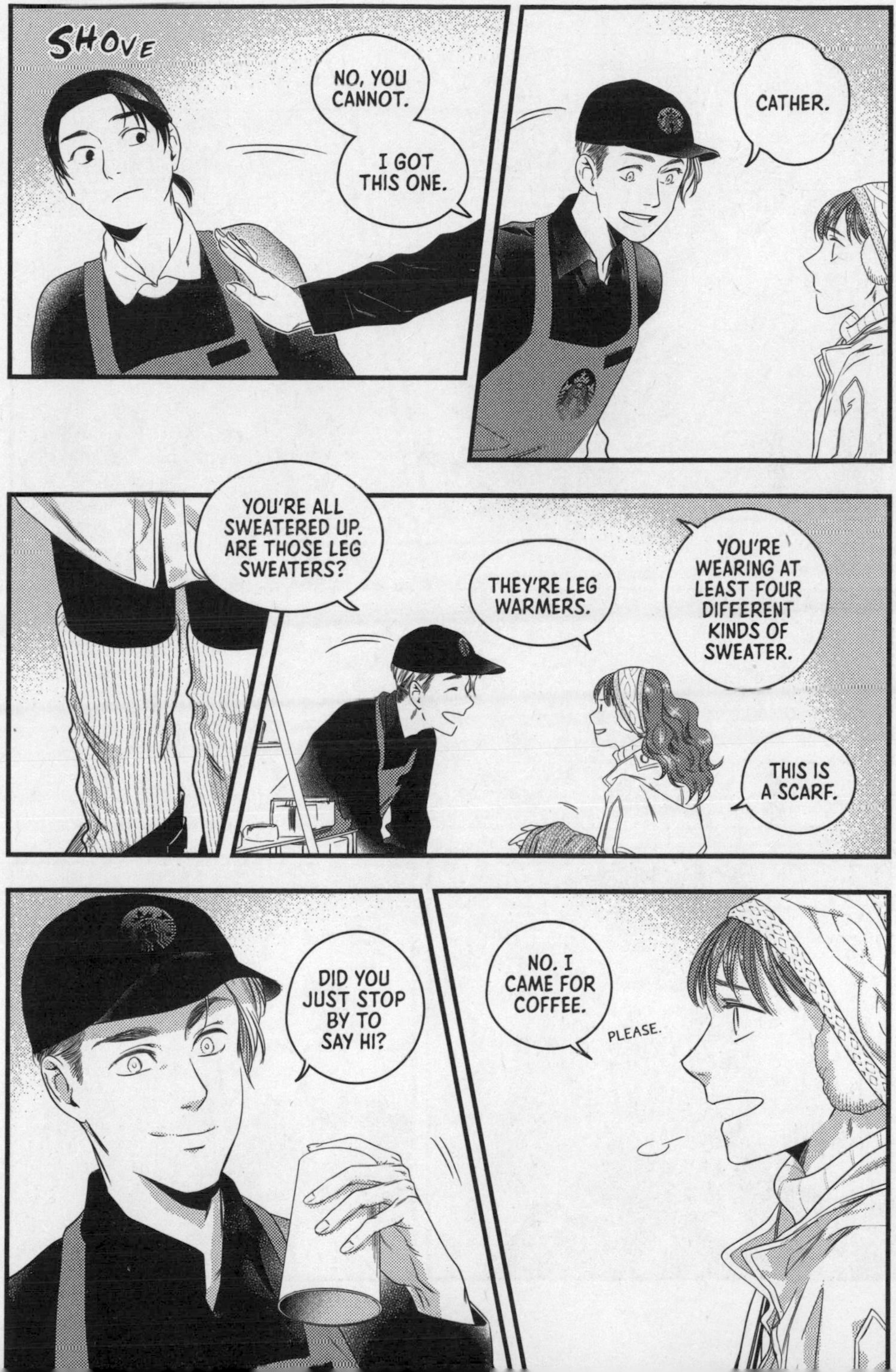
SHOVE
NO, YOU CANNOT.
I GOT THIS ONE.
CATHER.
YOU'RE ALL SWEATERED UP. ARE THOSE LEG SWEATERS?
THEY'RE LEG WARMERS.
YOU'RE WEARING AT LEAST FOUR DIFFERENT KINDS OF SWEATER.
THIS IS A SCARF.
DID YOU JUST STOP BY TO SAY HI?
NO. I CAME FOR COFFEE.
PLEASE.

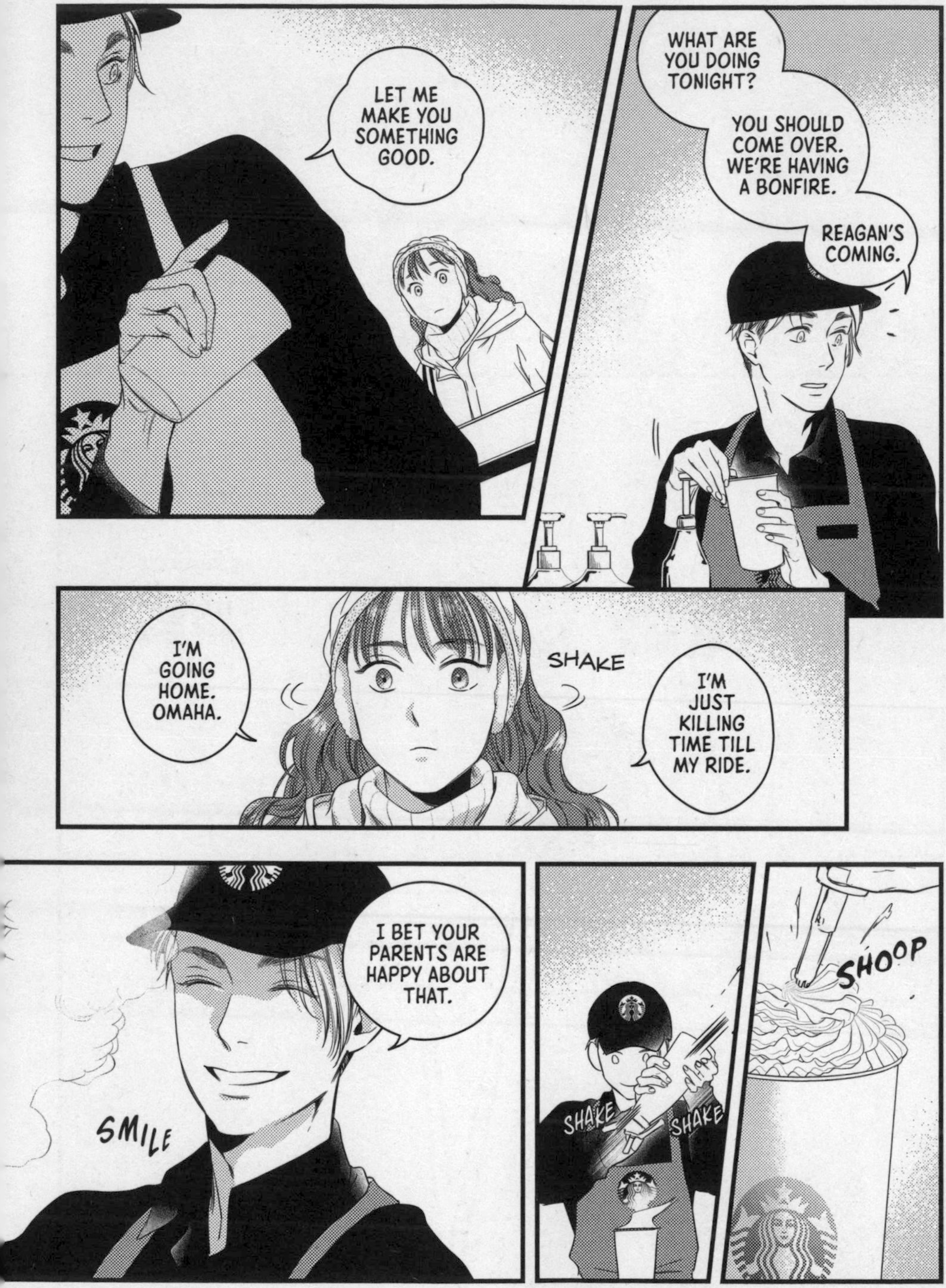
LET ME MAKE YOU SOMETHING GOOD.
WHAT ARE YOU DOING TONIGHT?
YOU SHOULD COME OVER. WE'RE HAVING A BONFIRE.
REAGAN'S COMING.
I'M GOING HOME. OMAHA.
SHAKE
I'M JUST KILLING TIME TILL MY RIDE.
I BET YOUR PARENTS ARE HAPPY ABOUT THAT.
SMILE
SHAKE
SHAKE
SHOOP

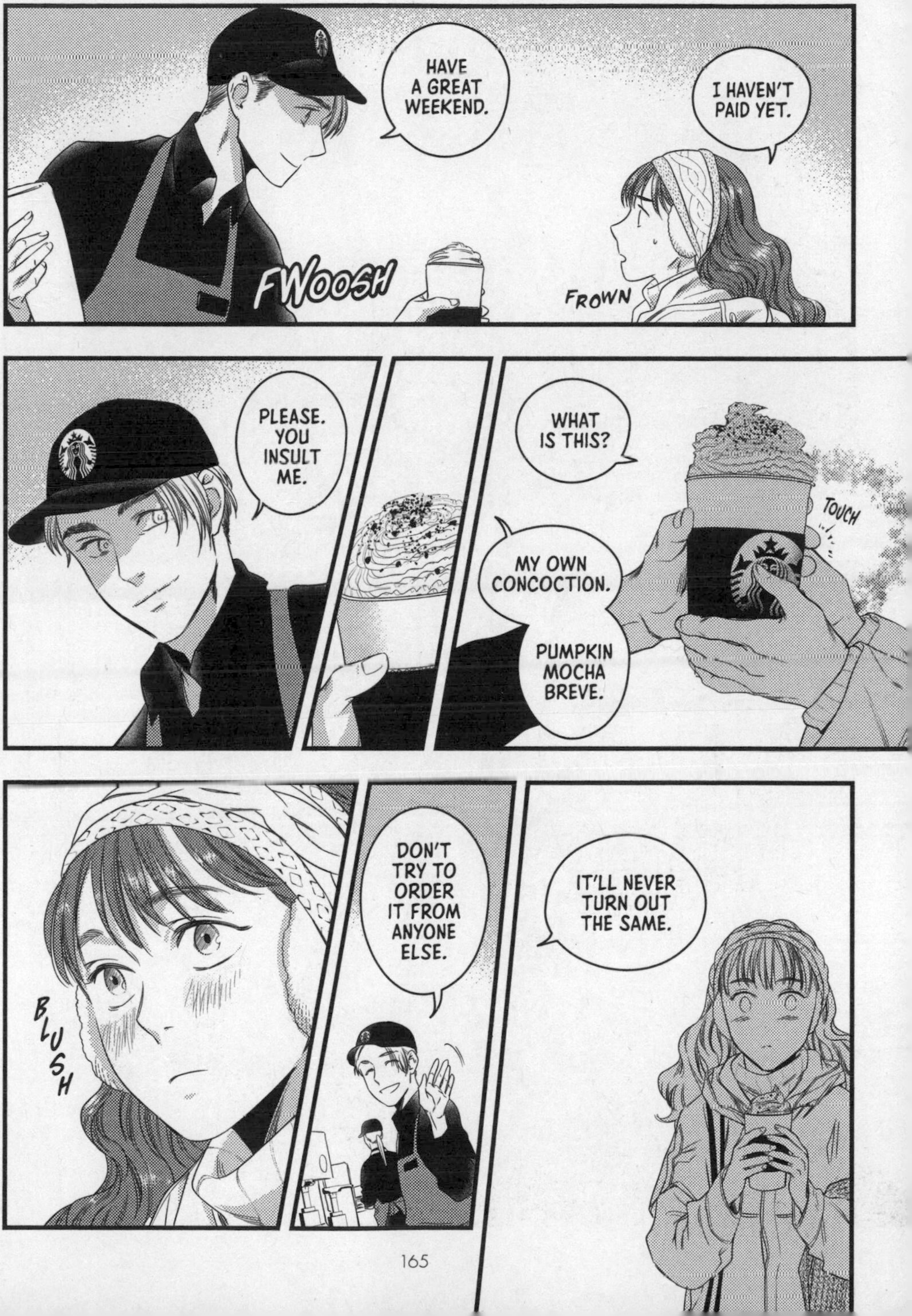
HAVE A GREAT WEEKEND.
FWOOSH
I HAVEN'T PAID YET.
FROWN
PLEASE. YOU INSULT ME.
WHAT IS THIS?
MY OWN CONCOCTION.
PUMPKIN MOCHA BREVE.
TOUCH
BLUSH
DON'T TRY TO ORDER IT FROM ANYONE ELSE.
IT'LL NEVER TURN OUT THE SAME.

Where the *magic* happens

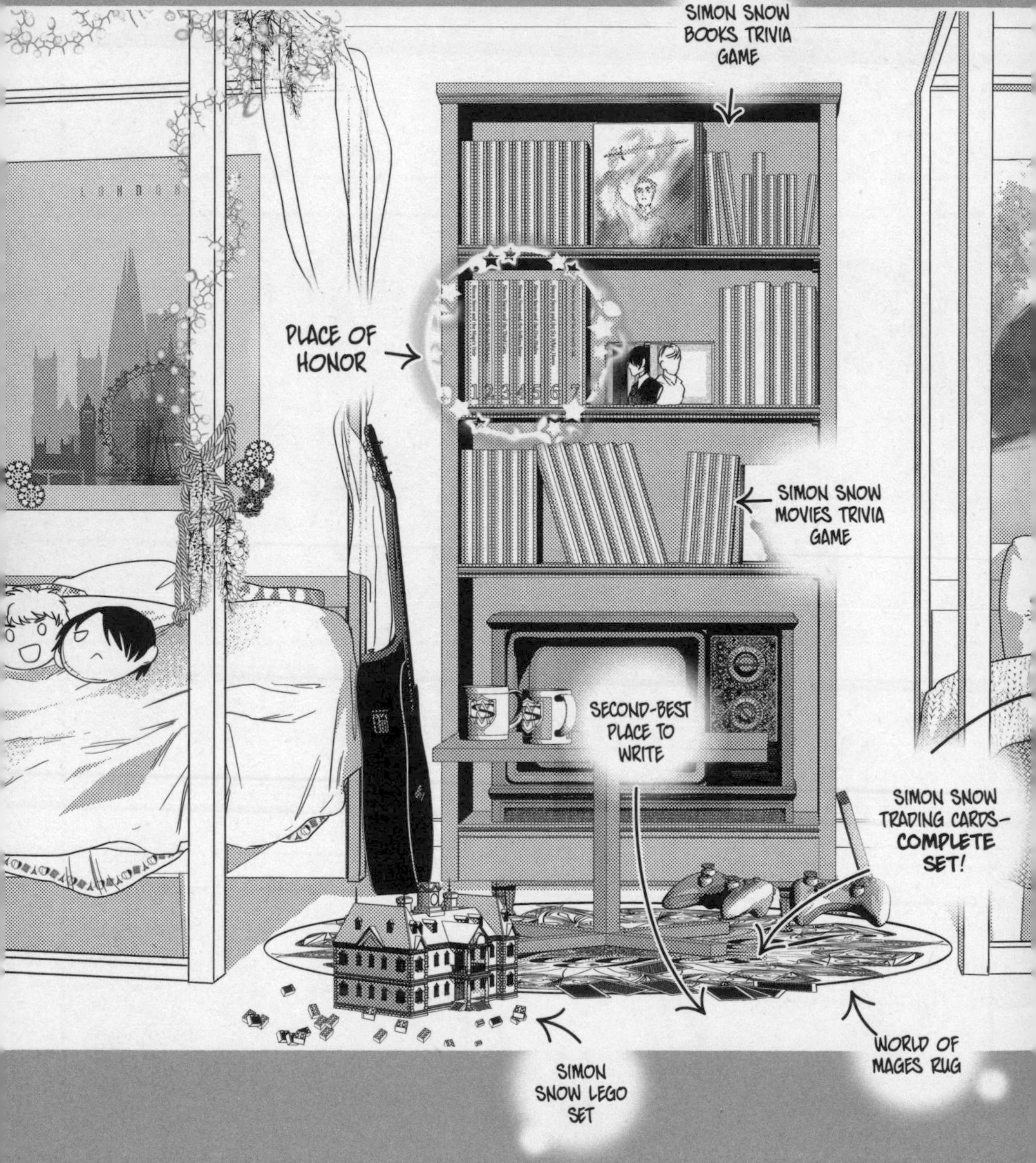
SIMON SNOW BOOKS TRIVIA GAME
PLACE OF HONOR
SIMON SNOW MOVIES TRIVIA GAME
SECOND-BEST PLACE TO WRITE
SIMON SNOW TRADING CARDS- COMPLETE SET!
WORLD OF MAGES RUG
SIMON SNOW LEGO SET

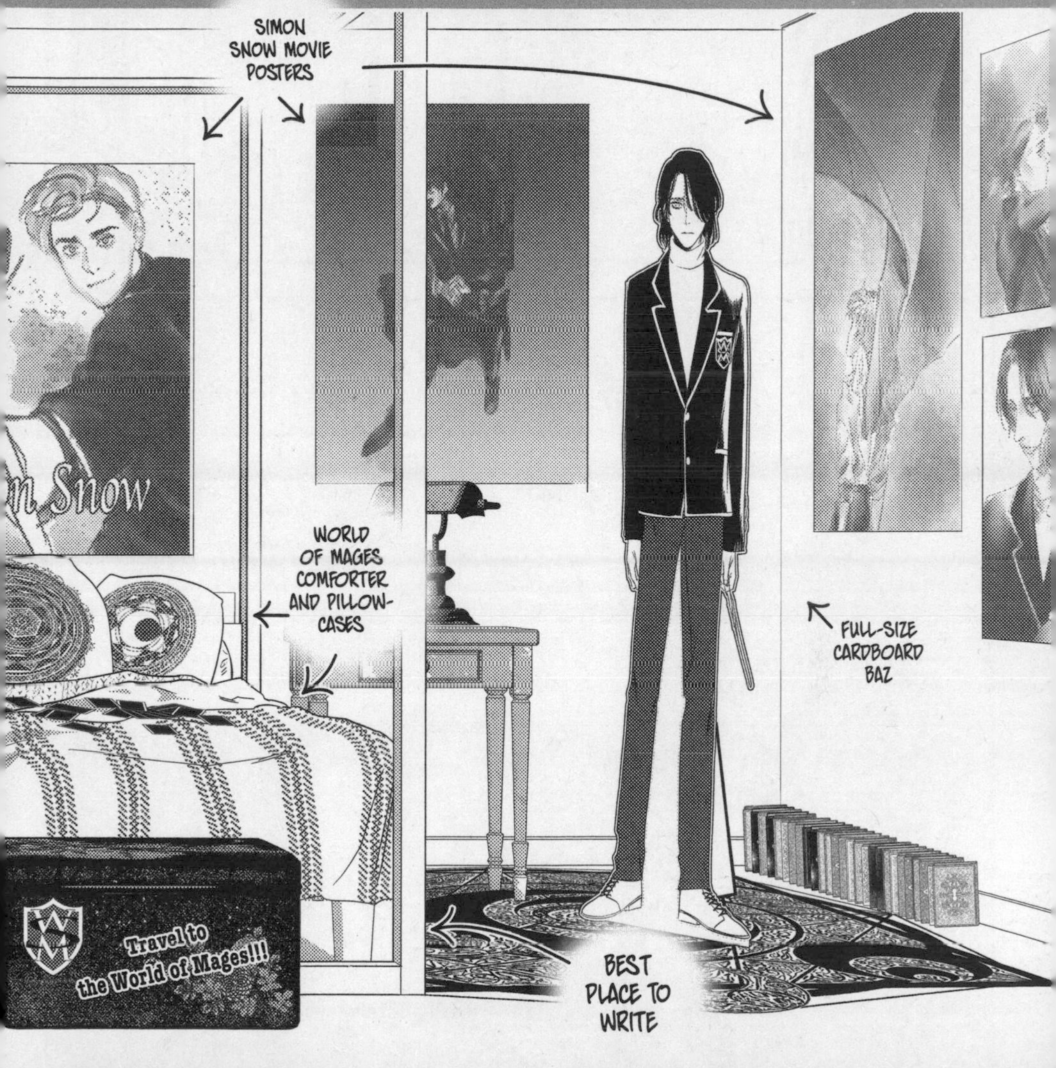
SIMON SNOW MOVIE POSTERS
n Snow
WORLD OF MAGES COMFORTER AND PILLOW-CASES
FULL-SIZE CARDBOARD BAZ
Travel to the World of Mages!!!
BEST PLACE TO WRITE

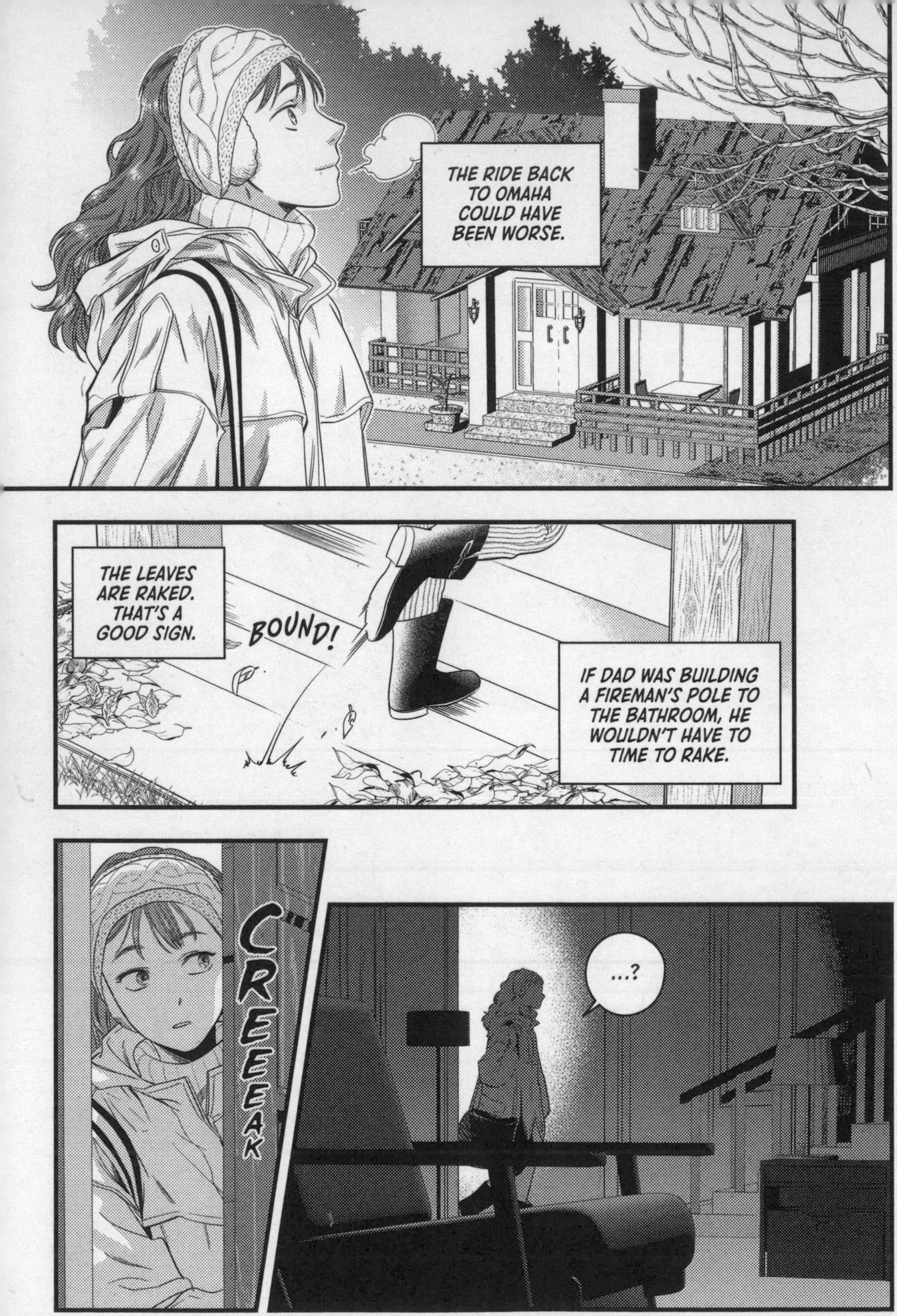
THE RIDE BACK TO OMAHA COULD HAVE BEEN WORSE.
THE LEAVES ARE RAKED. THAT'S A GOOD SIGN.
BOUND!
IF DAD WAS BUILDING A FIREMAN'S POLE TO THE BATHROOM, HE WOULDN'T HAVE TO TIME TO RAKE.
CREEEAK
...?

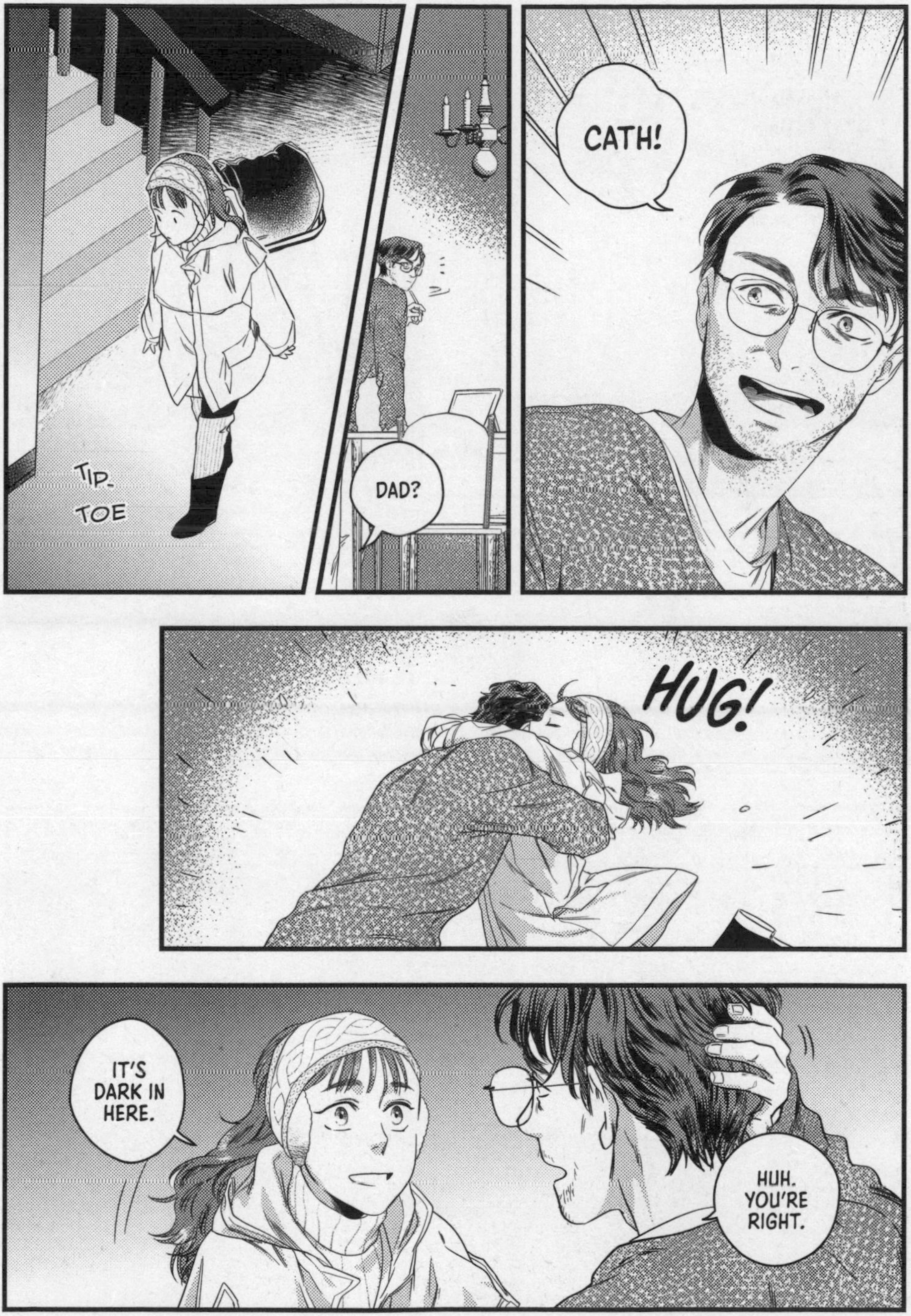
TIP-
TOE
DAD?
CATH!
HUG!
IT'S DARK IN HERE.
HUH. YOU'RE RIGHT.

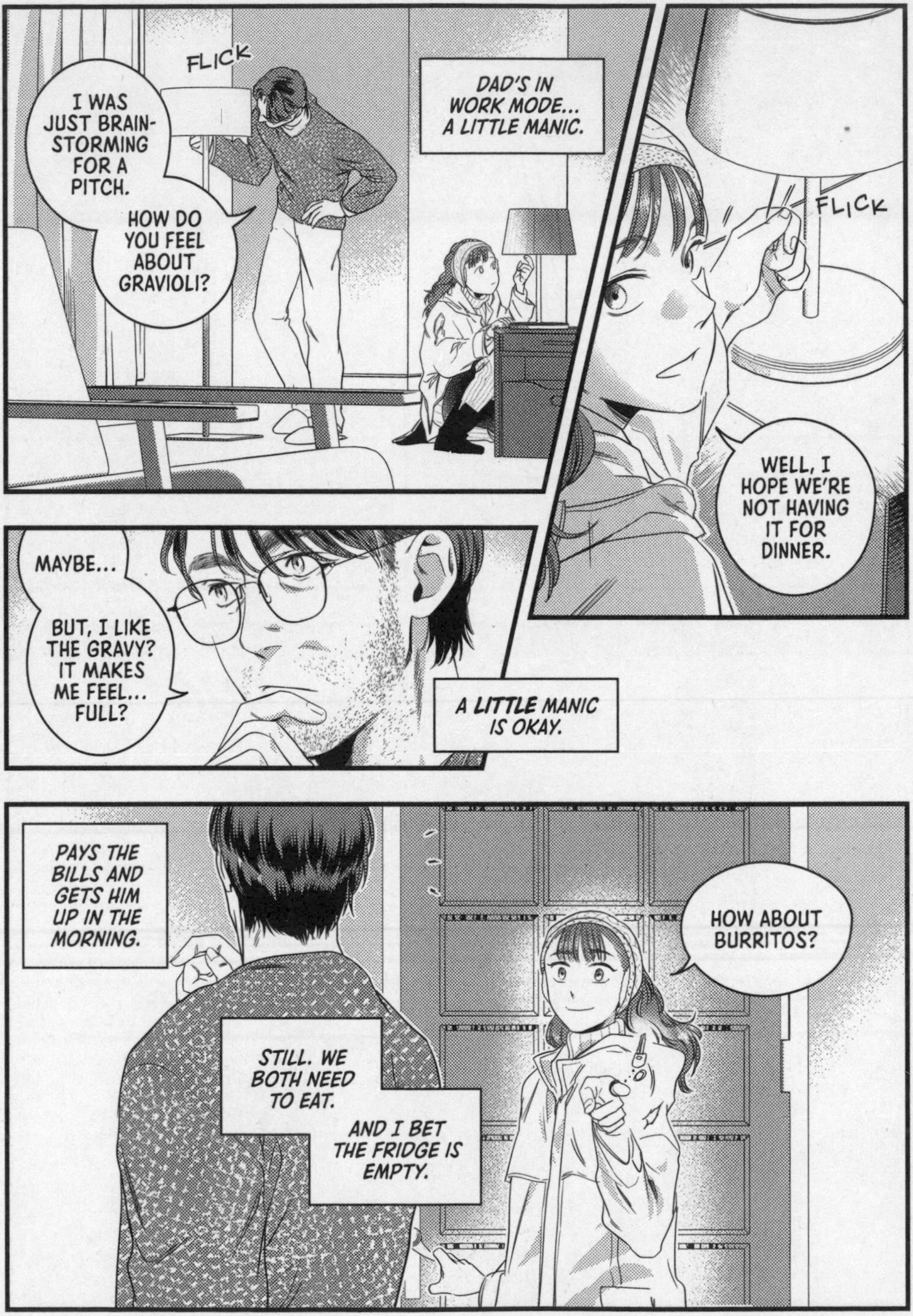
FLICK
I WAS JUST BRAIN-STORMING FOR A PITCH.
HOW DO YOU FEEL ABOUT GRAVIOLI?
DAD'S IN WORK MODE... A LITTLE MANIC.
FLICK
WELL, I HOPE WE'RE NOT HAVING IT FOR DINNER.
MAYBE...
BUT, I LIKE THE GRAVY? IT MAKES ME FEEL... FULL?
A *LITTLE* MANIC IS OKAY.
PAYS THE BILLS AND GETS HIM UP IN THE MORNING.
HOW ABOUT BURRITOS?
STILL. WE BOTH NEED TO EAT.
AND I BET THE FRIDGE IS EMPTY.

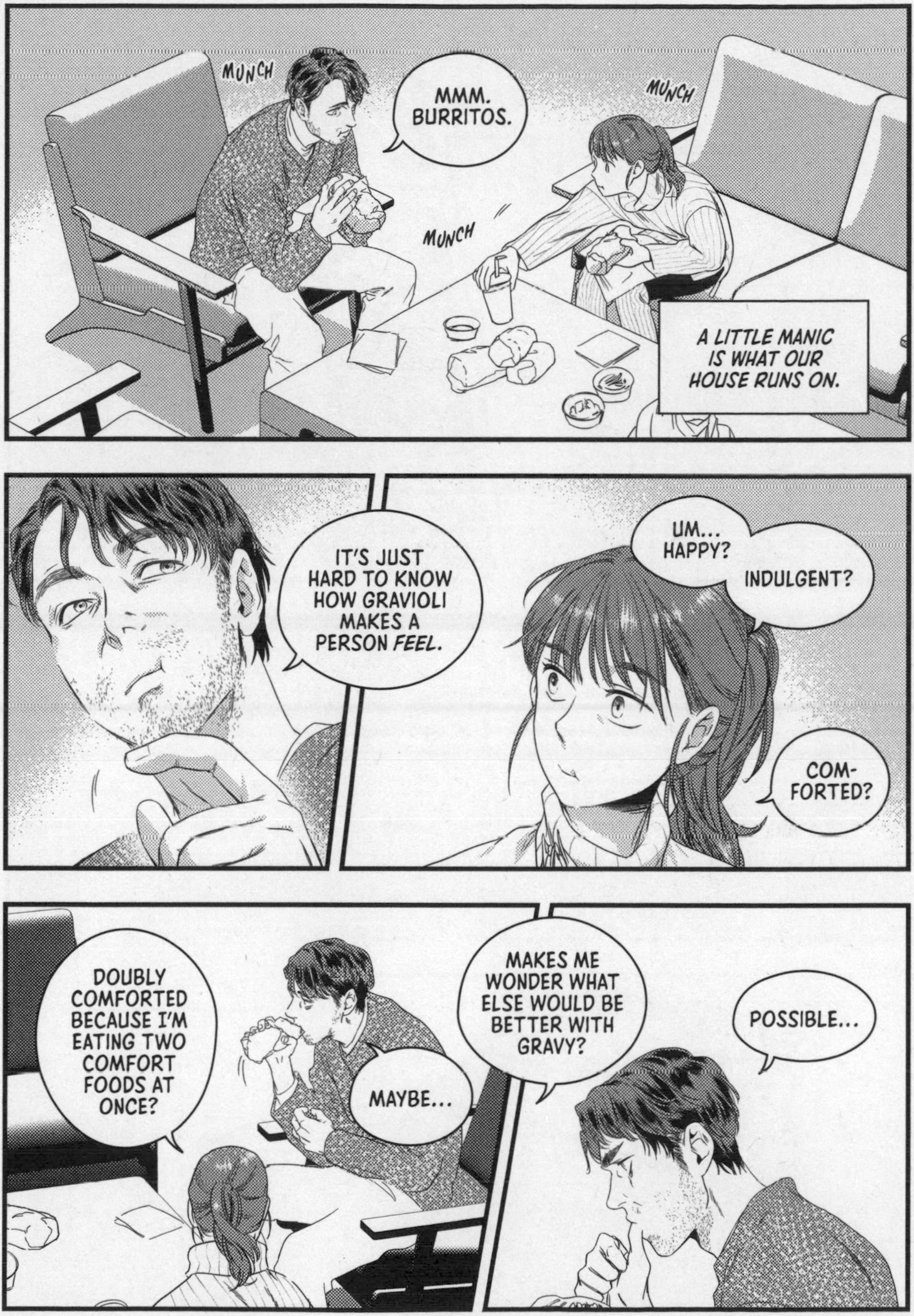
MUNCH
MMM. BURRITOS.
MUNCH
MUNCH
A LITTLE MANIC IS WHAT OUR HOUSE RUNS ON.
IT'S JUST HARD TO KNOW HOW GRAVIOLI MAKES A PERSON *FEEL*.
UM... HAPPY?
INDULGENT?
COM-FORTED?
DOUBLY COMFORTED BECAUSE I'M EATING TWO COMFORT FOODS AT ONCE?
MAYBE...
MAKES ME WONDER WHAT ELSE WOULD BE BETTER WITH GRAVY?
POSSIBLE...

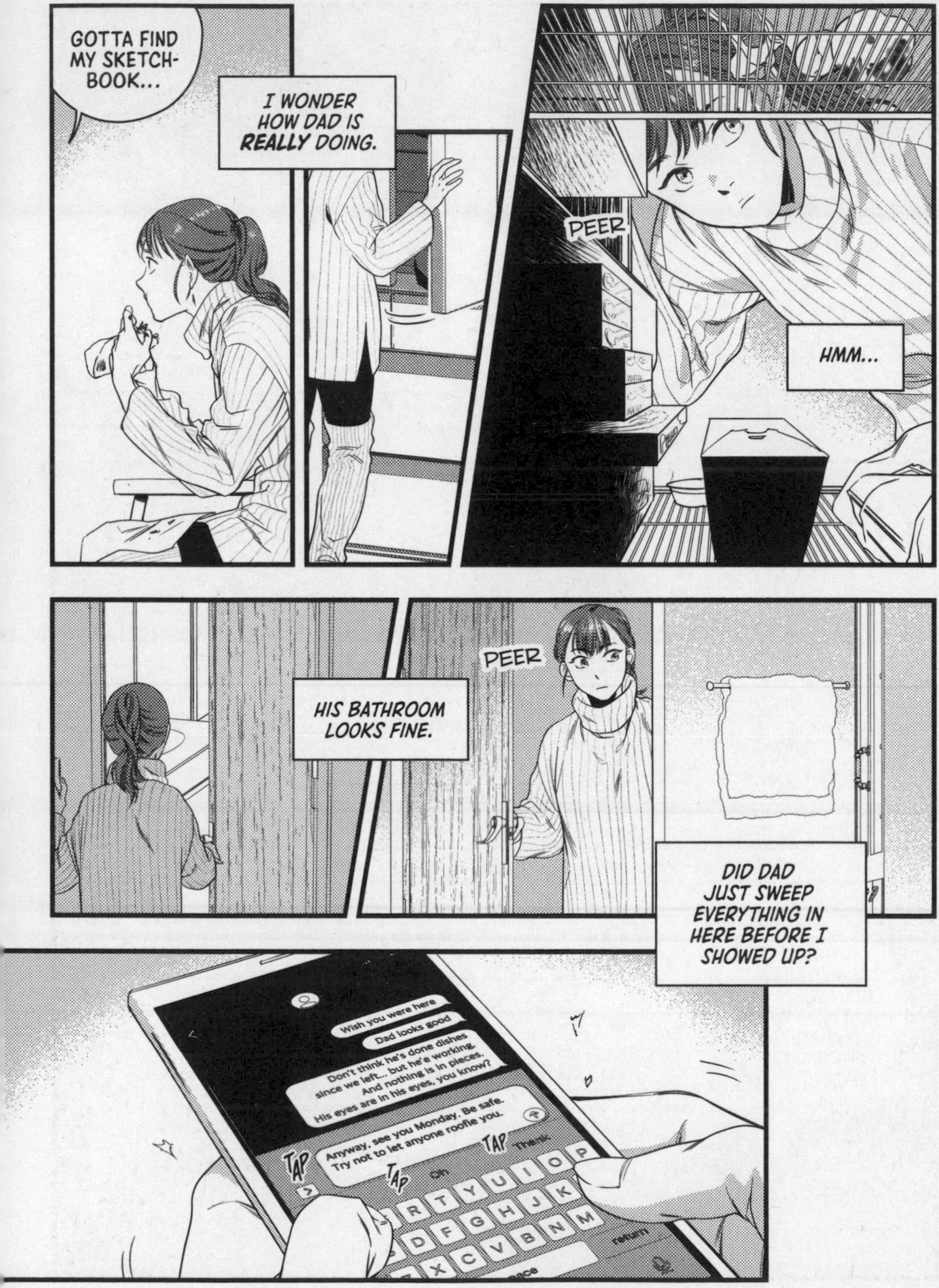
GOTTA FIND MY SKETCH-BOOK...
I WONDER HOW DAD IS REALLY DOING.
PEER
HMM...
HIS BATHROOM LOOKS FINE.
PEER
DID DAD JUST SWEEP EVERYTHING IN HERE BEFORE I SHOWED UP?
Wish you were here
Dad looks good
Don't think he's done dishes since we left... but he's working. And nothing is in pieces. His eyes are in his eyes, you know?
Anyway, see you Monday. Be safe. Try not to let anyone roofie you.
TAP
TAP
TAP

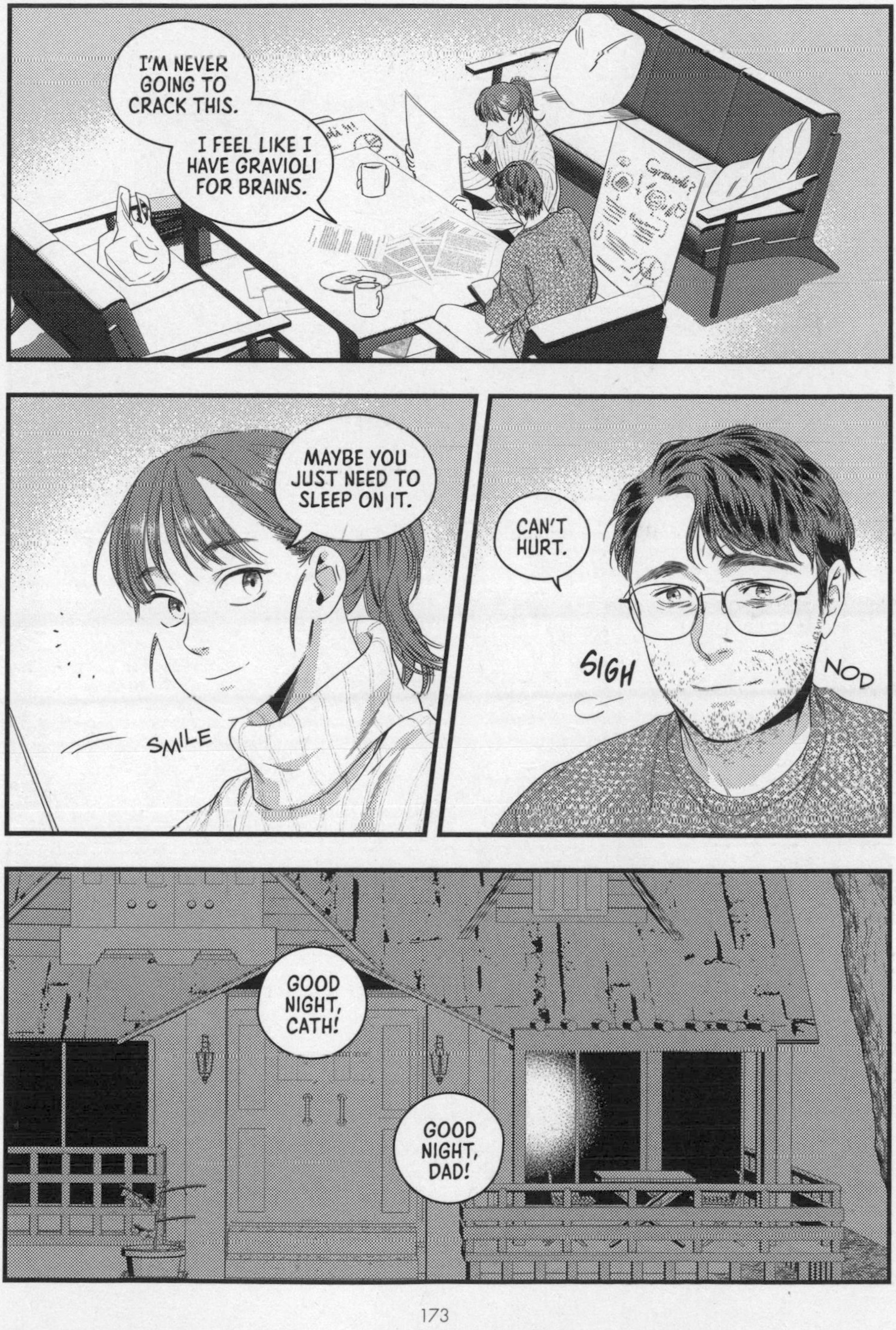
I'M NEVER GOING TO CRACK THIS.
I FEEL LIKE I HAVE GRAVIOLI FOR BRAINS.
Gravioli?
MAYBE YOU JUST NEED TO SLEEP ON IT.
SMILE
CAN'T HURT.
SIGH
NOD
GOOD NIGHT, CATH!
GOOD NIGHT, DAD!

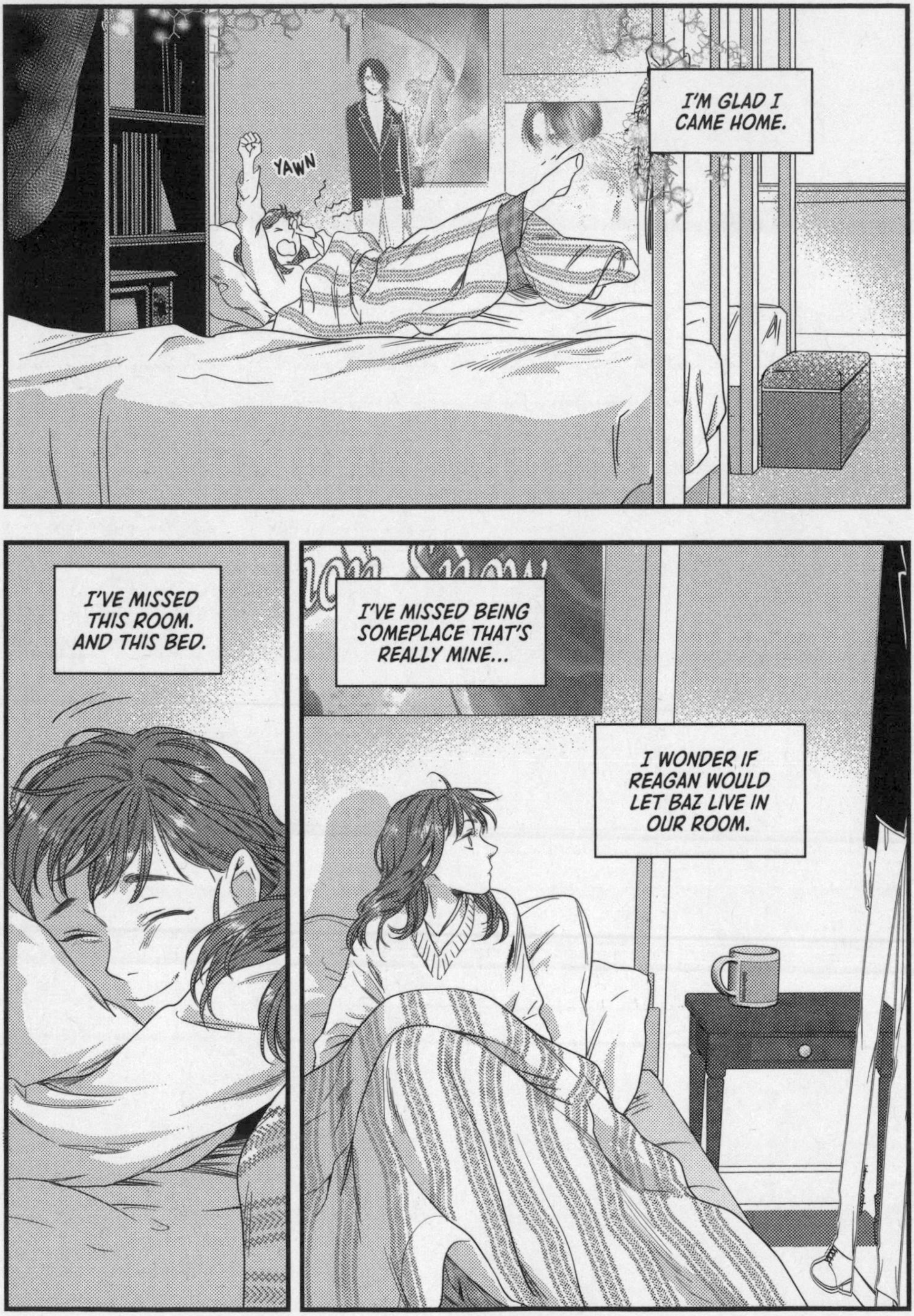
YAWN
I'M GLAD I CAME HOME.
I'VE MISSED THIS ROOM. AND THIS BED.
I'VE MISSED BEING SOMEPLACE THAT'S REALLY MINE...
I WONDER IF REAGAN WOULD LET BAZ LIVE IN OUR ROOM.

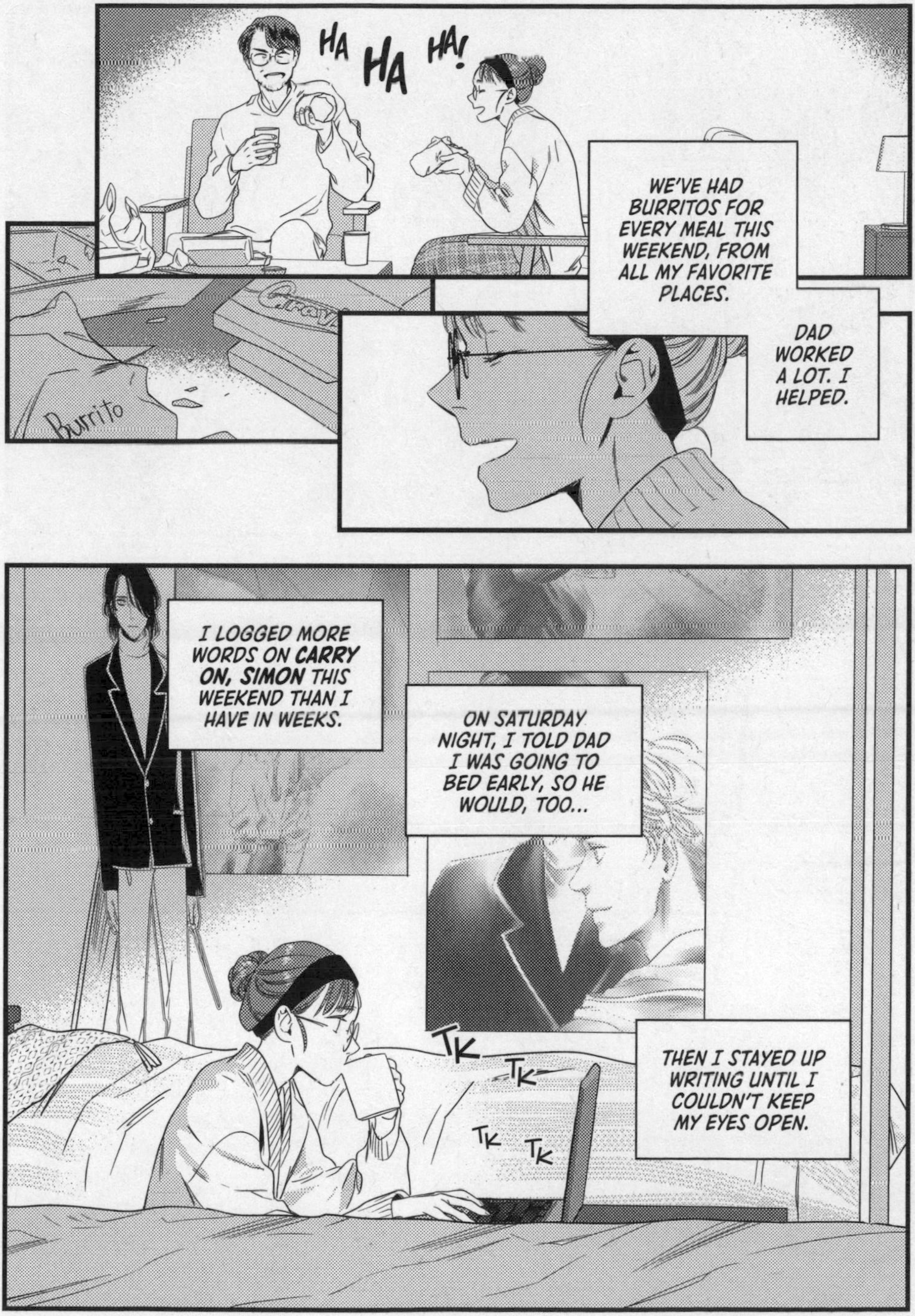
HA HA HA!
WE'VE HAD BURRITOS FOR EVERY MEAL THIS WEEKEND, FROM ALL MY FAVORITE PLACES.
Burrito
DAD WORKED A LOT. I HELPED.
I LOGGED MORE WORDS ON **CARRY ON, SIMON** THIS WEEKEND THAN I HAVE IN WEEKS.
ON SATURDAY NIGHT, I TOLD DAD I WAS GOING TO BED EARLY, SO HE WOULD, TOO...
TK TK TK TK
THEN I STAYED UP WRITING UNTIL I COULDN'T KEEP MY EYES OPEN.

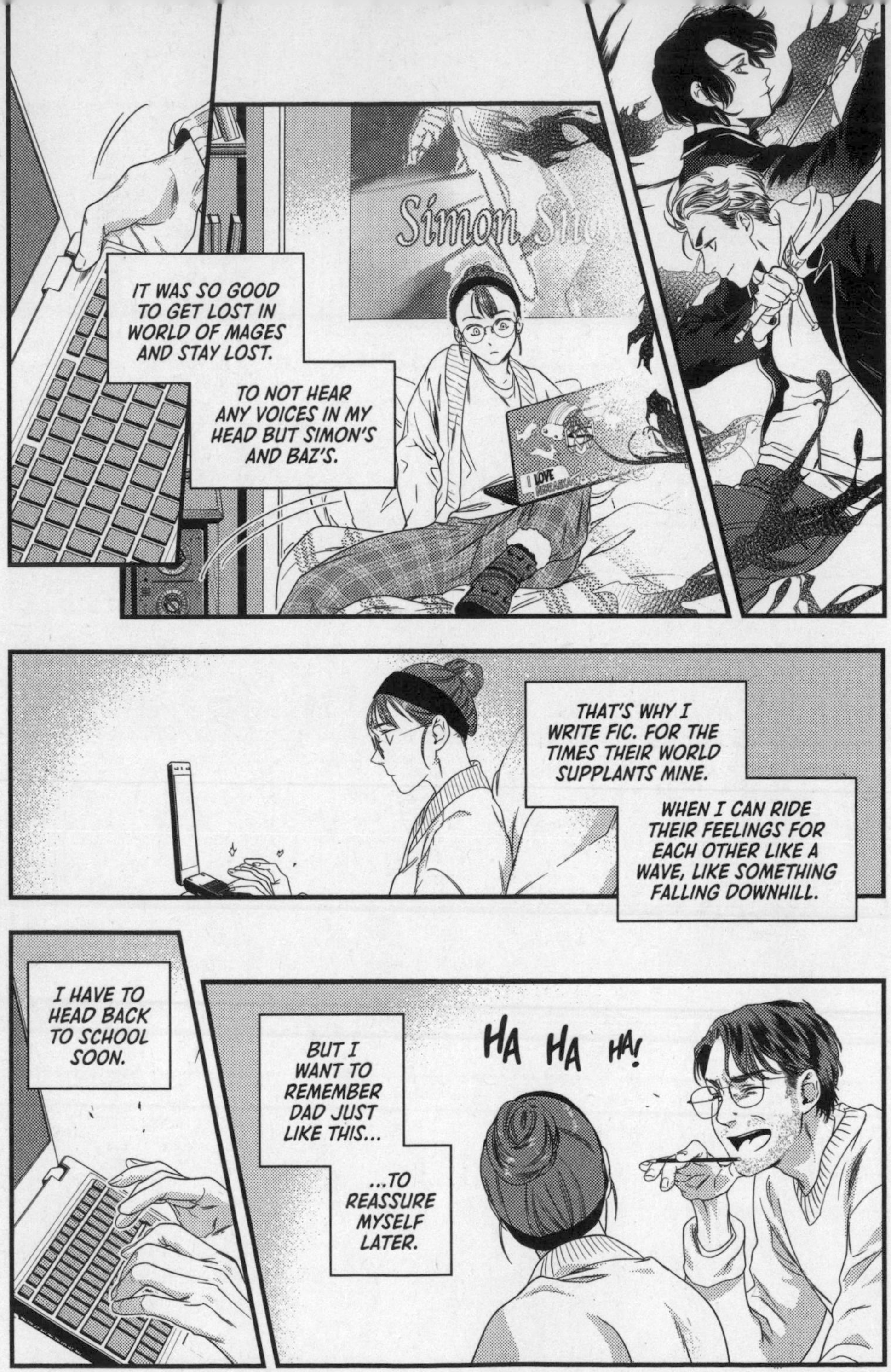
IT WAS SO GOOD TO GET LOST IN WORLD OF MAGES AND STAY LOST.
TO NOT HEAR ANY VOICES IN MY HEAD BUT SIMON'S AND BAZ'S.
THAT'S WHY I WRITE FIC. FOR THE TIMES THEIR WORLD SUPPLANTS MINE.
WHEN I CAN RIDE THEIR FEELINGS FOR EACH OTHER LIKE A WAVE, LIKE SOMETHING FALLING DOWNHILL.
I HAVE TO HEAD BACK TO SCHOOL SOON.
BUT I WANT TO REMEMBER DAD JUST LIKE THIS...
...TO REASSURE MYSELF LATER.
HA HA HA!

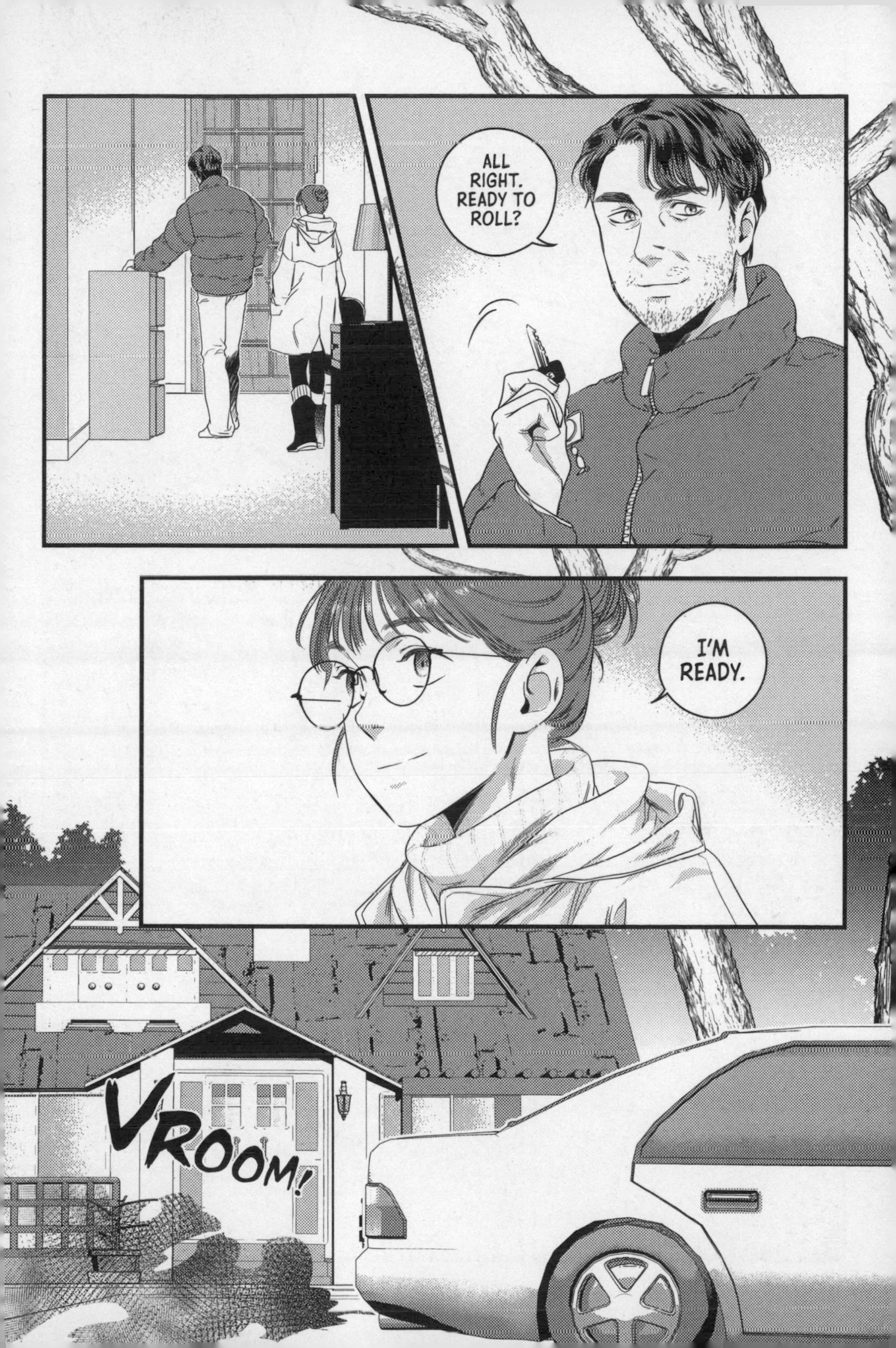
ALL RIGHT. READY TO ROLL?
I'M READY.
VROOM!

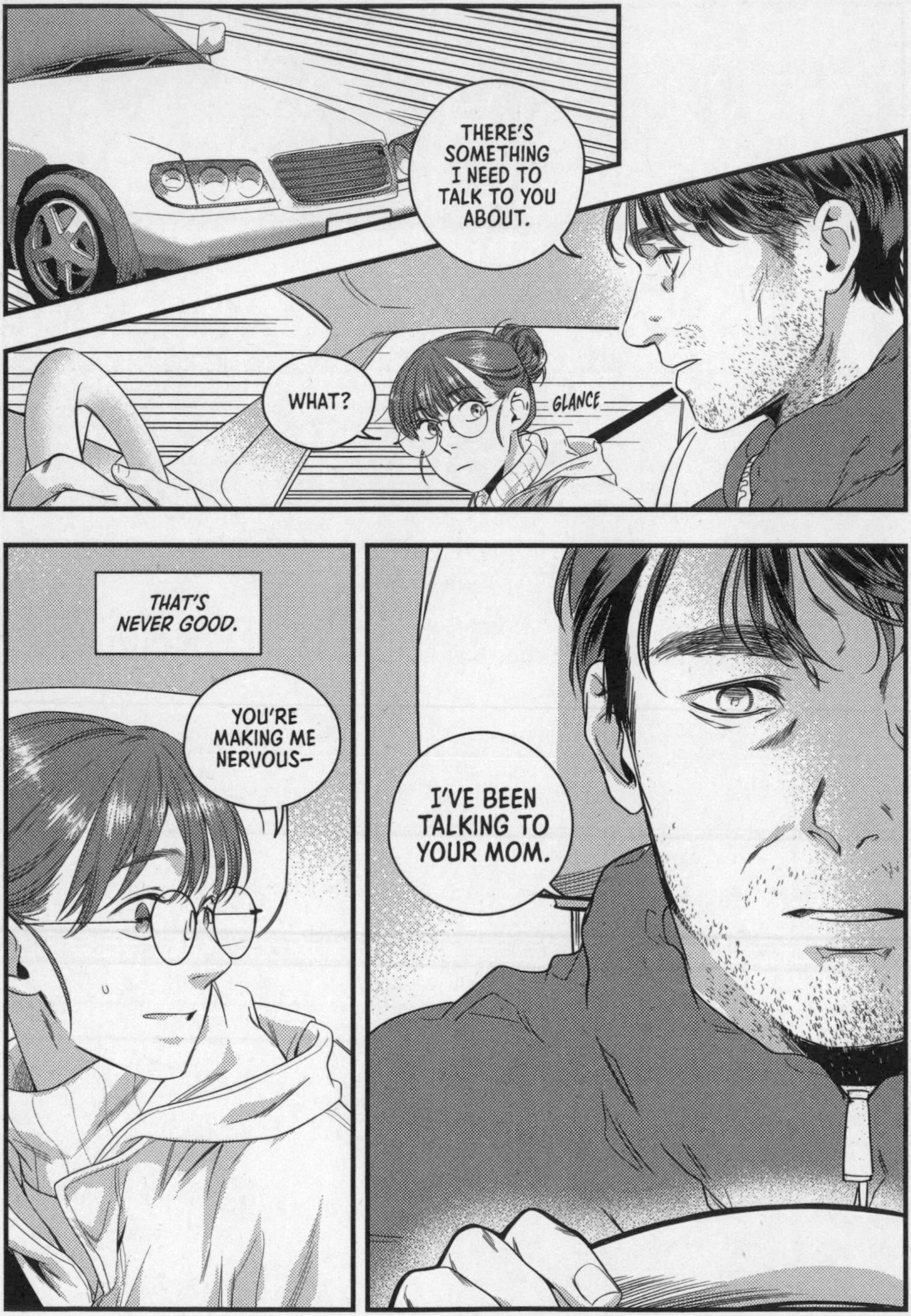
THERE'S SOMETHING I NEED TO TALK TO YOU ABOUT.
WHAT?
GLANCE
THAT'S NEVER GOOD.
YOU'RE MAKING ME NERVOUS–
I'VE BEEN TALKING TO YOUR MOM.

WHAT?

IT WOULD MAKE MORE SENSE FOR HIM TO BE TALKING TO A GHOST! OR A YETI!

MY... MOM?!

WHY? WHAT?!

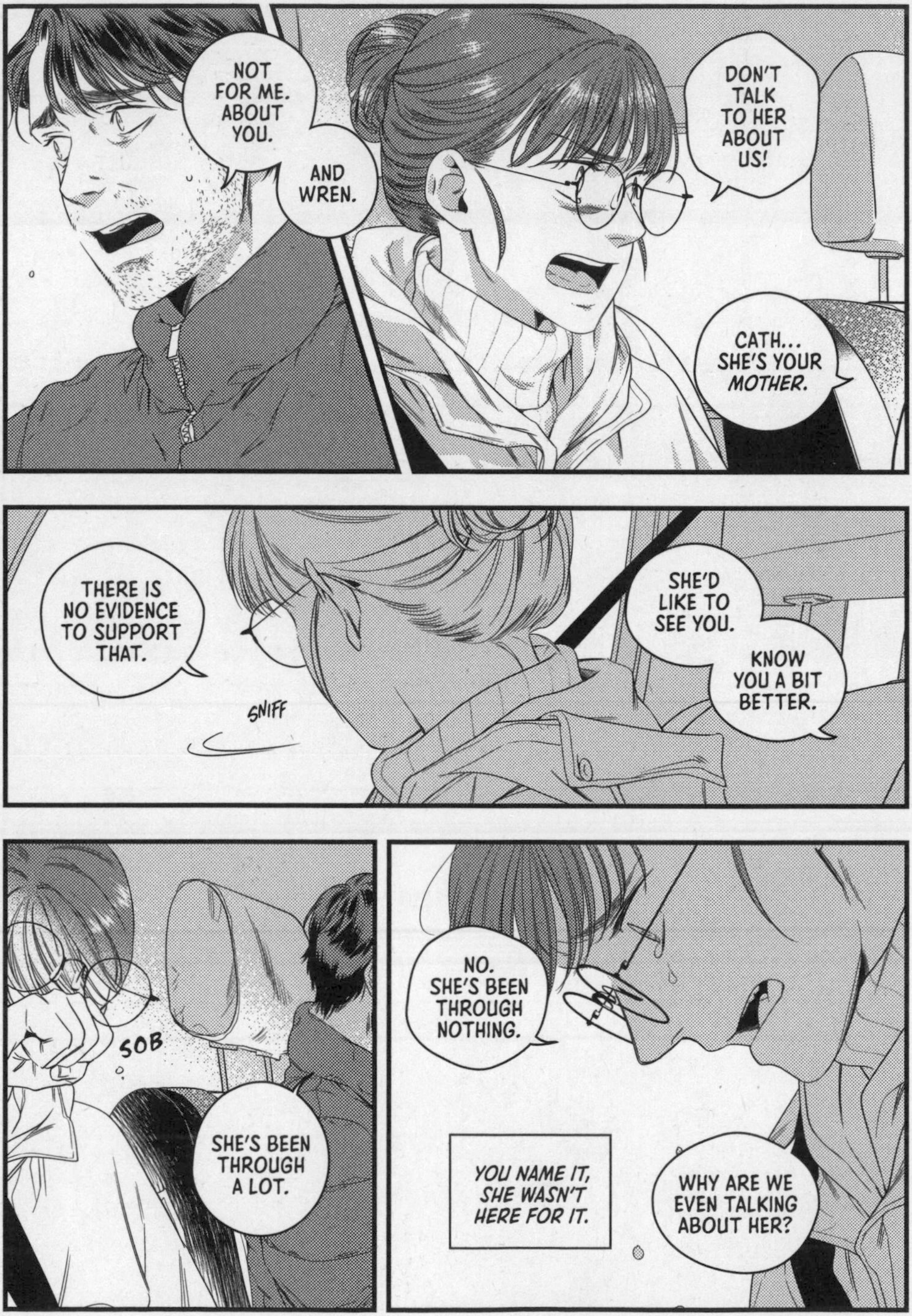
NOT FOR ME. ABOUT YOU.
AND WREN.
DON'T TALK TO HER ABOUT US!
CATH... SHE'S YOUR *MOTHER.*
THERE IS NO EVIDENCE TO SUPPORT THAT.
SNIFF
SHE'D LIKE TO SEE YOU.
KNOW YOU A BIT BETTER.
SOB
SHE'S BEEN THROUGH A LOT.
NO. SHE'S BEEN THROUGH NOTHING.
YOU NAME IT, SHE WASN'T HERE FOR IT.
WHY ARE WE EVEN TALKING ABOUT HER?

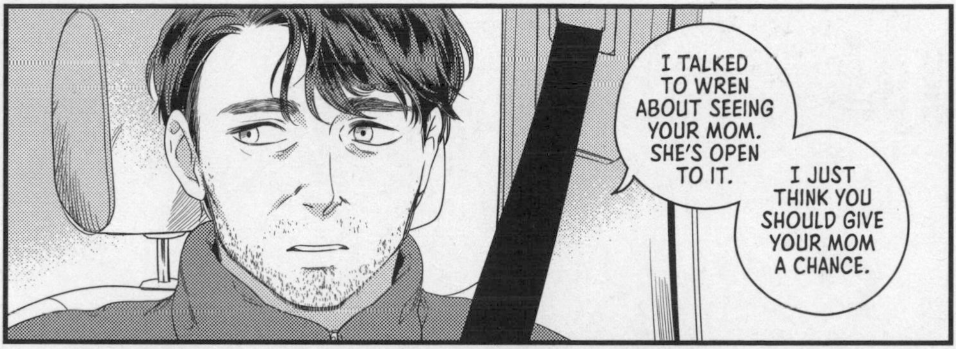
I TALKED TO WREN ABOUT SEEING YOUR MOM. SHE'S OPEN TO IT.
I JUST THINK YOU SHOULD GIVE YOUR MOM A CHANCE.

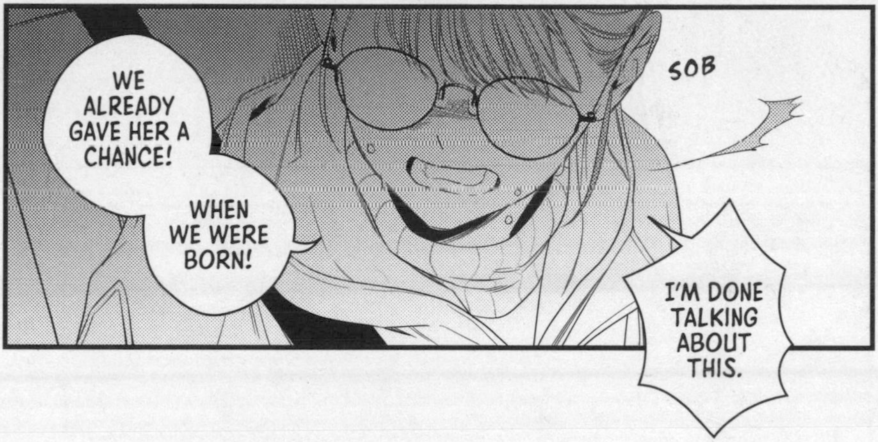
WE ALREADY GAVE HER A CHANCE!
WHEN WE WERE BORN!
SOB
I'M DONE TALKING ABOUT THIS.

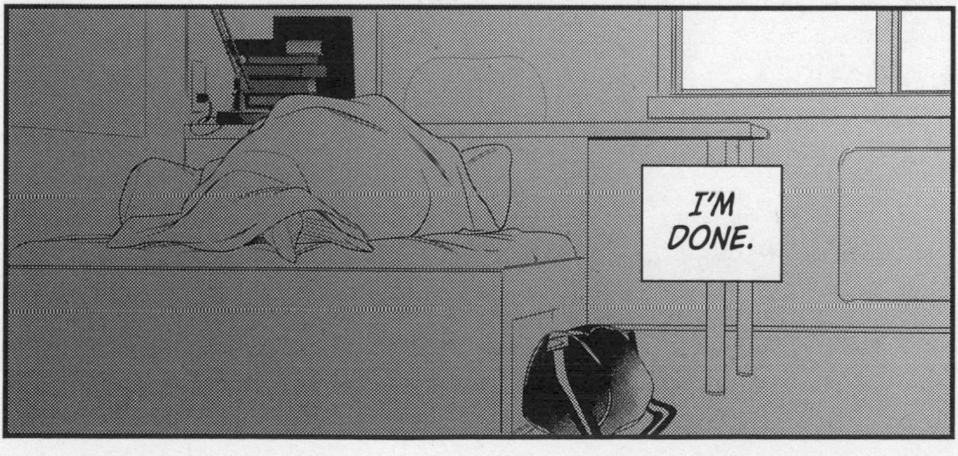
I'M DONE.

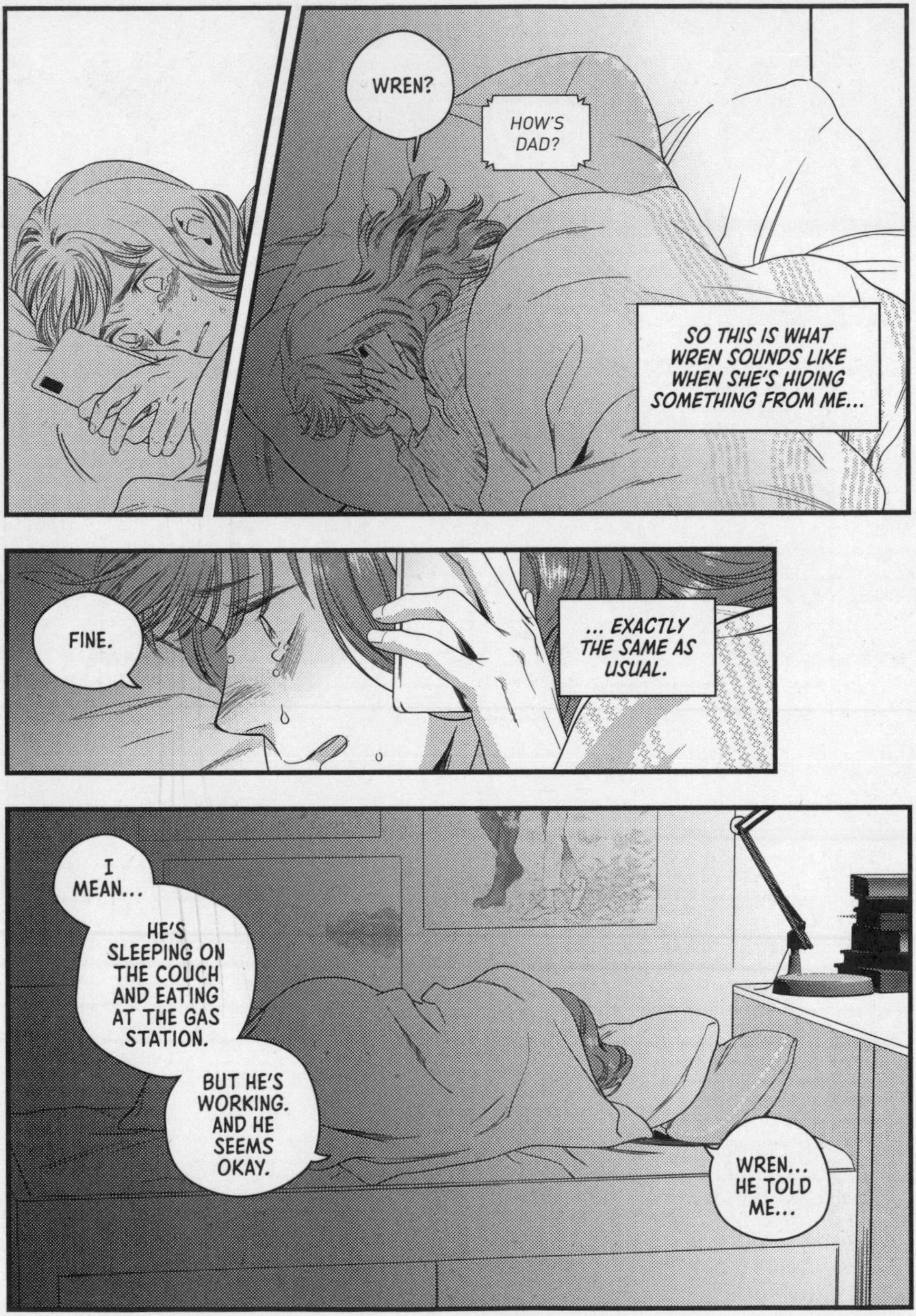
WREN?
HOW'S DAD?
SO THIS IS WHAT WREN SOUNDS LIKE WHEN SHE'S HIDING SOMETHING FROM ME...
FINE.
... EXACTLY THE SAME AS USUAL.
I MEAN...
HE'S SLEEPING ON THE COUCH AND EATING AT THE GAS STATION.
BUT HE'S WORKING. AND HE SEEMS OKAY.
WREN... HE TOLD ME...

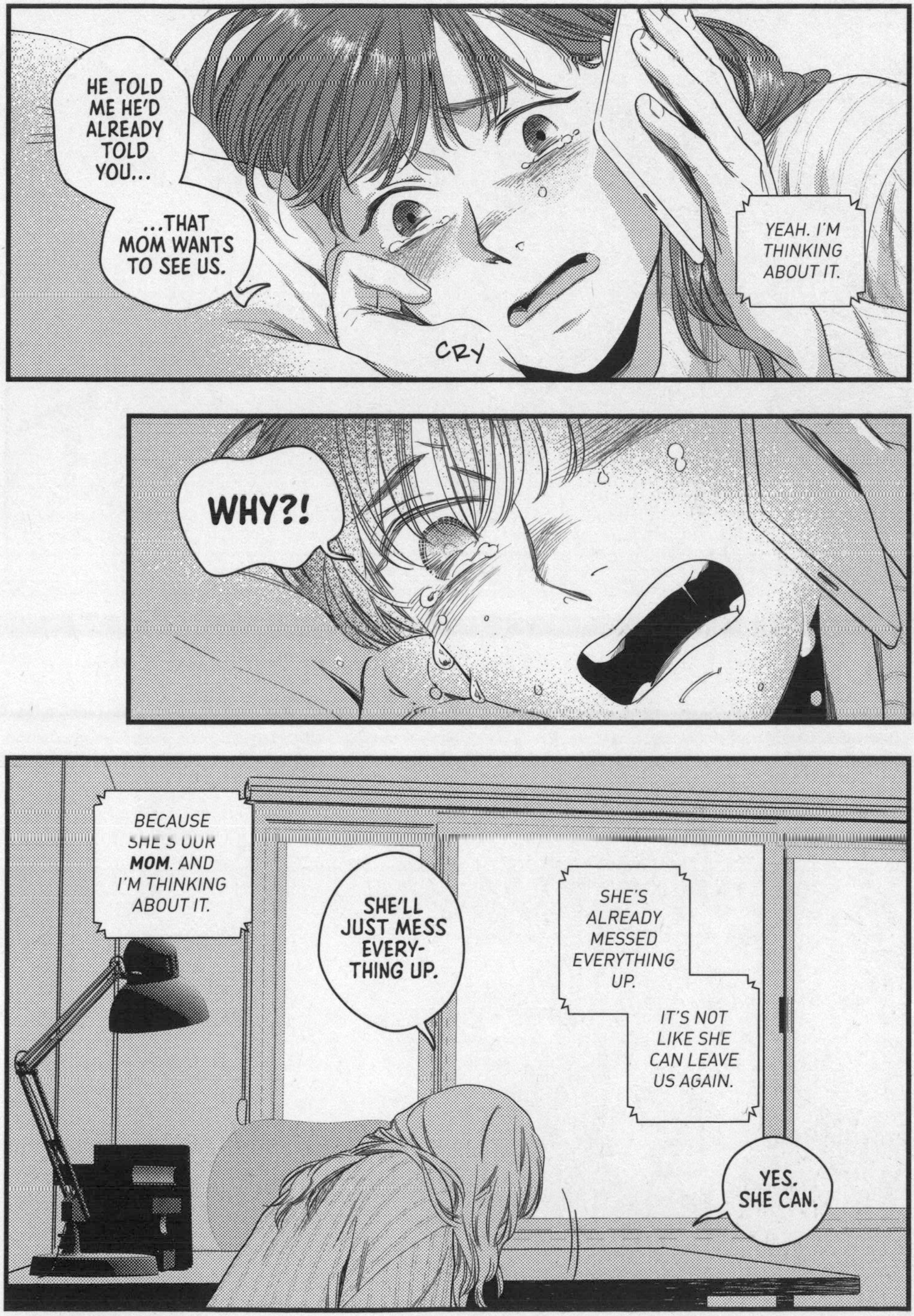

HE TOLD ME HE'D ALREADY TOLD YOU...
...THAT MOM WANTS TO SEE US.
CRY
YEAH. I'M THINKING ABOUT IT.
WHY?!
BECAUSE SHE'S OUR MOM. AND I'M THINKING ABOUT IT.
SHE'LL JUST MESS EVERY-THING UP.
SHE'S ALREADY MESSED EVERYTHING UP.
IT'S NOT LIKE SHE CAN LEAVE US AGAIN.
YES. SHE CAN.

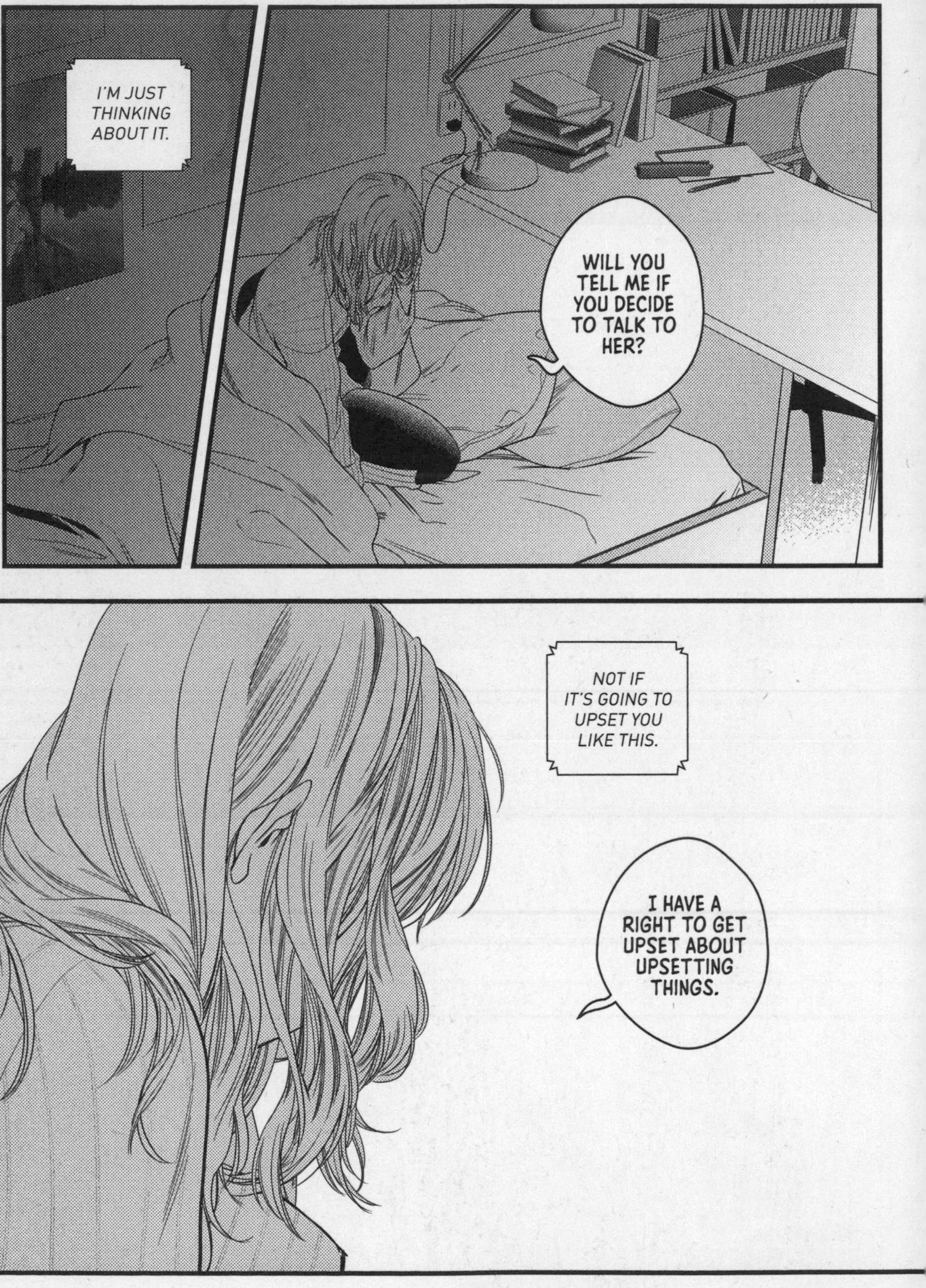
I'M JUST THINKING ABOUT IT.
WILL YOU TELL ME IF YOU DECIDE TO TALK TO HER?
NOT IF IT'S GOING TO UPSET YOU LIKE THIS.
I HAVE A RIGHT TO GET UPSET ABOUT UPSETTING THINGS.

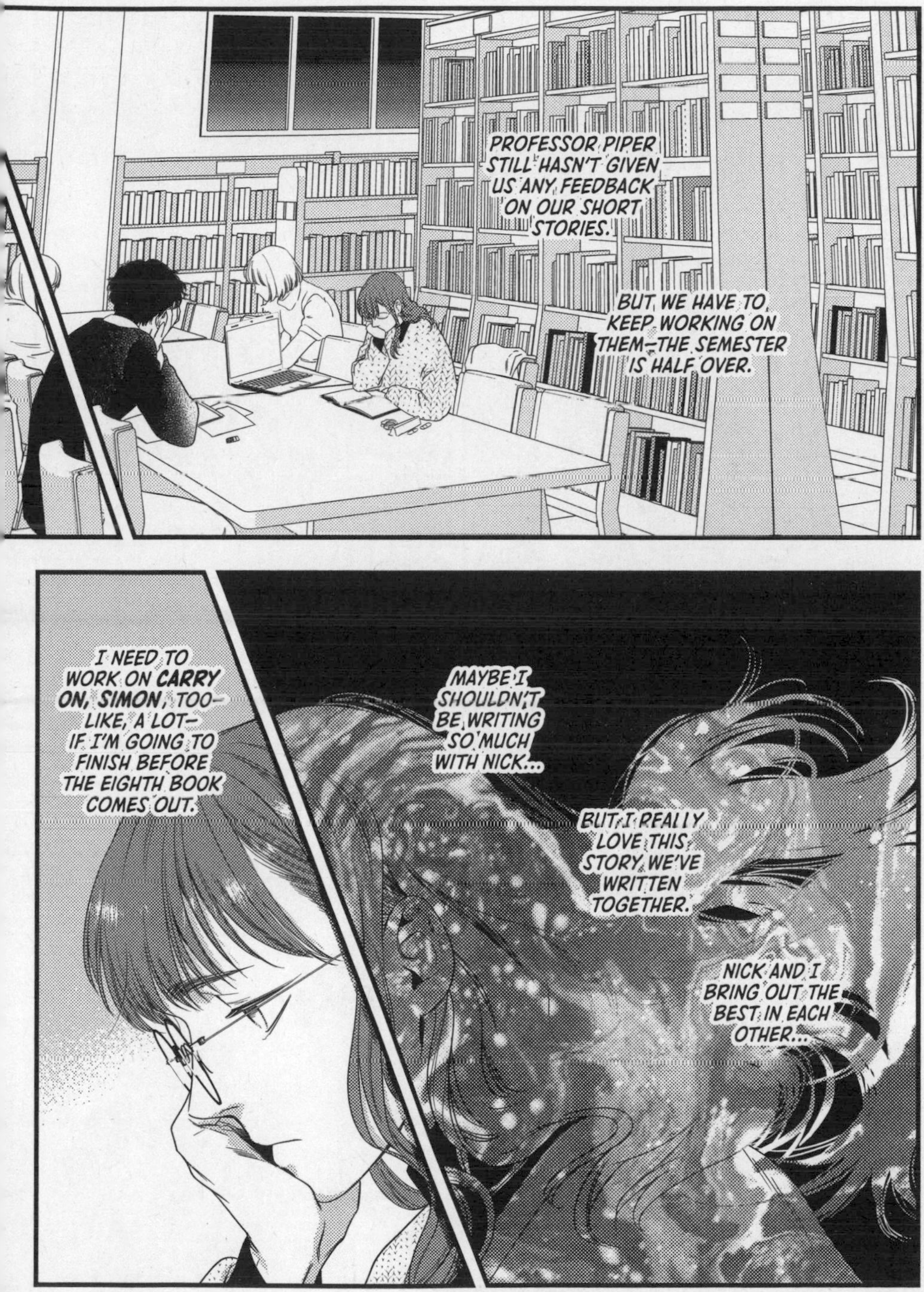

PROFESSOR PIPER STILL HASN'T GIVEN US ANY FEEDBACK ON OUR SHORT STORIES.
BUT WE HAVE TO KEEP WORKING ON THEM—THE SEMESTER IS HALF OVER.
I NEED TO WORK ON **CARRY ON, SIMON**, TOO-LIKE, A LOT-IF I'M GOING TO FINISH BEFORE THE EIGHTH BOOK COMES OUT.
MAYBE I SHOULDN'T BE WRITING SO MUCH WITH NICK...
BUT I REALLY LOVE THIS STORY WE'VE WRITTEN TOGETHER.
NICK AND I BRING OUT THE BEST IN EACH OTHER...

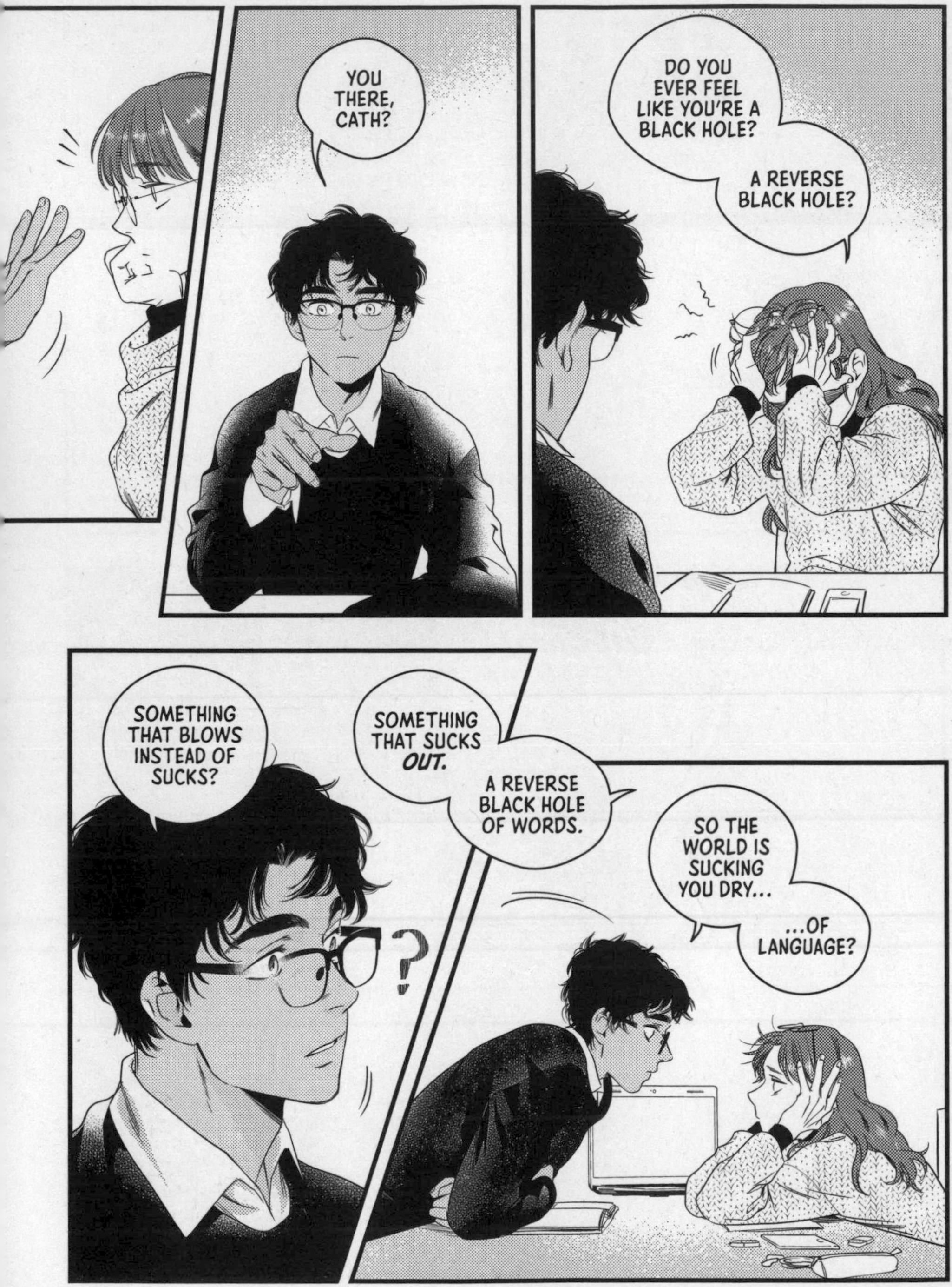
YOU THERE, CATH?
DO YOU EVER FEEL LIKE YOU'RE A BLACK HOLE?
A REVERSE BLACK HOLE?
SOMETHING THAT BLOWS INSTEAD OF SUCKS?
SOMETHING THAT SUCKS *OUT.*
A REVERSE BLACK HOLE OF WORDS.
?
SO THE WORLD IS SUCKING YOU DRY...
...OF LANGUAGE?

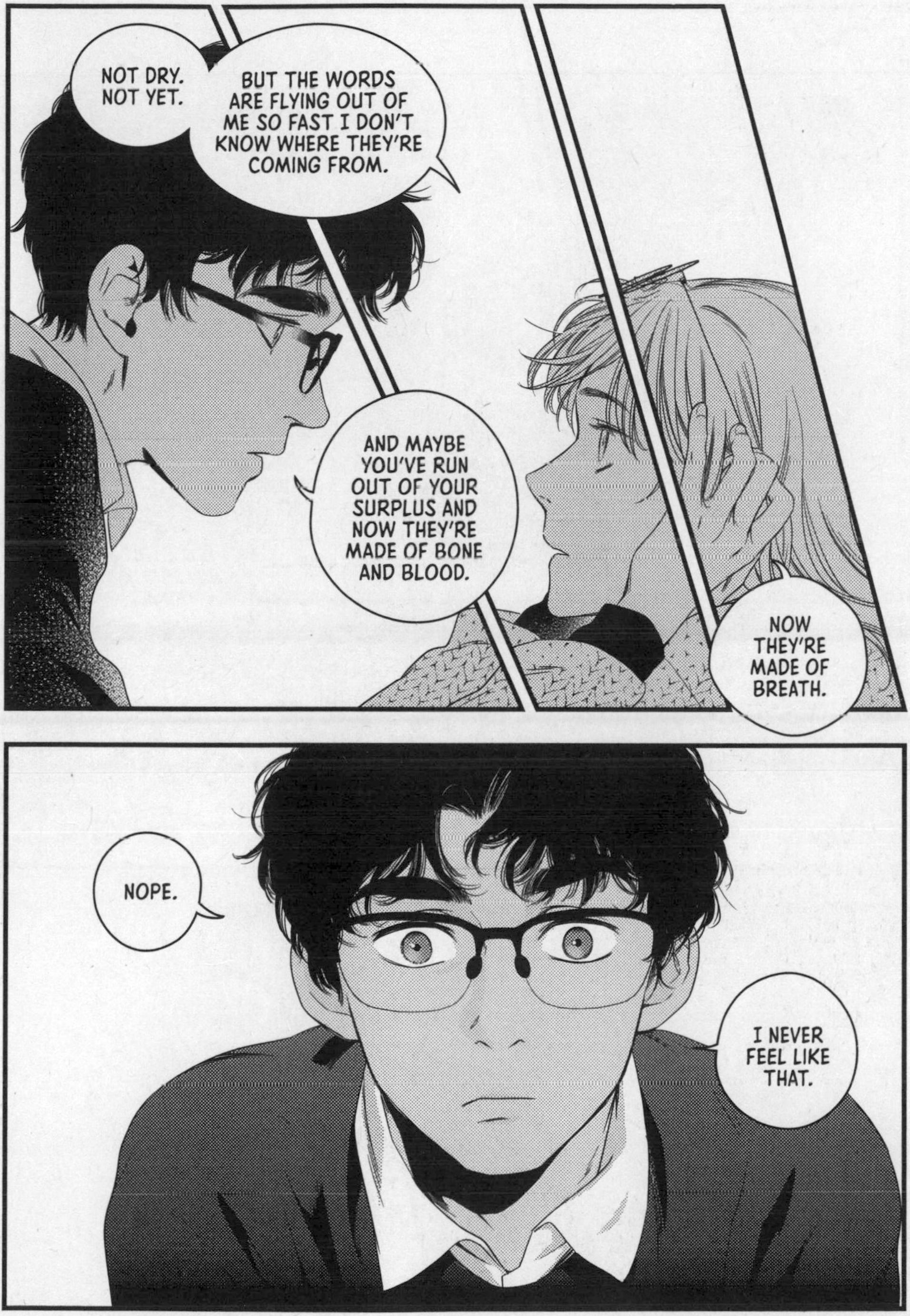
NOT DRY. NOT YET.
BUT THE WORDS ARE FLYING OUT OF ME SO FAST I DON'T KNOW WHERE THEY'RE COMING FROM.
AND MAYBE YOU'VE RUN OUT OF YOUR SURPLUS AND NOW THEY'RE MADE OF BONE AND BLOOD.
NOW THEY'RE MADE OF BREATH.
NOPE.
I NEVER FEEL LIKE THAT.

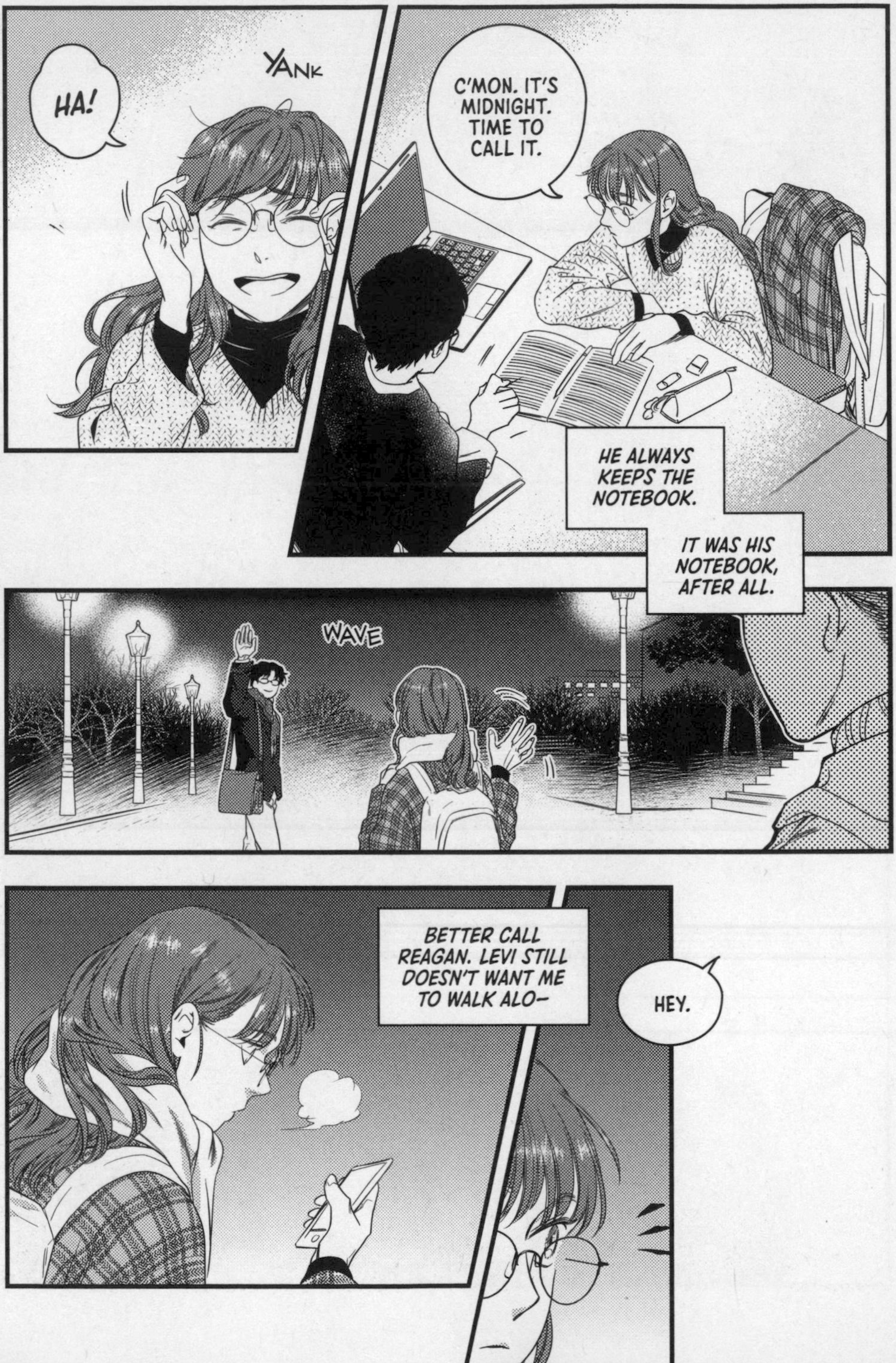

HA!
YANK
C'MON. IT'S MIDNIGHT. TIME TO CALL IT.
HE ALWAYS KEEPS THE NOTEBOOK.
IT WAS HIS NOTEBOOK, AFTER ALL.
WAVE
BETTER CALL REAGAN. LEVI STILL DOESN'T WANT ME TO WALK ALO—
HEY.

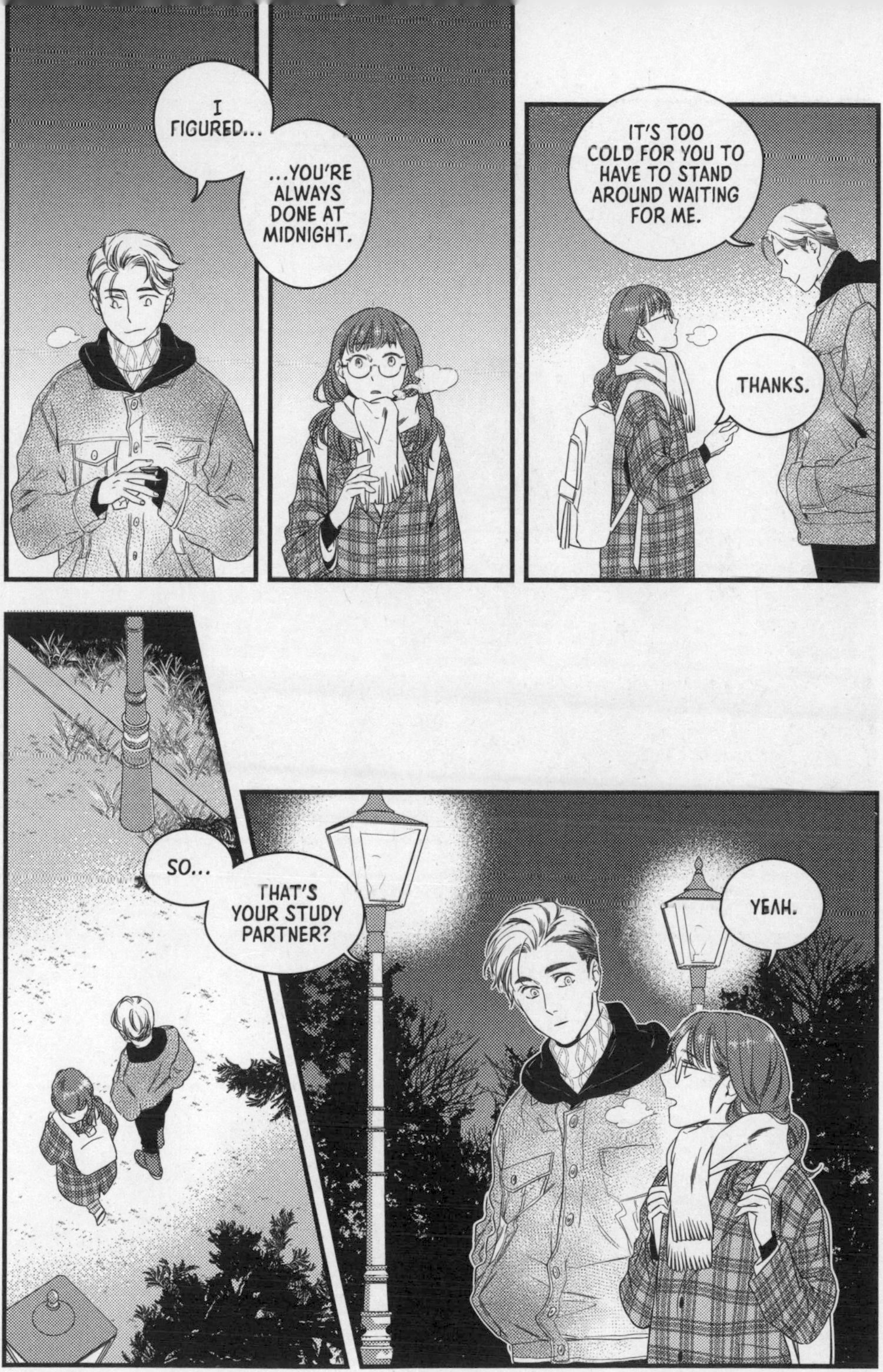
I FIGURED...
...YOU'RE ALWAYS DONE AT MIDNIGHT.
IT'S TOO COLD FOR YOU TO HAVE TO STAND AROUND WAITING FOR ME.
THANKS.
SO...
THAT'S YOUR STUDY PARTNER?
YEAH.

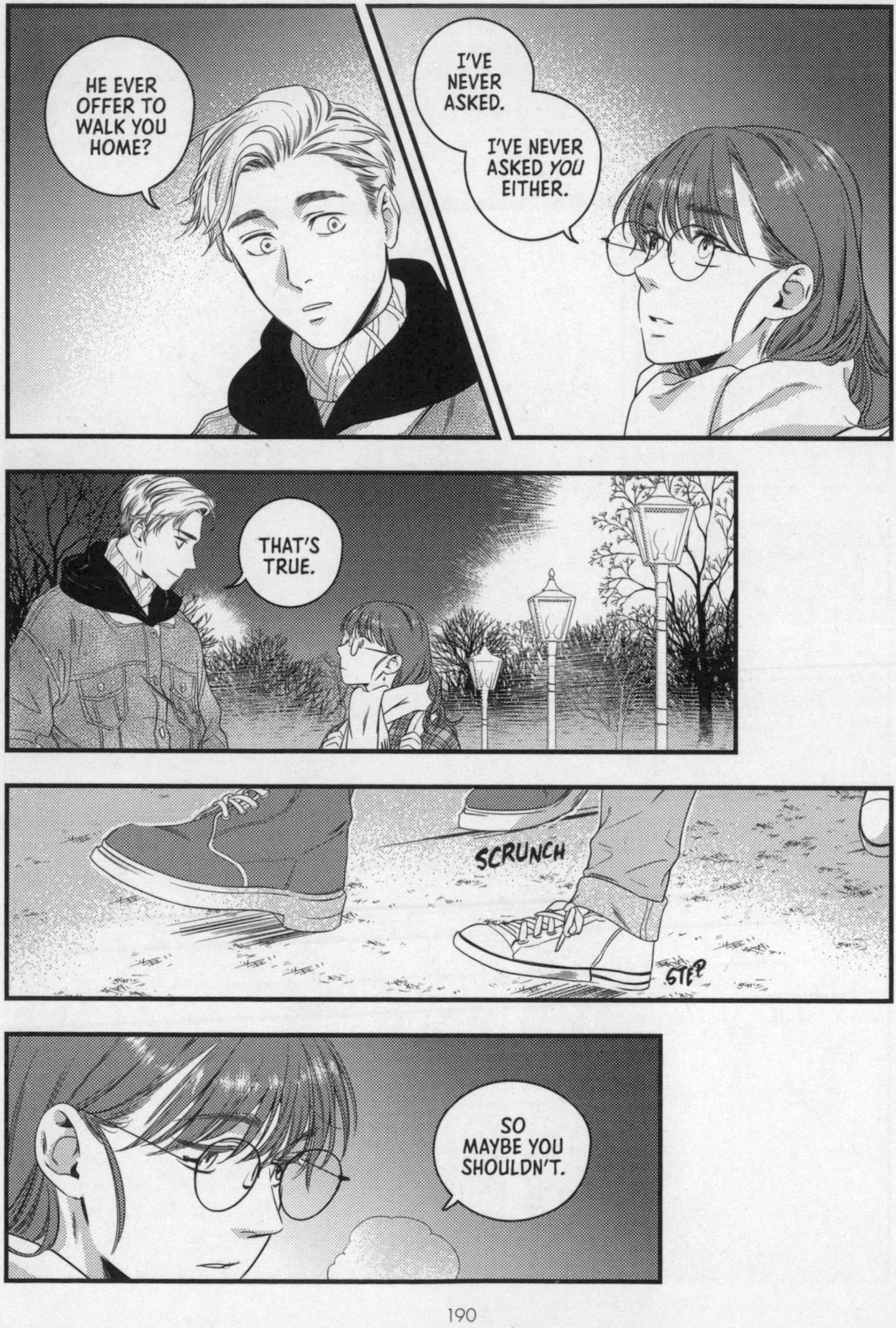
HE EVER OFFER TO WALK YOU HOME?
I'VE NEVER ASKED.
I'VE NEVER ASKED *YOU* EITHER.
THAT'S TRUE.
SCRUNCH
STEP
SO MAYBE YOU SHOULDN'T.

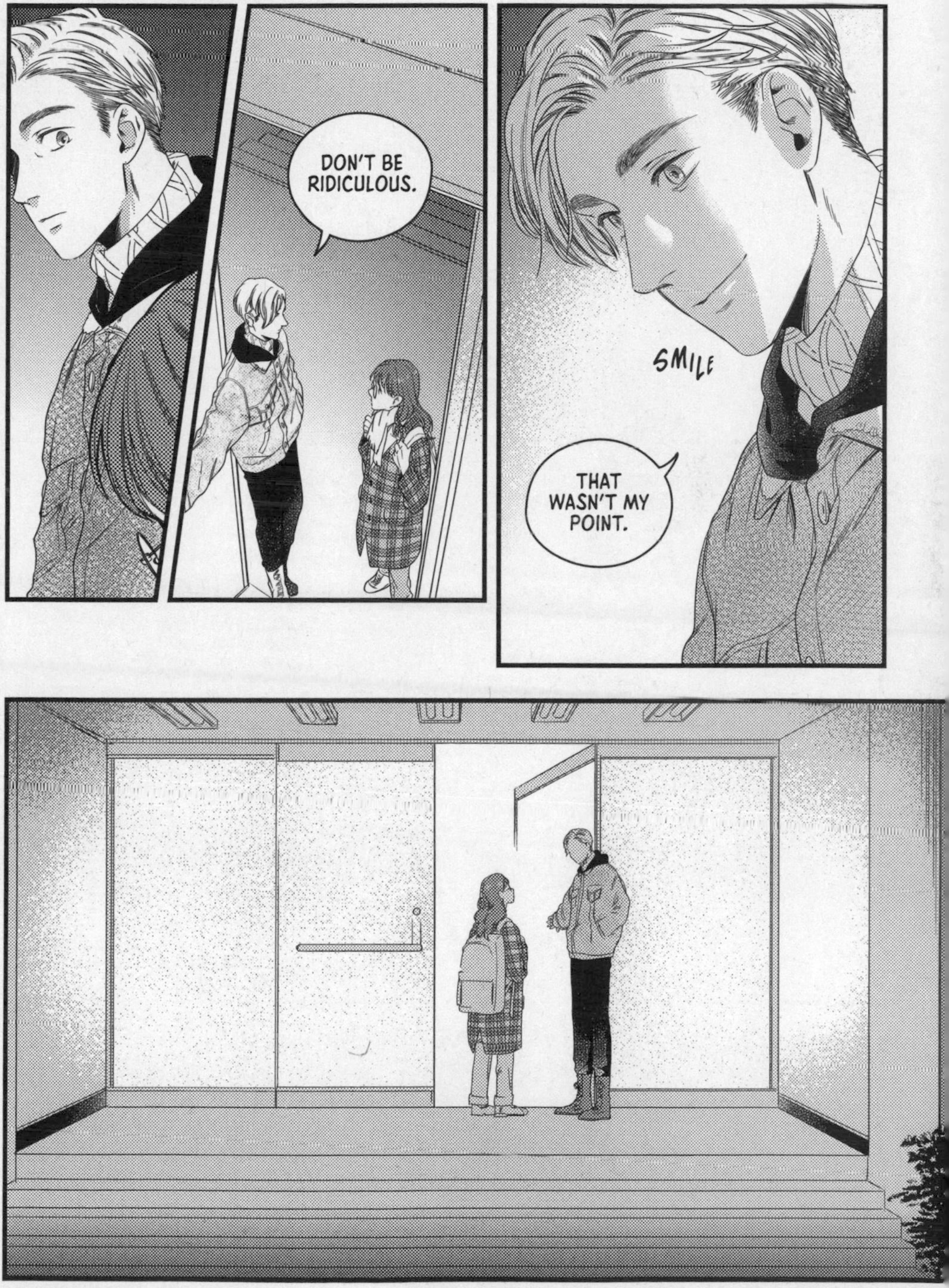
DON'T BE RIDICULOUS.
SMILE
THAT WASN'T MY POINT.

From "The Nemesis"

By Cather Avery

Fiction-Writing 300/Piper

Short Story – Progress Check

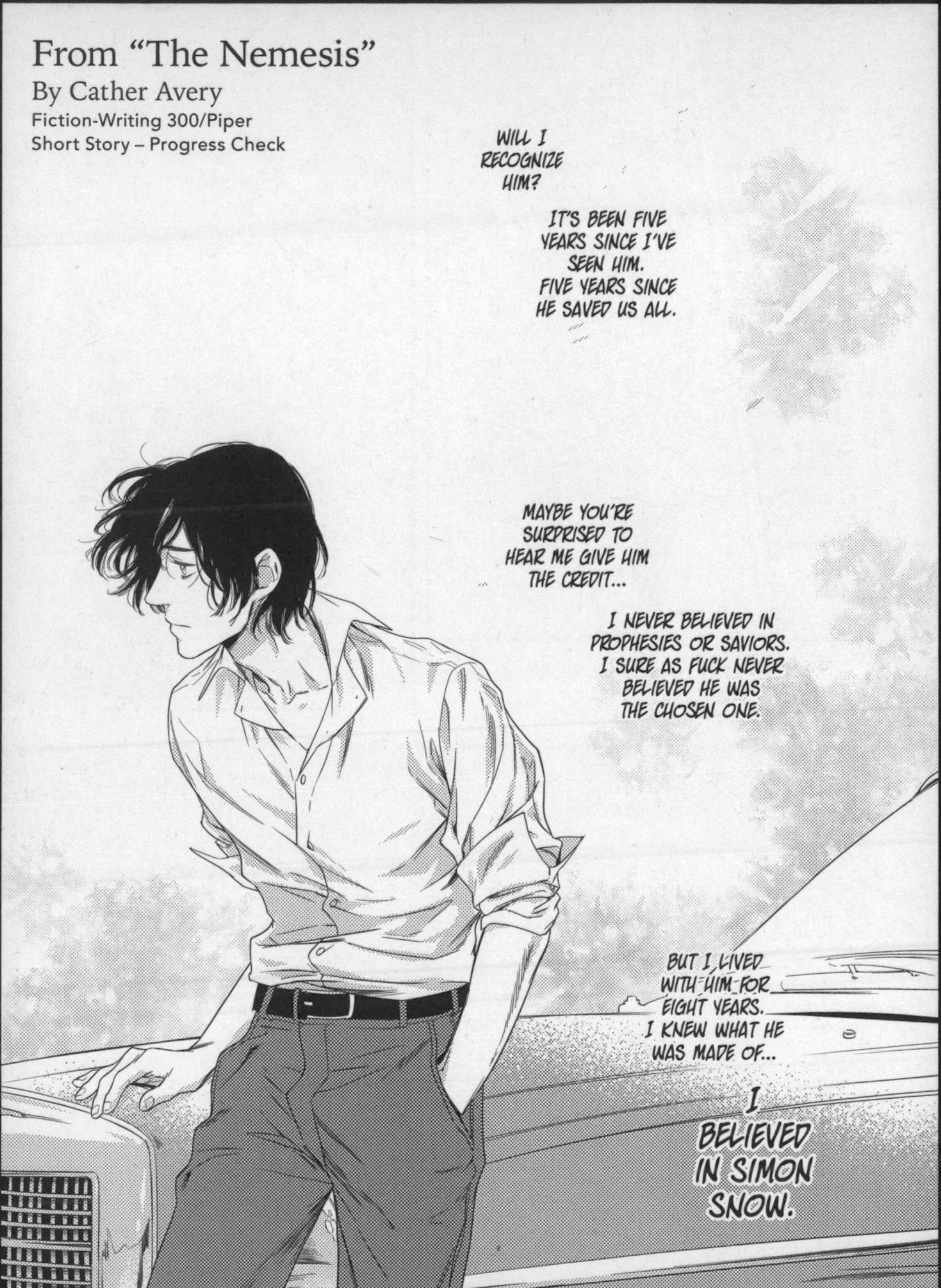
WILL I RECOGNIZE HIM?
IT'S BEEN FIVE YEARS SINCE I'VE SEEN HIM. FIVE YEARS SINCE HE SAVED US ALL.
MAYBE YOU'RE SURPRISED TO HEAR ME GIVE HIM THE CREDIT...
I NEVER BELIEVED IN PROPHESIES OR SAVIORS. I SURE AS FUCK NEVER BELIEVED HE WAS THE CHOSEN ONE.
BUT I LIVED WITH HIM FOR EIGHT YEARS. I KNEW WHAT HE WAS MADE OF...
I BELIEVED IN SIMON SNOW.

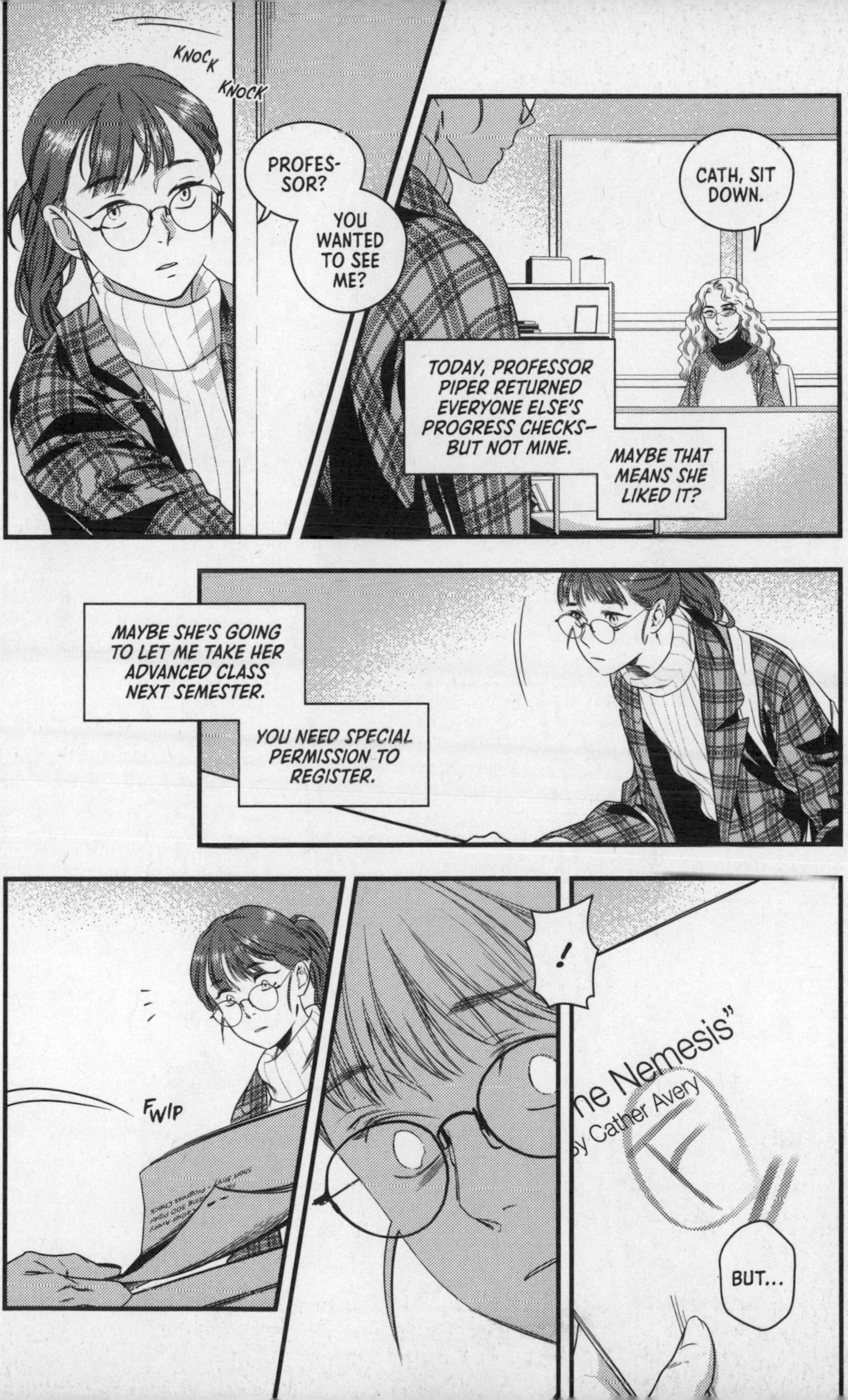
KNOCK
KNOCK
PROFES-SOR?
YOU WANTED TO SEE ME?
CATH, SIT DOWN.
TODAY, PROFESSOR PIPER RETURNED EVERYONE ELSE'S PROGRESS CHECKS— BUT NOT MINE.
MAYBE THAT MEANS SHE LIKED IT?
MAYBE SHE'S GOING TO LET ME TAKE HER ADVANCED CLASS NEXT SEMESTER.
YOU NEED SPECIAL PERMISSION TO REGISTER.
FWIP
!
he Nemesis"
y Cather Avery
F
BUT...

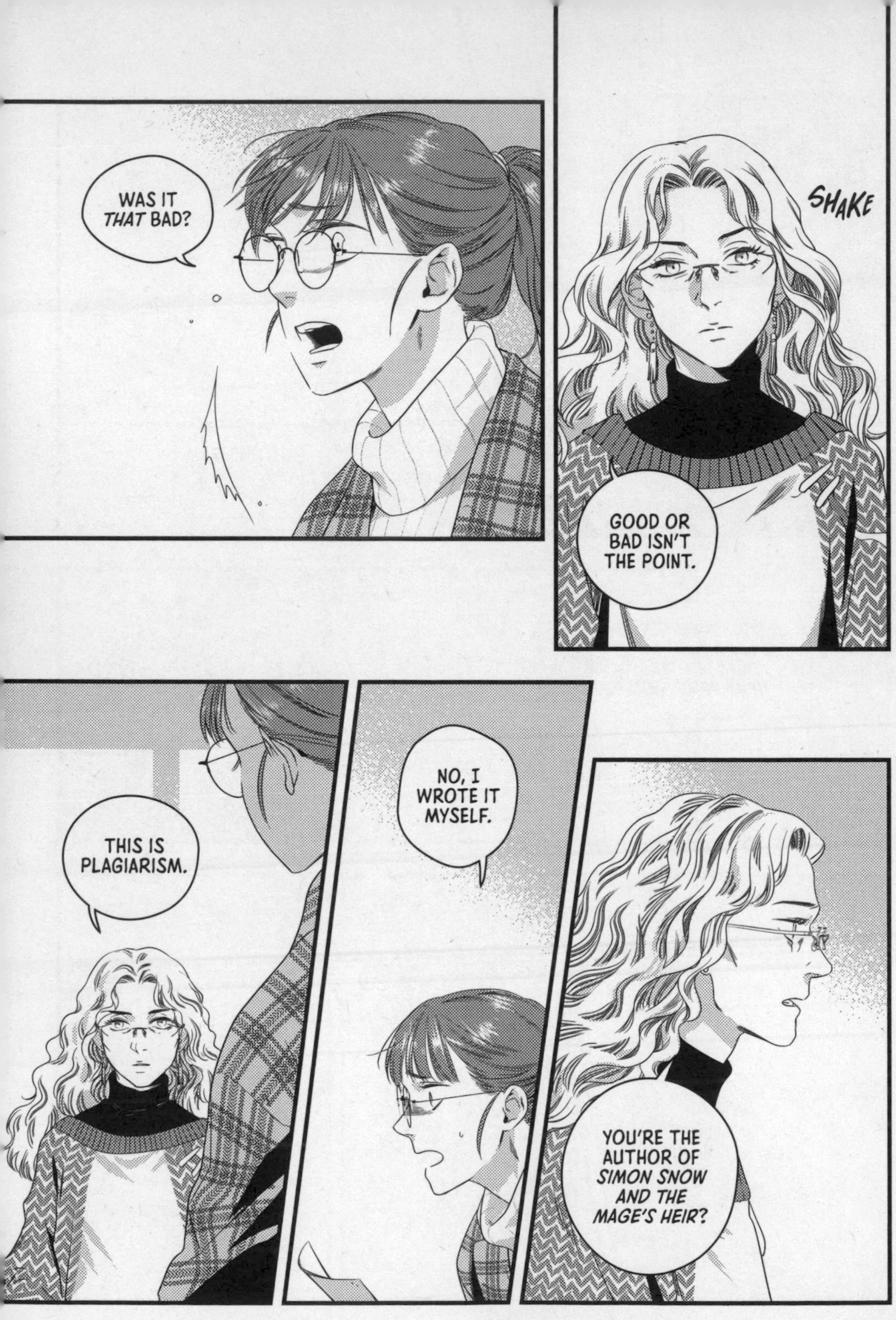
WAS IT *THAT* BAD?
SHAKE
GOOD OR BAD ISN'T THE POINT.
THIS IS PLAGIARISM.
NO, I WROTE IT MYSELF.
YOU'RE THE AUTHOR OF *SIMON SNOW AND THE MAGE'S HEIR?*

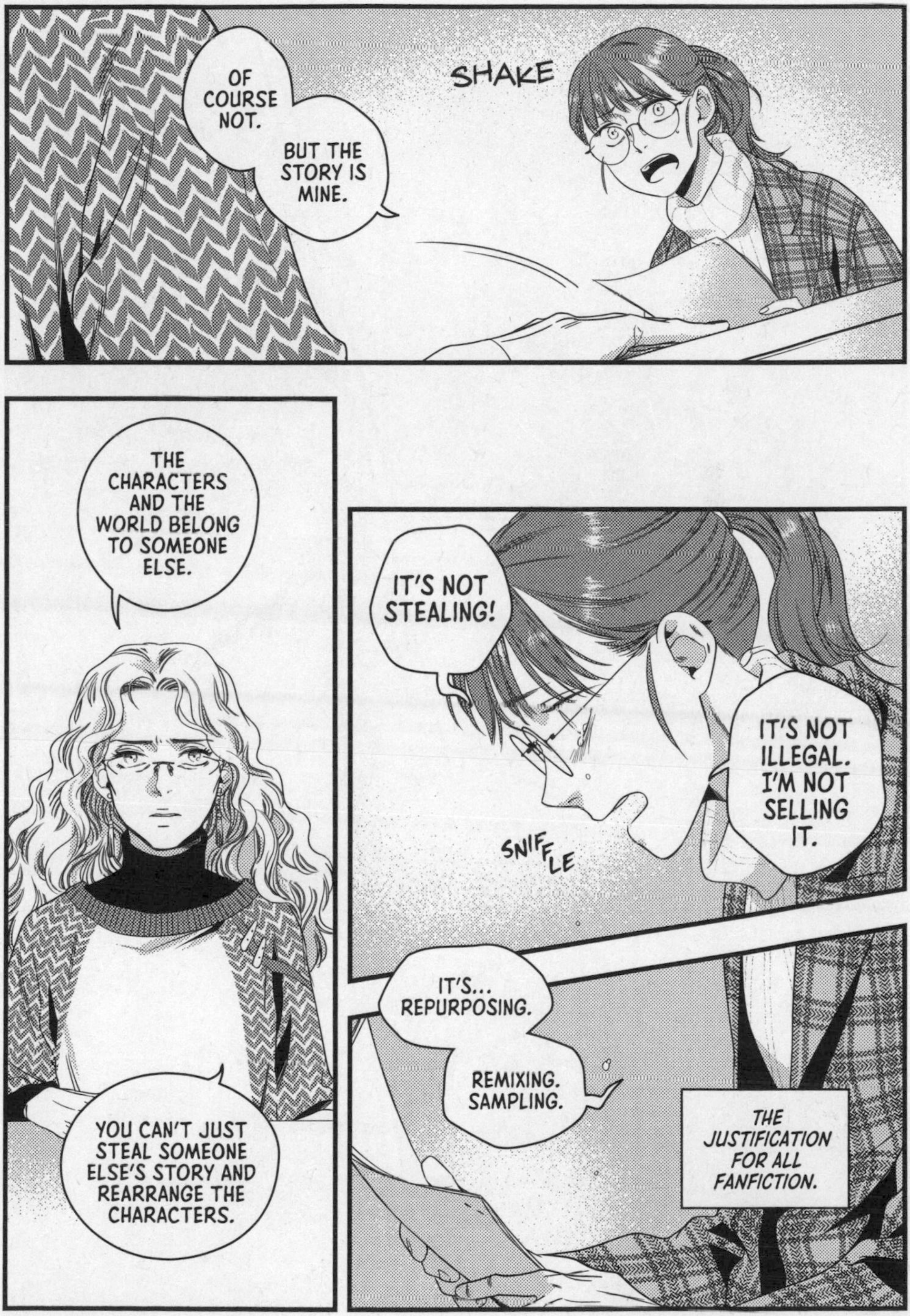
OF COURSE NOT.
BUT THE STORY IS MINE.
SHAKE
THE CHARACTERS AND THE WORLD BELONG TO SOMEONE ELSE.
YOU CAN'T JUST STEAL SOMEONE ELSE'S STORY AND REARRANGE THE CHARACTERS.
IT'S NOT STEALING!
SNIFFLE
IT'S NOT ILLEGAL. I'M NOT SELLING IT.
IT'S... REPURPOSING.
REMIXING. SAMPLING.
THE JUSTIFICATION FOR ALL FANFICTION.

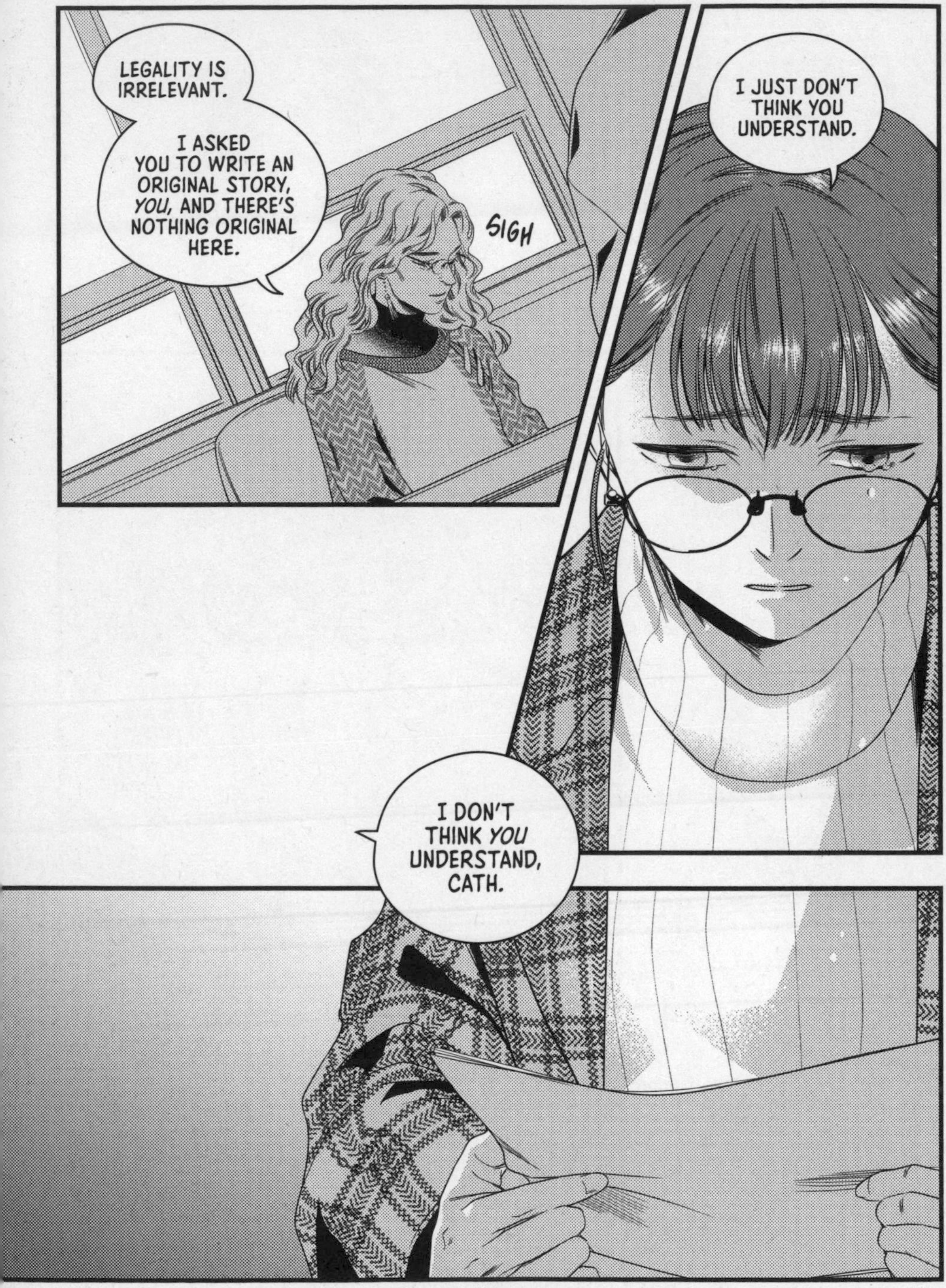
LEGALITY IS IRRELEVANT.
I ASKED YOU TO WRITE AN ORIGINAL STORY, *YOU*, AND THERE'S NOTHING ORIGINAL HERE.
SIGH
I JUST DON'T THINK YOU UNDERSTAND.
I DON'T THINK *YOU* UNDERSTAND, CATH.

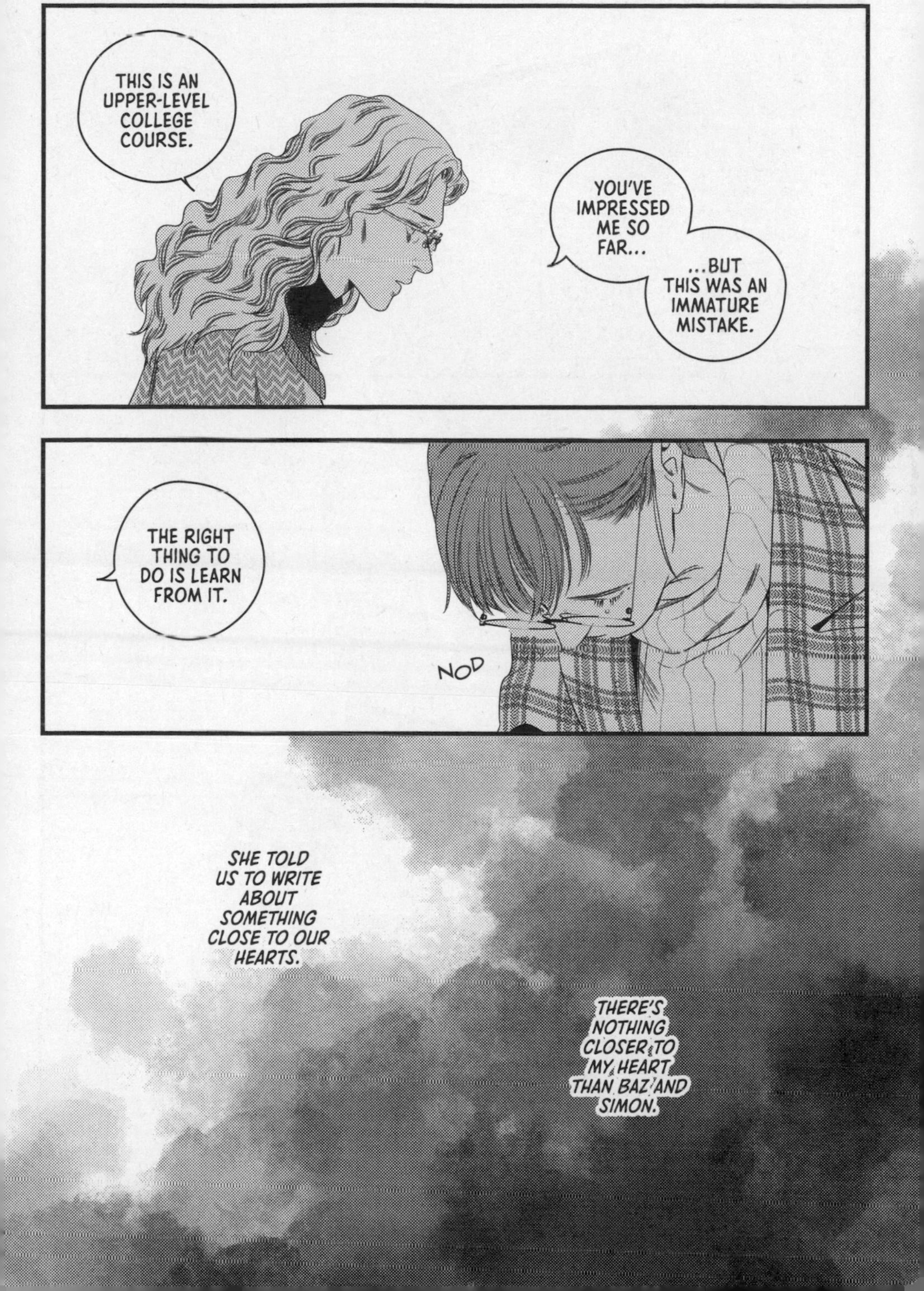
THIS IS AN UPPER-LEVEL COLLEGE COURSE.
YOU'VE IMPRESSED ME SO FAR...
...BUT THIS WAS AN IMMATURE MISTAKE.
THE RIGHT THING TO DO IS LEARN FROM IT.
NOD
SHE TOLD US TO WRITE ABOUT SOMETHING CLOSE TO OUR HEARTS.
THERE'S NOTHING CLOSER TO MY HEART THAN BAZ AND SIMON.

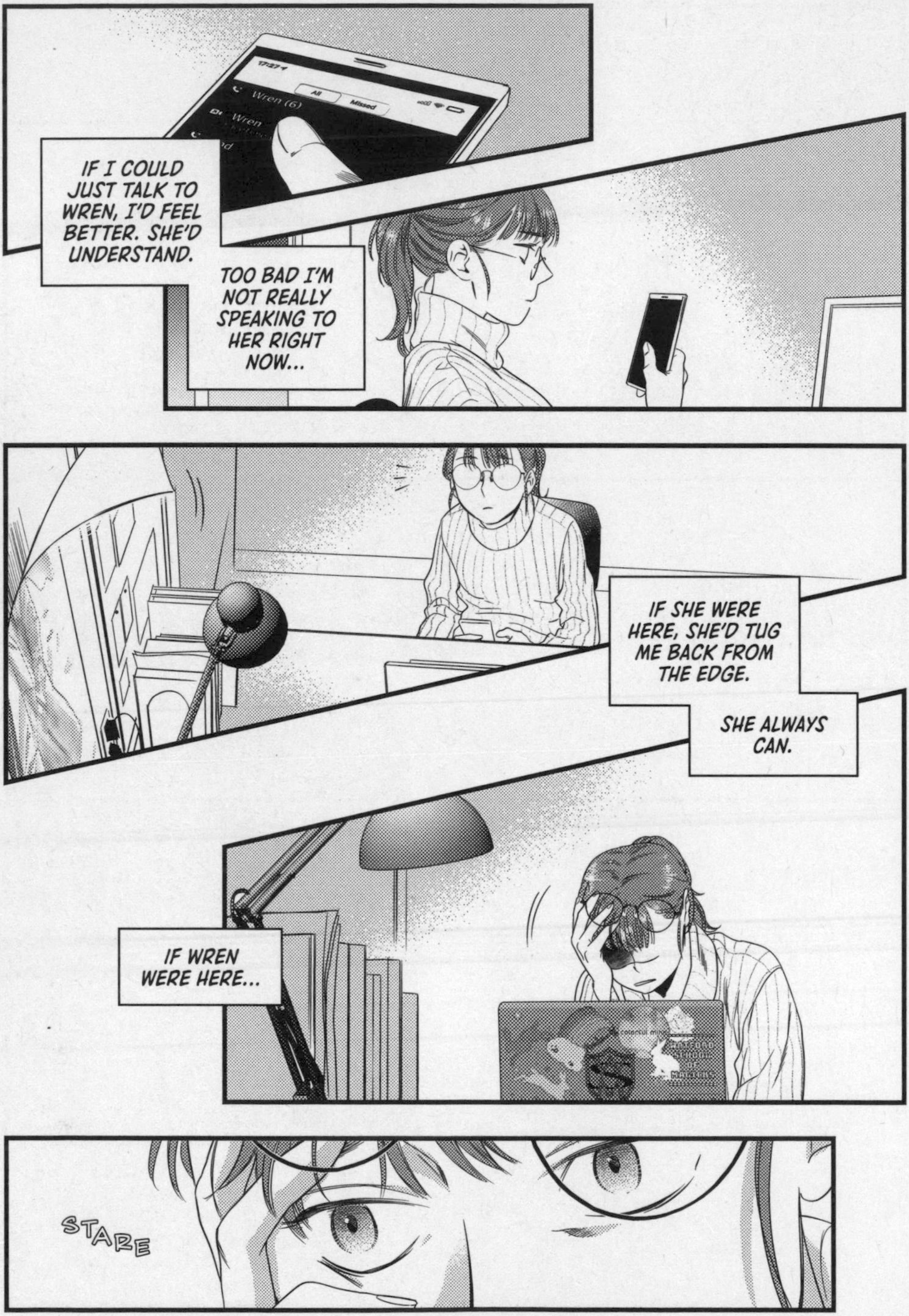

Wren (6)
All
Missed
IF I COULD JUST TALK TO WREN, I'D FEEL BETTER. SHE'D UNDERSTAND.
TOO BAD I'M NOT REALLY SPEAKING TO HER RIGHT NOW...
IF SHE WERE HERE, SHE'D TUG ME BACK FROM THE EDGE.
SHE ALWAYS CAN.
IF WREN WERE HERE...
STARE

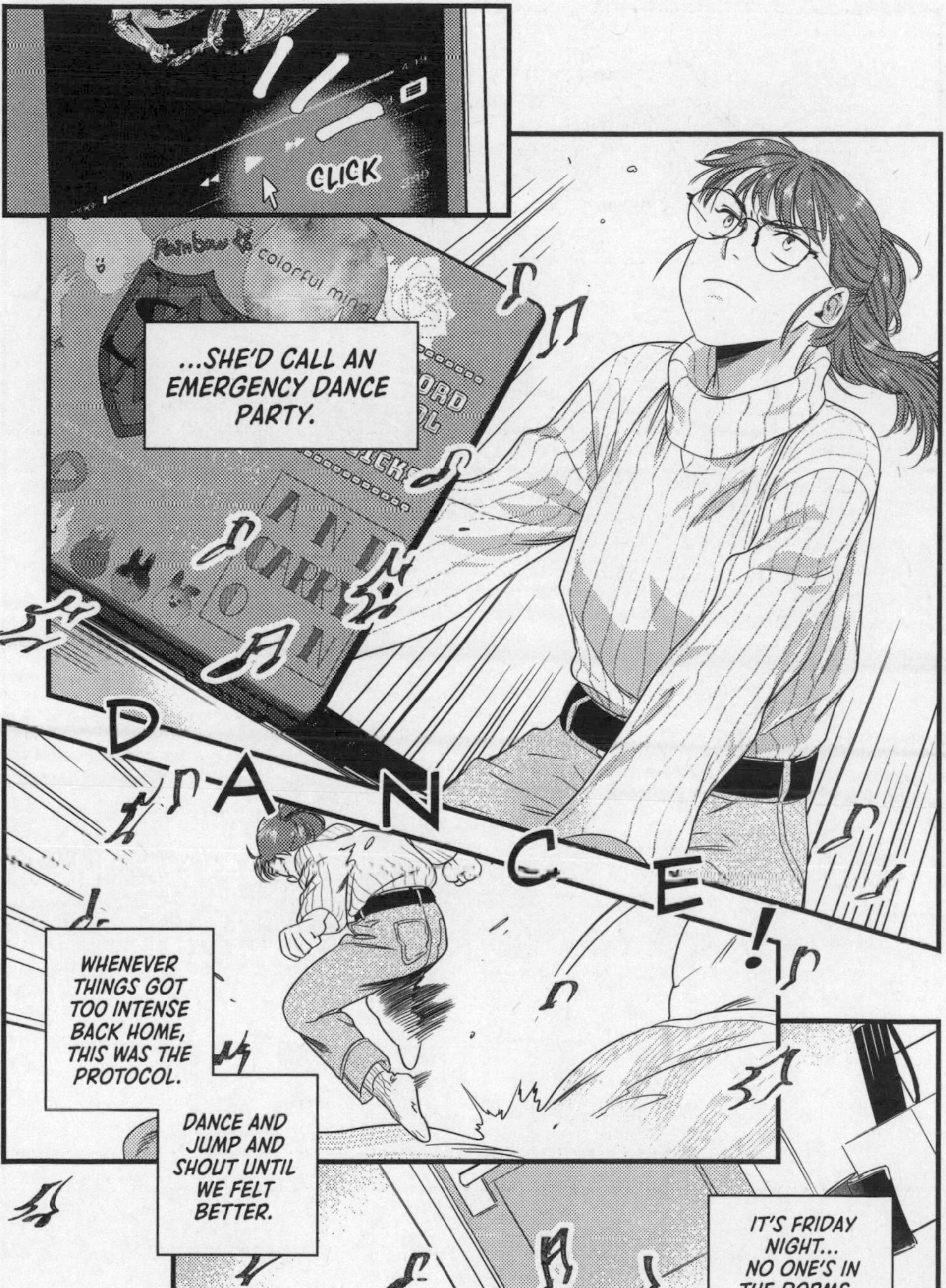
CLICK
...SHE'D CALL AN EMERGENCY DANCE PARTY.
DANCE!
WHENEVER THINGS GOT TOO INTENSE BACK HOME, THIS WAS THE PROTOCOL.
DANCE AND JUMP AND SHOUT UNTIL WE FELT BETTER.
IT'S FRIDAY NIGHT... NO ONE'S IN THE DORMS...

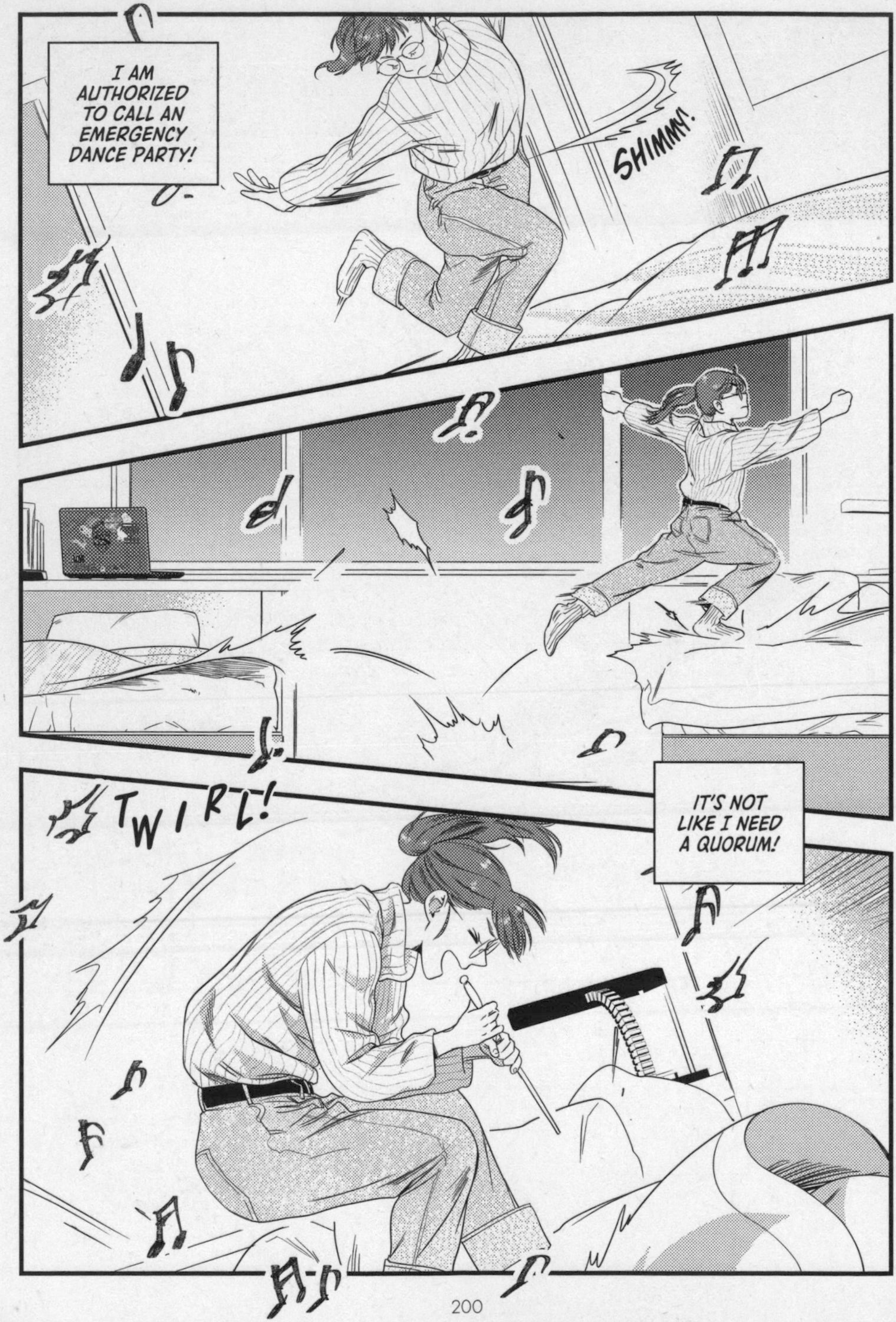
I AM AUTHORIZED TO CALL AN EMERGENCY DANCE PARTY!
SHIMMY!
TWIRL!
IT'S NOT LIKE I NEED A QUORUM!

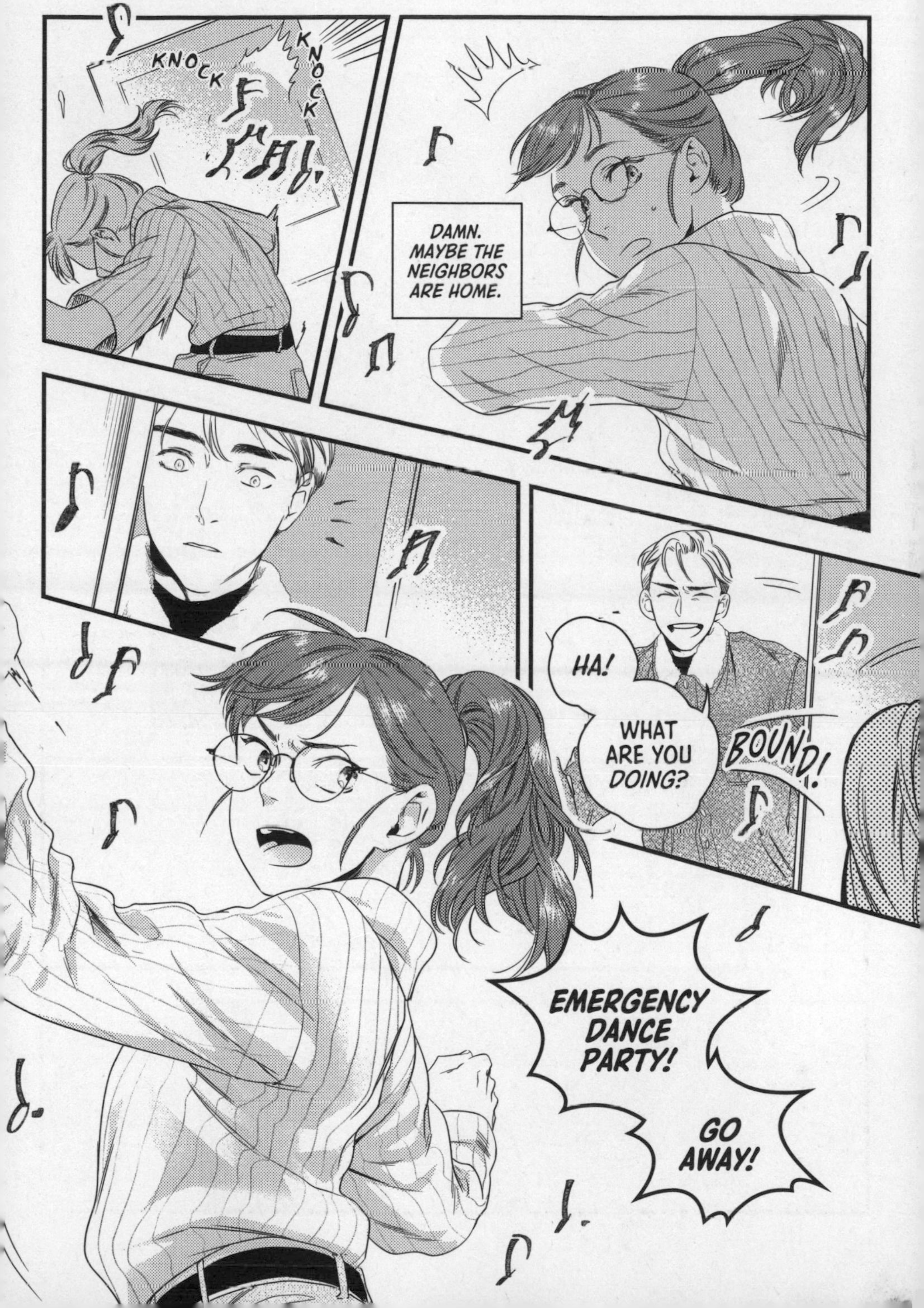
KNOCK
KNOCK
DAMN. MAYBE THE NEIGHBORS ARE HOME.
HA!
WHAT ARE YOU DOING?
BOUND!
EMERGENCY DANCE PARTY!
GO AWAY!

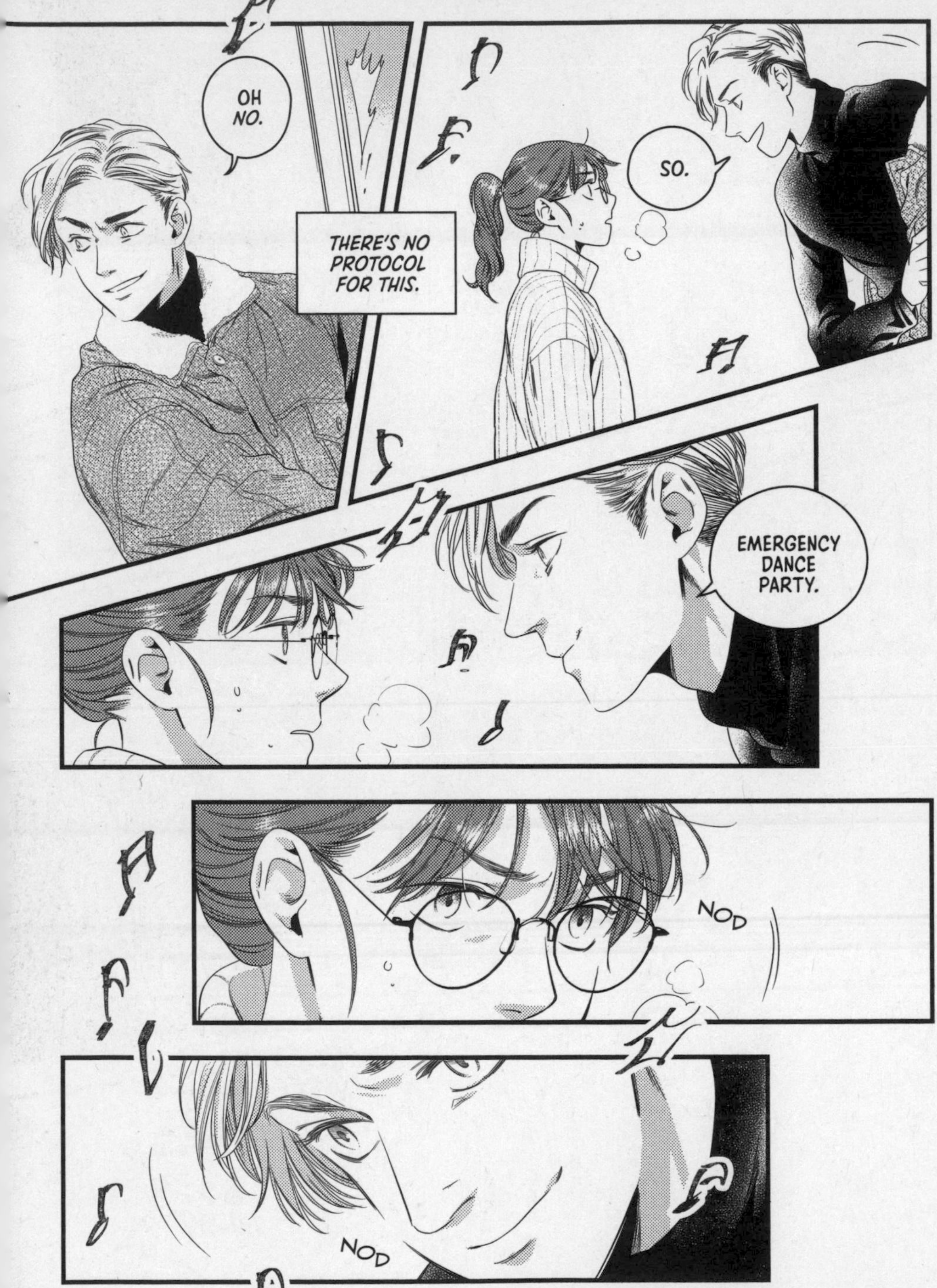
OH NO.
THERE'S NO PROTOCOL FOR THIS.
SO.
EMERGENCY DANCE PARTY.
NOD
NOD

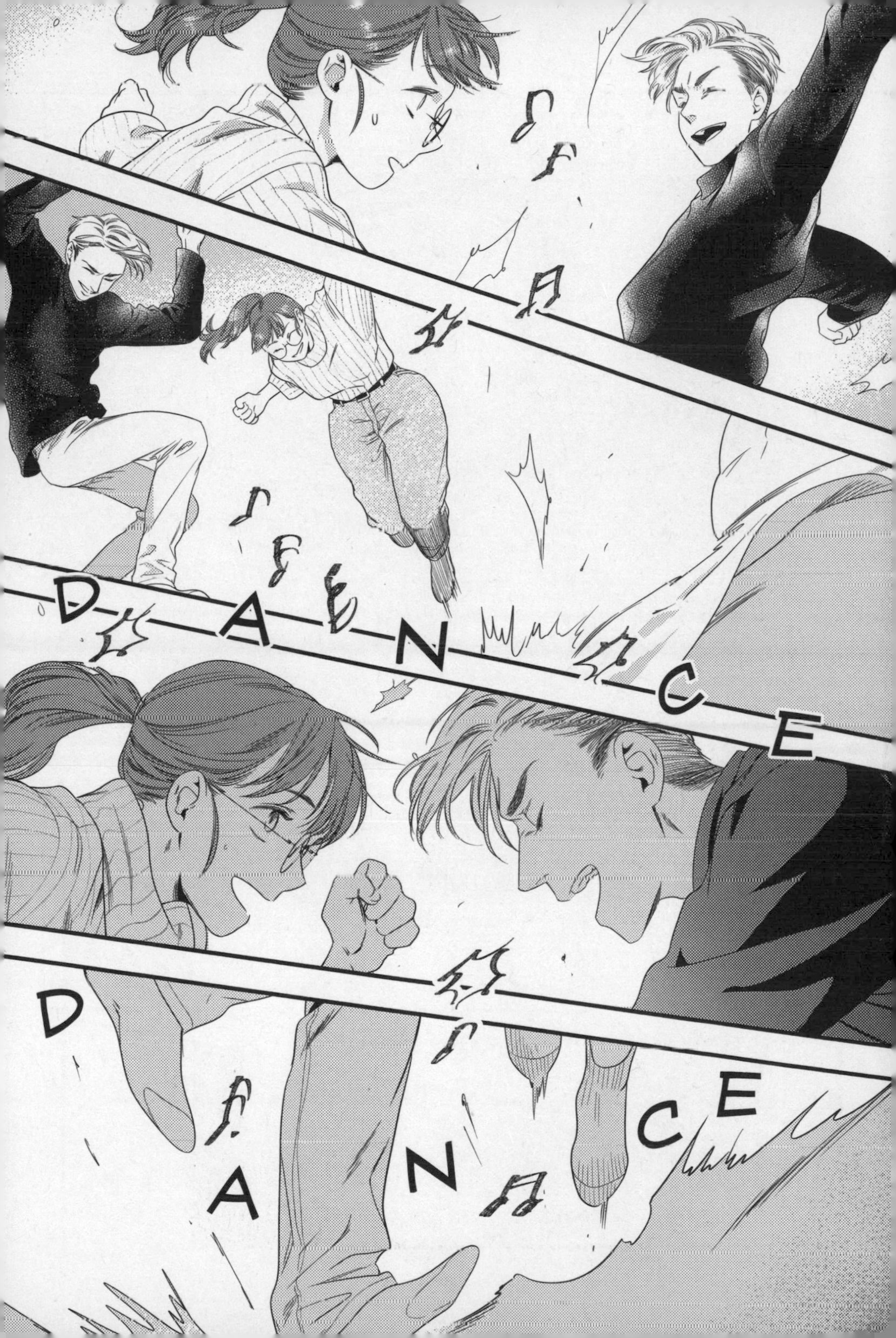
DANCE
DANCE

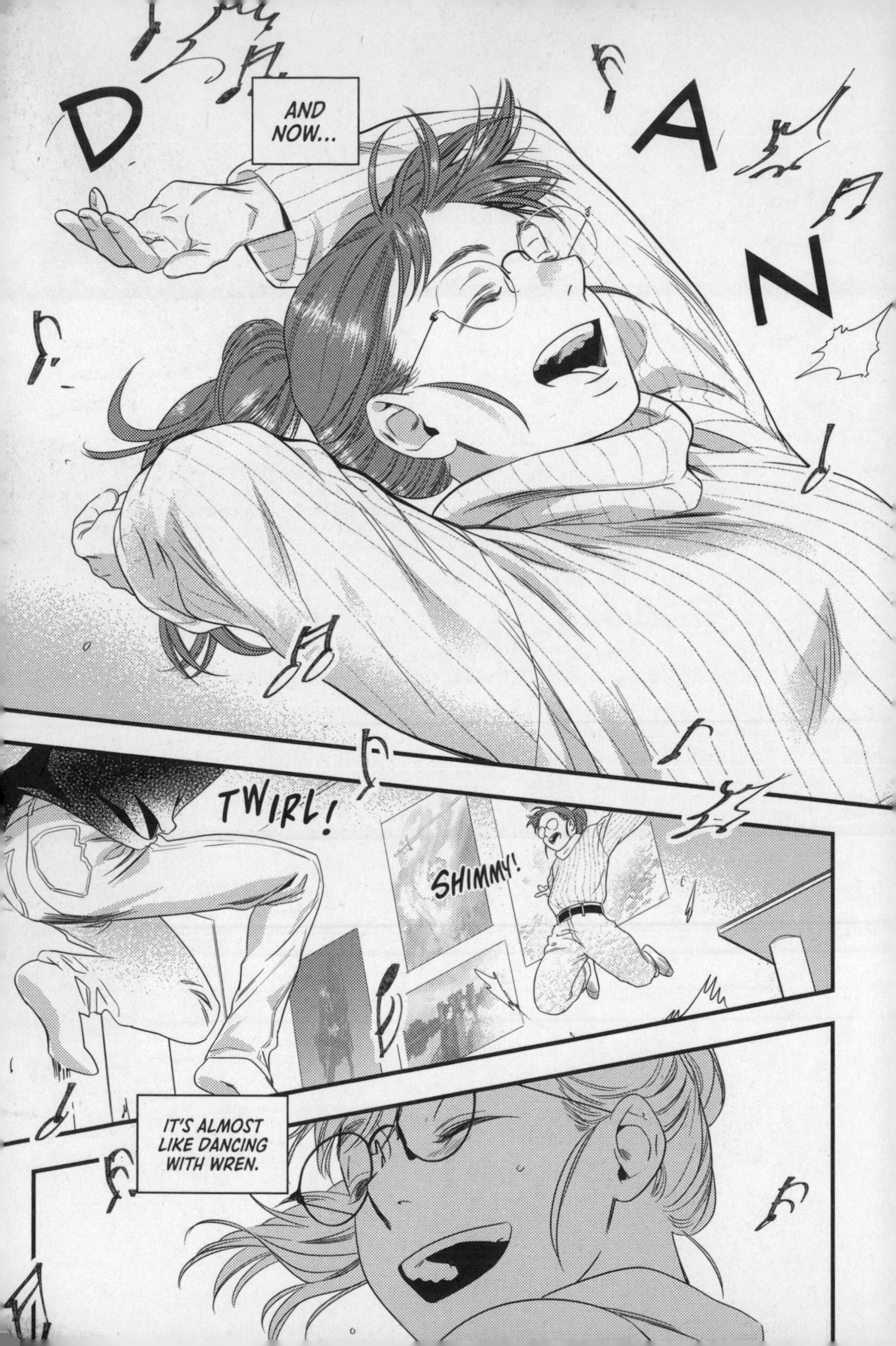
D
AND NOW...
A
N
TWIRL!
SHIMMY!
IT'S ALMOST LIKE DANCING WITH WREN.

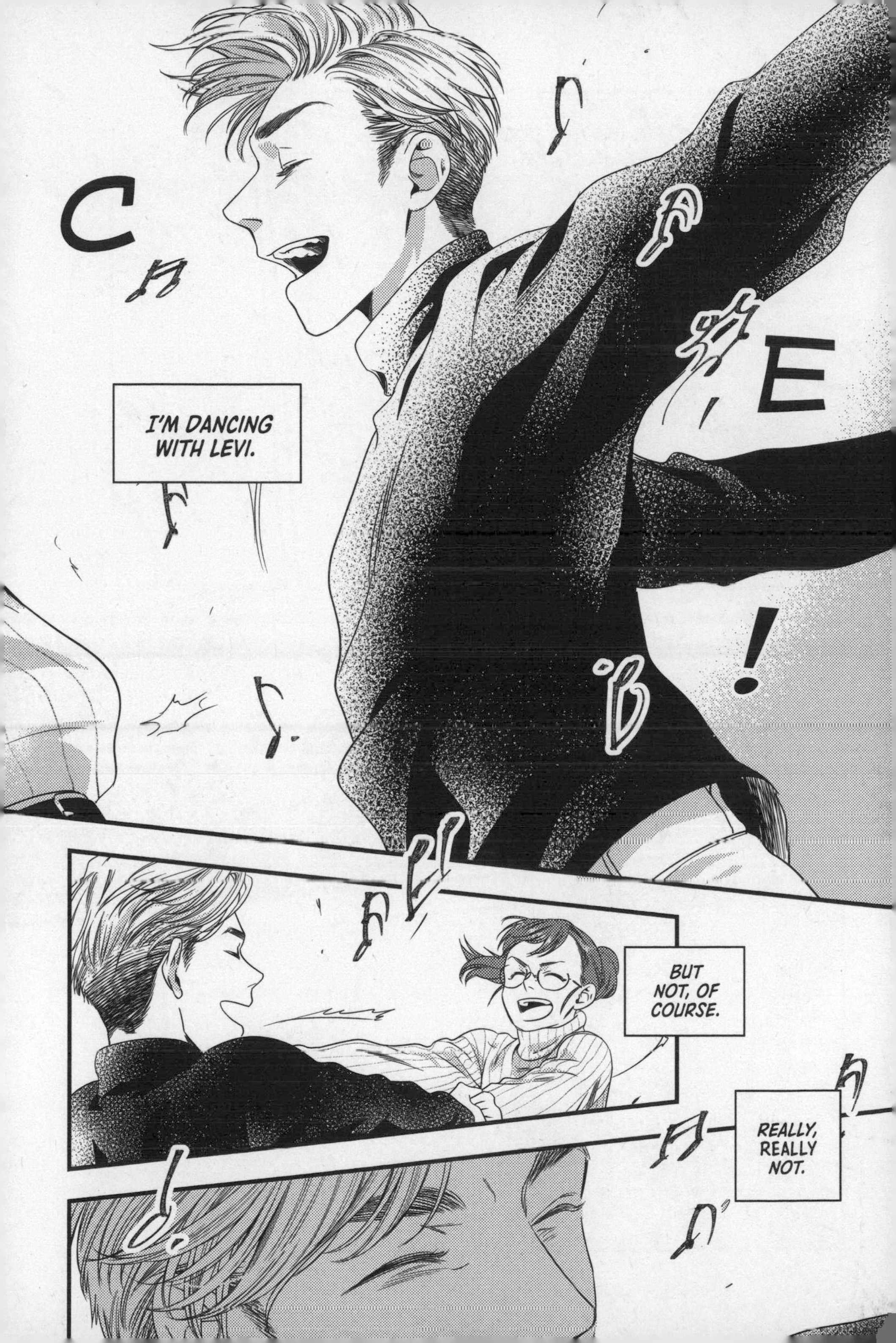

CHEE!
I'M DANCING WITH LEVI.
BUT NOT, OF COURSE.
REALLY, REALLY NOT.

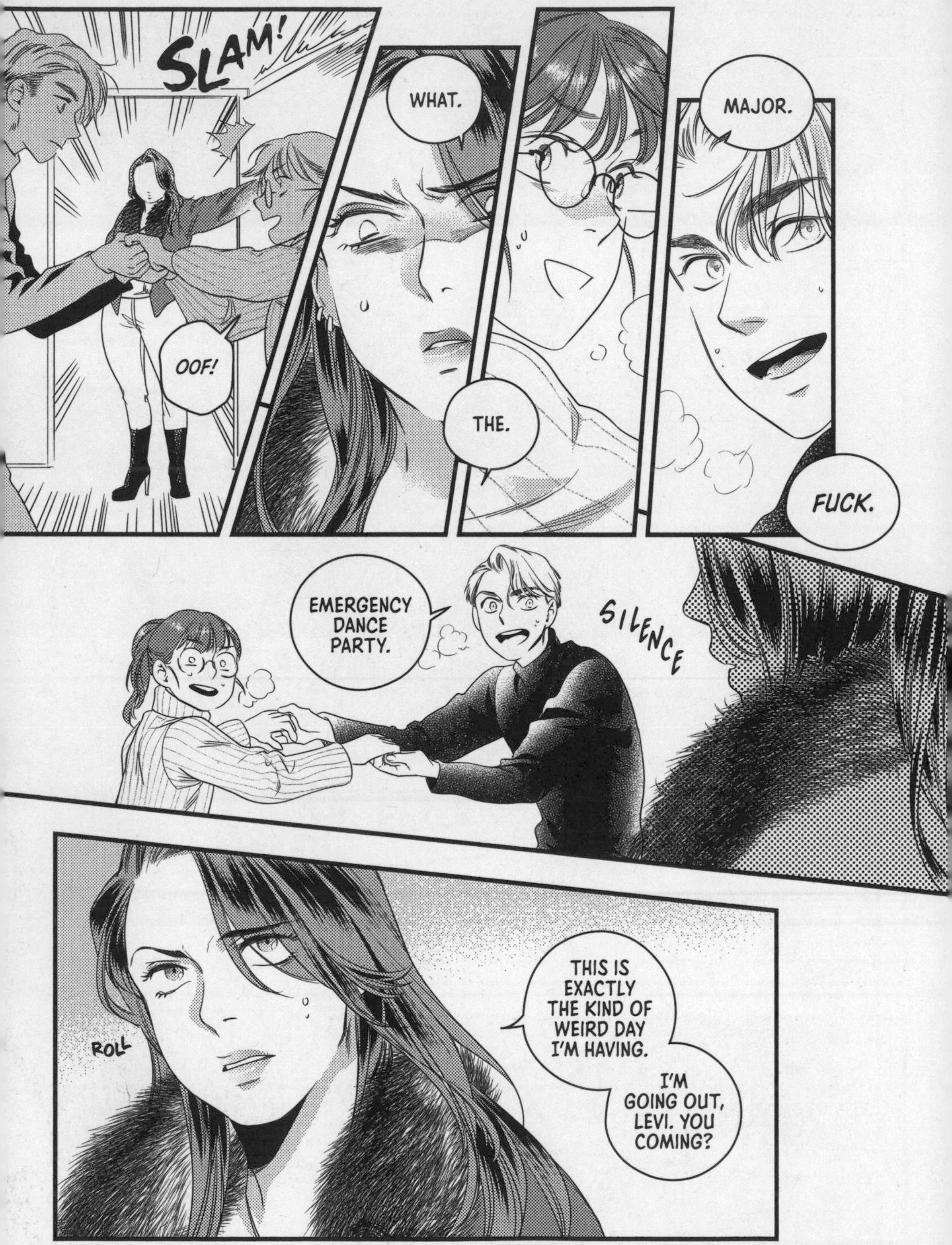
SLAM!
OOF!
WHAT.
THE.
MAJOR.
FUCK.
EMERGENCY DANCE PARTY.
SILENCE
ROLL
THIS IS EXACTLY THE KIND OF WEIRD DAY I'M HAVING.
I'M GOING OUT, LEVI. YOU COMING?

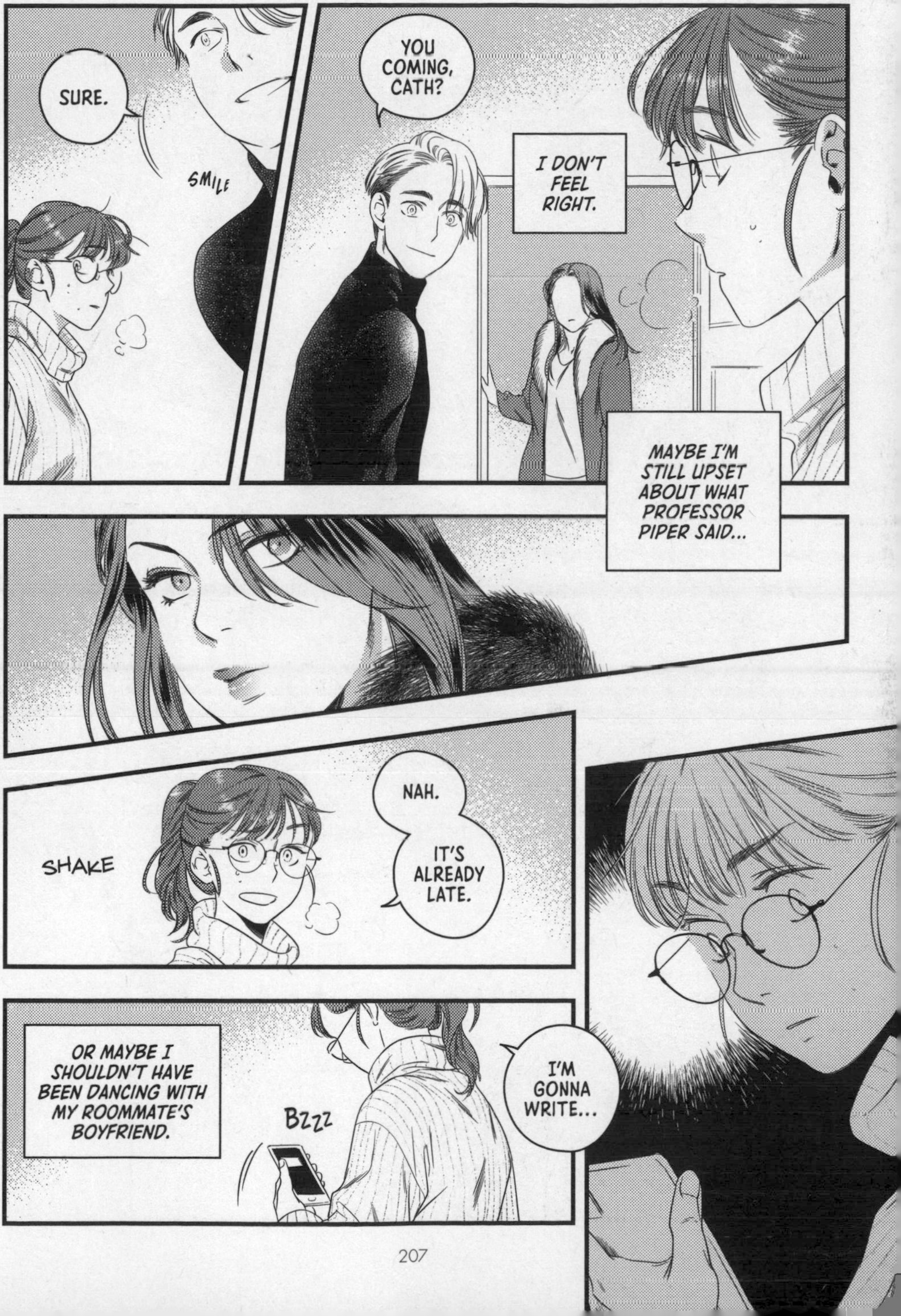
SURE.
SMILE
YOU COMING, CATH?
I DON'T FEEL RIGHT.
MAYBE I'M STILL UPSET ABOUT WHAT PROFESSOR PIPER SAID...
SHAKE
NAH.
IT'S ALREADY LATE.
OR MAYBE I SHOULDN'T HAVE BEEN DANCING WITH MY ROOMMATE'S BOYFRIEND.
BZZZ
I'M GONNA WRITE...

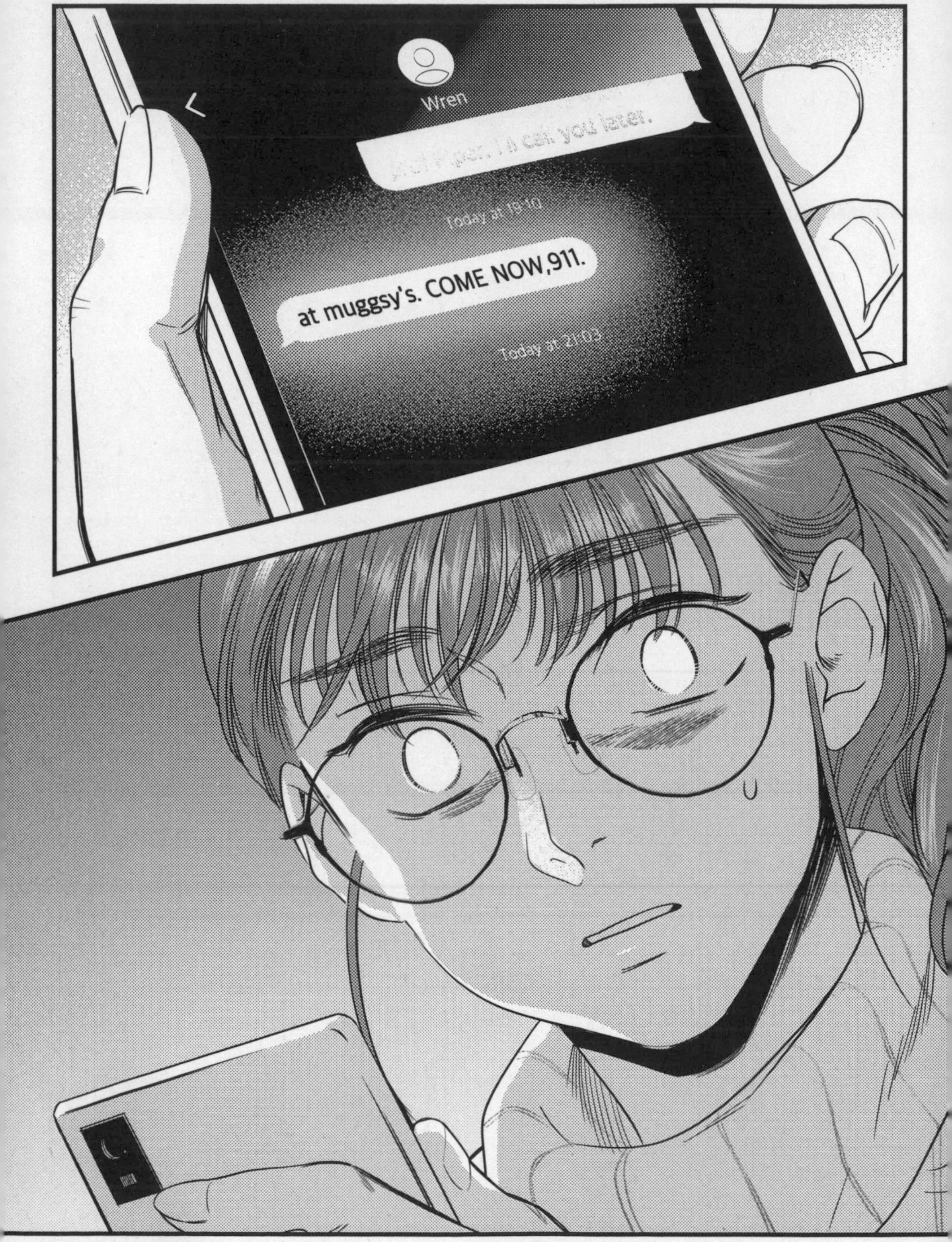

Wren
I'll call you later.
Today at 19:10
at muggsy's. COME NOW,911.
Today at 21:03

Fangirl: The Manga
Rainbow Rowell, Sam Maggs, Gabi Nam

Status:	Incomplete
Currently reading:	1/4
Language:	English
Tags:	Simon Snow, college, sisters, betrayal, energy bars

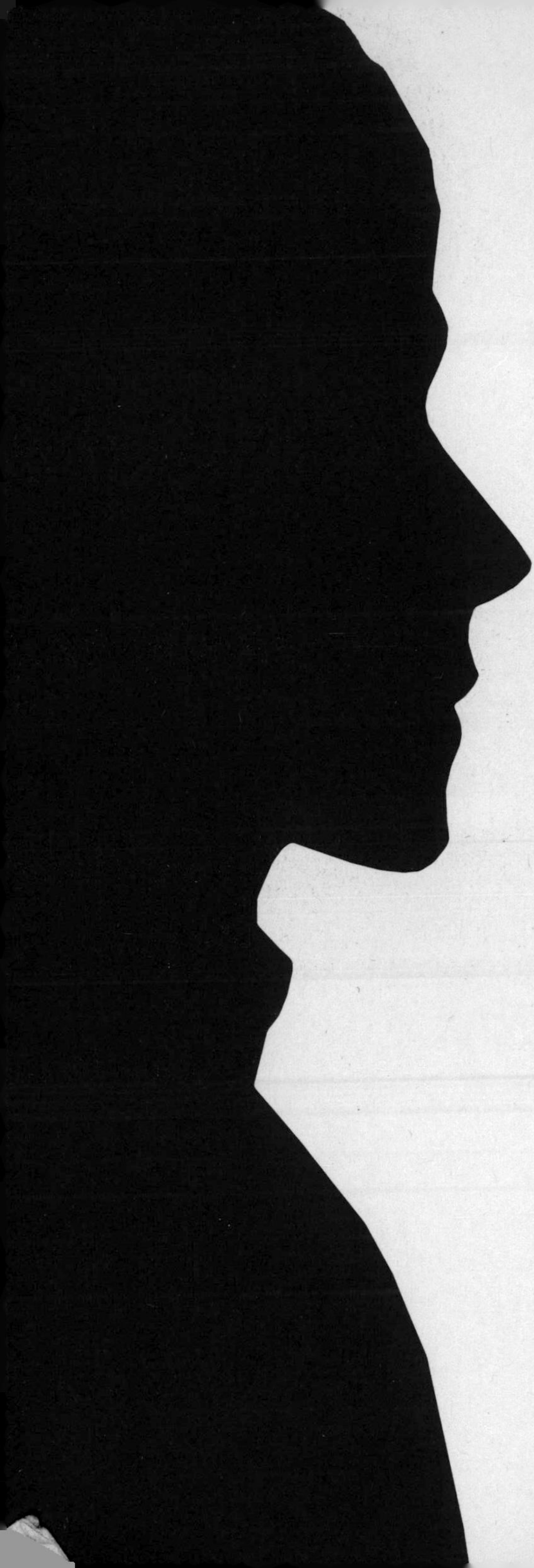

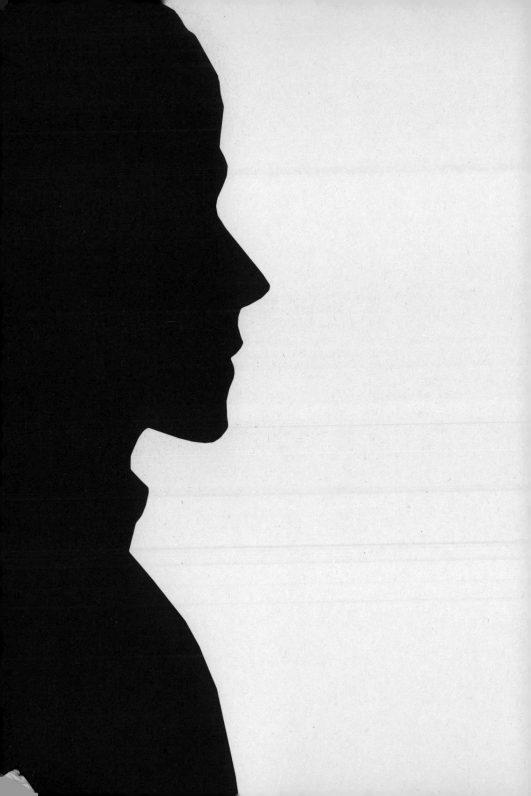

RAINBOW ROWELL
Creator

RAINBOW ROWELL lives in Omaha, Nebraska, with her husband and two sons. She is the #1 *New York Times* bestselling author of *Carry On*, *Landline*, *Attachments* and *Wayward Son* and the writer of Marvel's *Runaways* and the graphic novel *Pumpkinheads*.

You can visit her website at www.rainbowrowell.com

SAM MAGGS
Adapter

SAM MAGGS is a bestselling author of books, comics and video games. She's been a senior games writer, including work on Marvel's *Spider-Man*; the author of many YA and middle-grade books like *The Unstoppable Wasp*, *Con Quest!*, *Tell No Tales* and *The Fangirl's Guide to the Galaxy*; and a comics writer for beloved titles like *Marvel Action: Captain Marvel*, *My Little Pony* and *Transformers*.

You can visit her website at www.sammaggs.com

GABI NAM
Illustrator

GABI NAM is a South Korean artist who has lived abroad in Japan and France. She self-publishes her work in South Korea and specializes in the black-and-white manga style. *Fangirl: The Manga* is her English debut.

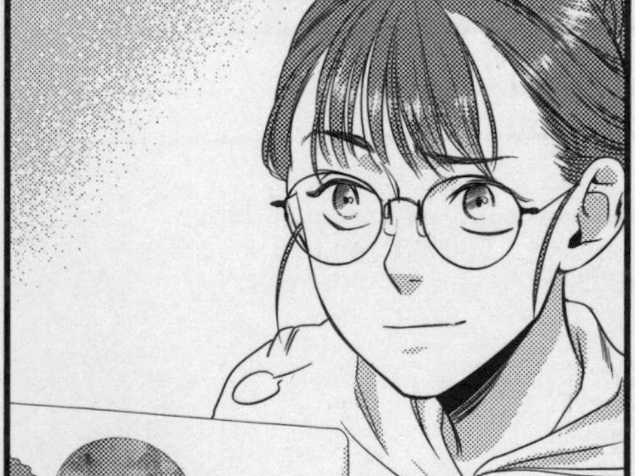
colorful

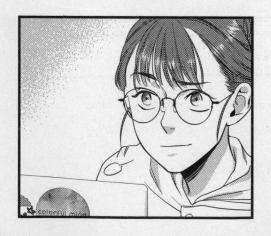

fangirl

THE MANGA

1

VIZ ORIGINALS EDITION

Based on the original novel *Fangirl* by Rainbow Rowell

Written and Edited by RAINBOW ROWELL
Adapted by SAM MAGGS
Illustrated by GABI NAM

Lettering: ERIKA TERRIQUEZ
Cover and Interior Design: ADAM GRANO
Editor: FAWN LAU

Printed in the U.S.A.

Published by VIZ Media, LLC
P.O. Box 77010
San Francisco, CA 94107

10 9 8 7 6 5 4 3 2 1
First printing, October 2020

viz.com